The Roach Family and Other Stories

Cindy Matthews

The Roach Family and Other Stories

First Printing: February 2024

Published by **DarkWinter Press**: www.darkwinterlit.com

ISBN: 978-1-7382734-6-1

The author acknowledges the financial support of the Ontario Arts Council and the Government of Ontario.

Dedicated to my readers and anyone else trying to fit in.

"[The stories in *The Roach Family and Other Stories*] have a strong gothic quality about them. I begin each story, waiting for the circuitous journey Cindy's words will take me on. There will be a twist, a new awareness, an unexpected consequence that amuses or frightens. An unravelling. A character freely exhibits a chasm of untoward impulses. The reader is caught off guard, in a series of dilapidated homes with uneven floorboards which throw us off-balance, makes us look carefully for defining moments which illuminate individuals' foibles."

JENNIFER FRANKUM, author of *Strong in My Skin* and *Dance More Often, Into the Wilderness: A Temple in Sharon, Now That You Are Two*, and a forthcoming poetry collection.

"Can a child learn more about family relationships from cockroaches than she does from her parents? The title story in Cindy Matthews' stunning collection of short fiction foreshadows the richly descriptive landscapes and complex characters that await in *The Roach Family and Other Stories*."

JANET TRULL, author of *Hot Town and Other Stories, Something's Burning, End of the Line,* and *Once a Storm.* She's a frequent contributor to the *Haliburton Echo*.

Table of Contents

Return of Voice

The father pulled a coat over his child's limp arms. "Straighten up, will you?" he said, the boy's hands snagged partway into the sleeves.

"I'll fix it, for Christ's sake," a female voice said, pushing the father out of the way. "We don't have time for dawdling, not today, anyway."

"I shouldn't even be up." The father pulled his bathrobe around himself before he shuffled barefoot back to the bedroom.

The mother loomed over her son, her lamprey-thin body already in her grey coat. She maneuvered the boy's hands through their corresponding sleeves, her methodical technique practiced, like threading the eye of a fishhook in the dark.

The boy stood still, his nose running. His half-closed eyes set too far apart on an otherwise narrow face gave him a goat-like appearance. The child had a God-given patience about him, similar to others they'd met at support meetings for the voiceless, the mother realized.

"You'll like this new school," she said, repeatedly nodding as if trying to convince herself. "I know it's not ideal to start in November but at least you finally got in."

The bedroom door whipped open. The boy's father stuck his head into the hall. "Goodbye, Cedric. Remember to draw us a picture of what it's like, okay, son?"

The boy jumped up and down, his spindly arms jabbing the air next to his ears like a Jack-in-the-Box.

Once mother and son were in the corridor the mother motioned at Cedric to go ahead and ring for the elevator. Their recently constructed apartment building was the only housing complex in their small town equipped with such convenience.

Long ash-coloured shadows cast by the Baptist Church and a used clothing depot prophesied a somber morning.

"Blue skies are on their way, I hope," the mother reassured the boy.

He looked up, his little wide eyes squinting, and left a trail of snot on his coat sleeve.

"Where are your manners?" his mother said, tugging a crumpled tissue from her pocket. She stooped and began the work of cleaning up his nose and lips.

"Blow," she said, and he blew.

They walked a few blocks into a stiff wind until they reached the storefront where they were to meet the short bus arranged by the new school. A school with the promise of smaller classes. Highly specialized teachers. Extra staff to bridle those who became unruly.

The boy stood facing his reflection in the stationery store window. He experimented with different looks: hands on his hips, fingers in his pockets with thumbs sticking out, fists knotted next to his legs, and when his mother looked away, pretend-smoking.

She adjusted her coat collar so it would meet the scarf resting on the back of her neck.

"Chilly for a first day of school, isn't it, Cedric?" she said, her lips pursed into a thin line.

She believed if he'd been the sort of child who spoke his mind, he'd say how much it sucked to be the new kid, how he dreaded becoming a target at recess.

The boy's name would not help his cause at the new school. It was one of those names passed down through generations, a raft of Cedrics graced with large hands and sturdy bodies on short thick legs. Lucky for him, his parents weren't inclined to use the pretentious moniker: Cedric the 5th.

Mother and son leaned against the store window and waited, each absorbed in their own thoughts, when Kevin Strupp loped down the sidewalk from the fifties-style diner on the corner. The mother had bumped into Kevin before, here and there when she was out and about in town, but Cedric had not.

Kevin's giant body listed left then right as he shuffled towards them. He had a curious habit of lifting a hand to his forehead as if in salute before the arm dropped to his side only to repeat the process all over again. With every arm fling, a guttural sound rumbled out of him, a sound like wild boars rooting around for truffles.

He wore matching brown clothes: an oversized coat, baggy splash pants, a toque barely pulled down enough to conceal ear lobes that appeared to have been bitten off. And rubber galoshes, the kind school-aged kids wore when Cedric's mother was a girl, with difficult-to-do-up silver buckles and a non-slip tread that didn't actually do much to prevent falls. His outfit reminded her of a clay-bottom river after a heavy rain.

She held her position, projecting herself as tall and confident, her back pressed against the store's cold glass. If her shoulders hunched forward, the fear coursing through her might expose itself and there was no knowing how Kevin would respond. She had her boy's interests and safety to consider. Summoning her husband to be there jumped into her mind but she nudged the notion away. He was at home, dead to the world, after pulling a double-shift.

All at once, Cedric leapt into the air, stamping and gesturing at Kevin Strupp, making shrill wordless utterances, squeals more likely to come from a sow's pen.

The mother tried to quell her son's outburst by giving him a stiff sideways glance, her eyebrows rigid, her parched lips pulled from her gums, her compact teeth like soldiers ready to rush into battle.

Kevin's stern face charged toward them. Not so close that he was completely in their bubble but near enough all the same to force a shiver to slink along the mother's long back. Her eyes darkened as she peered directly into Kevin's. He didn't even flinch.

Plaits of thick black hair poked from the edges of his toque, reminding her of drapes on a school stage. His face was mostly forehead with eyes, nose, and mouth slapped on the bottom like an afterthought. It was difficult to nail down Kevin's age as he had a childishness about him coupled with the movements of a timeworn elder, relentlessly listing from side to side, his muscles browbeating him to finally keel over.

What the mother dreaded were Kevin Strupp's eyes with their heavily veined lids over bloodshot sclera and irises the colour of soot, piercing her with naked surveillance.

"Good morning," the mother said, forcing a false welcome in the hopes it might endear Kevin.

He cocked a boot heel against the sidewalk before his hand shot to his toque, his arm forming a V before falling to his thigh. Then came the grunt. The mother remained rigid as she watched the spectacle, arms over her bosom, rooted to her spot as if she owned the sidewalk.

Cedric flattened against his mother's thigh, earlier jitters now under control. His helpless hands dangled from his wrists; his button chin thrust into his mother's coat. If Cedric could have, he might have had the notion to inquire about the bus, why it wasn't there yet, or if it still intended to come.

There were some people, purported experts, who believed that Kevin Strupp's only failing was his softness of mind, the direct result of a mother who sucked from a whiskey bottle her entire pregnancy. Others said, "No!" He was special because of his healing powers. That if those were channelled properly, the infirm could reap benefits. After all, hadn't he cured Beven Schellenburg after half his stomach had been removed? Kevin's single strike to Bevan's forehead left the previously stricken man able to once again hold down food.

Perhaps Kevin Strupp could cure Cedric; rid him of his muteness, a condition never before witnessed in her or her husband's families. The boy's silence certainly wasn't rooted in a hearing impairment or otherwise obvious medical condition. Cedric always returned promptly to the apartment whenever she hollered for him from the balcony.

If only Kevin Strupp could help Cedric locate his voice.

The mother began to feel peckish, the kind of hungry that comes from having only downed a few mouthfuls of cereal instead of a hearty meal of eggs, cheese, and toast. She glanced at the boy and wondered if he felt the same cramps in his belly.

But she couldn't be worrying about food with the likes of Kevin Strupp only inches away, a mouth of broken ochre teeth, an odour coming from him not unlike compost left too long in a pail under the sink.

The school bus was taking forever. Perhaps she'd gotten her son ready on the wrong day. But she doubted that. She was fastidious with details and scheduling. She had the boy there ahead of time as instructed by transportation services in case the driver showed up early. She resisted glancing at her watch lest Kevin Strupp get the wrong idea and reach out to steal it, or worse, maim the child with a blow to the noggin.

It wouldn't be the first time Kevin had foisted harm on others.

Once, he'd wandered from his parents' home and headed for the Mill Pond park. A school-aged girl was alone on the swings, launching herself skyward by pumping her legs. Kevin snuck up from behind as he was wont to do. Braked her progress by grabbing the swing's rusty chains. After the girl had slowed some, his palm cupped her chest, fingers lightly stroking the innocent skin beneath her blousy cotton top.

Some believed Kevin Strupp was only doing what was best. That the girl had been swinging too fast, that somehow, he knew she might be destined to crush her skull on the swing set's wide metal legs, or worse, land on the hard-pack below.

That Kevin Strupp had made the correct choice. He'd done right by stopping the soles of her shoes from brushing the sky.

The police and mayor had received angry phone calls. Complaints. That, despite his ties to the influential Strupp family, a gang with enough wealth to support the entire town, Kevin deserved severe punishment. Because Kevin had harmed a tender-aged child.

Despite the maneuvering by the mayor and his cronies in the name of justice, it seemed that money talked. Kevin Strupp ended up serving no jail time. Instead, he'd remained in a private room at a nearby psychiatric facility. Attended counselling. Complied by consistently taking fistfuls of meds to control his urges. The model patient received an early release.

Cedric's mother cottoned to the mayor's prudent approach. Allowing Kevin Strupp free-reign of the town's innocents could spark more tragedy. It was only a matter of time.

The apartment the mother shared with her husband and Cedric was half a mile away. She'd argued with the provincial school administrator that a bus stop so far from the boy's home would most certainly put the child at risk. The administrator insisted that rules were rules. There were others in town who also needed a lift and individual stops would lengthen the trip beyond what was permitted by legislation.

"Bus rides mustn't edge over the constituted limit," the school administrator explained. "If you prefer, your son could stay here all week and return home on weekends. For the price of room and board, of course."

She wasn't the kind of mother to permit her disadvantaged son to live far from home.

"I wonder where the other children could be?" the mother asked Cedric, not expecting an answer.

Kevin Strupp rocked from foot to foot, snarls leaking from his throat.

The transportation letter remained on the kitchen counter. If only she could phone her husband to check the details, but he'd dive into a funk if she dared wake him. Besides, there weren't any pay phones in sight.

Beyond Kevin's shoulder she spotted three boys of varying sizes, their cheeks sprinkled with freckles, their turquoise coats bopping up and down with each step they took. She was tempted to wave, inquire if they were scheduled to be on the bus, but Kevin kept lumbering closer, her view of the children suddenly blocked by his strapping shoulder.

Kevin undid the buttons of his coat, took it off, and folded it into the V of his arm. Light from the ascending sun gleamed from behind, draping Kevin in the wings of archangels. For a moment she considered other mothers around town who were said to leave their children unsupervised for brief periods of time. The bus was sure to be along shortly. It wasn't as if Kevin had even noticed her son. He seemed keen for her, not the boy.

She worried for her job. It wasn't as if she could afford to be kicked to the curb. They were saving for a down payment on a house. Her boss had permitted her this one-time-only opportunity to show Cedric how the bus worked, but that was it.

"He's nine-years-old, for heaven's sake, old enough to wait on his own," her boss had said, his thumbs doing a worry-dance.

She knew she had to get back to work. After all, payroll was due at the bank.

Kevin crept closer still, his booted feet bumping along as if plantar warts were causing him pain. His eyes flicked from side to side, causing the mother's chest to tighten, while Cedric remained oblivious, his voice clammed up inside.

The mother's gaze travelled to the opposite side of the street to see if she could spot the three brothers. She took care to appear as if she were admiring Kevin instead of soliciting help. She worried that if she gawked off into the distance too long Kevin might notice and do more than twitch and hover. He might finish them off right then and there.

"Stand up, Cedric," she told her son who had allowed himself to slip to the ground, a dazed look over his pale face, the point of his tongue locked between his lips.

Three things happened next. Kevin bundled the folded coat against his chest and rocked it like a baby. Next, a thin sound escaped from the boy's lips, not unlike the *b-b-b* at the start of the word ball followed by a long hiss much like the sound of brakes. Lastly, the short bus pulled up at the exact moment the mother yanked Cedric from the pile of cigarette butts, bottle caps, and wrappers in which he crouched.

After the door swung open, the driver said, "Figured you'd be here. Your boy's stop is actually Third Avenue A. This here's Third Avenue. I'll drop him off in front of the Empire Hotel this afternoon, four thirty sharp. You can count on lots of eyes being there."

As the mother watched her boy head off, the street shimmered in a crimson-yellow glow, pushing away the grey. Kevin Strupp didn't get to them this time and come tomorrow, Cedric would be waiting someplace new. She turned with bright eyes toward her day.

Sad Mommy

Within days of giving birth and once the euphoria of bringing new life into the world had evaporated, I inched through my days at the speed of treacle. My thoughts were muddled, my beet-blistered eyes oozing fatigue. My days post-birth now consisted of baby-shit and spit-up. It was clear that John was fed up with me. He told me that if I didn't agree to attend Sad Mommy Munchkin Group, his mother was destined to remain underfoot for the foreseeable future.

The arrival of Baby Maxine had left a stain on John too. Her birth had turned him into a seedy turd who offered zero help with the baby, especially when it mattered most, such as the middle of the night. No matter how hard I elbowed him, the end result was a shower of farts and a typhoon of snoring from his side of the bed.

I tried bringing up my frustration to him one morning after a particularly difficult night getting her back to sleep. "The least you could do is offer to get her from the nursery for the 2 a.m. feeding," I said, struggling to keep my hands from choking the life out of him.

"Then we'd be two exhausted parents instead of only one. Besides, you're the one nursing her," he said, the logic of his excuse something I elected to ignore.

Saddled with an infant during a global pandemic had caused me to feel shackled to our home. John was fortunate; he shirked the blinding daily monotony of changing dozens of dirty diapers by heading off to work at the hospital.

To make matters worse, Baby Maxine shrieked at the prospect of being confined to her car seat. So, taking her on leisurely drives in the country was out of the question. The Internet said many infants resisted their car seats but *in a matter of time things would improve.* If all parenting advice came with a mitten full of cash, we'd have enough for our baby's Montessori school tuition.

Because the group for sad mommies met in a park around the corner from where we lived, a location I could walk to, I couldn't come up with a single legitimate reason to miss it. So, I told John he could count on me to attend.

~

Days trudged by until the first date of the sad mommy group arrived. By the time I showed up at the park, the other moms and a token dad were already there. Because of pandemic health mandates, each participant sat six feet apart. There were hand-made quilts and crocheted blankets, babies and toddlers tucked against their respective caregivers' thighs.

The parents cracked weak-ass grins when the leader, a woman with salt-and-pepper hair tucked into a ponytail and sweat beading along her brow, nudged them to introduce themselves and their child.

Baby Maxine wore a long-sleeved onesie I'd designed and prototyped in my at-home art studio. Crimson strawberries with frowning, surprised, and bewildered emoticons dotted the otherwise pristine white fabric.

A mom whose red-rimmed eyes rivaled my Zombie slits pressed a nipple into her infant's mouth. "I honestly don't know how much longer I can do this," she managed to say before a flood ran down both cheeks.

Spoiler alert, I thought. *This group wasn't going to be any fun at all.*

I fidgeted with a hair elastic mined from the grass. My fingers wound their way through the stretchy band like a Romanian tumbler performing a never-before-viewed gymnastics routine. I wished I'd rehearsed what I might say before the talking stick found its way to me. Whatever I came up with, I'd have to work at keeping my temper in check. I could always wave the stick off by saying 'Pass,' an option the leader had offered.

I couldn't stop thinking about the bank statement for my design company that had arrived earlier by email. It indicated that my business account was grossly overdrawn. Now I had that to contend with on top of everything else.

John's mother had suggested earlier in the week that I try and nap when the baby was down. I'd lied and said that I had tried a time or two but that I ended up filled with guilt. Truth was I couldn't figure out how to look after the baby, my business, and the household chores that picketed for my attention. Never-ending mounds of laundry. Dishes to wash. Carpets to vacuum.

It didn't help that John's mother was completely useless. She simply had no idea. If she offered to assist in the day-to-day work, even doing some light housekeeping, I might actually start to feel like I was returning to the world again. It wasn't as if she'd worked a real job while John and his brothers were little. They always had hired help around. I shuddered with self-loathing when the words *real job* popped out of nowhere. Not only was I a lousy mother of a newborn, I was turning into a bitch on top of everything.

My mother-in-law didn't actually *do* anything to help me or the baby. She declined prods to rock Baby Maxine because it made her sciatica act up. Didn't cook supper or order in. Never even tossed a load of laundry into the washer. Just clucked her tongue, ribbons of disapproval etched on her face, the smell of her talcum powder plugging up my sinuses.

A waif of a girl in yoga pants and an oversized tie-dyed sweatshirt clutched the talking stick to her chest and said, "My baby's in the NICU at St. Mary's. I'm supposed to go every day. Stroke her skin, whisper that I love her. I try but it's hard, you know, really hard."

An avocado-sized lump threatened to close my throat. NICU—where babies with serious health issues were kept.

"It's an hour by bus to the hospital," the girl added.

I studied her from across the sad mommy circle. She looked to be about seventeen, eighteen at most. Some people shouldn't be parents. A bold thing for me to say, but I believed I was right in this case. She was nothing more than a child and now she had a seriously ill baby. The two of them didn't stand a chance in hell.

It saddened me to consider that hope lived in the misery of others. Next to the NICU mother sat someone whose female partner reportedly lounged around all day watching NFL reruns. Beside the leader, a toddler played peek-a-boo from behind his mom's gourd-shaped belly. And the token dad? His newly-adopted-baby-turned-vampire (his words, not mine) slept all day and cried all night.

When the talking stick headed my way, I took a moment to smooth my hair and roll my head side-to-side. I said, "Good thing Baby Maxine has a guardian angel. I've been obsessing about what life would be like if my baby were no longer here."

Around me, the members of the sad mommy group released a collective sigh. The leader's eyes flickered with a spark of panic before she said, "Honesty is good. If that's how you feel, I'm glad you told us. You're here and I see that you haven't done your baby any harm."

As she spoke, I felt my shoulders collapse; her reaction told me I wasn't completely nuts but not exactly normal, either. I certainly didn't feel gaga over my baby like the fucking perfect moms of goddamned Instagram. Internet Mommy sites were, in my opinion, toxic. I lowered my gaze to my lap where Baby Maxine was dopey with dreams of milk, naps, and dry diapers.

And just like that, group was over. Everyone scurried off in various directions while I slowly started to get myself organized to leave. It turned out I was the last one there. The leader was standing with her back to me, nodding at her cell phone. She spoke so loudly that I could overhear that she was making arrangements for after-school care for her children.

The idea of going back to face my mother-in-law made my eczema flare so instead of going home, I turned and headed in the opposite direction.

As I walked, I delighted in the sensory details of the fall day. People calling out, the far away hum of lawn mowers, dogs yipping, leaf piles smoldering. I followed a path along the

Avon River to a pedestrian bridge, then wound past a waterfowl sanctuary until I reached a gazebo located on the opposite side of the river.

A light dusting of frost still dotted the gazebo's north facing roofline. It didn't seem cold enough for frost but there was no denying its existence. I studied the shingles longer than I might have, as if doing so would permit me to delay yet another inevitable clash with what awaited me at home. Along the rectangular roof tiles were tiny human footprints, distinctive in size and shape but clearly made by baby feet. I tucked the idea away for a future receiving blanket design.

That's when I remembered that I had a baby and said baby was not strapped to my body. That at some point I'd undone the snaps and set Baby Maxine and the BABYBJÖRN carrier down on the blanket on the other side of the river.

"Jesus fucking Christ!" I cried. "What kind of mother forgets her baby?"

Get moving, I thought. I ran, my eyes wild, arms thrusting like pistons. Sweat pooled in my armpits despite the chill in the air. Soon I was where the group had been held. I scanned the grass for what was mine but all I saw were fallen leaves, a granola wrapper trapped under a yellow rattle, and depressions in the grass created by diaper bags, baby bottles, shoes, and blankets.

My first instinct was to call John. Admit I'd left the baby at the mercy of raccoons and molesters. No, that wouldn't do. He'd minimize things and tell me to calm the hell down, that there was always a logical explanation. *Babe, we'll get this all sorted out.*

I pawed my pockets. *Shit. Where was my phone?* It had to be in the diaper bag.

I headed home as quickly as my legs would go, the wind snapping my jeans against my shins. Once there I could gather my thoughts, make some calls. I had the group leader's phone number somewhere. Maybe she knew, had seen something.

As I neared the front steps of my home, something felt off. Like when you're out hiking a new trail through the woods and your nose picks up an unsavoury odour but you can't figure out if it's an exotic plant or rotting flesh. My spidey sense was going off. When I pushed the door open, my mother-in-law's face loomed from the dim interior, repugnance creasing the skin of her face.

"About time," she hissed.

I spotted Baby Maxine's diaper bag sitting on the floor by the wall. "The baby's here? She's here?"

"Asleep in her crib—no thanks to her mother."

"Oh my God. I was so worried." I could feel my eyes turn wet behind my glasses.

I stayed by the diaper bag as if rooted there as my mother-in-law towered over me with her thick legs.

Elephant tree legs, my mother used to call limbs like that when she was still around, not gallivanting the world with her latest hook-up.

"How did she get here?" I asked.

My mother-in-law's lip curled in disdain. "You want me to say the police?"

"No, I just want the truth."

"The leader. She had the foresight to have your address on a clip board."

"Does John know?"

"It's your job to confess to my son how negligent you've been. And for the record, I always thought you were pathetic." My mother-in-law turned and headed for the guestroom.

I wiped the back of my hand against my nose which was now dripping with snot. My mother-in-law was right; I *was* pathetic. Baby Maxine was lucky this time. I pulled my phone from the diaper bag and opened the contacts. It was time to make some calls.

~

A few days later a woman in a black blazer, white blouse, and nutmeg-coloured pencil skirt sounded the doorbell. I'd heard a car door slam so I was already lurking in the foyer.

"Who are you?" I demanded through the closed door though I knew precisely who she was. She was the monster who'd been sent here to apprehend Baby Maxine.

The woman glanced at her digital watch before pressing a business card against the sidelight, the Child and Family Service's monogram shrieking with significance next to her name in bright-gold font.

"I've got a headache, a migraine, actually." I said, a web of fingers loose over my eyes. "The kind that comes with auras. Call later to set something up."

When the woman didn't move, I realized that I didn't matter to her. She was here for the child.

"Where are your manners?" my mother-in-law said, a mannequin smile pasted to her lips. "Open the door and invite her in while I brew tea."

The woman followed me into the living room before sitting in an armchair across from the sofa. Her pudgy fingers kneaded the fabric of her skirt in order to push it over her thighs, her black leather briefcase oozing importance on the floor next to her.

"We need to have a conversation about what happened at the park," she said, studying my face with neutral interest.

Absence of small talk. A sure sign that Baby Maxine would be on her way out of my life.

I waited. She waited. For some kind of an explanation.

I needed to come up with a reason why I should be permitted to keep my baby. But the words wouldn't come; it was as if someone had stuffed cotton balls against the roof of my mouth. I couldn't explain away stupid. That I'd become doltish, a simpleton, merely from having given birth, as if a tiny vacuum had sucked away any remaining brain matter and had left vacuous holes in its wake.

"I only went as far as the gazebo. Not too far, all things considered," I said quickly, before my head bowed in shame.

The worker's mouth masticated as if she were gnawing on a tiny shard of willow. She must have thought I was both dangerous and daft, such a sorrowful combination. How abandoning my infant was not something Baby Maxine should have as part of her birth story.

But I knew fear. It was all I knew, in fact. I said, "I know you might not care but I barely feel human anymore."

I folded my fingers into fists, concealing nails bitten to the quick.

As the worker tried to maintain an impartial expression, the air between us thickened, the tepid tea in our cups no longer desirable.

"I'm dying here!" I said, my voice louder than necessary for the size of the room.

"Where is the baby right now?" the worker asked, her face oscillating between her actual face and that of a serpent.

"I don't know." I rubbed my eyes. "My mother-in-law—"

"You have a habit of leaning on others," the worker told me, her left eye now the size of a dime. "It has resulted in you detaching from your baby, all of which might explain what went on in the park."

The worker pulled out an electronic notebook and began to write notes. Clicking and clacking the fillable fields. Words to expose the terrible mother I was.

In spite of myself, I said, "You can't really blame me. Leaning on John's mother."

With the worker's face still pointed at the screen, I spotted traces of grey sprouting from the part in her hair.

"She's been here exactly two months and fifteen days."

The worker lifted her face and said, "I'm sure she's been a great—"

"I want her gone," I said, my hand cupping my mouth to block my mother-in-law from hearing.

"What's that?" the worker said.

"I need her to leave!" I said, the muscles of my jaw tightening. "I told John last night. I need to learn how to operate as a mother, independent of her, without her hanging over me, making me feel unfit."

The worker set her notebook aside. "Off-the-record, it's clear you need help. Perhaps your mother-in-law is not the answer, not the right choice moving forward but I have to think of Baby Maxine, her interests. These cases can be so complicated."

I detected the loud clatter of dishes in the kitchen, John's mother's way of saying she'd been eavesdropping and been hurt by what I'd said. I experienced a brief modicum of relief that at least she was helping put away the dishes.

My throat began to constrict. I fumbled in my pockets for a cough candy, anything to stop the overbearing tickle, the feeling that this conversation would be the end of me.

"You're going to take my baby from me?" I managed to squeak out.

"Oh, heavens, no. What happened in the park was a warning. By all accounts, the baby is fine. You, on the other hand, are not. I can help put some things into place—perhaps connect you with a doula to come in. Get some meals made so you can bond with the baby. Arrange for additional group

support. Get the doctor to start you on a trial of medication."
The worker smiled for the first time.

A gentle voice rolled around in my ear: *You're all right.*
You're going to be okay. I wanted to burst out laughing because of
course I *was* okay. I was alive, secure in my home, my baby
safely tucked away in her crib. I felt my shoulders soften as I
realized I might get to the other side and not perish before the
next day's dawn.

What's the Word on Meryl Streep?

Mink, with his wide-eyed acne-free face, is friends with everyone. He likes to fuss over the other students and laugh at their stories while doling out candy cigarettes and liquorice cigars from a stash he keeps in the side pocket of his backpack. His real name isn't Mink. His actual name is something northern-European and tricky to pronounce and spell. Mink doesn't dissuade people from using his real name but when they call him Mink, he breaks into a toothy grin few can resist. The use of the nickname means fewer mix-ups with his grandfather, Lars Kiiminki Sr.

Mink's grandfather is the town's undertaker. His chosen avocation fits the older Lars like a well-tailored suit on a dead man. He wears tuxedoes even when not working. He owns three, so one is always on hand when the others are at the cleaners. After taking a bad fall as a child, Lars Sr. waddles when he walks. As a result, people call him Penguin.

After Mink's parents are trampled to death while elk hunting, Mink moves in with his grandfather at the funeral home.

Weeks before Mink's eighteenth birthday, Penguin says, his brow bridled with concern, "We need to discuss your plans for after high school."

Mink's moist hands grip the edges of his seat. It's never occurred to him to contemplate a life beyond school. While his friends complete applications to universities and colleges or consider a trade, Mink sits there, stuck. He tries to come up with something, but has no clear idea of a direction.

He finally lets it slip to his grandfather that he missed the university application process. Penguin's fingers weave together as if releasing them might cause them to fling across the room and strike Mink. He waits for his grandfather to yell or shake him. Instead, his grandfather does something worse; he stews in silence.

A few days later, Mink says to his grandfather, "I was wondering what you'd think if I moved into the doll house?"

The doll house is a salmon-coloured shack tucked against a row of overgrown cedars. It and the hedge keep the funeral home property from encroaching upon the Methodist Church parking lot.

"I'd be out of your hair that way," Mink adds. "Maybe I could fix it up."

Penguin grits his teeth and nods in agreement. "But there's no lesson from living there for free. You need something to fill your days. Either ante up room and board or work it off by doing chores."

The menial jobs hold more appeal than handing over cash Mink doesn't have.

Within days Mink is staining weather-beaten siding. Mending loose hinges. Turning over the compost. Planting and tending the gardens. Mowing the lawn. Boring, mindless tasks that offer little in the way of joy or reward.

Then, in early May, on a day too breezy and hesitant to finally open itself up to spring, Kirk, a close friend of Mink's, alters the direction of their lives.

Unbeknownst to Penguin whose week has been slammed with three corpses in as many days, Mink sneaks out and climbs onto the back of Kirk's motorcycle. A rain-slick curve, speed, and driver error cause the bike to career off the road and down the escarpment. Kirk succumbs to his injuries at the scene.

Mink, many say, is luckier. He is confined to hospital for months. Sepsis of the right tibia necessitates amputation below the knee. Loss of limb, though, is not the reason he gives on his disability pension application. Instead, upon Penguin's advice, Mink uses macular degeneration due to the motorcycle collision as the basis for his claim. "People can get around with one leg. But to suddenly lose one's sight at such a young age …," Penguin says, his face stiff as if entombed in cement.

Mink's central vision consists of circular shadows, a condition more commonly diagnosed in the elderly. His peripheral sight is all he has to navigate the world. Stripped of his leg *and* vision causes the words *my life sucks* to coil in his mind like swirls of ticker tape.

Once Mink's stump fully heals and he's been fitted and trained in the use of a prosthetic, Penguin says, "You're all set, then, for the doll house."

But Mink isn't ready. He keeps repeating, "Who's going to take care of me?"

Despite having already grieved the loss of his parents, his friend, Kirk, and now the loss of his mobility and sight, Mink is tangled in sorrow. Doom, dark as black-out curtains, swallows his will to move forward with his life.

Penguin can't bear to lose Mink, too, like he did his son and daughter-in-law, so he encloses his grandson with a team consisting of a disabled-Olympian-turned-psychiatrist, a raft of counsellors, and an art therapist.

Mink finds himself with impenetrable cognitive fog. He isn't able to execute the steps involved in simple tasks such as taking a shower. Can't recall dates such as his own birthday, the day of the week, or even the month. Can't find anything. His possessions are flung everywhere: his backpack, boxers, jeans, and T-shirts, and stacks of magazines and comic books dropped off by well-meaning friends too timid to step inside.

All the while, Mink's life swells with experts resolved to pull him out of his funk.

The team tells him to try and meet them part way, to view his grief as a strand of wool unravelling from a pullover. To Mink, recovery from the loss of his former life feels like a betrayal. Though Mink resists, making art with the therapist is what finally sparks a renewed zest in him.

He begins by making rudimentary pencil drawings of everyday items in a sketchbook called *1016 BIG Things to Draw*. Later, with a tub of glue at hand, he clips headlines, images, obituaries, and comic strips from the newspaper and glues them to Styrofoam heads the art therapist finds at the Dollar Store. Moving on, Mink creates still-life paintings of his breakfast. What he finds most therapeutic is to portray what his leg looked like prior to amputation. In time, the old Mink begins to surface.

Months after the accident, Mink tells his grandfather over cartons of Thai takeout, "I feel ready to set myself up in the doll house."

In response, Penguin allows a smile to broaden on his face.

~

Along two walls of the doll house, workmen install shelving and cupboards. They connect a table-top microwave, a bar fridge with a compact freezer, and a tiny stainless-steel sink, the kind found in tent trailers. There's a futon and swivel rocker with a matching ottoman. These amenities provide Mink with a semblance of independence and comfort. He only has to return to the main house for washroom and laundry facilities, and to take his evening meals.

Opposite the kitchenette is the flip-top desk where Mink does his crafting, Penguin's word for what saved Mink from remaining in the bowels of depression.

Crafting. Mink despises the word. It grates that Penguin refers to his artistic pursuits as craft. The old man can't differentiate between a crochet hook and a stretched canvas. And Mink's artistic output, he's been told, is extremely creative: he paints using glue sticks, gel medium, torn paper, charcoal, a palette knife, and neon paint. He believes his work rivals that of American neo-expressionist Jean-Michel Basquiat.

If Penguin would tear his eyes from his embalming table long enough to observe what Mink has been doing, he might actually grow some respect for his grandson. But the undertaker business is booming and their times together are brief, so Mink feels there's little he can do to make his grandfather see what a prodigious talent he's become.

Penguin isn't the only one filled with doubts about Mink. Subscribers to Mink's YouTube channel frequently comment that the work demonstrates breath-taking innovation—for a disabled man—that is. *Hardly fair*, he thinks.

Every Thursday, Mink books the disability van to drop him at the library where he sifts through magazines in a crate labelled FREE STUFF. Hunting, automotive, and parenting magazines don't pique much interest, but *People, Animal Antics, The Photo Ark,* and *Us Weekly* do, as do tourist pamphlets and tattered road maps.

Every art project begins the same. He gingerly turns the brittle magazine pages, the paper and ink weakened by strong sunlight beaming through the all-glass library doors. He tears out bright bubble fonts. Columns of grey ink. Headlines. Smatterings of foreign words. Combinations of letters and numbers such as those found in formulas. After amassing stacks of clippings, he returns to the doll house to thoughtfully arrange and adhere the treasures to canvas.

After the first layer is dry to the touch, he sketches with twig charcoal. Butterflies, spiders, feathered friends such as Great Blue Herons. Whatever strikes his whimsy is crudely sketched on top of the words.

Mink then scours the magazines again, this time for images to add around and over the words and roughly rendered lines. Because his central vision is akin to looking through soot, the outer edges of his eyes do the seeing for him. Seated at his desk, the magazines a few inches from his cheek, his head becomes a periscope, his broken eyes mining the souls of famous people and animals.

Flustered by lips filled with Botox and noses straightened by plastic surgeons, he decides that eyes are what rouse his imagination.

Occasionally, if his schedule permits, Penguin stops by, not only to check up on Mink but to cheer him on. And each time he looks at what's been created, he begins to stutter and stammer, landing on, "What's the word on Meryl Streep today?"

It's unclear if Penguin's words are intended to be disingenuous or if this is his lame attempt at humour. Sensitive to the potency of his grandfather's criticism, Mink feels himself begin to shrink.

"I'm getting in touch with the medium, is all," Mink replies from below his desk, his sticky fingers pawing dust bunnies for a misplaced glue stick.

Mink abhors these impromptu visits. After Mink's release from hospital and while undergoing therapy with his at-home team, he languished in the clutches of darkness. At high school, he was a different person, someone accustomed to a constant bombardment of friends. Now, he acknowledges, no one bothers to hang with the crippled misfit, a term he's grown to use in reference to himself.

Sliding into a blue funk is something he must protect himself from. To guard himself during creative times, he hangs a sign on the door: ARTIST AT WORK — DON'T YOU DARE DISTURB, then sets the deadbolt, and dives into his collage work.

While sporadically drawn to the eyes of felines and other hairy beasts, famous people's eyes carry a vacancy that animals don't. Despite having successful film and TV careers, actors' eyes seem ever-searching, thirsty for what's out of reach.

Their eyes come in an assortment of colours: mocha, turquoise, and green with gold flecks. They boast countless shapes: almond, oblong, round as lichee fruit, while some are almost square. A few are so tiny they resemble slits. Some are behind glasses though most aren't.

Ann-Margret with her striking hazel. Mila Kunis with her one sightless eye. The crazy ink-coloured blinkers that catapulted Uzo Aduba into stardom on *Orange is the New Black*. Meryl Streep with her penetrating blue irises. Mink studies the eyes so long, he swears they wink back. He brings the paper cut-outs to within inches of his face and inhales their inky fragrance, then slips off his prosthetic and sprawls on the floor, hundreds of eyeballs monitoring his movements.

He loves the flow and process he's developed. Many evenings, he texts his grandfather to say that he'll be skipping the evening meal; then he gorges on pizza pockets he keeps in the mini-freezer, working well into the night.

Within two years and after many attempts at finding his artistic voice, Mink is selected to headline a one-person art show at a chic downtown gallery, a show he calls MINK ☻.

The installation consists of globe-sized eyeballs, their inorganic components sourced from costume shops and retired opticians. The eyes dangle from dehydrated entrails affixed to the gallery's redwood ceiling rafters. Thousands of artificial eyes suspended from fish line, some sourced from as far away as the Ukraine, leave visitors to quiver with dread. Special lighting and mirrors make a person feel as if they're bathing in vitreous liquid.

On opening day, sweat trickles down Mink's back, not because he's prone to excessive sweating, but because of the explosive interest in his exhibit. In him.

Children are encouraged to not only browse but to *fondle* the installation. Tactile experiences like this are unheard of. The youngsters' squeals fill the stuffy gallery with joy mingled with repulsion.

There are oceans of responses to the show. Awe. Pursed lips. Scrunched noses. Furrowed brows. Shrieks of disbelief. Collective squirming. Full-on nausea and vomiting. Then, the murmur of the words *utter lunacy* while making a run for the exit.

Despite the varied responses, every giant eyeball is spoken for within a week of his show's opening.

Through special effects, Mink floats amid the eyeballs as if he's a swan, his white cane striking patrons' heads while frantically inquiring, "Has anyone bumped into Lars Sr.?"

People nervously back away from the cane, muttering, "Not here. Not tonight."

The *NY Times* writes, "While intriguing and courageous, MINK 👁 lacks general appeal." Though it's a clear and honest review, Mink takes exception to the words *absolute rubbish* in a quote from a renowned critic on assignment from central Europe.

The experience leaves Mink with a crushing headache and swollen eyes, the latter a result of sobbing when his grandfather turns out to be a no-show. Later, Mink finds moderate relief by soaking his lids under wet tea bags.

Weeks go by until he can finally re-claim his artistic identity by heading back to the studio and digging in. He begins by coating huge canvasses in cut-outs. The final step, the palette knife smearing paint before it's pulled away to expose the *Weltschmerz* therein, triggers both pain and joy. Nothing tidy about the end result, but rather, a ferocious attempt at gaining control and tamping down chaos.

~

Years later, when interviewed by *USA Today,* thirty-year-old Mink doesn't shy away from the questions. He prides himself on having become a famous multi-disability artist amid controversy, doesn't conceal his blindness behind dark glasses, and manages to get around on crutches rather than use a prosthetic. He likes when people turn to look at him and say *Now that man* is *something!*

Mink believes if he hadn't been on that motorcycle that day, he might not have stumbled upon his artistic voice. That he'd most likely be a cart boy at *Plenty Fresh* or working as a mystery shopper. Instead, the government annually awards him the Double-D grant, Double-D standing for double-disability. If *he* isn't qualified, who is? In addition to his pension, the grant provides him a way to offer workshops for differently-abled creatives.

Whenever people ask who inspired his creativity, Mink wells up, the sight of his grandfather's now emaciated body shackled to a wreath of chemotherapy tubes at the forefront of his thoughts.

"My grandfather, a huge fan of what he called crafting, always said I had a way of making Meryl Streep look good."

When Penguin finally succumbs to his diagnosis, Mink feels he has no choice. The world must commit Penguin, like Mink will, to memory. So, Mink stretches out on his dollhouse cot, his good leg elevated and braced by the wall, and begins the painstaking job of coming up with something amazing.

He considers M. C. Escher's 1946 sketch of his own eye, evidence of a skull oozing from the pupil, as inspiration. Or perhaps the focus should be on Penguin's eye colour. A mural consisting of a simply rendered blue painting. Staged in a public space. Something similar to *The Eye of Horus* as depicted in the Tomb of Sennedjem, ca. 1250 BC. Or should he take wisdom from Salvador Dalí's *The Eye*, a 1945 piece commissioned by Alfred Hitchcock himself?

No! He must come up with something completely original.

After many hours, while deep in a trance-like state, Mink sits up and shouts, "I've got it." He'll honour Penguin by deconstructing his grandfather's dot matrix printer and desktop computer. His idea is to repurpose their components, items that would otherwise end up as e-waste.

He imagines himself constructing replicas of Penguin's various glasses worn throughout his life. Capacitors, Molex connectors, and power jacks melted and reshaped into funky overlapping frames. A pyramid of frames worn by an oversized rendition of Penguin's head. A crafting activity if there ever was one, a creation to make his grandfather proud.

The Stars Have It

While Kim was in the care of a babysitter, her parents' vehicle collided with a freight train, so her mother's brother took her in. Even though Uncle Wink had never before looked after anyone but himself, he willingly shared his small cabin at the edge of Storyville with his niece.

Within days, Uncle Wink hung Kim's natal chart on the wall next to the wooden table where they took their meals, moon and planet phases clearly marked with her exact moment of entry into the world. Kim didn't think to ask how her uncle knew the details of her birth, considering that he and her mother hadn't spoken in years.

Time soon passed and with it Kim's skin broke out into purple pustules and a labyrinth of blackheads. When she complained about the acne, her uncle simply shrugged his shoulders and said, "That's your destiny, I suppose."

With her birthday in December, a Saturday no less, according to Uncle Wink, Kim was destined to be predictably sorrowful and besotted by everlasting grief. She was ordained to slink through life like the scrawniest of runts, cursed by a carefully crafted playbook.

She gnashed her teeth against Uncle Wink's astrological babbling. The more she battled, the calmer he became, speaking as if scripted. "Some people believe the stars are just up there in the sky offering a great view but are devoid of meaning. I believe that the stars are a predetermined road map of our lives, steering us away from life's endless chaos."

Uncle Wink was a devout follower of CHAM radio's *Astrology Now*, a call-in program on Saturday afternoons. Her uncle would call in to defend astrological principles, his face shiny with flush as his right fist pounded the kitchen table with each point he made against the naysayers.

One Wednesday, the stars aligned against Wink. A hit-and-miss vegetarian, Wink was told by an internist to increase his intake of animal protein. Wink began to devour meat with the wild abandon of an adolescent boy. His teeth, tongue, and lips dove into poultry, beef, fish, lamb, bacon, as well as wild game. On the fateful day in question, a cunning chicken bone porpoised from the back of his tongue toward his lungs. A hung-over paramedic was unable to forcep the wily bone out. Wink didn't stand a chance.

Kim, besotted with grief, took to committing the family's star charts to memory. This helped soothe the initial melancholy that choked her. After Wink's cremation, she returned to school, a fake smile pasted on her droopy face. When proposed, Kim readily accepted the headmaster's offer to cover the entire cost of the year-end trip, a tour of Times Square, Broadway, and other Big Apple sites.

The morning of the trip, the charter bus departed under the shadow of an unfavourable star.

Upon entering the Turquoise Sand and Straw Sculpture exhibit at The New Museum of Contemporary Art, rather than paying attention to the numerous faults and cracks in the concrete floor, Kim's eyes ricocheted everywhere. Her mouth agape, her neck swiveling, she wondered how the curator had managed to cram so much into one display.

By Day 3 of the trip, Kim allowed herself to blunder; she abandoned her customary cautious approach and began waltzing around with the confidence of an urbanite. She strode about with nary a care, her head stuck in the pillowy cumulous clouds dangling from the gallery ceiling. She gazed while she walked, and walked while she gazed. As a result, a body check into the accessible washroom came from nowhere like a judder from an electric socket.

The constellations were to blame.

It came as no surprise when Kim found herself with child after the unexpected sexual assault in the aforementioned accessible washroom. A thankfully short-lived but fierce penetration. If Kim had had proof of the man's identity, she'd have immediately reported the assailant, but his characteristics and any distinguishing marks were unknown, something that comes from being taken from behind.

Kim realized it could have been anyone. The skateboarders. The bald panhandler. The executive with the exquisite handlebar moustache. No matter, she'd mocked them all only moments before skipping up the ramp and pushing through the turnstile into the gallery.

After a rather uneventful pregnancy, the baby arrived earlier than predicted, or Kim wanted. Without benefit of pain medication or delivery coach, the newborn dove from Kim's nether regions like an Olympic platform diver, institutional green walls in the baby's sights, his rubbery appendages lagging behind head and shoulders, the delivery more afterthought than outcome.

"What a fine-looking lad. Nicely proportioned face to go with those rather prominent ears. A head as round as a full moon," the on-call midwife said, before whisking him off to be weighed and wiped.

All Kim could think was *What if?* What if the little bastard had been born just a few minutes later? He'd have missed arriving at the same time as the dreaded full moon at its brightest and roundest. What if he'd waited until Sunday, the first of January, to be born? He'd leapt from her privates as if hurdling off stilts. *Dang stars*, she thought. *Goddamn it to hell,*

Uncle Wink. Look what I have to contend with now! And all on my own.

Kim took Wade home a couple of days later, to Uncle Wink's cabin on the edge of town past the torn-out rail lines, a home now hers to share with the baby.

An older maternal type who lived a few houses away reviewed the basics. What to do when the baby cried, how to feed, burp, and care for him. Kim learned how to stroke his plump cheek with her nipple as a way to coax him to suckle at her overly full breast.

After burping him, she rocked him to sleep, holding him as if he were a fallen star, precious and fragile. Once he'd begun to dream on the mattress next to her, she'd listen to his breaths, his short, quick inhales, and wish with all her heart to feel something, anything at all, for the baby. Instead, there was only emptiness, like a pond void of water.

When he nursed, when he wound his fingers around her thumb, when his face broke into a smile likely brought on by gas, Kim bristled with the hollowness of it all.

If Kim's uncle were still alive, he would declare that fate had dealt baby and mother shared providence, that destiny would drive them apart, like lavender repels bugs on a muggy night.

There was no cure for the curse of sharing similar sun signs.

Rotten luck coursed through the baby's veins and into hers. Because of him, Kim had been unable to accumulate enough credits to graduate high school. Because of him, their life was split between poverty and boredom. If only she'd hung on and birthed him a moment or two later. If he were a New Year's baby, publicity of being first would have blessed them with a modicum of luck and a decent amount of media attention. Some sorry sap might have felt pity and showered them in dollar bills.

Sleep deprivation was next. Frazzled with fatigue, Kim feared catastrophe around every corner. It was only a matter of time before tragedy would erupt. Every hiccup, cry, and whimper from the baby felt like a chain of transport trucks rumbling past. A month after his birth, Kim's milk dried up, her breasts slack as punctured balloons.

Kim located a wet nurse, a generous soul willing to breastfeed the baby for free. Kim leapt with joy every time Wade left the cabin to stay at the woman's house. She secretly hoped the woman would offer to permanently take Wade off her hands.

With his feedings looked after, Kim began venturing out. She discovered a pop-up rummage shop in the basement of an otherwise empty building. A sandwich board between the front steps and curb indicated it was called *The Penny Hoarder*.

While it took getting used to, it wasn't long before Kim stopped noticing the staleness of the place. It reminded her of her damp jeans and sweatshirts pegged next to the wood stove. Kim soon found herself drawn to the back of the shop. Past the racks of gently used clothes, and stuffed foxes, rabbits, and fish. Beyond the bins of Lincoln Logs and Lego, plastic dinosaurs, and farm animals.

What she was drawn to were the dolls.

They were in various stages of disrepair. Their heads, made of vinyl, had beady eyes that followed Kim around the shop. Some wore dirty dresses and torn socks. Many had suffered haircuts at the hands of a knife-wielding butcher. A few had begun to smell. There was, after all, no Laundromat for dolls. Yet, at some point in their lives the dolls had had purpose.

These were not the sort of dolls collectors of rare finds sought out. Nor would hobbyists be bothered with the likes of these. There weren't any made of bisque or wood or wax. None that could be classified as antique or vintage. Most were shoeless. Some had suffered permanent tattooing at the hands of a toddler and a few had endured battles with tubes of crimson lipstick. Some eyes winked whether they wanted to or not.

A wooden carrier at the rear of the table was jammed with epoch Barbie dolls, carefully crafted ones from the late fifties to early seventies, some with chewed feet and a few with their heads snapped off. The hamper was little more than spare parts.

The laundry basket packed with Cabbage Patch Kids was what drew Kim's interest. Uncle Wink had saved enough money once to find her a used one, a boy, his adoption card pristine inside its yellow vinyl holder, a doll that bore a striking resemblance to Wade.

Kim returned to the shop many times. She said nothing to the clerk or the other customers, just waved as she came and went. She never bought anything. Her time was divided between the doll table and the heavily-thumbed paperbacks even though she didn't consider herself much of a reader.

One night, while she held the baby and swung him back and forth, his tiny body pressed against hers, she stared into his wide brown eyes and wondered. Was he looking at her, or through her? How could she tell what was in his little head? Even at this tender age he seemed to harbour secrets, an uncanny ability to keep his thoughts from Kim's reach.

The next day when the wet nurse messaged that she was unavailable to look after Wade, a rush of resentment mixed with relief washed over Kim. Destiny had selected this day. Kim warmed up some milk before stirring in a spoonful of corn syrup. After, she wrapped Wade in swaddling clothes.

Next, she slung him to her hip before heading for the shop. Her feet moved with light steps, lighter than ever before.

Once the bell over the shop door jingled, Kim headed for the dolls. There seemed to be more kids than last time. She wanted to ask why but thought better of it. With the tops of her thighs pressed against the table's edge, she slipped the baby from the swaddle and nestled him among the other life-size dolls there.

She loved that the kids had realistic faces, had once been loved, and possessed accredited adoption papers. With nary a thought, Kim floated on buoyant feet to the front of the shop, barely offering a perceptible howdy-do at the cashier. Before heading out the door, she left the swaddle to fall onto the floor. She stepped away from the shop and headed in the opposite direction of the cabin, toward the four-lane highway, abandoning the influence of stars.

I Never Dream About

My parents stand at the east-facing window and watch winter melt. Soggy paper, depressed leaves, and grubby piles of soil sit where last year's garden once stood. Their boots, still caked with mud, wait by the door.

My mother can't linger inside a moment longer. She's wearing earth-stained track pants and a spring jacket she's had since high school. She heads outside to pull out sprouts of twitch and immature dandelions while the neighbour's cat hunches over to take a dump in a clump of dirt.

Tiny buds have begun to unfurl from the forsythia. Skipping ropes and marbles belonging to winter-weary neighbourhood children appear from wherever they've been napping all winter. I head for my swing set. Despite how wilted the muscles of my left leg are, I still manage to hang from my knees on the crossbar, thoughts of Susan crowding my mind.

~

One afternoon a few weeks back while Susan and I were on our way home from school, I undid the buttons of my jacket. It was one of those warm enough days that juts out from between weeks of cold and wet. The skies were bright and hopeful with the flurry of birds flocking north.

Susan was supposed to keep an eye peeled so I wouldn't get out of hand. I was the sort of kid who didn't look both ways when crossing the street and got distracted by snapping turtles mating in a swamp.

It was my parents' idea to hire Susan to watch over me. She was a privately-contracted spy who scrutinized my every step. In return, she provided them with a detailed written account of my comings and goings, and for this my parents forked over five dollars every week.

"Hurry up," Susan commanded from the hill, her hands squeezing her hips. "I don't have all day, squirt."

I was standing on the bridge that crossed a wide ditch in the woods behind the new subdivision. I'd been limping along, trying to keep up, but my left leg, weak and wasted due to a genetic condition on my mother's side of the family, stopped me from making good time. Besides, the bridge had wobbly wooden slats where bottles and broken jars sparkled from the dark underbelly of the ravine.

I scooted under the bridge on the look-out for treasure. I hoped for a story to fold into my palm. Something flickered from the depths of grass and mud. Using a stick, I pried a bottle cap free and placed it, muck and all, into my jacket pocket. I could hardly wait to get home, rinse it off, and hold it to the light, its rusty edges rippling with secrets and skeletons.

Susan was suddenly stomping on the bridge, her voice dripping with self-importance. "What's taking you so long? If I'd known minding you would be so tiresome, I'd never have agreed to it."

"Nothing." I crawled out from under the boards.

"What's that you've got there?"

"I already said nothing."

Once I was back on the bridge, she gave a shove to my shoulder.

"Ouch! What'd you do that for?"

"Show me nothing right now, you little brat."

"It's just some old thing. You won't like it."

She gripped my chin as if it were a ball of clay and peered into my soul. "You sure are giving nothing the time of its life."

I pretended to whip the cap into the forest so she couldn't rip it from my hands and claim it as hers. "There, now it's gone. Happy?"

She turned and trudged off toward the crest of the hill. "About time. You better not make me late for the rerun of *Gilligan's Island.*"

I pressed the foiled edge of the cap against my hand as if doing so would imbue me with power. Once I'd pushed long enough, blood began to bloom.

~

Another school year ends. Daylight lasts past bedtime and moist heat slumps over the neighbourhood like a clammy coverlet. My parents make pitchers of cherry Freshie with crushed ice, the caustic smell not unlike weed killer. My father arranges to take the summer off so he can wade through the latest academia on cell division research while my mother entrusts yard care to a teenager who lives around the block.

My father snaps a used car-top carrier to the roof of the VW Beetle. He's wearing a yellow polyester shirt with a white pocket protector on the left side of his chest. Two University of Toronto ballpoint pens jut out from the pocket. His horn-rimmed glasses have greasy fingerprint smears on the lenses. His costume reeks of geek but I don't care. Spending time with him once we've finally reached our destination is what I'm after.

It's cramped in the back of the car. My knees press against the driver's seat; my legs are twigs, one gaunt, the other robust like any other kid. As my father pulls out onto the street, Susan appears next to our driveway, gawking. When the car moves away, she lifts a hand to say goodbye. I don't wave back.

Soon we're headed for the highway. My parents want to make it to the nature camp by late afternoon. The other night I'd overheard them saying that the location offered a cathartic approach to camping and something we could do as a family. I meant to ask what cathartic meant but didn't want them to know I'd been listening in.

The nature camp is way up north in a part of the province that's so large it requires the back of the road map to show all of its features. When I turn and look out of the back window at the city, I wonder if Susan has abandoned her spot by our house, or if she's gone home by now. I watch the city fall behind us, like a smudge of ash on the horizon.

A song by Joni Mitchell spills from the cassette tape deck. Soon the air turns crisp, the trees shorter, their lime leaves smaller than those in the city. There's a black bird on the shoulder of the road pecking at something squished into the gravel.

"A raven," my mother says when I ask what it is.

"No, what got run over?" I feel a flash of sorrow as my father's eyes burn into me from the rear-view mirror.

The mess on the shoulder is replaced by granite swelling from the ground, the road cutting through rock faces. Our tiny car is a skater gaining momentum. Dead trees poke through periodic intervals of wetland.

"Raccoons," my father says, steering into a long curve. "The world is overrun with them. Rats with fancy tails."

He pulls into a gas bar equipped with a small convenience store. He tanks up while my mother slips inside to satisfy her craving for something sweet. The car soon smells of fuel and Aerobar chocolate. A family of five scatters from their camper van, the kids elbowing each other, yelping, "Me first, me first."

My father squeegees the windshield, headlamps, and brake lights. The gas bar sits on a wide section of road next to a long bridge that spans a fast-flowing river. I'm still in the back of the car, the Coleman cooler crushing me from the right. If only I could cool off in the river. I want to know its name but the sign is snapped off. The windows of the car are rolled up because of the bugs. They creep along the glass, their underbellies flashing red, their backs buckled over. If any of them worm their way inside, I'll stomp them dead with the heel of my palm.

~

The camp is on the north shore of Lake Superior. As we pull in, I notice that there's barely anyone around. The lake is enormous and black. According to a tourist pamphlet at the clubhouse where we check in, over the years the lake has swallowed freighters and killed people.

"It's clothing optional until you get used to being here," the manager explains.

I don't bother telling him that I have no intention of going bare-naked.

The cabin where we'll spend the summer is on the edge of woods at the back of the camp. Shards of blue paint have peeled off the wood siding and some of the window screens have holes which my father says can be fixed in a jiffy using the Duct tape he packed. My mother uses words like reasonably-priced and charming to describe the place.

My teeth clench as soon as I realize my bottle cap is back at home. I limp from the porch into the kitchen where my parents are filling the pantry and fridge with provisions.

I whimper about my bottle cap. "We have to go back and get it."

My father chuckles. "There's more where that came from." He pulls a brown bottle from the cooler and uses the back of a church key opener to pry the cap off. He finishes his first beer in a few gulps. He flicks the cap at me but I'm at the wrong angle to make a respectable attempt at the catch.

After putting away my T-shirts, shorts, snorkel and mask, underwear, stamp album, toothbrush, and a stack of Nancy Drews on extended loan from the library, it's time to check out the lake.

My mother grips me by the shoulder and aims me toward the porch where she sprays me head to toe in bug spray. I think about the highway signs that warned of bears and moose and wolves.

"Race you to the lake," I call, only no one answers back.

It's strange to realize that Susan's eyeballs won't be clocking my every move while I'm here at the camp, that my parents regard our subdivision as more dangerous than the great outdoors.

I wade up to my knees in the lake's freezing water. When I look down, my legs resemble those wooden chopsticks that accompany Chinese food take-out.

The first night my dreams fill with enormous snouts. Wolves and bears, their long sharp claws tearing at the window screens, coming for me. It's just a matter of time.

I spend the next few days crouched on the ridge that coils along the edge of the pebbled beach. The ridge consists of smoothed out boulders flecked with blue, green, and grey crystals. The rocks remind me of enormous humpback whales. When the sun heats up the boulders, I pull off my towel and sit on them with my bare bum. It took a few days before I realized I was comfortable going around with no clothes. Like my mother, I'm going for an all-over tan.

Beyond the rocks is a patch of low-growing plants dotted with bright purple blooms. Moss dense and green as our living room carpet covers the forest floor. I'm careful to avoid walking in any tall grass after my legs got shredded by their sharp edges. Birches, pines, and poplars try to crowd each other out. My mother's warning about the woods being filled with poison ivy swirls in my head.

I stumble upon a dead bird, some kind of jay, flatter than a dead bird should ever be. I poke what's left of it with the toe of my sandal, finally succeeding in flipping it over. Maggots have eaten holes into it and it smells like compost after meat and cheese have been added to it. I try to look away but oddly can't.

It's not like I haven't experienced death before. Mr. Markes, my grade five teacher, had rows of Mason jars filled with dead frogs, a rat, and even a small pig. One of the specials didn't listen when the teacher reminded us to look with our eyes, not with our hands. The boy bumped the container that contained a preserved snake, its body spongy and waterlogged. The jar crashed to the floor, a pong not unlike pickle juice filling the air. Next thing we knew, Mr. Markes evacuated the room so the head custodian could air the place out and get things cleaned up. The shelves were empty after that.

I poke the bird again, this time with a stick and realize no matter what, nothing can get to it now.

The camp is silent most days other than the sound of waves striking the shore and loons calling, sometimes laughing, sometimes emitting a soft moan. It turns out I'm the only kid enrolled at the camp. In fact, there aren't many people at all. My parents are the sort to stick to themselves.

There is no dock. That makes fishing a challenge. Besides, we don't have any gear other than my dad's fishing hat. We didn't think to bring a boat, so instead of fishing, I start thinking it might be nice to collect butterflies.

My father spends most of the time parked on the couch, stacks of papers he brought from the university piled on the floor next to him. When I'm inside, my mother orders me to be quiet so I don't disturb him but I prefer to spend my time outdoors.

When I tell him over hotdogs and beans about my interest in making a butterfly display, he springs to life. He sets aside the document he's been reading and winks at my mother, letting us know how thrilled he is with my sudden fascination with biology. He rummages around until he locates a box of straight pins in the cupboard above the fridge. Then begin the lessons on proper insect-mounting technique.

Once I've collected a bunch of butterflies and moths with a net I found hanging on the back of a door, I exhibit them on bloated chunks of Styrofoam found washed up on the shore. I'm mindful to not rip the wings with the straight pins. I refer to *Butterflies and Moths of Canada*, a book left behind in the nightstand of my room. I tear strips of newsprint from dated issues of the *Globe*. In my best printing, I record the names of my captures with one of my father's university pens. Great Spangled Fritillary. Red Admiral. Silver-spotted Skipper. No Monarchs, though.

The wall calendar by the fridge changes to August. Along the forest edge are hundreds of blackberry plants. They pitch forward with the weight of the dark fruit, like canes in prayer. The berries are plentiful but tart, so sour they dry the spit in my mouth. My mother says, "It's been a mostly rain-free summer. That's what happens in nature. We'll make something wonderful out of them, you wait and see."

I collect a bunch of berries and mound them in an old vinegar jug my mother has cut the side out of. Picking takes all the concentration I can assemble. The barbs on the canes, under the leaves, and at the base of the fruit leave my hands and arms looking as if someone used a grater on them. Once my mother rinses the berries, I gingerly pick rogue leaves and twigs out of the sieve. Then, she simmers the berries in a pot rigged over a fire pit in the front yard.

"This is so much work," I say as she strains the berry mash through cheese cloth into a waiting bowl.

"If we skip this step, Moira, we'll be cursing our laziness all winter."

She stirs in sugar and something she calls magic powder, then carefully pours the mixture into clean Mason jars that she later seals with hot wax. The jam is plum-coloured. It's all I can do to resist eating it all.

A few nights before we're supposed to head home, I start dreaming as if it's a job, as if I'll earn a noble wage for what my subconscious can invent.

In one dream, my jacket hangs in the hall closet, the beer cap in its pocket. The cap is cold, like the water of Lake Superior. When I grip the cap, it grows wings before jetting off. Instead of remaining small, something that can fit into my palm, it becomes bigger than the boulders running along the edge of the beach. Bigger than the forest behind the cabin. Bigger than the lake, in fact. When I wake up, my sheet and blanket are on the floor beside my bed, stained, a dank pile of sweat.

Other nights I dream about the bridge on the way home from school, the one over the ditch where Susan left me when she should have waited. There's a voice, stern and scared. It whimpers but in a loud way. The voice belongs to my mother, I think, but I can't be certain because my eyes no longer see.

I stumble and strike my head. I'm confused; my mind becomes flooded with maggots. There's a portal into my skull, round and wide like the opening of a Mason jar that's the size of the CN Tower. When my hand brushes the maggots away, they tumble over me like popcorn kernels striking a lid. The maggots' clacking fills the air.

When I wake up, my pillow is dark with worry.

My dreams, though, are never about Susan.

On the final days of summer, my father finally decides to abandon his pile of papers so he can tutor me on the attributes of the perfect skipping stone.

"The best skippers are flat on both sides and fit snug against your palm," he says. "Don't pick a stone that's too big or too small. Something the length of your thumb is what you're after. Skipping takes trial and error, and above all, perseverance."

"Perseverance?" I say.

He answers by lumbering along the beach, eyes combing the rocky shoreline for perfection. He stoops over, cranes his neck, and swings his head to and fro like a giraffe. No, more like a bear. I hope to hold this memory of him forever, for when we're back in the city, before his face finds its way back into stacks of papers.

He bends to pick up a stone and tosses it at me. My hand leaps into the air where I manage to snag the toss with my non-dominant hand.

Ships float along the lake, smoke trailing behind them. The sun, mauve and calm, begins its descent. I begin to locate what my father calls textbook-perfect stone specimens. I don't fling them, though; instead, I slip them into the pockets of my shorts.

On the final night, we fill the remaining moments with a campfire and sing-along. We sit on logs washed up by the motion of the waves. We roast wieners my father cuts into thin slits with his pocketknife. When the flames strike the meat, the slits curl around themselves like spiders pinned to a display board. I watch sparks from the fire rival the brightness of the stars in the night sky. I look up so long my neck threatens to lock into place. My mother smiles from the other side of the fire, gazes at me with a rare flash of fondness.

The next morning when we take off for the city, my face has fewer smooth edges and there are indentations on either side of my mouth. Dimples. I have succeeded in getting an all-over tan, even in the crack of my bum, a hard place to get brown, according to my mother.

We're back home by the Sunday of Labour Day weekend. It's cool enough for a thin wool blanket at night in the far north but not back home. The city is still sizzling and moist, noisy with cars and trucks, and the smell of smog and roofing tar. In our house, the water pipes thump and clunk when we first turn them on, the first rush of water from the tap coming out rusty.

The next morning, Susan is on the steps of our house. She's taller and her head appears rounder, maybe because of the black-rimmed glasses she now wears. She's in a blue skirt and a colourful halter top. There's a fresh patch of freckles on her cheeks and a few on her shoulders, too.

There's a mirror in the pocket of her skirt, a plain oblong one with a collapsible handle. She holds it in front of my face and says, "Just look at yourself. You've turned into a bohemian." Her voice sounds loud and bossy, like a circus announcer.

Her lips curl in disgust as if she's bored, already fed up with me and my face, as if my face has gone and done something horrid. I glance into the mirror. It's my same old face, not the same but not all that different, except for its golden sheen and new-found sleekness. It's me, all right, just with rosy cheeks and slightly fuller lips.

"You look dumber than ever," Susan says, giving me a shove.

I feel my spine slump, crumbling into nothing.

I don't want to fight with Susan so I run into the house where my mother is checking flyers and writing out a grocery list.

"Tell me what to do," I say, powerless to be rid of this girl my mother and father hired to be my keeper.

My mother looks up briefly before folding the shopping list in half and slipping it into her purse. All we have to eat are stale cereal and some canned fish. She turns a metal key on a tin of sardines before releasing the bread-tie on a loaf of bread we picked up on our way home.

She whistles while putting together a sandwich for me. I like salmon better than sardines but not if there are onions and too much mayonnaise. I'm still amazed that a person can eat an entire sardine, spine and all. Same with salmon out of the tin, the fish's backbone made flexible and soft during the canning process.

My mother wipes food crumbs off the counter before saying, "Your father's decided you won't be needing that Susan anymore."

As I bite into the sandwich, everything feels just right against my tongue.

Black Hole

Early one afternoon, two teenagers climbed over a barbed wire fence. They waved off assigning importance to the red circles dotting the wooden fence posts. When Olivia got the lining of her calf-length coat caught on a barb, she cried, "Help," but Dave was already too far ahead to hear. The centre of his attention was on the dilapidated farmhouse beyond the hill. Once she'd freed herself from the fence, she shadowed Dave through mud-packed ruts and snapped-off corn stalks.

As Olivia crested the hill, the two-storey farmhouse poked from the landscape like an afterthought. Making out on the floor of the empty house would be a more memorable location than the backseat of Dave's Austin Mini.

When Olivia reached the house, she waited for her heart to slow down before gingerly stepping onto the wooden steps of the porch that tilted towards her. Traces of yellow paint flaked from the building. With a few strikes of his boot heel, Dave smashed the rusty padlock weakened over time by the elements. When he pushed the door open, the house released a musty belch.

A month prior, Olivia and Dave had met standing in line for foot-longs at the fall fair. She, a sucker for boys with long silky hair parted down the centre, thought that Dave's tapered nose gave him a distinctive ethnic flair not evident in the other boys at their high school. His lanky build emphasized by his skin-tight blue jeans and multi-coloured long-sleeve T-shirt was irresistible.

Dave took Olivia's elbow and guided her into the house. She felt a mixture of longing sprinkled with panic. She groped for the light switch on the cord hanging from the ceiling but the place had long been abandoned and the power was off. Dave pointed at the broken bulbs, smashed fixtures. and chain-pulls wagging in puffs of wind coming in through busted windows.

Where a kitchen table had once stood was a large gaping hole, blackness beckoning from below.

"Watch out," Olivia said, seizing Dave by the back of his shirt to keep him from tumbling in.

"I guess I should be more careful. Good thing you're here." Dave made a grab for her.

"Hang on," she said, flashing a weak smile. "What's your hurry?"

"You like?" he asked, gesturing at the building.

"It's wonderful," she said, standing on her tippy-toes to plant a kiss on his cheek. "Thank you for bringing me here."

Dave folded their coats into thirds, creating a mattress of sorts for the wooden floor. She reclined on the pile, thankful she didn't have to put up with splinters of frayed wood stabbing into her. They made out quickly, keeping most of their clothes on in case someone happened by. Despite the bed of coats, she could feel the bones of the floor, the history of the place, against her spine. They fell asleep in a tangle of arms and legs.

Later, she awoke with a start. The room was shadowed with the grey of late afternoon. She felt achy and stiff, similar to a time she went camping—the ground hard and unrelenting against her tense body. She groped around for Dave, expecting him to still be beside her, breathing deeply with heaviness of interrupted sleep, but he was nowhere to be found.

"Dave? Quick goofing around."

The hole in the floor next to where they had slept yawned like a velvet pond, the wooden edges of the hole soft and juicy. Had Dave rolled over in his sleep and fallen in? Surely she would have heard a crash if he had. She pressed her ear to the floor and waited for the sound of his voice but all she could hear was wind like the exhale of a monster living under a child's bed.

"Dave, can you hear me?" A momentary hush filled her ears. She shivered when she imagined the debris, or worse, animal bones, poking into Dave's broken body.

"I don't like practical jokes," Olivia said.

The dark had terrified her ever since she could remember. Many a night she derived benefit from her mother's warm arms wrapped around her so she could fall asleep. With evening imminent, it was futile to remain at the farmhouse a second longer so Olivia started to make her way back to where they'd left the car. Once there, she fumbled in her coat pockets.

"Fuck! He's got the god-damned keys."

It took a few hours trudging under the moonlit sky but eventually she returned home, weary from melancholy and defeat.

~

Years later …

Olivia came around the corner into the primary corridor of the school where she'd recently been appointed as a fulltime teacher. A man wearing a faded Blue Jays cap sat hunched over. With his elbows pressed against his thighs, he struggled to stay balanced on the child-sized chair under him.

When he lifted his eyes to hers, he broke into a smile of immediate recognition. "I'd know that face anywhere," he said.

"Dave?"

"Olivia? I haven't seen you in years."

"What are you doing here? I didn't know you had a son or daughter here."

"My great-niece attends this school. I'm meeting my nephew for the parent-teacher conference." He looked briefly at his shoes before continuing. "The girl has significant learning issues and he thought I might be able to help."

Dave stood and pulled her against him. She could feel his inhale catch against her hair. "You smell how I remember. Cherry Blossom lip gloss."

She pushed him away. "Seriously? I haven't used that in years."

Olivia didn't want to be here in the hallway with Dave. She wanted to kick him in the shins or wrap her hands around his throat and choke the life out of him.

He slid an arm along her shoulder in an apologetic way. "I shouldn't have pranked you like that, disappearing that afternoon."

She spotted her reflection in the black window across from where they stood, her eyes dark hollows gobbling up her face.

"It was mean," she said, taken aback when she shuddered at the memory of it. "You simply vanished."

"We moved. My dad took a job in Calgary. I couldn't think of any other way to split up with you without breaking your heart."

She'd heard things, rumours shared in corners of the high school, people winking, laughing, elbowing each other. That Dave had dumped her. That Olivia was an easy lay.

"Have you been back?" he asked.

"Huh?" She felt the temperature in the hall drop.

"To the old farmhouse."

"No, I never had the urge," she said.

That night, in bed, Olivia thought about their brief intimate encounter in the old farmhouse. How Dave had folded their coats into a cot-shape creating somewhere soft where they could be together. How quickly the love-making had started and how quickly it had ended. Her first time, a smudge of blood left behind, next to where her coat's silky lining had snagged the barb wire.

How Dave had disappeared like a sliver of wood into skin, leaving intense pain where nothing else showed.

Now you see me, now you don't.

What he'd done had hurt so much at the time.

Dave's friends had managed to keep the secret even after her belly had begun to swell and her once nimble gymnast's figure evolved into something swollen and thick.

The community had stepped up, found a loving home where her child could grow up. A boy, their son.

~

When Olivia woke Sunday morning after her encounter with Dave, her muscles ached. She climbed from bed, and made her way to the bathroom to wash her face. Her appearance shocked her. Spiky brown hair sprinkled with sprouts of grey, coarse against her fingertips. Thin folds of skin beginning to droop from her neck. Dark circles under her eyes where supple blemish-free skin had once dominated.

Later that afternoon, Olivia started her car and returned to the property where she'd left childhood and become a woman. Row houses now stood where broken corn stalks once prevailed, the house where she and Dave had done something dramatic together, now a mere puff of memory.

The joints of her fingers stiffened as she tapped Dave's name into Safari on her iPhone. He needed to know what happened to her. She would disrupt his quiet Sunday, make him experience the crush of being pushed into a hole.

Consent

According to a podcast about the future, the coming year will be in the 'lap of the gods.' Leah hasn't heard that expression since growing up on the family farm near Woodstock. Her mother often expressed herself in clichés rather than taking the time to come up with something original. The podcast predicts that cities will have no choice but to implement curfews in response to civil unrest. That protesters will stop at nothing; they'll torch police cars, loot, and wreak havoc by shooting peacekeepers at point-blank range.

Leah doesn't like to put faith in doom and gloom predictions. The seriousness of the commentators' voices, though, causes her breathing to quicken. Yet she's drawn to the program like a goldfinch to thistle. She takes notice of a particular prognosticator who goes so far as to crystal-ball a global pandemic. If that were in the cards, certainly scientists would have prodded world leaders to draft a critical response by now.

She pulls an overripe banana from the bunch next to the toaster and lets it plop into the blender. She adds frozen blueberries, half a cup of hemp hearts, some yogurt, and a splash of milk. She makes the smoothies in advance of when she intends to drink them, fearful that the required ingredients may no longer be on hand. The idea of settling for toast in the morning leaves her antsy.

Other aspects of her life are more unremarkable than her breakfast routine. She brushes her teeth prior to and immediately after consuming food and beverages, her electric toothbrush whirring against a mouth of mostly straight teeth. She completes a series of stretches she comes up with herself, switching from upper body to lower every other day. Her brief meditative practice involves mantras of gratitude while keeping feelings of pride in check.

~

Leah's life wasn't always predictable and neat. Growing up in a century two-storey clapboard house surrounded by tobacco fields, she suffered from debilitating night terrors. One toe dipped in fantasy while the other was firmly rooted in reality. Once she permitted herself to finally fall asleep, she soon found herself pinned to the bed linens while two-headed beasts, slithering serpents, and scaly creatures snapped at her, threatening to gobble her up. By this point in the action, she'd begin to scream, startling her parents from their reverie. These terrors were bent on doing Leah in until father, mother, or both accompanied her from her sweat-drenched sheets to the safety of their double bed.

In the morning Leah would deny everything. But the evidence was clear. One or both parents would sport a black eye or a serious welt across the mouth. Warm soup or weak tea did nothing to quell the demons plaguing Leah. That is, until puberty took hold and vanquished the night terrors' grip on her.

~

The plan is for Tito to spend the first part of his sabbatical on the Amalfi Coast of Italy by himself. After a couple of months have passed, Leah is to join him there.

So, while her husband is away, Leah plans to take care of her sexual urges as per the schedule Tito will leave next to the takeout menus. With a dollop of warming gel on her fingers, she'll bring to mind Tito's limber body, his baritone voice, and his repertoire of sexual techniques.

~

As predicted on the podcast, the newspapers' headlines warn of an insidious enemy making its way across invisible land borders. Country-by-country, a modern-day plague takes innocent people hostage with its highly transmittable characteristics.

When the government orders the country locked down, nothing too significant changes for Leah. She simply carries on. When her social media fills with friends' gripes about boredom, the attack on personal freedoms, and the unfairness of it all, she finds herself quietly rejoicing.

Her world is finally still enough that she is able to concentrate and make art without interruption. She has time to ruminate. She foresees innovation and creativity drifting through her as if coursing through the four-part digestive chamber of a bovine.

With too much quiet, though, she finds herself uninspired. She waits in anticipation for her paintbrush to make a mark on the gessoed surface. Positioned before her easel, her mind is as blank as the 4-foot by 3-foot canvas standing before her.

Lying on her hammock in the backyard, a normally perfect place for ideas to twist and coil, the creative blockage persists. New tubes of paint languish unopened on the enameled steel painter's palette where she once experienced the joy of mixing colours.

~

Before Tito left for Italy, Leah offered to kneel between his thighs and take him with her lips. But he would have none of that. Instead, with her eyes trained on the grains of the headboard, he took her from behind. Never once did their eyes meet.

After, she brought a suitcase down from the shelf in their closet and packed for him. Under his boxers, she placed the Polaroid of him sporting a pair of her edible panties like a beret over his thick gunmetal-grey hair. Beneath his golf shirts, she tucked a photo of her with a downturned mouth with the caption: *l'onanisme*, French for climaxing solo. The third surprise, a bottle of chocolate-flavoured massage oil, she folded between the legs of his trousers.

Tempting as it is to hook responsibility for their fetishes on Tito, it's Leah who possesses a proclivity for kinkiness. It all started one July when a fourteen-year-old German-exchange student smuggled a stack of porn into the summer camp Leah's church-loving parents enrolled her in. While Leah couldn't read the German photo tags, the brightly-coloured, highly explicit images nurtured the beginning of her sexual experimentation.

~

The days begin to blur. Leah can't honestly remember which day is which unless she consults the calendar next to the fridge. Each evening she uses a Sharpie to scribble that completed day from memory.

Time is broken up by occasional Zoom calls with family, grim-faced cousins she hasn't bothered with in years crowding the screen of her laptop. Leah feels confused as they talk over each other, then overwhelmed, and finally irritated. She invents wild excuses to skip subsequent virtual meet-ups:

recipes gone mad, plugged drains, and painful constipation brought on by consuming too much home-baked bread.

Plans to join Tito are crushed when the government bans travel in and out of the country. Leah's world is further flattened when a higher-up at the university calls inquiring if this is a good time to talk.

Tito's work calling her at home is highly unusual. The possibilities of the call cause her chest to break out in heat rash while sweat soaks the back of her T-shirt.

"I don't know how else to broach this. Tito is positive for the virus."

Leah can't breathe.

"He's one of thousands in the country to have developed symptoms."

She imagines her husband strapped to a gurney in a corridor, one of many lining the hallways of the overcrowded Italian hospitals shown on the evening news. Or perhaps he's already on life support, his every need tended to by an intensive care nurse situated in an observation zone outside the specialized chamber.

She asks before hanging up, "When can I speak to him?"

She derives no comfort when the man says, "I'll see what I can do. But I'm not holding out much hope."

That night before going to sleep, Leah replays her husband's colleague's words. "While it is hoped that Professor Tito will make a full recovery, there could be limits to the level of care he receives. As you are most likely aware, the Italian health care system has been slammed by this plague."

Unable to do anything for Tito from their isolated cabin by the lake, Leah's shoulders feel weighted down as if carrying a backpack filled with doom.

~

Other than bi-weekly updates from an Italian nurse with rudimentary English skills, Leah permits all other voicemails to pile up on her phone. She cloisters herself in the cabin, arranging for meal kits to be dropped at the door. When toilet paper becomes unavailable, she makes do with tiny squares she creates from shop flyers piled up on the porch.

Connection with the world comes in the form of a CBC newscaster beset with sharing the virus's daily case counts. Because the January podcast now feels too authentic, Leah removes it from her playlist. When mountains of body bags blacken the television screen, she cancels her satellite TV package.

Her cell phone, normally quiet, begins ringing. Canada Revenue Agency threatens her with the slammer if she doesn't immediately wire thousands in overdue taxes to an off-shore account. There are other calls with multiple ideas on how to enlarge one's penis size. Then it's the blood bank. "Hello," Leah says, her voice soft and wispy from lack of use.

"We've noticed you haven't donated lately. Truth be told, our supply is desperately low," a male voice says louder than needed.

She imagines the caller grimacing at the word *desperately*, his round reading glasses reflected on a screen showcasing her donation history.

"It says here you're needle averse."

"Yes, I don't much like—"

"Yet, you've still managed—"

"I know. But with the pandemic —"

"Such a rare blood type: AB negative."

"Yes, yes. That's right."

"Fifty-seven. That's how many times you've given. Impressive! You're in line for a plaque once you reach seventy-five," the caller reminds her.

Leah takes in the lake scenery outside the large window. Off-shore waves lather the sandy shoreline, an elephant-sized Tito emerging from the water. She shakes her head. It's not the first time he's popped up there. Only last week he called from the front door, telling her to "Open the Christ up" so he could come in and put away the groceries. She finally helped him, emptied the bags, and started frying up some eggs for lunch.

78

She admits there is comfort in having Tito nearby. At her elbow, telling her to watch her caloric intake. It never once occurs to her that he is make-believe. When she reaches out for him, he feels so real, his skin so soft, the hair on his arms bristly and long. His hurried inhales quickly followed by another and another. But more than once, when she takes a platter of food, enough for a party, to the dining room table, he isn't actually there. And it's then that she realizes that their earlier conversations, at least his side of it, are complete fabrications brought on by pandemic loneliness and despair.

Her chest tightens before plugs of mucous threaten to close her throat.

"But we're still in lockdown," she tells the man from the blood bank.

"Here's the magic. We'll come to you. Rest assured; our nurses wear proper PPE."

Oh, yes, Leah thinks. Personal Protective Equipment, or PPE, one of the many acronyms to become part of what social media refers to as the new normal.

She sits with the phone receiver wedged between shoulder and ear, the fingers of one hand forming a fan shape against the windowpane, as if doing so can keep the virus at bay.

While the caller reviews the plan in copious detail, Leah feels her attention wane. Exhausted, she consents. "Yes, yes, of course I'll do it."

~

Leah finds herself doubting Tito, a characteristic she doesn't admire about herself. She tasks herself with scrubbing away the notion that Tito likely played around on her during the early days of his European sabbatical. Tito was a man with an insatiable sexual appetite and urges that needed to be met. After all, that was how they'd come together. Twenty-five years her senior, their lives collided when she became Tito's teaching assistant. As Leah's mother was wont to say, the rest is history.

Was that how he contracted the virus? Schlepping around art galleries and museums, painting *plein air*, all the while setting his sights on penetrating new young meat?

Leah remembers when Tito introduced the safe word, an utterance to reveal to her that what was happening was too much, that the sex had gone too far and needed to stop. It happened a few months after they'd moved in together, right before she'd completed her graduate studies for a Masters of Fine Art. They'd only required its use a few times, when Leah exceeded what Tito regarded as a firm sexual boundary.

~

The following Wednesday, a pretty 30-something-year-old wearing purple scrubs emerges from a white vehicle parked on the driveway of Leah's cabin. A red plastic ice box is in one hand and a tote of disposable medical paraphernalia is in the other. The car offers nothing to distinguish it from others in the area; no official blood bank logo or wrap, leaving ropes of doubt to weave through Leah.

Standing on the porch, Millie, as her plastic name badge states, seems no-nonsense in her sensible white shoes and medical-grade face covering and shield. Upon closer inspection, Leah notices that Millie's left eye is modestly rounder and bigger than the right, and is, in fact, a prosthetic eyeball.

After exchanging pleasantries, Millie says, "You'll need to lie down for the procedure."

"Follow me," Leah says, readjusting her homemade face covering.

As Millie makes preparations to plunge a needle into Leah's arm, she talks about her step-daughter's recent acquisition of an Angel fish.

Leah hates needles. Always has. Likely the result of a botched vaccination attempt when she was four. But her urge to donate blood over the years is stronger than her fear. Her toes curl toward her shins in anticipation of the needle's jab. She helps manage her emotions by visualizing a snowstorm, fat wet flakes that materialize out of nowhere, the kind that stick to the windshield when you're driving, the sort of scene that makes Christmas cards and snow globes so magical.

This time, though, instead of melting her anxiety, the imagery threatens to choke Leah. Her breathing becomes laboured as the steady pressure of a gloved finger bears down on her vein.

"There, there," Millie says, "I've almost got it. You're doing awesome so far."

Awesome—a word teenagers and flight attendants use. Like cool and rad, or hot, to mean sexy.

Leah takes a sideways glance at the bag that should be filling with her rare blood type, only it's empty. The hairs on her arms stand at attention. She bristles with annoyance. She wants to scream: *This is not what I signed up for.*

"Something isn't right," Leah says, her voice meek with angst.

She tries to sideline her panic by thinking about the soiled bed linens, towels, panties, shorts, and T-shirts piled in front of the washer. The idea of opening the tiny detergent drawer is exhausting. Filling the laundry drum: overwhelming. The clammy air makes the already tiny room feel even smaller. Tito was the domestic one in the relationship. Looked after everything. Washing. Ironing. Polishing the hardwood. Grocery runs. Did the bulk of the cooking. Disinfected the toilets, shower, sinks. Buffed the windows and mirrors.

But that was then, and this is now.

"You'll feel a little poke," Millie says.

"Ouch!"

Millie unfurls Leah's fingers. "Keep your hand open. There we go. Let's fill that bag so I can be on my way."

Millie's gloved hand against Leah's forearm feels oddly comforting. She's so close; Leah's skin is hyper-aware. If only Millie could stick around and caress Leah a while longer. She imagines Millie's fingertips combing her legs, hands, face, and scalp. A gentle brush against her clavicle and breasts. But during the new normal, being able to give and accept unwarranted touch has come to a swift close.

The place where Leah normally goes to give blood is a century-old stone church on the corner of Main and Wilson. It has vine-covered basement windows and dull cement floors. Despite the dimly lit location, the blood drawing team has a warm, caring approach. They envelop her hands with theirs, skin to skin, before stepping back to pull on the standard blue latex protection. They take time to dab the inside of her arm with an alcohol swab, then make light by saying, "You'll feel a little prick."

And feel it she does. "Damn it! How come you're poking me again?" she asks at the same time that Millie withdraws a syringe from Leah's upper arm.

"Oh, that. That's your complimentary pseudo-vaccine. While I had you here, all relaxed, I thought I'd—"

"You gave me a vaccine without my go-ahead?"

"It's not a *real* vaccine. Consider it an immune booster of sorts. You know—Vitamin C, amino acids, that sort of thing."

Once Millie packs up and is headed for her car, Leah can't help but feel dirty.

~

Later that evening, Leah develops a headache, joint pain, and a low-grade fever, so she heads to bed early. Her dream state comes on fast and her visualizations are vivid. She's next to a body of water, floating along the shore on a puff of wind. Not Lake Huron, though. Some place different. Perhaps the Mediterranean judging by the turquoise swells. Her arms are in front of her, zombie-like. But they're spinning in a front-crawl motion as if she needs to get somewhere fast.

Ahead of her are horses. Black stallions. Sleek and quick. But she is faster than they are and she manages to catch up. She pulls herself aboard one that is lagging at the rear of the pack. She guides the horse toward the setting sun. When the horse turns to look back at her, she realizes that it's actually Tito. Where eyes are supposed to be, though, are dark empty sockets.

Leah wakes with a start to realize that Tito is gone.

~

Two days after the blood bank visit, the square Band-Aid still on the inside of her arm, she thinks, I need to change our will now that Tito . . .

She traces the skin from elbow to wrist, over and over, until she feels herself spacing out. She can't remember where the will is kept. Tito looked after everything. And anyway, how does one meet with a lawyer during lockdown?

If only Leah felt energetic enough to be able to take an actual run along the beach. Inhale the moist air coming off the lake. But lockdown means the only people allowed to move about are essential workers and dog walkers. The government orders all others to stay home. Neighbours squeal on neighbours, turning them in for reward money. There are reports of a mayor of a large city tweeting "Stay the f*ck home," which causes a backlash from constituents. People *can* exercise at home, Leah knows, but who the hell wants to. She threatens to smash her TV when antiquated fitness videos created during the Vietnam War are made available for free download.

She still can't paint. Has zero ideas. No problem: art has been deemed non-essential. Art galleries are shuttered. Museums. Dance studios. Concert halls. Theatres. What would Monet say about art being classified as unnecessary? Or Shakespeare, who turned to writing poetry when the plague closed theatres? Or Dr. Tito, fine-arts-professor-turned-husband?

If only she could run among the beach grasses that hug the dunes. Stumble upon a coyote or a fox. Or even a black bear ripping through the neighbour's garbage. Eye-to-eye with wilderness. Feel a beast's observation of her.

Then she notices. The tears. The sickly surge of sorrow. Despondency so strong it tightens the backs of her eyes, courses through her veins, down her spine, into her belly, finally coming to rest in her bowels. Tears for Tito. The loss of agency, the rawness of it all. Brine-filled droplets dribble down her cheeks and chin to pool against her clavicle.

"Why can't this be over?" she says, pounding the kitchen table with the heels of her fists, the past few months aging her like years.

Once she composes herself, she pulls up the World Covid site on her iPhone. It doesn't take long before she finds the latest case count for Italy. Where Tito is. Where he was when the plague hit and busted a hole in their lives.

She longs for him, his lean naked body touching hers. She imagines them in a park, her unclothed back pressed against the trunk of a tree. Their muscles stiff, their nerves raw. Making love as if it were their first time. A thoughtful lover, a compassionate man, he likes to surprise her with unexpected, novel techniques to make her body hum.

Tito always had a knack for gaining her agreement to the queerest of sexual positions. She only occasionally barbed at his maneuverings, but eventually found herself willing, likely because, in the end, she couldn't resist the knack his body was capable of. She loved that he left his chest, leg, arm, and back hair long and fuzzy. Her furry little man. And he gave off an insatiable scent, a combination of garlic, basil, and the lavender-infused cologne he paid a fortune for.

She always returned the favour by servicing him with her mouth after he intoxicated her with shameless titillation. She pined for Tito to howl, to feel his shoulders, spine, and buttocks quiver, his skin to pimple with goosebumps. A notable tremble followed by a gush of release, his firm muscles and tendons rippling beneath her.

But in the end, Tito, like so many during lockdown, had been destined to become a statistic well before his time.

Leah's chest aches. She knows what it means to hate, to be at war, to despise an invisible enemy, her heart chilled.

~

Two and a half years later . . .

Quadruple-vaccinated and with a government sanctioned vaccine passport in hand, Leah plans to hop a plane for Italy to retrieve Tito's remains and what's left of his personal belongings. What a term: remains. What remains for her is the lake they shared. The tiny log cabin they built themselves and called home. The sway of the two-person rope hammock as they rocked together in the westerly breeze.

Memories. Something no one can take from her.

She carries the sound of voices, too. Tito's nurse, her broken English. Her final words before confirming to Leah that Tito had succumbed: *I have sadness for your Tito.*

Leah would give anything for Tito to enter the cabin and call out *Hello* one last time. His voice deep, a lilt at the end of each sentence, a sensibility to his vocabulary.

In the nights leading up to retrieve Tito's ashes, nightmares plague her. She opens her eyes, her hand patting his pillow next to her. "You're still here?" she asks. "I wasn't able to feel you." She waits for Tito to answer but all that remains is emptiness.

At other times, she manages to waken mid-dream. She tears herself from the sticky sheets, and calls up Tito's number so she can listen to his voice mail message. She listens to it on repeat, until exhaustion replaces dread.

Leah hopes she will be able to meet Tito's nurse assuming no harm has come to her. That she's come through on the right side of the pandemic, without residual trauma. There are gifts for the nurse in Leah's suitcase. Requisite symbols Canadians feel a piranha-like urge to share whenever they go abroad. Postcards of RCMP in their regulation red regalia, the Rockies, Niagara Falls, Cape Breton. And Canada flag pins, enough for the nurse, her family, and all of her shift colleagues. The crimson maple leaf centred against a white background between rectangular blazes of blood-red. Leah hopes to memorize a few phrases of Italian while on the plane, words she hopes will convey that she too has deep sadness for Tito.

Dead Writers' Society

The last place I wanted to be was at the airport. But the director of the literary festival I had volunteered for left author transportation up to me. Apparently, Thom knew the writers; that's why they had been selected.

The authors looked as exhausted as I felt. The man, bearded and tall, was slumped against a post, puffing a cigarette. The woman had a pear-shaped build that reminded me of hay bales.

In addition to luggage, the man had several banker boxes containing his last three novels, books I was supposed to sell on the weekend. As I filled the back of my van with their belongings, the authors briefly bickered over who would get to sit in the front until they decided to share the bench seat behind me.

Once we'd left the labyrinth of asphalt winding around the airport and were headed west, I stole a glance in my rear-view mirror. Neither of them wrote the sort of books I was accustomed to reading so I knew little to nothing about them.

I tried to connect with them on how they knew Thom. They seemed unwilling to elaborate much beyond 'met at school' or 'worked together one summer' so I took their brief responses as an indication of jet lag. Yet, they seemed alert enough to chat together.

"I shudder at having to traipse all those boxes home again," the man said.

"You'd sooner fret about your stupid books than what you're going to talk about?" she asked.

"Just worry about yourself."

"Why not let the local book sellers coordinate sales?" she said.

"And lose 30% right off-the-top?"

"Always about the money."

Their conversation made no sense to me at the time.

Yet, the manner in which they spoke revealed that they likely had a shared past. I later learned they'd once been married. To each other.

Three hours later, I dropped them at a B&B in town. The hostess must have heard us drive in because she was waiting for us on the porch.

"Sorry we're so late. The traffic—"

"Our guests are here," the hostess yelled to someone in another room. "Come help get them settled."

A teenager on metal crutches entered the foyer. When he spoke, there was a hitch between his words, as if his mouth needed time to catch up to his brain.

"Bryan Banks! I've been an admirer of your work for years," the boy said, pulling a paperback from the rear pocket of his jeans. "The Wild West mixed with love and adventure are so—"

"Western?" the female author said. "I'm Holly LaForge."

"*The* Holly LaForge? The one who just won This Country Reads?" the boy asked.

"The same!"

~

Later that night once I was home and in my pajamas, I reflected upon how Thom and I had met. It was the tail-end of the Vietnam war and the early days of the Middle East oil crisis. I was living in Belmont Village, working on an undergrad geography degree. Thom was the script writer/director of a university theatre troupe where I was a set painter.

Thom had been married to his high school sweetheart for a while. As we came to learn, though, he'd been living a lie. After he was found in bed with a male classmate, his wife kicked him out.

Instead of Thom crumbling under the embarrassment of a broken marriage, he became driven. He spearheaded the first Walk for Pride. Allies and queers alike carried placards and banners on the dusty road that circled campus.

Thom oozed charisma. Everywhere he went, people trailed in his shadow. Everyone wanted to be invited to be part of his inner circle, and I wasn't about to be left on the outside, no matter what.

The local police had been conducting raids on public bath houses, spaces men used for hook-ups with other homosexuals. The raids became front page news, arrestees' names published. Married men, outed to their wives, family, employers, and the community at large.

Thom became a casualty of one of the raids. By then, he'd had enough of the closed-mindedness of our city. So, he purchased a small bungalow a couple of hours west of the city.

Thom and his male partner adopted two orphans from eastern Europe. No longer feeling the urge to be on stage, and consumed with the need to grow roots, Thom secured a job promoting the arts across three counties.

Fast forward to my early retirement. Trudy and I sold our house and moved to the cottage. When Thom found out, he suckered me into becoming his wingman for a new literary festival he was putting together.

This litfest was our fifth. Thom and I had had our share of disagreements over the years. There were multitudes of issues to work through including establishing a stellar line-up of authors. It was always my belief that there should be a tight match between the writers we invited and the interests of patrons.

Case in point: two years back, the entire author line-up consisted of those who identified as queer, trans, bisexual, or questioning. This rubbed the members of the five local book clubs the wrong way. It wasn't that they were opposed to the lifestyle per se; they just didn't necessarily want to "read about it ad nauseum" as one elderly member put it.

Lord knows I took many calls from them. They griped that there'd be nothing, absolutely nothing, for them. I begged them to trust us, to attend the festival anyway.

They wouldn't listen to me and ended up snubbing Thom by not going to him, either. They demonstrated their rage by refusing to purchase tickets. Sales plummeted.

In the dying days ahead of the event, I tried to salvage things by setting up a few readings at five local high schools. Twitter, Instagram, and Facebook soon filled with selfies of gay teenagers delighted with the attention the authors gave them.

I didn't think it was unreasonable to receive some gratitude for saving the festival that year. While Thom often referred to ours as a business partnership, 'partnership' was a misnomer. It was clear that Thom thought he was way above me in the pecking order and didn't allow anyone to forget that.

He took the glory when things succeeded and was quick to jab a critical finger at me when things screwed up.

Trudy became terminally ill leading up to this year's festival, causing any friction between Thom and me to congeal into a roux. I called him up on the phone and pleaded for compassion.

"You can't leave the bulk of the work to me. There's too much to do," Thom said.

His molars clacked together in a maddening tell that showed he was pissed.

"Don't you get it; Trudy needs me. I can't leave her now."

"But," he said, "the show must go on."

So, I kept drilling down, as best as I could, on the dirty little details that Thom apparently had no idea how to navigate.

Trudy passed away two weeks before the launch of Year 5 but Thom was relentless.

"Why in heaven's name would we postpone now?" he said when I asked for compassion. "It's not as if it would bring Trudy back."

~

As Bryan Banks' Saturday morning workshop at the local high school approached the mid-way point, I rose from my seat so I could set out coffee and tea before taking the fruit tray out of the fridge. It was loaded with three varieties of seedless grapes, apple slices, chocolate dip, and just-picked local strawberries.

As soon as I lifted the lid from the fruit tray, an earthy bouquet filled the air, a culinary delight for the nostrils. I was fussing with the food and drinks when I heard gasps coming from behind me.

Bryan's face was the colour of a coral snake and his lips were three-times their usual size. He panted like a diseased dingo before collapsing to the floor, his hands clinging to his throat.

It was clear he was having some kind of severe reaction and I was doing shit about it. "Back up, people," I yelled. "We've got a situation here."

Among the twenty or so people milling about, two faces were familiar: the boy from the B&B and Principal Elizabeth Watts.

"Beth, run back to the office, will you? We need the school's EpiPen. And young man, pull out your cell phone and call 911."

~

The ambulance attendants praised us for our quick response to the patient's symptoms. Then they rushed him to emergency for a once over.

All attempts to locate Thom had failed, so when a reporter stuck a microphone and camera my way, I had no choice but to become the face of the festival.

What happened with Bryan became front page news. My photograph appeared above the fold, although it was considerably smaller than the picture of Bryan Banks.

Days later, once the media had found a new story to follow, I took time for myself. I headed into London to pick up Trudy's cremains. Thom stopped by while I was considering what to do with her ashes.

"You just couldn't stay out of the limelight, could you?" Thom said, thrusting a copy of the newspaper at me. "You had to carve your own human-interest story, I see, by almost killing one of the authors."

"Hey now. It's been a hell of a week and all you can do is chew me to bits?" I said, my voice louder than it needed to be.

"You fucked up, that's all."

"Me? How do you figure that? It's YOUR festival, Thom."

"You're the detail guy. You must have known about the allergy."

"Now wait one second. There's absolutely nothing about allergies in the author's contract."

"Well, I—"

"How was I supposed to know Bryan Banks had a deadly allergy to goddamned strawberries?"

"He could have died. You almost killed him."

"But he didn't die. The key word is almost."

"No, the key word is killed. And it had to be Bryan fucking Banks, the number one writer of Westerns in the entire country. Jesus, Peter."

"Just hang on a minute, Thom."

"You and me, we're done!"

And with that, Thom turned and left.

In small towns you can live with people sticking their noses into your business or you can jump ship. I chose the latter.

Thom and his doubts crushed me. I hated that he thought nothing of pushing me in front of an oncoming train. It was clear he'd be talking trash about me forever.

I packed a few changes of clothes and my toiletries plus Trudy's cremains, and aimed my van east, travelling as far from the lake as I could get in one night. I didn't care where my vehicle took me, didn't care if I ever stopped. I couldn't be under Thom's thumb anymore. If I stayed, I knew he'd cause me to do something the town rumour-makers would chew about long into the future.

I leased a room in an old house north of Pembroke. The first days were spent in bed. I was too exhausted to do much more than read, complain to Trudy about how unfair Thom had been, and eat take-out dropped off outside the door of my rental.

A few weeks later I returned home to list my house with my cousin who was a realtor. There was a gift on the porch, a still-life painting of a fruit basket with a note that said: *For heaven's sake, call me. We've got another festival to start planning. T.*

I tossed his gift into the trash and headed inside to begin staging my home.

Not Husband Material

When people asked to hear about the time Colleen first lived away from home, she would say that in most ways it was all right. That she and Stu met at a bar, when, in fact, they'd met in the residence cafeteria. She didn't want it out there that she had lived on campus during Teachers College. Didn't want people viewing her as a tender-foot instead of a woman who was on her way to completing her second university degree by age twenty-one.

Instead, she told people that she and Stu met at Ralphie's Trough, the on-campus bar located in a three-storey chalet overlooking the Niagara Escarpment. From the seats next to the floor-to-ceiling windows, patrons could observe songbirds darting through the branches of maples, birches, and wild grape vines.

It was said that when Colleen and her classmate, Gracie, arrived at the bar, Stu felt drawn to Gracie, although he was later heard to deny it. Gracie was Amazonian in stature, taller than every girl in the joint and the majority of guys. She had straight black hair worn halfway down her back and jagged bangs that brushed the tops of her bushy eyebrows. She looked like one of those watercolour Cleopatras you'd find in grade school history texts. When she walked, the hardwood groaned in response to her weight.

As soon as Gracie opened her mouth to tell Stu that teaching was a second career, he gasped and turned toward Colleen.

"She's got a mother of a lisp, doesn't she?" he said.

~

For their first date, the forty-five-minute drive from campus across the border into Buffalo was the least Stu figured he could do for Colleen. She had her heart set on a place that specialized in ethnic noodles. Even though it was a long drive on a school night, he was willing to do it because he wanted to show how nice he could be by letting Colleen choose where to eat.

The restaurant was more or less dead with only three other couples in a place that could seat around fifty. Stu liked that Colleen couldn't keep her eyes off the older man briskly rubbing garlic cloves against a large wooden bowl as he prepared a fresh Caesar salad at their table. The conversation between Stu and Colleen was stilted, he thought, so he flagged someone and ordered a couple of highballs.

He couldn't help but notice Colleen's eyelids droop once he started talking about the campus clubs he'd joined. Rocky Horror Picture Show Admiration Society. Badgers Against Homelessness. Anime Club.

"Anime offers an introduction to anime, manga, and, of course, Japanese costumes," he explained. "You should come."

Colleen kept glancing at her bitten-off fingernails, then twisting the tails of her blouse, so he decided to try a different tactic by asking questions about her. Her responses were shallow and distressingly disinterested. In fact, she didn't loosen up until after he'd paid the bill and aimed the car at Canada.

Once they were on the overpass heading towards campus, he asked why she liked the noodles there so much. She said, "Well, they *are* homemade. Besides, didn't you enjoy how they snaked down your throat and danced in your belly?"

"Want to go out again sometime," Stu asked, his eyes aimed at the damp streetscape ahead.

"Oh, sure, why in heaven's wouldn't I?"

~

Colleen found Teachers College tedious. All that cutting out of laminate. The laborious lesson planning. Acting as though she gave two shits about the children. But, ever since meeting up with Stu, she no longer held regrets about her chosen career path that would certify her to teach ten different grades.

The university had not issued Colleen a private dorm despite hours of heated pleading. She had rattled off a myriad of reasons why they should issue her a single room. She was an only child and unaccustomed to sharing. She'd grown up in a small town and needed a quiet space to retreat to at the end of each day. She couldn't possibly be expected to sleep on a single bed; she had a Queen-size at home, for goodness' sake. And, as a mature student who had already completed one degree, she shouldn't be subjected to cohabiting with, gulp, kids.

With her voice raised a few notches higher than some would say was warranted, the residence clerk threatened to lodge a harassment charge against Colleen if she didn't immediately back down.

Because Colleen's roommate was still on a flight from Hong Kong on the day Colleen moved into residence, Colleen took the bed on the far side of the room. She dragged the desks and chests of drawers to form a barricade between her bed and her roommate's.

At least the roommate Colleen got stuck with wasn't first year! The biochemistry major was blessed with such a tiny stature Colleen would brag that she could fold the girl up three times and slip her into the breast pocket of her best teaching blouse. A female version of Flat Stanley. The night the roommate arrived, she said a quiet *Hello* that sounded like *arro*. Then she warned Colleen that she was happy that Colleen had arranged the furniture like she did since the roommate was a night owl. The girls had two things in common: they shared a love of jumbo shrimp and both slept in fleece nighties that hung to their ankles.

In her spare time, Colleen liked to doodle. The back-and-forth action of fine-tipped markers soothed her riled up temperament. She did her colouring at the table in the common area opposite the co-ed showers. Her latest poster featured The Colosseum. She intended to frame the poster if she ever got it finished. She'd never been to Rome but it was a Top Ten Destination to visit by age thirty. The word *Invictus* appeared in bubble letters near the top of the poster. According to one of the history majors that lived on Colleen's floor, *Invictus* meant unconquered, a concept she wished she could better relate to. After a long while she decided that the only fitting colour for *Invictus* was cardinal red.

Stu could usually be found at the colouring table, too, sucking from a brown stubby of Molson Canadian, a carton of twenty-four on the floor next to his slippered foot. Whenever Stu offered her a sip, Colleen waved him off, not caring much for a drink that left her belly bloated and her teeth furry.

~

Prior to Teachers College, Gracie had worked as a dental hygienist. Standing over people all day long caused her upper back to hunch and her sciatica to act up. So, she quit and headed back to school for an undergrad degree. Now she was in Teachers College. She didn't much like kids and what she really hoped was to meet a nice guy, perhaps a doctor or something. But the only university that accepted her didn't have medical, law, or engineering departments. Sure, there was a decent business department on this campus but the male students she'd seen around resembled ferrets. She figured before long she'd just have to settle.

Her apartment was located in a walk-up at the bottom of the escarpment. She shared it with a guy who worked as a sous chef at a national restaurant chain. Fortunately, the bus stop was right outside their building and the bus dropped her off at the entrance to campus. Otherwise, she'd have a forty-minute walk up the mountain every day and there wasn't even so much as a sidewalk along the narrow hairpin curves. So much time gallivanting in the cold wind was sure to crack her skin into something resembling a Nevada desert.

~

Stu wished he could generate the right words to persuade Colleen to help him with his homework. He was in second-year geography; he'd pretty much flunked out of first year and here he was a year later not doing much better. He'd picked geography for no other reason than it was his best subject in high school. What he had not counted on was having to take math and Elizabethan English.

If only Stu could fashion a career out of his passion, which was freshwater surfing. While in high school Stu took every other weekend off from his dad's hardware store and headed for the lake. Once there, he pulled on an insulated wet suit and rode the waves of Lake Huron. The rush of danger coupled with frigid temperatures pounding on his body made him feel alive.

From grades ten to twelve Stu dated the same girl. Everyone expected they'd get married. She was always saying that she didn't feel smart enough for university but since he'd always planned to go, he broke it off with her days before prom. He hated hurting her that way but didn't see the point of dragging things out.

Lately, Stu had begun dreaming about her. In fact, he had a spate of recurring dreams where he ran into her at the Chinese buffet located across the street from his dad's store. She was at the hot plate, steam circling her freckled face, a dinner plate in hand, greasy fingers shovelling deep-fried scallops into her mouth by the dozen. Suddenly the plate clattered to the floor, her sticky hands gripping her throat, her face turning into a puffy eggplant. When Stu reached out to help her, the soles of his shoes were on ball bearings. That's when he woke up.

~

Every summer Colleen took a different job. One year she worked security at Canada's Wonderland. Another year, squeezed into a period costume, she led tours of a two-hundred-year-old home where she operated a spinning wheel. Before Teachers College, she ran an ice cream shop at the beach while boarding with her aunt. Kids were so predictable, always ordering baby cones packed with Cookies 'n Cream and Bubblegum flavours. Most adults went for Fudgy Pudgy, Chocolate Swirl, and Mint Chocolate Chip. It got so Colleen couldn't stomach the smell, the stickiness on her hands and arms, or the explosive crunch of Styrofoam-coloured cones.

When Stu's roommate moved out but didn't let the university know, Stu gave Colleen a key to his room. One afternoon when Colleen's Ethics in Education professor called off class, she found herself with free time. Instead of tackling lesson plans or working on her Colosseum poster, she headed for Stu's room.

She inserted the key and busted in, ready to shout surprise. The room was dim but she was fairly certain she recognized the knees gripping Stu's head as belonging to Gracie.

"Next time, bitch, at least ask before using my scarf for bondage," Colleen said, unknotting Gracie's wrists before slamming the door.

~

At times, Stu regretted breaking up with his high school sweetheart. When early morning classes at the university were cancelled, he sometimes allowed himself to remain in bed where he'd try to resurrect the dream about the Chinese buffet so he could rewrite the ending. Rather than choking on scallops, his ex-girlfriend would turn into a toddler, sucking on a highchair tray filled with mango, blackberries, Cheerios, and banana.

~

With so much free time on her hands after giving Stu the boot, Colleen threw herself into the metric system, a new method of measurement the prime minister was ramming down the throats of taxpayers. Colleen found it so confusing and got everything muddled up: she tried to turn grams into metres, mixed up litres with decibels, and tried to divide kilometres by minutes. Her practice teaching reports reflected her ineptitude.

Colleen believed her associate teacher had had it out for her since the beginning. If only she hadn't agreed to sign up with him for two sessions. She offered to volunteer at a fall camp he ran as a way to ingratiate herself with him. In the second practicum, she tried to make amends by keeping some children in at recess for extra help. But that backfired. After recess, those students acted out by shooting spit balls at her and calling out the most profane nicknames she'd ever heard in her life.

It didn't seem to matter what she did. The associate teacher was having none of it.

"You need to master the metric system if you have a hope of getting hired," he said. "Besides, what children with learning issues need at recess is to blow off steam, not sit across from you rolling their eyes."

~

Stu beat himself up for the hook-up with Gracie which had, with good reason, chased Colleen away. He finally managed to coax Colleen to meet him at Side Street Pizza so he could try to make it up to her. He knew she liked their thin crust veggie special, loaded with mushrooms, green olives, and hot peppers.

"Allow me to indulge you," he had said on the message he'd left on her phone.

Stu, ever punctual, arrived at Side Street twenty minutes early. When Colleen entered, he was in awe at the skimpiness of her outfit despite the coolness of the early spring day: hot-pink tank top over soot-black knickers, something she later revealed her mother had sewn.

~

To Colleen, Stu appeared pale, as if he were afraid, or was hiding something. She figured he had lured her to the pizzeria in a weak attempt to rekindle things. She planned to let him know just how much she enjoyed life now that she was single. Sure, he had been a good enough guy to hang around with but in the long run, no way. It wasn't as if he were husband material. And the sex on a good day was merely average.

After putting a third slice on her paper plate, Colleen revealed to Stu that she'd received an offer to teach at a fly-in reservation in the northwest corner of the province.

"I had no idea you had any interest," Stu said before taking a long pull of his lemonade.

"The proposed salary isn't what I would get paid in the public system, but there are perks such as free accommodation. Let's face it, having nowhere to spend my money means I'm sure to save most of it. Besides, it's the experience I'm after. My jobs until now have been so … uninspired."

Colleen had never done anything like this. One requirement was that she try to learn the language of the indigenous peoples located there. She was damned if she could remember the name. The hiring committee had been so encouraging during the phone interview and hadn't gotten bogged down on the deficits speckled throughout her practicum reports.

She wiped her hands off on her knickers. "Well, look who's about to drag herself in." She nodded to her right. "Why in heaven's name would you invite her?"

Stu's nervous silence wasn't enough answer for Colleen so she kicked him in the shin.

"You asshole," Colleen said, careful to keep her volume down. No knowing who might be listening in. "What gives? It's not like she and I are friends anymore. Not after what the two of you did."

Stu's eyes widened like a lynx caught in a leg trap. "You're right—I did invite her. I hoped you two might want to patch things up."

"What do you think we're going to have here, Stu? A little family meeting? God, you're more of a dork than I imagined. I'm so glad we're D O N E done."

Stu fingered a cigarette from his pack and rested it between his lips, unlit. When Colleen looked at him, his chin drooped further down his chest.

Despite being in the same program, Colleen had managed to sidestep running into Gracie. Until now.

Gracie took her time entering, hesitation seeming to chain her feet to the sidewalk. Perhaps she had something to hide. Colleen watched her former friend stoop down to maul a tangerine-coloured cat mewling for a handout. Colleen wondered why Gracie hadn't caught on that the cat was likely full of fleas, mange, or worse.

When Gracie finally approached, Colleen excused herself for the restroom. She checked the stalls for tissue but every roll was empty. What a pitiful place. She took a long strip of paper towel and made do. After splashing her fingers with water, she used the same toilet to hoist herself up. After three attempts, she managed to shimmy out the window but ended up snagging her blouse on something sharp on the way out. But, in the end, it was worth it.

The Opportunity Shop

Part I

The Opportunity Shop:

For reasons that will become clear, Baron Van Ael went nuts for the Opportunity Shop. Set back from the street, the shop was around the corner from where he and his twin sister, Karin, lived with their widowed mother. The shop was the sort that most people would be inclined to hurry past if they had occasion to find themselves in that part of town.

Before it became a shop it was the only tombstone masonry business around. Built in the 1940s by Stanley Crawford Skelton, Skelly's Memorials offered the finest in grave markers. At first, interest in high end monuments was non-existent. Flat markers, also known as grass stones, were what grieving family members of Linton preferred. After all, flat markers were reasonable in price and did the trick. But as the town grew and attracted more affluence, gravestone styles and sizes evolved. Slant markers replaced flat and bevel stones, and soon all but the poorest willingly paid top dollar for grandiose monuments to mark their loved ones' graves.

With the surge of interest in high end tombstones, Stanley added on to Skelly's until the building became a lopsided mishmash of roof lines, peaks, and chimneys.

When it was in fashion to do so, Stanley painted the windows shut. The brick exterior was painted over, too, some garish purple and gold, the original brick poking through here and there.

Of course, young Baron was not interested in learning the history of his favourite shop.

At age seventy-three, Stanley Crawford Skelton decided that he'd lived long enough. It was said that he took his life by way of an attic beam two storeys above the business. His death came at the same time as three other residents of Linton selected suicide as a way to end things: the town's cobbler, Doc Hambly, and a Presbyterian clergyman, their lives snapped in two by their own hands.

Then came Butch:

Not a single Skelton was interested in taking over the tombstone carving business. A distant relative, though, who went by Butch after *Butch Cassidy and the Sundance Kid,* decided to turn the building into retail space and low-rent studio apartments.

The main level windows, which were draughty, small, and dusty, were swapped out for larger ones, like those at the butcher shop where convincing replica pot roasts, mutton chops, and pork rinds were displayed. After renovations were completed and a close shave with a nervous breakdown rattled

Butch, he filled the studio apartments with suitable tenants. The sizeable retail space went to Oxford Hemingway, who signed a five-year lease with a fixed $175 per month rate.

Ox, as his name suggested, was a gigantic specimen of a man. His long sausage fingers dangled from hands the size of pizza boxes. He dressed in black pants, custom-made to accommodate his camel-length legs and expansive girth. Ox often ate at the local diner, scarfing down a platter of hamburgers at a single sitting.

His shirts were made of shimmery fabrics, gold or silver being his usual colours, with obscure patterns like gingerbread houses or ghouls. He preferred garments with the feel and lightness of silk, equipped with snap buttons and a breast pocket.

Ox was known to wear face powder, highlights on the tip of his broad nose, gloss on his lips, and blue eye liner around his kernel-sized eyes.

Baron:

In the big display window was a headless mannequin wearing a black lacy evening gown, a spider web shawl, and snake-style bracelets coiled up both arms. If the mannequin's head were still intact, it would only be right that her lips be painted black to match the dress. At least that was what Baron

Van Ael thought time and time again when he stumbled past the display.

Circling the front yard was a ring of repurposed mannequin parts—legs, arms, torsos, and even an occasional head. The parts were collaged with postage stamps, dried flowers, pages of old novels, dictionaries, road maps, atlases, and encyclopedias, and something that resembled the ears of dead animals.

Mannequin heads affixed to spring-loaded posts kept an eye peeled on passersby. Sadly, many of the eyes had been worn away by sleet or hail, or decimated by youth wielding slingshots.

It was said by many longtime residents of Linton that the Opportunity Shop's mannequins in their various states of disarray could leave a young man nervous and twitchy. And that was true of young Baron. When the sun shone, light glittered off the mannequins' voluptuous fake breasts, causing Baron, a combination of raging teen hormones and questionable sensibilities, to blush and his breath to quicken.

One afternoon Baron found himself deep inside the Opportunity Shop when he should have been serving a detention for mooning his classmates during English. He'd been dragged there by his one and only guy pal, a guy who went by the name Alice, after the shock-rocker, Alice Cooper.

Alice, Baron's friend, not the famous Alice, had a missing front tooth, knocked out during a skirmish at elementary school. Often when Alice spoke, a soft whoosh completed his sentences, like the sound automatic doors made when they closed. Alice's neck was long and his skin tone resembled an octopus, giving him the appearance of an ostrich on the look-out.

The Opportunity Shop:

Inside the shop were the usual things one expects in a store offering gently-used items: old recipe books, stamp albums, heavily used sewing patterns. Knitting needles. Toasters of questionable toastability. Flimsy end tables. Yard sticks and protractors. Chairs with backs gnawed by toddlers. Foldable metal and wooden step stools. Pink and yellow skipping ropes. Already-completed paint-by-numbers, ready to hang.

Ox's shop, though, offered much more than the run-of-the-mill thrift stores. Items so ancient and bizarre, shoppers could taste and smell the lineage. All a person had to do was stand in the aisle and breathe deeply to experience the possibilities.

The shop offered what every teen boy craved: piles and piles of worthless junk.

On the day that Baron and Alice found themselves in the Opportunity Shop, the hobby of bestowing life to junk had just started to trend.

At the back of the store were the linen hankies. Next to them were the tarnished tins of throat lozenges that came across the ocean from England via the Savannah. There were hardcover English-Spanish dictionaries. Shoes, most in pairs, but some not. Decks of playing cards in their original boxes, fastened with blue elastic bands, the kind so often found bundling broccoli. Some decks were missing a card or two; for that, they were reduced five cents.

There were baskets of red suspenders that resembled knots of red liquorice. Loads of collared men's shirts. Billowing blouses for women. A yellow dildo-shaped bottle with daffodil-scented cologne that Baron couldn't resist holding. Rusted out tweezers. Umbrellas poking from a pail like United Nations' arms without hands.

Baron was partial to the golf balls, mostly white, some pink, a few glow-in-the-dark.

There were two porcelain postage wells still full of water that Alice kept using to slick back his unruly bangs. A jar of plastic combs, strands of previous owners' hair still evident. Jars of home-made mustard. A gold-plated hand mirror. Tins of buttons. A half empty package of printing paper.

Alice considered buying the back scratcher with the wickedly sharp cactus-head.

The items were organized as if Ox had spent his youth stocking shelves at the local hardware store instead of in and out of juvie for soaping windows and peeing in alleys. The shop offered a certain predictable yet creative flow, like those big box stores in every town and city. The crochet hooks and balls of yarn strategically sat alongside pedal-operated sewing machines and seam rippers.

There were racks and racks of wearables. Tweed jackets. A handful of kimonos. A number of beaver pelts. A few taxidermied raccoons and even a hat made of red squirrel. A carton of handcuffs. Some roll-on deodorant. A pile of wool blankets so itchy even a rhino would say "No." A full-length skirt comprised of quilt patches which Alice considered for his mom.

Metal and wooden skewers. Oyster forks, rusted knives, dozens of fishnet stockings, a shoe stretcher, a leather horse whip, and four curling irons. A number of crock pots, various binoculars, a Ziplock of ballpoint pens, a case overflowing with tubes of oil paint. Magnifying glasses. Masks all the way from Mexico, according to a computer-generated sign.

Baron felt Ox's eyes boring into him. No matter where Baron stood, Ox gaped at him from behind a lockable glass cabinet where the high-end hair clips, refillable lighters, and sparklers were stored. Baron had never felt the urge to steal from the Opportunity Shop and this day was no different. Besides, if he or anyone did, Baron suspected that Ox would flatten them with a single blow from one of his massive paws.

More stuff:

Alice and Baron mauled and gawked at the junk with the officiousness of feral cats. The board games had a special place in their hearts. Scrabble, Checkers that doubled as Chess, Chinese Checkers, Monopoly, and *Mensch ärgere Dich nicht,* a 1914 edition all the way from Germany.

There were hundreds of pastel butt-ends.

And outerwear: navy blue capes, beige frocks, quilted parkas, pea coats, all of which were missing buttons. Black velvet blazers. A white tuxedo. Double-breasted overcoats. Puffer coats, two dusters (one female and one for a tall man). A number of yellow and orange high-visibility-vests. One red coat with a black patch, shoulder strap and cuffs, and plain silver buttons.

The jacket didn't fit Baron. Too bad. It went well with his eyes and mocha skin tone.

A size 2 empire wedding dress, priced-to-sell, never worn.

Pink baby shoes, the palmed-sized box sealed shut.

Three laundry baskets of hats: bowlers, a trilby, a rainbow of ball caps, toques, visors with Velcro fasteners, beanies, sun hats, and bike helmets of questionable reliability.

Bottles of pills, vitamins. Mason jars with nuts, bolts, nails, staples, shearing pins. A half a bag of kibble.

Two boxes of beige-coloured hearing aids.

A tiny jar of fingernail clippings.

Permanent hair dye: red, monotone silver, turquoise, midnight black, and violet, which Alice was partial to.

Toothpicks: reusable and throw-away. Dental floss. Toothpaste for humans and a few tubes marked 'For Canine Use Only.'

Baron couldn't resist giving the doggie paste a taste.

Q-tips, many still in the original box, and a few dozen in see-through baggies.

A bag of twist ties. Another jammed with bread tags.

Ox:

Throughout the day, Ox took snorts of mouthwash and swished it around his mouth. After a reasonably long time, he opened the front door and spat into the flowerbed to the right of the entrance. Nothing of value ever grew there.

More about the stuff:

There were forty-seven tie pins, various clip-on earrings, and a tangle of bracelets. Tins with metal keys: sardines, oysters, high-end cat food, and halvah.

Board books with chewed-off corners. A six-quart basket of harmonicas. Alice and Baron took turns playing the harmonicas and didn't wipe them off before returning them. Black and white photos of miserable looking people at church, in front of cemeteries, and along stretches of fence wire.

Plastic kites and a number of pea shooters. Sling shots (the nice ones with a leather strap). And a sign: Parental permission required.

Baron:

For an hour, Baron had been eying a pair of pink hot pants, a blue and yellow striped tube top, and a shearling coat that was a smidge tight across the shoulders. And a pair of multi-coloured platform shoes that fit perfectly. The ideal get-up for his band. The items cost $15.50 but he only had a ten. Twelve minutes of haggling before Baron sealed the deal.

Baron considered himself a percussionist: a sort of tambourine-triangle player. His vocals were decent enough but he found himself challenged to commit lyrics to memory.

Alice had adequate keyboarding skills but was an abysmal guitarist. His joints were trash from juvenile arthritis so after pounding the ivories, his keyboarding control turned haphazard. Their band needed a drummer and two guitarists. They'd even considered soliciting a saxophonist from the school band.

No one thus far had replied to notices tacked up at the local grocers, the Co-op, the bulletin board by the music room, or the community centre.

Alice:

Alice and Baron hadn't made traction gaining cred at school. It didn't help that they were both duller than a drawer of rusted potato peelers. Being in a band, they believed, would fetch sexual favours from the finer sex, and might even earn them some dough. But without enough musicians to form a band, they thought they'd shelve the idea. Well, Alice did.

Baron decided he'd wear his band costume to school anyway so no one could accuse him of being mediocre.

A need for cash:

Baron was desperate to form a band, that much was clear. But what he needed was to earn some money so he could enroll in music classes. What sucked was the boy had zero experience at doing anything. By June everyone was supposed to have completed volunteer hours in the community, but Baron and Alice still hadn't gotten around to it. Theirs were lives of lost opportunities.

The boys soon replaced band practice with reading Kafka and playing Pick-up Sticks, a game they found at the Opportunity Shop for 10 cents.

Ox was always trying to find ways to ingratiate himself with his regulars. So, it wasn't much of a stretch when Ox, steadily dialing the wheel of his wireless mouse, stumbled upon what appeared to be a legitimate study seeking all-male test subjects.

"Hey guys, have a look at this." Ox scrolled down the page, then tilted the monitor to face Baron and Alice. "I was just scrolling the university website and there's a study right up your alley. All you have to do is take drugs and then write about it."

"Seems simple enough," Baron said.

The Nitty-gritty:

After a brief psychological quiz, suitable subjects were selected for a month-long trial during which they were handsomely remunerated. Subjects would micro-dose on Fridays without knowing if they were getting LSD or a placebo. Fridays were optimal so subjects could recuperate in time to return to normal life by Monday.

After every 'trip,' subjects completed a multi-question online survey, after which, money was e-transferred to their accounts.

Part II

Mid-August, Micro-dose Session #7

Baron and Karin Van Ael:

Karin decided to make a birthday cake. She was measuring ingredients into a steel mixing bowl when Baron loped into the kitchen of their aunt and uncle's cottage.

"You're making cake! Sweet," Baron said, dipping a pinkie into the batter.

"Get lost!" Karin elbowed him out of the way. "About time you got up."

"What else you got planned for our birthday?" Baron said from the sliding door, the lake at the bottom of the hill lapping the rocky shore and dock.

"Nothing much. Mom said she's heading up after work. Ribs for the grill and that bean salad you always rave about," Karin said.

"Mom's specialties."

Baron could feel Karin scrutinizing his face.

"You sure partied hard enough last night," she said. "I could hear you giggling, which was weird because you were by yourself. What were you on?"

"I'm not supposed to talk—"

"Seriously? We're twins. I know everything there is to know about you."

"It's that new paper mushroom called Natalia's Dream. Pure fucking gold. I was out on the dock all night watching the cascading replicas trailing from the stars."

"Huh?" Karin asked, spooning batter into the cake pan.

"I wasn't getting a buzz so I took a second hit. The study allows for that." Baron stretched his arms behind his back to form angel wings. "Then, it hit me. Enormous mushrooms over Rankin's boathouse. Purple, blue, pink, yellow, mauve—"

"You said that already. Purple is mauve and mauve—" Karin bent down to pop the cake pan into the oven.

"Anyway, quit correcting me. I've been getting flashbacks and my brain feels like sourdough bread."

"How much did you say they're paying you for this so-called research?"

"I didn't." His fingers brushed over his stubbly chin. "This is on the QT. Alice and I split a grand every time we take part. An overseas bank wires an e-transfer once our survey responses are uploaded to the Cloud."

Karin twirled a strand of hair. "It's all so risky, don't you think?"

"Listen to you. Ever cautious."

"And you, ever reckless. Tell me more about the psychedelic clouds while we wait for the cake."

Baron grabbed a beach towel from the tree stand. "Right after I get my shit together with a swim across the lake."

"And back, right?" Karin smiled.

"Ah, sure. That's what I said, isn't it?"

The lake:

The truth was, Baron hadn't been honest with Karin. She was right; the experiments were taking their toll. Flashbacks were coming more frequently and with more intensity. And for days after, Baron felt as if he were floating in darkness, like a stingray on the bottom of the ocean. He'd mentioned all this to Alice, who answered by giving Baron a shove and calling him a pussy.

Baron felt particularly groggy after this latest dose of Natalia's Dream. Two tabs hadn't been a great idea but he'd gotten impatient with how long it was taking to start tripping. And besides, there was no way to know if they were getting the actual drug or a placebo.

Alice had tried that version of Natalia's Dream the previous week and still wasn't able to keep food down or stop wobbling. That was why he wasn't at the cottage sharing in the celebrations.

Last time Baron had micro-dosed, he forgot about the online survey and almost got kicked out of the program. When the supervisor offered him a way to stay in, Baron bit. All he had to do was extend the length of the trial past the end of September. Sure, it was taking its toll but whatever. By then he'd have saved a few grand to enroll with a decent guitar teacher so he figured, *So what?* No one else seemed to give a rat's ass about his grey matter becoming Swiss cheese.

What Baron needed was the cold lake water to clear his head, the lake where he and Karin had spent their summers ever since elementary school, a wonderful place owned by their uncle and aunt, two workaholics who rarely used the place.

After leaving his towel on the dock, he dipped a toe into the water. The temperature was just right, not too warm but not too frosty, like it sometimes was by late summer. Baron straddled an inflatable mesh floatie and dog-paddled toward Rankin's boathouse, a modest corrugated aluminum structure pock-marked with corrosion and shotgun pellets.

In Baron's early teens, he placed first in every swim race across the lake. He was so fast there'd been talk of training for the Olympics.

But all that hype blew away with the wind once Baron's father, the local cobbler, took his life.

Karin:

Karin watched her brother start out. Thankfully he had the floatie with him.

She was the worrier of the two. When she and Baron were in kindergarten, instead of pants and a shirt, one day he wore pajamas to class. After Karin pointed it out to him, she burst into tears, fearful he'd get into big trouble. But when the teacher saw, she didn't even care. All she did was knuckle the crown of Baron's head and say, "Don't worry about it. Something like that could happen to anyone."

Karin worried about the long-term effects the drugs would have on her brother. Sure, he and Alice were doing this for science. What if micro-dosing became a viable option for people with cluster headaches or moderate to severe depression?

Karin thumbed the focus wheel on a pair of Bushnell binoculars, zeroing in on her brother's hundred-and-sixty-pound stick-of-a-body bobbing in the waves, not seeming to gain on the opposite shoreline. What the hell was he up to?

Baron:

Winds out of the west threatened to tip the floatie. Baron had already spent half an hour trying to reach the boathouse but he was in the same spot.

He squinted at the horizon which was still impossibly far away.

There was something else Baron should have told his sister. He'd learned that the drug trials were funded by the federal government. If the drug's positive impacts gained traction, there were plans to push for legalization, get the drugs into authorized storefront and online dealers, and reap tax revenue under the medical-micro-dosing umbrella.

As he was thinking, this was when things got wonky. All of a sudden, a salmon-coloured mushroom almost as big as the lake floated overhead, slender black snake-like creatures spilling onto his body. He blinked and rubbed his eyes a few times to be certain of what he thought he saw.

"Jesus-fucking lampreys," he said.

He sat back and tried to calm his breathing which was coming fast and irregular. He closed his eyes briefly, allowing the waves to rock him. The wind took him right into the arms of another lamprey-infested cloud, the creatures' jawless mouths opening and closing as they latched, their raspy teeth and file-like tongues tearing his skin to shreds.

"Get the hell off me," Baron yelled, pawing madly to get them away.

Karin:

From the sliding door Karin could see that her brother was in trouble. His arms were flailing around like he was quarterbacking a political protest. He bobbed up and down in the same spot, not gaining any on the boathouse.

Karin considered seeing if she could start the trolling motor on the boat. She wasn't good at pulling the rip cord and besides, she couldn't leave. The cake wasn't done.

She raised the field glasses and watched the blunt ends of the floatie. Thank goodness Baron had had the wherewithal to take that with him. She worried, though, that before long he'd become hypothermic.

What's he doing now? she wondered.

He was plucking at his body as if under attack. She'd had to do that during mosquito season. But Baron was doing more than swatting insects. It was as if an enemy were blitzing from overhead.

She was torn between taking the cake out early and running down to help her brother or using a wait-and-see approach.

Ten minutes on the timer. Enough time to get to the dock and back.

Baron:

Strings of dark blue clouds streaked the afternoon sky as lampreys continued showering Baron, threatening to drain his body of fluids.

"Help!" he cried to deaf ears.

Lampreys whipped against his weakening muscles. His heart hammered in his chest. His breathing laboured. His dry mouth gasped for air. His only hope: Karin, sweet innocent Karin. Baking them a cake while he was freaking out.

Calm down, he told himself. His fingers hooked the mouth of a lamprey and tried to pry it from his chest. The more he pried, the more the bastard hung on.

"To hell with you," he said. He straddled the floatie and using a cross-country ski stroke, aimed toward the boathouse, the vigorous arm and leg action coaxing the remaining lampreys to let go.

As the pink cloud started to shrivel, another cloud took its place, this one twice as big, with an ominous cobalt sheen.

Behind the cloud, the forest shivered as it took in air. The trees leaned back with each inhalation and folded forward to exhale, the force of their breath pushing Baron away from the boathouse. Behind the trees were enormous skulls with bone structures that were oddly familiar.

"Mom! Karin! You're dead? And Dad, you're there, too?"

The lampreys, with their bellies now full of Baron's blood and pus, slithered onto shore, their funnel mouths sneering as they wormed through eye sockets and nasal cavities.

Baron was screwed.

Karin:

Once Karin lost sight of Baron, panic took over. First, she paced the dock. Then, there was a quickening in her chest, as if being squeezed by a constrictor. She was in the race of her life, uncontrollable terror closing in. That is until she recognized the faint buzz of a timer.

"Shit, the cake!" Karin yelled, taking the outdoor stairs two-at-a-time.

Once she'd set the cake on the wire rack to cool, she returned to the lake. Her tongue probed the corner of her lips, the site of a recent cold sore, while scanning for Baron.

She caught a flash of orange—unless the change in sunlight was playing tricks on her. Hard to say for sure even with the binoculars.

All she knew was time was running out.

Baron:

As the lampreys snaked through skyscraper-sized skulls, their beady eyes flashed trouble. It had to be the drugs

133

fucking with his brain. He was tempted to get ahold of Alice and tell him to shove the drug project up his ass. Phone Alice? Baron was in the middle of a fucking lake!

He thought about Karin, alone at the cottage, Baron out in the water, being an idiot, going off the deep end over a few lampreys. When he stroked his shoulder, his fingers sank into shredded flesh. He *was* right to be afraid. The lampreys *were* real.

But how had they gotten here? Hadn't he always thought that lampreys were only in the Great Lakes?

The mushroom cloud, that's how.

He began to suffocate, as if his throat and chest were dense sponges. He took two weak-ass breaths, and tried to focus on staying alive.

Karin:

Karin held her cell phone up and snapped a few pictures, using her fingers to enlarge the images. Baron's arms were overhead as if he was fending off monsters. What the hell?

Baron:

Wind and waves crashed against the floatie, sucking the...

Karin:

Sitting in the back of the boat, Karin knew she had to do something fast. She yanked the rip cord until her shoulder burned. Then she switched and used her non-dominant arm. *Stupid, stupid, stupid,* she thought. *Why did I never learn how to make this stupid boat go?* It was pointless. The gas lines were obviously fouled up with gunk.

Baron:

. . .

Karin:

Karin raced to the neighbour's and knocked. No answer. She headed for their dock where a tandem kayak was moored. She drained the rainwater out. It had been years since she'd operated a kayak but her arms found their form right away. Left-right left-right. She established a steady rhythm and soon made it to the centre of the lake.

"Where are you? Baron, call out!"

Baron:

Baron barfed up the head of a loon. Then he clawed his teeth and gums with webbed fingers before starting to feast on the floatie.

Karin:

When Karin finally found Baron, he was ripped to shreds.

EMS shook their heads when she told them that her brother had been tripping on Natalia's Dream, the deadliest psychedelic to hit the nation.

"He was a test subject for the university," Karin explained.

"Yeah, sure, lady. And mushroom clouds are made of paper."

EMS wheeled Baron up the hill on a stretcher designed for outdoor rescues. Baron tried to speak but only managed to snarl like a raccoon.

Part III

Karin:

After Baron's physical injuries were dealt with, he was committed to a long-stay psychiatric hospital.

When Karin went to visit, she always brought presents, and tried to keep her stays brief.

"I'm allowed to sit outside today," he told Karin soon after she arrived.

Karin tensed, thinking that what Baron was suggesting was likely against the rules. Her jawline tightened when she glanced up at him. Then she waved a worker over so she could make sure.

A sound like a wolf howl erupted from Baron's throat.

"Never mind," she told the worker. "We're okay now."

"You almost ruined it!" Baron said.

"I believe you, okay? Be cool, Baron."

They ambled in the direction of the exit.

"Did you bring it?" Baron asked.

"Of course." She placed a small nougat treat against his palm.

"No, you know what I mean."

Karin reached into her handbag. "This?" she asked, flashing the cover of a brand-new word-search at him.

"Yes, but not that. You know."

"I'll give it to you right before I go."

"No, you have to give it to me now."

Her hand dove into her bag to retrieve a photograph, a Polaroid. She turned it over so the back faced up.

"It's a very old picture. You probably won't like it."

Baron:

Baron resisted ripping the photo away from her. In therapy, he'd been practicing being patient. Taking it one step at a time, the counsellors called it.

137

He wondered if the photograph was of the old cottage they used to go to. Since micro-dosing, he'd completely forgotten about it. Electroshock therapy did that to memory.

Karin had mentioned last visit that they used to swim in a lake at a cottage. Baron had become quite agitated, told her that was impossible. That he didn't know how to swim.

The psychiatrist had encouraged Baron to stop going over and over that last LSD trip at the cottage because that was where the incident that caused him to lose his mind had happened. Baron *had* lost his mind. Lost it, as if he'd misplaced it or forgotten it on the school bus or dropped it into the sewer. The therapists warned patients to not use words like: insane, crazy, nuts, loco, bonkers, mental case.

Baron hadn't told the doctors that he didn't remember anything about a cottage.

When the wind tore the photo from Karin's hand, Baron felt excitement surge through him, that feeling right before something amazing is about to happen, like riding on the Zipper at the Ex. Baron glanced left, then right, before the photo flipped over. The scream that escaped from his lips caused a nearby orderly to jump into action.

Ox, proprietor of the Opportunity Shop:

As Ox slid the skeleton key into the door of his shop, he wondered what had happened to the two nice boys who used to lurk around. Baron and Alice. Prancing about in those ridiculous costumes from the get-up table. Outfits they raved so much about, like a couple of randy dandies.

No one knew how the boys had gotten mixed up in all that shit. Ox kept it to himself, of course, that it was he who had set Baron and Alice up with that wacko prof at the liberal arts university in Ripley. He'd convinced the boys to enroll in the trial and take *LS* fucking *D*. What was that nut bar prof thinking? Acid was no easy-peasy pot, now, was it?

All Ox knew was he still experienced flashbacks from shit he'd taken back in college.

One good thing, though. The Opportunity Shop being so close to the high school meant that before long, one or two more curious lads would stumble in. They wouldn't be able to resist the mannequin fences and the intoxicating window displays. And fresh young boys, just like Baron and Alice, would be hooked. And once inside, they would be Ox's to play with any old way his little heart desired.

The Moment Everything Changed

In 1967, Montreal had Expo. Modern schools were taking the place of one- and two-room schoolhouses. Mothers and children became unintended casualties of the war in Vietnam. Our country's one hundredth birthday was on the horizon.

1967, the same year children around me began vanishing. The most appalling: the disappearance of Carolyn Arnold.

On the afternoon Carolyn went missing, I was sitting on the school bus next to my bestie, Steph. We were going to her place so we could take turns riding her horse. I didn't bother telling Steph that I despised the horse for biting me last time I was there. I knew if I did, she'd only tease me for putting my fingers in the horse's way.

A light drizzle was falling as we got off the bus. The driver called me back, insisting on a note from my parents.

"I showed you before." I pulled a crumpled note dated weeks earlier.

"Okay, okay, I guess you did," he said, the doors sighing as they closed.

Because of the rain we stayed in and played Barbies in Steph's bedroom. When her mom busted in with a plate of cookies, she let us know about the abduction. "It just happened. A little girl your age. Over in Taran."

I shivered.

"I hope they find her." Concern lined Steph's mom's face. "All those rocks and crevices at the base of the escarpment. And the woods and marsh."

I didn't ask Steph's mom why she thought the girl had ended up in the forest. It wasn't until later that we learned that the girl had been spotted getting into a car. That she'd been wearing blue shoes threaded with red laces to match her jacket.

According to reports made by her friends and classmates, she had recently been granted permission to bike to and from school. The day of the abduction she'd dumped her bike in favour of jumping into a car with a man with a large head and pale face. Some said that he'd been wearing a grey hat. The car was reported to be of European make, dark in colour, navy or perhaps black.

The bicycle was found nearby, barely a scratch on it, the front wheel spinning in the mid-April breeze. While this emergency gripped our district, the news was filled with reports that the Beatles were about to release an album, and that women were still not allowed to run the Boston marathon.

According to the police, the victim was a brown-haired, mild-mannered ten-year-old. Innocently heading home after a day like so many we could relate to: a day of memorizing math facts, conducting experiments with baking soda and vinegar, and writing thrillers about our pets.

Minutes after dismissal, her pipe cleaner-thin legs pumped hard, intent on reaching her modest insulbrick home at the end of a dead-end road. Too early still for trilliums; the wettest sections of the woods still mushy underfoot.

Carolyn's red jacket was reported to have been zippered to her chin on account of the briskness of the breeze. Last seen on Main Street in the hamlet where she lived with her parents and little brother.

Carolyn Arnold. Hide and seek no longer child's play.

Spotted standing next to the driver's door, her bike to her left. So tiny, she was barely able to see into the car. Grinning as if the driver were familiar, a dad, neighbour, uncle, according to a witness stopped at a traffic light en route to a medical appointment. Then lickety-split, around the rear of the car she went, the bicycle ditched, quickly and quietly slipping into the back seat.

The school I attended was a half hour's drive east of where the abduction took place. So close I felt I knew her, as if she'd spent the past few years occupying the desk in front of mine or the one directly behind. As if the teacher regularly grouped us together for read-aloud or social studies.

Her disappearance left me chilled. That night in bed, I called my mom to bring an extra blanket and tuck me in all over again. At school the next day, everyone was talking about Carolyn. Scout troops from neighbouring towns joined up with Taran's to perform extensive grid searches.

Parents started picking their sons and daughters up at school rather than letting them walk home as they usually did. Within a week, an anonymous donor offered a sizeable reward for the girl's return. The teachers lectured us non-stop about 'stranger danger.'

European-made cars began showing up on every corner.

My parents forbade me to play at Steph's. Said that getting there on my own was no longer safe. I missed going there because Steph had more dolls than I did. And bubblegum. And Nancy Drew mysteries. Her father was a full-time firefighter. He'd been the one to help organize the grid search. We took whatever he said about the case as gospel.

I managed to fill my newly-found free time by playing on my swings, riding my bike on the front yard, and writing stories I could never seem to finish. So much scrunched up paper tossed into the wastepaper basket.

Once on the way home from school ...

and

A little girl climbed into a dark car, never to be ...

and

Instead of going home like I was supposed to ...

My writing upset my mother so much she started sending me to bed earlier and earlier. Carolyn's disappearance had taken hold of me.

~

One day, one of her blue shoes with its bright red laces was found by a family of hikers on a trail outside of Bolton. Images of the sneaker were plastered on every television in the country. After that, everyone at school strung coloured laces through the eyelets of their shoes.

Helicopters circled overhead, binoculars dialed onto heavily wooded areas. Adults took vacation time to help with the search. It got that there were so many people choking up the roads in and around Taran that the police had to set up roadblocks and turn people away. The chief of police appeared on the evening news to beg people to stay home and start praying.

I pleaded with my parents to let me go to Steph's. I made promises I couldn't keep, like pledging that Steph's mom would watch us at all times. My dad said my being grounded so long was taking its toll on the entire family. They agreed for me to go for a short visit.

It was Steph who came up with the idea of a new game: *Track the Missing Shoe*. It was a combination of Pin the Tail on the Donkey, Buried Treasure, and Hide and Seek. It began in the forest that ran behind her house. I agreed to be first to put on the blindfold, which turned out to be one of her dad's old neck ties. She spun me around a few times before pushing me to the ground. Then she ripped off my right shoe and sock. While running away, she counted until I couldn't make out her voice anymore. That's when I tore off the blindfold and started hunting for my shoe.

For the first few minutes, I felt as if anything were possible.

It soon became clear that the game would be an epic failure. Steph was primed to win. After all, she'd come up with all the rules.

I soon got mixed up. All the trees resembled each other with their repeated trunk patterns and totem pole height. No way to know which way was which. I was confused when the wind whispered my name. I got turned around by what I thought was the hum of a car. The smell of decayed leaves and animal pee made barf rise into my throat.

Never before had I tried to get around by only hopping on one foot.

I located a sturdy stick. To defend myself. To lean on. Latch onto.

It was fast approaching dusk when I wiggled out of the woods' tight embrace. The skin of my arms was clawed to shreds. I was so thirsty; I could have drunk an entire tub of water. Steph laughed so hard, she sounded like raccoons cascading down a tree for a night of fun and games.

Later, my parents pointed out how vicious her prank had been. That true friends didn't act that way. That's when they stopped leaving the front door unlocked.

~

A couple of months went by when I overheard my parents whispering one evening. That Carolyn Arnold never stood a chance. That everything was changed now — forever.

After a while, the news no longer featured the face of the missing girl. Things began to evolve; life began its slow return to normal. My parents invited friends over for cards, drinks, and appetizers my mother spent hours fussing over.

I passed from one grade to the next, and received a dollar for every A on my report card. Summer flew by and a new school year began. A new family moved in next door. They had only one child, too, just like us. Their little girl didn't blink. My parents told me to not ask about it

The only thing left to talk about on the radio and TV news was the Vietnam war. The unnecessary deaths got my mom so upset, she pulled out her old manual typewriter and wrote what my father called a 'nasty bit of business' addressed to the president of the United States.

We kids got back to how things were before the girl got taken. The bus started to drop me off at my proper bus stop half a mile from home. No one thought it strange anymore to see a couple of young kids on the Lower Baseline without an adult hovering nearby.

One Thursday in mid-October after the bus dropped us off, I started for home. It was warm for that time of year and I wanted to ride my bike before supper. My jacket was off, its sleeves tied around my waist so I wouldn't have to carry it as well as my lunch pail.

I often toed a pebble along the road in front of me and this day was no different than the rest. It was a way of keeping from racing home, a way for the slow neighbour girl to keep up without me having to constantly harp at her.

There was a white van off to the right. It appeared to be having some kind of engine trouble or a busted-up tire. There were no words painted on the outside like on my dad's van. Nor were there any windows in the rear. When we had almost caught up to it, the van started creeping ahead, keeping pace with us.

The van's engine purred. Deep grey smoke choked from the tailpipe. The neighbour kid started to lag so my fingers curled around hers and schlepped her along. My focus now was on checking our mailbox which was on the other side of the road. And getting home to my bicycle.

The driver's window was rolled most of the way down. By now we had almost caught up to the van, which had stopped. The driver had a broad head, small ears, and pale skin. His arm, which hung partway out the window, was covered in long dark hair like he was part chimpanzee. He looked to be no older than my dad. On his head was some sort of hat with a black velvet band.

"Nice day," he called out to me. "I need help with something. There's a treat in it for you as well as for your little friend."

Stranger danger had taught us that this was a trick some predators use. But curiosity got the better of me. Besides, what could happen? We'd learned that abductors didn't prefer taking more than one kid at a time.

I dropped the girl's hand and climbed onto the running board. I could see inside except his arm was kind of in the way. Crumpled bags of take-out sat on the seat next to him, and a pair of muddy rubber boots were on the floor. The air around him smelled of onions, smoke, and sweat. When he finally pulled his arm back, my fingers wrapped around the lip of the open window, enabling me to tip my head in.

He wore painter's overalls. They were covered in splotches of grey, blue, and orange. The orange paint was near his crotch.

"Can you help me with the zipper?" he asked, breaking into a sheepish smile. "It's caught."

He began to stroke himself.

"Come closer," he said, his voice barely a whisper.

The neighbour's kid started sneezing, making it the perfect time to make a run for it.

~

The police were nice. When they came to the house, they showed me binders of mug shots. The police said all the men I identified as 'maybes' were harmless, that they weren't interested in kidnapping a child. That me watching him touch himself was how he got his thrills.

I thought about the kind of thrills I went for: skipping rope, blowing the biggest bubble possible so it could be added to the Guinness World Book of Records, tossing flat stones into the pond, colouring inside the lines, collecting twigs and taping them into my art journal.

For a while after the incident, I started to wet the bed again. I recorded descriptions of every strange vehicle I spotted. Shared this with my parents who were obsessed as I was. The creases between their eyes deepened and they started whispering at each other behind open palms.

People down the street organized a neighbourhood watch but finding enough volunteers became a losing proposition. The special kid next door got sent away, perhaps to live with her grandparents. It didn't take long before their property went on the market.

My parents referred to the white van incident as 'the almost abduction,' an expression whose roots remain with me.

Even though I've been a mother and a grandmother, I still have days when I need to remind myself that the world is more or less a good place. That life goes on, and that most days nothing too horrid happens. That is, until I bring forth the memory of 'the almost abduction.'

When Things Run Afoul

A middle-aged man and his wife sat on the porch reading the Saturday paper when a drifter came along the country road. The dead-end property was concealed enough that the man and his wife had skinny-dipped a few times in the pond located to the rear of the house. The man slid to the edge of his rocker to get a better look at the drifter. Gaining a clear view posed a challenge because of the angle of the sun. All the while, his wife nattered on about a pair of pandas recently sent over to the Toronto Zoo from China.

Years before, after immigrating to Canada from Europe, the man got hired at a cardboard processing plant. It was tedious work that only a numbskull could withstand but it paid handsomely and promised a defined pension and benefits when he retired, for which he was beholden. In the meantime, he had slipped on packaging tape, leaving him with a good-enough disability pension, as well as a head injury that resulted in periodic incapacitating headaches and night terrors.

The drifter didn't seem to be someone to fear. He walked with a pronounced limp and his left pant leg was folded in such a way to indicate evidence of a shortened limb. He was blessed with a complete foot that required a special kind of shoe with a thicker than usual sole. As he hobbled along, his wizened figure listed as if elbowed by the wind.

Despite a roof with wind-lifted shingles and a crumbled chimney, the man and his wife took pleasure in their property. Behind the house were a couple of rundown barns, a shed, and the aforementioned pond dug by the previous owner. If he had been of able body and head, the repairs might have been something the man would have tackled but while free of the demands of his factory job, sitting and musing were now his follies. He imagined himself something of a hobby farmer, despite his lack of knowledge to differentiate a peahen from a cock or a doe from a buck.

As the drifter came into full view, the man saw that he carried a beige carton equipped with a flimsy handle. His oak-coloured hat was turned up in the front but did nothing to conceal the long black ponytail jutting onto the collar of his blue button-up shirt. The man didn't adjust his position on his seat until the drifter was in the front yard where he set his box before tipping two fingers to his brow.

"Beautiful morning. What I wouldn't give to see that sunrise every day," the drifter said, the sun forming a halo behind his head. "I'm here in search of work. Anything you've got, I hope you'll consider me."

The man's wife, thin as a reed, made excited wordless murmurs from behind the newspaper she kept in front of her face.

The man, his arms crossed over his chest, studied the drifter as if he were a curious young chipmunk that had dared come up close. The drifter's pale face swiveled left, then right, taking in everything in the yard—the hand pump next to the porch, the weeping willow with its busted limbs, the drive shed with the butt end of a rusted tractor poking out.

"Still run?" the drifter asked, jabbing a thumb at the shed.

"Used to. Haven't had cause to get it going."

"Hoping that'll change?" the drifter said.

"You from these parts?" the man asked.

"Sort of. I'm Daniel King," the drifter said with a hint of a sigh.

The man said, "Pleased to meet you, Daniel King. I go by Findlay Thompson and this here's Laurenda."

"Call me Lucy." She sat up tall, folded the newspaper along the crease, and took in Daniel King for herself. "You never did say where you're from."

Daniel didn't answer. His face carried no expression. He leaned against the partially collapsed fence and moaned.

"Come on. No need to make a fuss here," Findlay said, patting his wife's hand.

"We don't know you from nothing," Lucy said, a frown making her already narrow face droop lower.

"A person can be from here or there, ma'am," Daniel explained. "If I told you where I stem from, I could be lying or I could be telling the truth. There's no way of knowing for sure."

Lucy gummed a strawberry seed that had wormed loose from one of her teeth. "I can hear our grandbaby rooting around." She shuffle-walked inside.

"Don't mind her none," Findlay said, nodding at the house. "Lucy was built suspicious."

"None taken," Daniel said, his left eye twitching.

Daniel explained he'd worked a lot of places: as an assistant to an undertaker, an organist in a band, and a porter on the train to and from Vancouver.

Findlay wondered if a partially lame man could fix the roof of their house. Collect and candle the eggs if he and Lucy had the mind to get into laying hens like they'd always wanted.

"If it's like you said and you're here to work, I can offer room and board and a small monthly allowance," Findlay said.

Daniel opened the lid of his cardboard box. Inside was a bouquet of red, peach, and yellow plastic blooms on the end of pipe cleaner stalks. "For the wife," he said. "Trust she, like most women, enjoys flowers."

It didn't matter to Findlay where Daniel was from. He knew an honourable man when one stood in front of him.

~

Within a week, the changes Daniel had made around the property became apparent. The roof patched up. The well pump mechanisms lubricated. The front fence mended. The barn cleaned up and readied for a quota of laying hens. It was Lucy who pointed out to Findlay the benefits of having Daniel around.

Mornings, before heading out to the barn, Lucy got things organized in the house. She chopped vegetables for soup and fed her granddaughter, a child she and Findlay looked after ever since their daughter became missing-in-action.

Lucy slipped a harness over the bony toddler's shoulders and tethered her to the horsehair chesterfield. From there, the child could watch *The Friendly Giant* and other favourite programs while munching on cheese-coloured crackers shaped like fish and whales. While Rusty and the Friendly Giant worked out solutions to problems children faced, Daniel weeded and tended the vegetable patch while Findlay and Lucy scythed the weeds next to the pond.

In some ways, it felt as if Daniel wasn't even around. Sure, he joined Lucy and Findlay for dinner and took a shower once a week. But he wasn't underfoot in the evenings as he liked to bunk in the shed where the rusted-out tractor was. He kept a razor in the box he came with and a bucket of cold water he pumped from the well himself. There was a shard of glass he'd scrounged somewhere that he rigged into a mirror. Most evenings, Daniel amused himself. Once he'd been there a while, he got into the habit of walking into town to the Baptist church where he sang in the choir and helped perform small chores such as sweeping out the vestibule after parishioners left.

It wasn't long before Findlay and Lucy acquired some chickens. Laying hens like they'd always wanted. And a few meat birds, too, pecking grubs from the front yard.

Usually, it was Lucy who candled the freshly gathered eggs. This was done in the basement. Since her eyes were better than either Daniel's or Findlay's, she could detect blood-spots on the yolks with eagle-eye accuracy. From the back of an old delivery van, Findlay peddled eggs to restaurants, stores, and private customers in the city. Lettering on the side of the van claimed they were the biggest darned eggs in the country. Likely he had meant it to say county, but what it said worked just fine.

Despite chickens being known for their quirks, Findlay decided to allow his laying hens free-range of the barn where they spent the day roosting or scratching around. They had the whole place to themselves but that didn't mean they got along.

Chickens were primed to fight, especially if they'd already tasted blood.

It turned out that a chicken's cannibalistic tendency was due to a design flaw. Its cloaca, the multi-purpose pee, poop, and egg-laying hole, remained partially inverted immediately after pushing out an egg. Such a hole was mouthwatering ambrosia to the rest of the brood.

Despite being de-beaked as baby chicks, the hens' beaks eventually grew back. Once chickens resorted to killing each other, it was imperative to de-beak again. Findlay hated de-beaking and tried to foist the chore on Daniel to do on his own. "You're the hired hand," he told Daniel, "I'm paying you to work."

Daniel agreed to help but refused to do it by himself, saying it was a two-man job. While Daniel gathered up the birds, Findlay clipped a quarter inch off each beak and stored the tips in a large jar. The beak tips were a reminder to the birds to bug off.

De-beaking was so stressful on man and fowl, the farm turned still the day of and the entire week following the procedure.

Though the feeding trough held mash and hen scratch, before long the hens scattered the feed. Raising chickens was troublesome, especially come winter when Daniel and Findlay spent much of their time, propane torches in hand, thawing frozen water pipes. Laying hens depended on a steady clean source of water as eggs were mostly composed of liquid.

One morning when Findlay and Daniel staggered into the barn, they stumbled upon forty dead birds.

"Coyotes," Findlay told Daniel. "Look at all the feathers."

"You always say that," Lucy said, joining them in the barn. "There's no way for them to get in. I check each and every time to ensure that I've latched the door properly."

"You're sure?"

Lucy clamped her mouth shut.

"Maybe I shouldn't have changed the feed," Findlay said.

"But it's far cheaper."

"Yet, if the birds were stressed by the change, we won't be any further ahead."

"At least the child didn't have to see this. Think of the nightmares the kid would have," Lucy said, wringing her chafed hands in front of her chest.

"It's not the food or stress. It's vent pecking," Daniel said. "We didn't go deep enough." He pointed at the tiny tips of beak piled in the jars on the sill.

Lucy performed the autopsies. She liked figuring out what the birds died of. Holding the organs against her palm.

Determining how many birds had had heart attacks. Which ones had enlarged livers. After, she carried the dead birds by the feet and tossed them in a mass grave next to the pond.

That evening instead of going to church, Daniel stuck around to sit with Findlay over a pitcher of iced tea. Lucy could overhear them talking.

"Don't take this wrong. I'm only suggesting this because I've got such pride and personal interest in this place. You and the wife are, after all, like family," Daniel said. "But what if you sell the remaining chickens to a soup processing plant and get into something new? Some free time will give me a chance to get that old tractor of yours moving."

~

"What about rabbits? There are people in Little Italy who like them in a stew," Daniel said one evening over homemade soup and toasted bread. "Rabbits are easy. They don't need much attention."

"And I suppose you think the meat tastes like chicken," Lucy said.

Findlay decided to start with one young buck and a couple of does.

Because Daniel had the most legible handwriting, Findlay charged him with keeping mating records. Rabbits in heat took part in strange rituals. When the doe was ready to be mounted, she rubbed her head against the walls of her cage, and smiled. This drove the buck bonkers. He climbed on, rubbed himself against her, and immediately fell to the ground, looking quite dead. Afterward, he leapt up ready for a replay, his tiny nap reviving him. It was at that moment that Daniel recorded date and time of conception.

The buck's effort resulted in sixteen baby bunnies.

"That's far too many for two does to feed," Lucy said, stunned to see four hairless newborn bunnies floating in a pail of water.

It was Lucy's idea to fast-multiply the brood. Because a doe can mate within hours of giving birth, the buck inseminated the two original does and their sexually mature offspring. Findlay liked to call this *keeping it in the family*. Before they knew it, they were overrun with bunnies.

The rabbits didn't need much in the way of a home. Each hutch consisted of a small wood-framed structure with a roof, and a wall dividing it into two sections. One part was wire mesh, and the other had wooden walls. Because the does were pumping out dozens of bunnies, no one could keep up with the demand for hutches, so Daniel abandoned his other chores including getting the tractor up and running, and offered to help.

Lucy noticed that her favourite doe was going bald. Findlay said, "Don't be such a worry-wart. She's making a nest for the babies."

A few days later the newborns' blind hairless bodies were shivering in a clump inches from the mother. Lucy did what any caring person would do. She reached in and nudged the babies closer to the mom. The doe took one look at Lucy, nuzzled the babies closer, and swallowed them whole.

Turned out, Findlay and Lucy knew less about rabbits than chickens. They fed the rabbits anything and everything. Alfalfa. Red clover. Birdsfoot trefoil. Bread crusts. Pellets. Pieces of salt lick. Water from a special drinking nozzle. Twigs to keep their teeth from growing over their jaws. And vegetables sourced from a restaurant implementing a farm-scrap program.

"Think of the money we'll save," Lucy told Findlay.

The rabbits devoured the scraps with enthusiasm until they developed the runs. They peed and shat everywhere. Their poop went from round and firm to watery like cow patties and carried a stench fit to put a damper on the hungriest person's appetite.

As the bunny population exploded, Findlay and Daniel had trouble keeping up with the number of hutches required but, in the end, didn't wind up using them. The restaurant scraps caused six-weeks of nonstop runs. The stink, no longer contained to the hutches, seeped into the house. The wet rabbit bottoms became an irresistible breeding ground for insects. This resulted in a condition called fly strike which was an outbreak of fly maggots. It chopped the population in half.

Later, when the local farm and tractor store had a sale on wood chips, Findlay took the van over and loaded up.

"Just think how clean and sweet smelling the hutches will be," he said over dinner one evening. "Using straw as bedding has left the does with itchy ears."

He and Daniel disinfected the hutches before sprinkling them with wood chips. Soon the now healthy does were squeezing babies out again. Only thing was, the babies couldn't tolerate the wood chips; the chips left them gasping for air.

Before long, a bunch died. If only Findlay had thought to mention to the store clerk what the wood chips were for. By this time, Lucy had grown tired of performing autopsies so the deaths were chalked up to a stroke of bad luck.

It became Daniel's job to pile the carcasses by the pond. After all, getting into rabbits had been his idea.

~

Findlay and Lucy needed a new focus. They considered setting up a tree farm with healing trees like willows, yews, and birches. Only trouble was, trees took forever to mature. Lucy made a plea for goats. The health section of the newspaper said that goat's milk was a viable alternative to cow's milk. Besides, they needed something different to keep their granddaughter's eczema in check.

Lucy told Findlay, "Raising goats is good for so many reasons."

After Lucy took the baby to town for her boosters, Findlay went to the shed and sought Daniel's views on raising goats. Daniel, wrench in hand and enough tractor lubricant on his skin to grease a rhino, weighed in. "A farmer worth his salt keeps records. If I were you, I'd head over to the livestock auction and look for a nanny who's a good milker. Don't hesitate to ask for her production records. That way you don't need to train her how to milk."

Findlay clamped his lips shut for a moment before saying, "Come with me to market."

"I would but I've been hired to put hay up at the Bishop's place this afternoon. The rounder a goat is, down there, the better."

"Down there?" Findlay said.

"The udder." Daniel's face flushed at the mention of the word. "The best nannies have a straight back and a broad rib cage."

Findlay drove to auction and set his sights on a lively nanny with a sleek grey coat and up-to-date inoculations. He was overjoyed when the owner tossed in a male goat, too. "I'm doing you a favour," the owner said. "He's cantankerous but he'll grow on you. His name is Billy."

When he got home, Findlay threw Billy into the same pen with Nanny.

The goats could sure eat. Leaves. Branches. Weeds. Shirts and pants. To make milk, Nanny needed corn, oats, and wheat bran, but Billy always forced his snout into the bucket before she could get near. What nobody knew was goats needed grass and cured hay first, then grain, or else they'd bloat up something fierce.

At first, Daniel referred friends from the church to buy goat milk from Findlay. Pickup trucks of farmers lined the concession road waiting for their chance to get their hands on some. That is until customers started complaining that the milk was off. "Blaine Bishop gave it to his Naomi. He said she's not one to complain, but she couldn't finish it."

Lucy had been drinking it for a while, and hadn't noticed anything. Sure, there was a fustiness that took some getting used to but her belly cramps and diarrhea had completely stopped. And the baby didn't need the prescription cream for a spate of elbow rashes anymore.

Daniel offered to check on Nanny. "Oh, oh," he told Findlay.

"What now?" Findlay said, shrugging his shoulders.

"They're in the same pen. That's why the milk tastes off."

When word got out about the milk, Findlay took a notion to blame Daniel. "He acts all high and mighty," he told Lucy one evening over supper while Daniel was at a church meeting, "but he doesn't know what he doesn't know."

~

After they sold the goats at a loss, Findlay and Lucy figured they'd sit low for a while, allow themselves extra thinking time before investing into their next notion. Daniel needed a part or two to get the tractor going. Findlay agreed he should go get whatever was required to get the thing running once and for all. For the rest of the week, shrieks and moans issued from the shed while Daniel worked on and greased the beloved tractor. He kept at it so long he didn't even pause for dinner some nights.

One evening, rocking in their chairs and reflecting on things, Findlay and Lucy smiled at each other like weary reptiles after a day spent sunbathing on a rock. All of a sudden, the rusty nose of the tractor poked from the drive shed, coughing and sputtering but working all the same.

"Finally got it going by the sounds of things," Lucy said, turning in her seat to face the drive shed.

Findlay's eyes filled with tears. "He's a tenacious bugger. Got to give him that."

Lucy thwacked him on the arm. "What are you getting all misty-eyed about, you old goat?"

As the sky turned the colour of rutabaga, Daniel pointed the refurbished tractor down the laneway. Neither Findlay nor Lucy felt concern until he turned onto the concession road where he was never seen in those parts again.

The End of Pillow Talk

You begin the semester trying to meet someone new. You roam campus where you started taking a couple of 'interest' courses. You love hanging out at the mall, too. You linger outside stores girls like to frequent. Some people enjoy shopping at church bazaars. Yes, you think, standing next to a table piled with Barbie doll clothes. That girl is a good option. You admire how she clutches a macramé purse like she made it herself. By the look of her fingernails, she likely cleans teeth for a living or preps food at a high-end restaurant.

The girl has broad shoulders and small breasts. Maybe she was once a gymnast or played goal for her high school soccer team. She has a page boy cut with thick bangs that form a wedge over dark bushy eyebrows.

Her face blooms when you ask her name. "Ursula," she says. "I'm German on my father's side."

You ask her out. You feel her eyes all over you while you sip lattes at a small metal table on the sidewalk of your favourite café. You haven't felt desirable in a while. Not since what's her name. You leave a larger than normal tip before guiding this girl by the elbow, the heat of her arm nourishing your palm.

Around her you feel an intense sense of desire and belonging. A few weeks in, you don't recall which one of your friends suggests it might be time to move in together. When you broach the subject with her, she nods yes. Suggests you move in, that her place is nicer.

She bristles when you say you want to establish a 'let's see how it goes' arrangement. Leave things willy nilly. Go month by month.

"I want both of our names on this lease," she says, tapping an official stack of papers. She wants exclusivity.

You finally shrug okay. It's not as if you've been suggesting that the two of you live like sluts.

She moves hangers along the rod in the closet, making room for your clothes. You don't ask for much. You only bring one suitcase.

Her smell reminds you of childhood, a home filled with love and sentimentality. Vicks ointment. Cinnamon turnovers, ginger snaps, and vanilla cookies. Sage dressing. Maple syrup. Steak sauce. Popcorn, lots of butter.

She nips your earlobe. Your toes. Your collarbone. She nibbles her way down to your bush. She sings for you. Dances. Wears olive-coloured tank tops and matching panties. Tells jokes about chickens crossing the road. You think—how old are you, anyway?

On the weekend she stirs eggs with milk and white flour and butter. Giggles as wet combines with dry. You lick the back of her neck as batter steams and sputters between heated waffle plates. She pushes you away in the name of safety. She pulls the plug on the waffle maker before nestling her lips against your nipple.

It turns out that the pristine condition of Ursula's fingers lied about who she is and what she does. She isn't a hygienist; she runs a second-hand store. Sometimes, when she spends the whole day there, she smells like dust and mildew.

You work in an office. The office employs a cleaning staff. Your place of work always smells fresh and clean. She wishes she had a job like you have. She studied acting way back when and sometimes role-plays for you but isn't all that convincing.

Sundays are for staying in bed. You lie on your right side, your arm serving as a pillow beneath your head. You're naked except for your glasses. Hip hop fused with blues plays in the background. Ursula is dressed in a short plaid skirt, something from the store where she works. Her small breasts are behind a lacy black bra.

You and she dance against the mattress. Slowly. You have all afternoon. She keeps her eyes closed the entire time, hums when she gets close, calls to God when she climaxes.

Time passes. Weeks become months. You introduce her to your mother. Your father is long gone by this time but your mother still tosses her influence on your life wherever she can. You take your girl to the cottage where the lake water slurps at the dock pilings in the dead of night.

Your mother flinches when you kiss your girl's cheek in front of her. A small flirtatious peck in front of the woman who birthed you. *This* is the person you've been keeping from me, your mother's sad eyes say.

The lake is dark. Your girl won't go in. You urge her to try skinny-dipping. "You know I don't swim," she says.

You ponder what would happen if you just pushed her in. Fears should be tested.

For lunch your mother serves cold cuts, sliced cucumber, and potato salad with bacon crisps and red onions. Your girl takes three servings of salad.

"Finish it off," your mother says, pushing the plate in Ursula's direction. You shrug when your mother raises her eyebrows to say, *see.*

Your mother gives you a hard angry look when your girl goes off to take a nap. Shakes her head. Your mother still cannot believe you're a lesbian, thinks if you tried, you'd find a nice man to marry.

You pull photo albums from a shelf behind the couch. You start paging through, remembering. Your girl joins you, her hair wild from her nap. Her bare leg is sticky and warm against yours.

She points out a picture of fourteen-year-old you, your sun-bleached bangs and the gap between your front teeth. You feel embarrassed. That the pictures don't have an organizational flow like some people's albums. That some pages are cluttered with overlapping photos, put there without thought or a plan. Your girl doesn't seem to tire of the stories that accompany the sepia images.

She jabs a finger at a boy wearing blue shorts standing next to a red trike. The boy is a year younger than you are. "Gregg," you say. Grey eyes narrow when you mention that you have no idea where your brother is.

Instead of feeling rested at the cottage, you're restless. Your mother starts in about politics. She's a Trump supporter despite living in Canada. You fill with a smoldering discontent, a yearning to return to the city. The bustle. The noise. You want new girls to gaze at while waiting for the pedestrian signal to change.

A few days after the cottage, you start seeing someone on the side. You wonder what her breasts feel like as she passes by. You turn around, call out to her. She mentions that she's a student from Northern Europe. You can't get enough of her wide cheek-bones and luminescent smile.

This girl likes to quote Emile Durkheim, the father of modern sociology. You make moves to sleep with her. Afterwards, you both cry. She, with tears of unexpected pleasure. You, because to stay with her shouldn't be in the plans. You brush your lips on her cheek before running home to Ursula.

When you arrive at the apartment, Ursula tells you she no longer has a job. Something about the building owner tearing down the existing structure for a condominium project. Nearly new stores don't jive with the proposed condo vision. You lean forward to brush your lips against her hairline but stop yourself short. What if she detects the student's scent on your skin? You turn away and say you're going to have a shower.

You spend too long in the bathroom. Ursula doesn't ask questions. She climbs into the stall with you. She's naked and hot, and soon you unleash your passion spurred on by your recent infidelity.

Under the covers, Ursula says that losing her job is a sign. She wants a family. You've noticed her interest in babies. Whenever you're out, her fingers seek the heads of little kids, stroking their hair.

"The first IV procedure is free," she says.

A sigh escapes, punctuating your lack of desire for anything related to family. Not now. Not ever.

Months go by. She finally conceives.

More doubt starts to creep in.

Ursula can't sit still; wants to go shopping. "For the baby," she says. As she passes storefront windows, she marvels at her baby bump, the reflection against dark glass vivid and pronounced. You don't want to know the sex of the fetus so she fills carts with blue, pink, and yellow onesies.

She squeals with delight as she snips the price tags from the sleeves. "Won't you be returning the ones you don't need?" you ask. The room she's decided to turn into a nursery fills with purchases.

You think about leaving. Packing your bags and slithering away, out the door, in the dead of night, a rat on the run. Before the baby shows its face

At least Ursula will have someone to hang out with.

But you don't leave. Your girl looks so good right now. Flashes a healthy luminosity.

You read. Books become an escape. Poetry. Prose poems but also free-form and rhyming. She asks when you'll start into the pile of parenting books towering next to the bed. You wink before formulating your lie. "What makes you think I haven't?" you ask.

She eats all the time. You never noticed before how loudly she chews. Ketchup chips, her favourite, crumbs on the sheets and under the pillows.

You start to plot your escape.

The final trimester. Ursula pounds back carton upon carton of mint chocolate ice cream, complains that her feet ache. She's prone on the bed, the giant lump that is her belly obscuring her face from where you sit. You go to the bathroom to soak rags in cold water and wrap them around her lower extremities. Doing so causes her to croon.

She wears tent dresses. No panties. She complains that they pinch her thighs.

You no longer fit together. You see that now. The future will bring baby shit, crying, and sleepless nights. Your girl threatens you with nighttime bottle duty.

"I'll pump," she says. "That way you can be involved, too."

Only you don't care to be.

She gets up and goes to the kitchen. You pace the apartment. You mutter that you're unhappy. She mouths *I love you* then begs you to reach for canned pasta sauce from the cupboard. You think she says, "Why can't I ever be enough?" only you can't be sure over the whir of the electric can opener.

The apartment walls close in. You say you need to head out for a while. "I'm making dinner," she says. You mutter that you're not hungry.

"I need air," you say. She insists you take your cell phone. In case.

In case of what, you wonder. You slam the door, louder than intended.

The air is cold. You begin sniffling, not because you're sad but because you need to be alone. You did not choose this life, never wanted it, any of it. She did. You stop outside a bar, the thump of music seeping through the walls. You go in. Just one beer. Maybe two. A man in a bright pink shirt and Mickey Mouse necktie tries to gain your attention. It's been forever since you've touched a man that way. You stare into your drink. Blink away the future.

You and the man have quick sloppy sex in the ally next to the bar. Then you head home, one last time.

The ambulance attendants say these things happen. There's so much blood. The fluids are dark and stain the floor, bathmat, towels.

You can't leave now.

Endless tests. Tears. Lost dreams. Advice given and ignored. As she wails you tuck your face against her clavicle. You feel a flash of love. Not all the time. Just at moments like this.

You cannot help but think, at least there wasn't a baby.

What if your girl had died?

You begin to plot your departure. For real, this time.

You start by finding a new lover. On Kijiji of all places. You begin to tell Ursula lies.

While she goes for tests, you go about your day in search of orgasms.

You fuck a person whose name you keep messing up: Siobhan. "It should be Si-ob-han," you say, "not SHI-VON." You tell her this as if you know better than she how to pronounce her name.

She says, "You're a fucking idiot. Now get over here and make me come."

After you creep home, Ursula seems unaware. Thank God she can't see the butterflies flittering in your belly. You tiptoe around like you're on stage, dancing Swan Lake or the Nutcracker. It doesn't matter. She doesn't suspect a thing.

You begin to hate her for being so dumb.

At work you shuffle from desk to copier, forgetting why you're there, what you're supposed to do. Others notice but are too polite to say anything. You're so distracted your boss takes you into her office for a little talk.

"Everything okay?" she asks.

Your thoughts are in chaos, like January blizzards. You feel as if you've been cast to dance in an ensemble. The night of the opening, your arms are open overhead but a glance downwards shows that your legs are missing. Only your ballet shoes are there, waiting to be told what to do.

Later that night, when you reach for Ursula, she's not there. The sheets are damp and wrinkled. You find her roaming the apartment. You press against her. She holds tight, arms around your waist, not able to let go. You keep it from her, what a shit you've been.

She finds a new job. Something with flowers. Delivery by bicycle. You start to work from home. That's what you tell everyone. You sit in your rocking chair by the sliding door and bask in the early morning sunlight. You wear your hair down so you can soak in the warmth of the sun on the strands.

You decide to make a special dinner for Ursula. The time to share your plans has finally come.

That night, over homemade cannelloni, she wants to know why.

Perhaps you should lie and say it's all on you. The end of pillow talk. But you can't. "There's nothing left," you say.

"When?" Ursula asks, her eyes surprisingly dry.

"After I moved in, I think."

The wait is over.

She doesn't eat much. Picks at the homemade pasta tubes that took the better part of a day to make.

"Where will you go?" she asks.

To my mother's, you want to say. "Does it really matter?"

She nods in agreement before taking the dishes away.

Change in Plans

Edna's daughter, Amy, was maneuvering onto a cloverleaf to access the highway when a call came to her cell. Now, instead of heading to the principals' conference, she was in the parking lot of her mother's long-term care home wrestling Edna into her Civic.

Once Edna was strapped in and the wheelchair safely stowed, Amy plunked a Ziplock baggie holding her mother's top and bottom dentures on the dashboard of the Civic, the false teeth the reason for suspending her road trip north.

Despite putting on a significant amount of weight the last few years, Edna's gums had managed to shrink and as a result, the dentures had begun slipping off her gums. As Amy pointed the car toward the street, the long-term care facility filled her review mirror.

Amy couldn't recall the last time she'd seen her mother. Could it already be six months? She found whenever she went to the home, her chest would tighten and she'd end up coughing to the point of almost throwing up. She blamed it on the caustic disinfectants used to mask the smell of pee, poop, and death. The puke-coloured interior walls didn't do much to cheer her up, either; she couldn't imagine living there herself.

The chairs, while functional and likely easy-to-clean, were unbearable to sit on.

It didn't help that the windows were painted shut and the sills cluttered with Edna's collections. Amy considered the items junk: tiny porcelain figurines that had come in boxes of tea, various foreign currencies found here and there, and nestling dolls layered in dust.

The facility windows reminded Amy of the first apartment she and her mother had lived in after Amy's father took off for who knows where. They couldn't open, likely because the unit was located on the third floor. Perhaps the landlord was terrified someone in the throes of despondency might take a swan dive out the window.

As Amy engaged the turn signal, she filled with envy at the thought of her principal colleagues already at the resort with their feet up, sipping cocktails, sharing war stories about crazy parents, and other tales of woe. Some would be playing golf while others would surely be rigging sailboats on the lake where the centre was situated. She couldn't stomach the idea of not getting to the Muskokas. She hoped to get Edna to the denturist and back by late morning so she could be on the highway a few minutes past noon.

Amy noticed that Edna was squinting at the streaky windshield. When Amy repositioned the visor to stop the sunlight from blinding her mother, Edna's hand snapped from where it gripped the edges of the passenger seat, and nudged Amy's arm away.

Edna said, "It's been forever since I've been out." Because her mother didn't have her teeth in, the words came out broken and sticky, as if coated in maple syrup.

Edna leaned her head against the passenger window and groaned.

"You okay?" Amy asked.

"Go faster," her mother said.

The appointment wasn't until ten and it was only half past nine. Just as they were about to pass a coffee shop with a drive-thru window, Edna yelled, "Turn around."

"Jesus, Mom. You scared the crap out of me."

"Get me a doughnut," Edna said, only it came out *det m dum nut.* "Never mind. Two would be better."

In old age, as in middle-age, Edna was riddled with health issues. Bad eyesight. Type 2 diabetes. Stopped-up bowels made worse by cancer. Complications from a hysterectomy. A generally weakened constitution that necessitated the use of the wheelchair. Amy knew that the care home staff would get them both in trouble if Amy allowed Edna to gorge on sweets. *But, really,* Amy thought*, what difference would it actually make at this stage of her life?*

After obtaining their order, Amy parked facing a farm scene mural painted on the back of the coffee shop. There was still plenty of time for Amy to enjoy the latte she'd purchased while her mother nibbled on her sweets. When Amy handed Edna the paper sack containing two sprinkled doughnuts, she noticed how puffy her mother's fingers were, pale and plump like uncooked breakfast sausages.

Edna's hand dove into the paper sack. With her tongue poking from between her thin lips, Edna used her fingers to tear bite-size pieces from doughnut number one. She inspected each morsel before placing it into her yawning maw. She chewed slowly, gumming the morsels like a bovine noshing its cud. The doughnut leapfrogged around her mouth until she finally let the slimy mess go down her throat. With each swallow, she sighed deeply, partly, it seemed, from exertion, and partly, in joy. After a while, Amy offered her mother a sip from her water bottle.

"What do I need that for?" Edna barked, rainbow sprinkles pimpling her plus-size blouse.

~

On the weekends, seven-year-old Amy had been known to crawl into bed while Edna napped. She would snuggle against her mother's partially clad body, trying to turn herself into a mini-version of her mother. Edna's deep breathing provided great comfort to Amy until Edna began to stir.

Naps would often cause Edna to wake up feisty. She'd tickle Amy's neck, gently at first, then building to harder jabs strategically aimed at Amy's bony ribs. Edna's thumbs and pointer fingers pressed so deeply into Amy's sides, it felt as if her organs would dislodge. The tickle game always seemed to end badly, though, the bed linens damp with urine.

~

By the time Amy pulled into the denturist's parking lot, her mother had managed to choke down half of the second doughnut.

The wheelchair was easy to assemble but transferring Edna from the passenger seat to the chair was cumbersome and consumed all of Amy's patience. "You're making us late," Amy snapped, madly brushing the remaining crumbs from her mother's blouse.

"More doughnut," Edna said, her fat fingers gripping Amy's arm with the brawn of a lobster.

"No more. Maybe later."

"Now!" Edna said. "They don't feed me anything good at the home."

"There's good reason for that."

Doughnut confetti dusted the passenger seat and floor mat. Now Amy would have to swing by a car wash to vacuum the interior before heading north.

Edna pointed at her daughter's water bottle. "Thirsty," she said, her hands clutching her throat. As she drank, her parched lips pulled on the straw like a butterfly sipping nectar after migration, its over-taxed wings beating down time.

~

After her mother's appointment, Amy noticed that an hour remained before Edna was expected to sign back in at the facility. For a moment she considered dropping Edna off early but stabs of guilt coupled by the anticipated accusatory stares from staff caused her to rethink that idea.

"Mom. Do you want to go see the swans?"

Amy parked next to a newly constructed high-tech self-cleaning washroom that had recently been featured in the newspaper. She wheeled her mother down a grassy slope to the lightly pebbled trail that rimmed the Thames River. When Amy was small, they'd go there on Sundays, stacks of stale bread in a knapsack. That was until aviary activists ruined the fun; feeding bread to waterfowl had become frowned upon and had fallen out-of-fashion. Instead, patrons of the park were encouraged to purchase dried corn from dispensers strategically situated along the river.

Light flickered from the slow-moving water, as if tinsel were caught on the rocky bottom. Upon closer inspection, Amy saw it was actually a fish in distress. A long specimen with metallic scales and a tapered snout kept flipping onto its back.

"Put that fish out of its misery," Edna said.

"Huh?"

"Wring its neck. Step on its head with the heel of your shoe."

Amy recalled the Ukrainian family who lived down the street from her childhood home. After Edna and Amy gave up the apartment, her mother rented a wartime house on a dead-end street. The salmon and cream-coloured houses with their tiny wooden fences offered more room and privacy than the apartment ever could.

For years the Ukrainians raised hens until city council passed a bylaw that forbade the practice. Until then, every fall the neighbours anxiously anticipated the slaughter of the chickens, their innards and feathers stripped from the carcasses in a process called 'getting dressed.' Edna saved up all summer so she could buy one or two of the oversized birds. There was nothing as juicy as the meat from a freshly butchered free-range chicken.

Amy stooped to get a better look at the ailing fish. Poked it a few times with the end of a stick.

"My bag needs to be emptied," Edna said.

Jesus, Amy thought. *How did I not plan for that?*

"I'll take you back home. We're only twenty minutes out. I have to get going anyway."

"We passed a washroom," Edna said, lifting a knobbed finger in the direction of Amy's car. "Up there, near where you parked."

"Mom, I—"

"You've got this."

Amy didn't have children of her own. Had never had to deal with other people's shit. Not even when she was still teaching and certainly not in her role as school administrator. One of the reasons Edna lived in long-term care was the need to have her colostomy bag emptied multiple times a day. Because of her ever-increasing girth, she could no longer manage it on her own.

"We should hurry back," Amy said. She quickly calculated different routes she might use to carve a minute or two off the return trip.

"I know my body," Edna said, fumbling with the wheel lock on her wheelchair in preparation for Amy to push her up the hill.

"Okay, okay," Amy said, grabbing the handles of the chair.

She wheeled Edna up the uneven hill and into the fully accessible building. Once inside, the door slid closed of its own accord, belching a loud click as the automatic locking

185

mechanism fell into place. Piped-in music soon filled the small room. Because the floor was slick with some kind of unspecified liquid, Amy gingerly made her way to the toilet, using the wheelchair handles for support.

Once there, she lifted her mother's blouse to expose the colostomy bag. Edna was right; it was full to the brim. She maneuvered the chair until it was braced against the outside lip of the toilet bowl. She hiked her mother's blouse higher so she could gain a better view. If only she could get the screw top on the bag to turn. Then she could drain the damned thing, and get them the hell out of there. But the stupid cap wouldn't budge. It must have been torqued by fingers belonging to Goliath.

"Sometimes the girls use their teeth," Edna told her daughter, offering a momentary smirk.

Amy shrank back in horror. "Mom, I can't do this."

"You have to. I can't manage on my own."

"Taking you out was a ridiculous idea."

"Hurry up, Amy. Or else the shit will rip the bag right off the stoma."

Tiptoeing on one foot, Amy braced the other against the wall. Then, she reefed on the cap with every bit of grit she had. Finally, the cap began to give. Fearful of getting splashed, she leaned back before aiming the spout toward the spotless toilet bowl.

The washroom had only recently been constructed. Its self-cleaning mechanism was housed inside cinder-block walls painted contemporary grey and light blue. The lighting was bright, too bright, in Amy's opinion. The draining of the bag took longer than she expected, so long that she couldn't imagine the bag needing to be emptied again until mid-afternoon. With luck, she'd be miles away by then.

The smell was overpowering, like fermented sugar. There was a sharpness to it, too. Amy imagined particles of it clinging to every surface of this high-tech washroom before a powerful power washer would scour away every trace.

What a shame her mother had to live this way.

After tightening the screw cap, Amy shifted her mother's blouse so it once again covered her belly. Next, she lifted the toe of her shoe toward the flush handle. Too late. The automatic flush mechanism activated and whooshed everything away.

After washing her hands with soap and warm water, she turned toward her mother. Edna's face was droopy, the skin on her neck forming small Ns under her down-turned mouth. She looked like one of those sad-faced clowns at the circus. Perhaps her mother's resting face would ease up once her new dentures were ready.

The no-touch exit sensor promptly rejected Amy's frantic hand gestures. The unresponsive door cried for more traditional methods such as brute force. Heaving her 150-pound frame against the door resulted in nothing more than a sore shoulder.

Amy took a deep steadying breath. She found a partially unwrapped stick of gum deep inside her pocket, popped it into her mouth, and began chewing. Pounding on the door did little except trigger her chest to tighten. She called for help, yelling that the door was locked, that they were trapped, that if they didn't get released in the next five seconds, she would become certifiable.

Suddenly the music stopped and was replaced by the shriek of an alarm. Next, an angry voice ordered occupants to vacate the space immediately. Mysteriously the door opened, a blast of sunlight streaming in. She grabbed the handles of the wheelchair and plunged into the light of day.

~

When Amy was little, their family would have been classified as working poor. Edna had a low-paying cleaning job at a hotel a few streets from where they lived. Yet, despite how little Edna made, she took care that Amy never went without. She made Amy clothes from ladies' dresses she found at the nearly-new shop. Edna slept on the couch while Amy slept in the bedroom, a quiet space where she could concentrate on her studies and get a good night's sleep.

Despite Edna giving Amy her all, Amy had pushed her mother away, spending less and less time with her. Eventually, even special occasions were ignored.

~

As she wheeled Edna through the automatic sliding doors of the care home, Amy wondered if Edna would thank her for taking her out. The air in reception smelled of antiseptic mixed with fish soup.

"Oh, goodie. We're having chowder," Edna said, her hands seeking the rear wheels so she could roll herself to the dining room.

"How could you possibly eat? You just had—"

"Oh, there you are!" a voice dusted with enthusiasm said to Edna and Amy. "You're just in time for our lunch sitting. Will you be joining your mother?"

"No, she will not. There's Bingo after lunch," Edna said before Amy could open her mouth to answer.

The staff member took control of the wheelchair, leaving Amy no choice but to back away. Amy eased towards the exit, the soles of her feet shuffling along the linoleum. She had, after all, somewhere to be.

"Take care," she said to her mother, her fingers scraping the bottom of her purse in search of a breath mint. "Take care until next time."

Tailspin

The patio of the old mill was crowded. Tasha tucked herself into a corner recently vacated by a server pushing an appetizer cart. She watched as the young waitress offered jumbo shrimp and canapés topped with black olives to the wedding guests. Fingers with manicured nails snatched at the food with gusto.

Tasha gulped from her glass of red wine. This was the second wedding of her husband's youngest sister, a sibling he infrequently talked to. Tasha didn't mind that her husband and his sister were distant. She found she had nothing in common with Brad's sister and didn't care for the way the woman had constantly wallowed in self-pity over the breakup of her first marriage.

The siblings' relationship improved once his sister fell for someone she'd met during a river cruise on the Rhine. Their wedding, her second and his first, was more extravagant than Tasha's commitment ceremony with Brad, a man with the means to throw a three-day bash, never mind a simple one-day event.

Tasha wondered where Brad was. It felt as if he had allowed Tasha to end up alone on the patio to fend for herself.

Perhaps it was because he was in the wedding party and she was not. Her toe started tapping but not in beat to the background music playing from the main event room. She couldn't figure out why she was becoming so peeved at him.

The guests were dressed in black as per the bride's instructions. Tasha tended toward black for formal affairs anyway. But here she stood out. Her black strapless gown was sprinkled in cough-drop sized pastel dots and topped with a creamy yellow shrug with half-sleeves and a pearl button. The outfit offered the only spot of colour at the entire venue. Even the servers were decked out in *noir*.

She soon figured out why she was so pissed. The black and white invitation had spelled out the rigid dress code. When the notice arrived by mail, Brad had stuffed it who knows where. Thank goodness he'd had the wherewithal to note the time, date, and location of the wedding or they might have completely missed it.

~

Tasha watched as the bride made the rounds, floating among the patio guests as if riding a magic carpet, the groom nowhere to be seen. Tasha was no prude but she couldn't keep her eyes from the bride's protruding black velvet belly. *What kind of bride wears black to her own wedding?* Tasha was tempted to ask, gulping instead from her near empty glass, its notes of dark chocolate with hints of blackberry and pepper fast becoming a distant memory.

A dozen or so guests were now shoulder-to-shoulder with the bride. Some starting chanting, "Carla, Carla, Carla," as if she were the star performer at a strip club.

Guests closest to Carla peppered her with questions about how she and the groom had met and, of course, about her due date and other baby-related questions.

As Tasha's ears filled with the bride's jubilant responses, resentment rushed through her. When Tasha and Brad had hooked up, she was already well past her prime reproductive years. In her late twenties, thirties, and early forties, unable to bring a pregnancy to term, Tasha had abandoned motherhood.

The barrage of questions about the bride's baby soon became too much for Tasha. Suddenly, a soloist broke into a delicate version of Celine Dion's "A Mother's Prayer," followed by throngs of people breaking into applause. By the end, Tasha wanted to puke.

"A little obvious, don't you think?" Tasha said to no one in particular, not keeping her tone in check.

Carla sailed over and asked, "You didn't like it? It was your husband's choice."

"Brad? Whatever for?"

"It's just that he's the—"

"Uncle! Why not get the soloist to sing 'Song for my Niece' then?"

"I'd no idea you'd respond this way, Tasha."

"Of course, you knew I'd find it—creepy."

By this point the guests around them craned their necks, intent on not missing a thing, then exhaled a collective *whoa* at the word creepy.

"Why are you doing this?" Brad asked, his fingers pressing into Tasha's upper arm.

"Ouch, let go. You're hurting me."

"*You're* making a scene."

"You abandoned me."

"Seriously? Since when do you remain by my side at a party? What's come over you?"

"Leave me," Tasha said.

She cringed at the omission of the word 'be.' Only then did she recognize how fully drunk she was. She left the party and hailed a cab to the hotel.

~

The next morning Tasha pulled the pillow from under her achy head and flipped it over to its cool side. As she came to, she thought she could make out shrieks coming from the hotel corridor. She couldn't be certain who the voices belonged to. Through the dense foam pillow, she gleaned that someone was missing. Tasha peeled away the blankets, and wiped sleep from her eyes.

Brad emerged from the bathroom with a steam-filled halo around his head. His eyes were red slits of disbelief. His brow furrowed as if he needed time to decide what to say.

Tasha knew the look. She went to Brad and pulled him toward her. A patchy account of what happened hissed from his lips. Shortly after the cake cutting and what was supposed to have been the last toast, the groom had simply vanished. As Brad spoke, Tasha felt the weight of her husband's head on her shoulder.

"The police are out searching for him now," Brad said.

They had pieced together that the groom had boarded the hotel shuttle without a whisper to his bride about his intentions. The driver reportedly dropped him off at a public golf course where he changed from his tux into street clothes. A few minutes later, he pressed a hundred-dollar bill into the driver's palm and told him to keep driving until told to stop.

"Isn't he diabetic?" Tasha asked, concern flooding her face.

"I think so. I just don't know what could have gotten into him," Brad said, resting his face against Tasha's cheek. "In hindsight, I should have gotten to know him better."

~

194

Weeks after the wedding there was a lead. That the groom might have shown up at a turnip farm. After interviewing the foreman, the police learned that the man had stumbled onto the farm in search of work. When asked to describe him, the foreman said he wore nondescript clothes, was of medium build and height, and had no distinguishing marks, tattoos, or piercings

"Just your average Joe," the foreman said.

"The man we're looking for goes by Hardeep."

"This guy told me he'd take cash as payment and to call him Harry."

The officers looked at each other and smiled. "Sounds like our guy."

The turnip farm consisted of endless fields and three grey buildings. One held the foreman's office, one was a two-storey bunkhouse/mess hall, and the largest building was the turnip processing plant. Hardeep, who now went by Harry, had been hired as a minimum wage labourer, a job anyone could get but few wanted, according to the foreman.

The bunkhouse had rows of cots where the seasonal workers kept their personal possessions and rested after their long shifts. The space smelled of deodorant, pot, and dirty socks. There was barely anything in the dresser next to Harry's bed: just a change of underwear, a few grey T-shirts, a pair of jeans, and a glucose testing kit.

The foreman said the reason he took a chance on Harry was he'd been the only person showing interest since the opening was posted on Kijiji.

The police decided they'd wait until end of shift for Harry to return from tilling. If he wasn't back in time, they'd return the next day and the next until they squeezed some answers out of him.

The foreman acted as though he were some kind of expert on human behaviour. To hear him tell it, he believed Harry was a loner. Instead of joining in on conversations with the other men, he kept to himself, sitting at the corner table he'd staked out his first day, his nose pressed into one of the paperbacks kept on the shelf next to the cooler. He never joined in when the other workers enjoyed a couple of cold beverages before bed, either.

Harry wasn't at odds with the men but he also wasn't popular.

"That's fine by me. I could care less if the men are friendly or not as long as they don't drag their bickering onto the work site."

The police returned later in the afternoon but had to leave for a vehicle roll-over a few miles north. When they got back to the farm, the foreman said, "Soon as you left, that guy you're looking for packed his things and buggered off."

~

In the weeks leading up to the due date, Carla stayed with Brad and Tasha. They'd agreed to put her and the baby up until things got sorted out. Mom-to-be kept herself occupied by knitting piles of baby socks, sweaters, and blankets. As her needles clicked and moved the pink, blue, and yellow yarn along, Tasha sensed that her sister-in-law was pissed. Flushed cheeks, audible sighs, loud clacking coming off the knitting needles. No, it was more than run-of-the-mill anger. Tasha's sister-in-law was steeped in disappointment.

She encouraged Carla to stand on the back deck with its view of Chicopee Hill and take long deep breaths but she barely lasted five minutes. As Tasha sipped from a cup of tea, her sister-in-law suddenly jumped up and headed for the vegetable patch near the back of their yard. She squatted down to weed between the tomato plants and around the red beets and carrots. Hoed the green onions. Harvested some yellow and green beans.

"What you've got is what they call nesting fever," Tasha said, following her into the house. "The baby will be along sooner than you can sing 'Rock-a-Bye Baby.'"

"I just can't seem to stop moving," Carla said, whistling notes from the lullaby.

~

Despite their efforts, the police never did determine Harry's whereabouts, although rumours raged through the community. That he'd used his bride to worm his way into the country and now that he didn't need her, he was in the wind. Brad promised to wring the man's neck if he came within an inch of his sister and the baby.

He wasn't the only one who was pissed. They'd heard that the foreman wanted to slaughter Harry, too. Never before had he seen an entire crop suffer from damping-off syndrome, a condition that turned the leaves luminescent-pearl and resulted in the turnips going punky. According to the farming grapevine, it was only a matter of time before Harry found himself face first in a pile of manure he wouldn't be able to dig himself out of.

If You Love Somebody

The spring I turn twenty-one, my boyfriend of seven months leaves me behind and heads west for a job on an oil rig in northern Alberta. After getting hired as a roughneck, Mark begins sending long letters he's written on lined paper, the kind torn from a scribbler, and only uses cobalt blue ink. His handwriting is a cross between writing and printed capital letters.

I long for the arrival of his letters that tend to appear towards the end of the week. As I read the words, I realize that everything he writes is already behind us, that I'm playing catch-up, that he's moved on to another adventure by the time I am privy to his news.

Mark writes: *They have me working seven nights in a row, then seven days. Twelve-hour shifts. I'm so tired by the end, I can't tell my toes from my head. Then I get a week off. Only it's not much of a week off because you have to subtract the travel days. The bus from Brooks to Calgary takes seven hours. It feels like forever because the driver stops in every hick town along the way. I stay with Stan when I'm in the city. Donna's there, too. I pretty much keep to myself. Sleep a lot. Think about you.*

I read his words over and over until the light outside my window starts to dim and the sentences swim on the page. I keep the letters behind a stack of paperbacks leaning against the wall, books I've already read and plan to reread.

His next correspondence contains no letter, only a photo someone took with a Polaroid camera. Mark is in his work gear: a yellow hardhat, grease-stained coveralls, steel-toed boots. A squint in his eyes and a boyish grin on his bronzed face. A wrench as long as his forearm in his right hand. The skin on his arms scraped and scarred. The picture is a glimpse into his new life, one filled with risk to limb and dangling bits. I try not to spend all my time worrying.

In his next letter: *The crew is from all over—Newfoundland, Nova Scotia, Ontario, BC, and Alberta. They are hardworking and hard drinking. The guy I bunk with is six-foot nine, smokes three packs a day, and wears a woolly mammoth tooth on a leather cord around his neck. His name is Kai which doesn't match what he looks like. We work opposite shifts so we hardly see each other.*

I imagine Mark, slouched over, trudging from the rig to the trailer he shares with Kai, wordlessly passing by, perhaps giving each other a weary nod of the head.

In another letter Mark writes: *The cook is the only female for miles and trust me, she is nothing to look at. She's as tall as she is wide. She was born somewhere in Europe and speaks three languages. When she talks, it sounds as if she's growling, a deep gravelly sound coming*

directly from her throat. She bakes fresh bread every day and even made
jam out of Saskatoon berries that grow behind the camp. Stuff tastes nutty,
kind of like almonds. She keeps the black bears away by hanging her
enormous panties from anything she can reach. Reminds me of those
Mennonite farms back home only I think the cook doesn't wash her
underwear before she hangs them out.

Our plan is to get married as soon as he returns from the rig. Not some attention-seeking ceremony but something small and intimate. I plan on wearing an off-white cocktail dress, something I can wear again later. He'll be in a suit, likely brown. We'll invite a handful of people or perhaps we'll just elope. But our plans are for the future and this is now.

Another letter: *Yesterday the sky behind the Jack pines turned a strange indigo mixed with lime. The foreman screamed at everyone to go back to their trailers, that we'd ride out the storm off-rig. I'll always remember the concern in his voice, that and the noise of the hail against the metal roof of the trailer. Hail the size of grapes. Wind and rain so strong windows got blasted out of three trailers. Glass flying. Metal siding stripped off here and there. Quick as it started, it was over. Prairie storms, something to revere. Not one word about it, though, on the news.*

I'm working as a data entry clerk even though I have a three-year fine arts degree and a year of Teachers College. It's my sixth summer in a row doing the same kind of office work and it's boring as hell. The full-timers need holidays just like anybody else so I'm there to fill in. Besides, I work with a motley crew of women.

Mark writes: *Stan took me to the Stampede today. Christ, was it ever hot. You should have seen me dressed up like a cowboy: Levi's, snakeskin boots with spurs, a plaid shirt with two buttons undone, and a Stetson. I should have got him to take a picture. People dressed in regular clothes, you know, tied-dyed and embroidered stuff, stick out more than us cowboys.*

We ate at a food truck. There were potatoes and steak and cream corn and Cole slaw and a buttered roll and it only cost $4.99. Stan paid even though I offered. Later, we watched bull riding and calf roping. You should have been here, all I can say. It was amazing.

He actually used the word amazing. Things that are amazing are: weddings, princesses, sunsets and sunrises (in that order), newborn baby smell, and autumn colours. I don't care how much Mark gushes about it; I don't care for the idea of rodeos. Bulls and horses and sweat-stained cowboys farting and carrying on. Shrill noises and flashing lights from the arcade. A smell hanging over the place like they'd trucked in a lagoon of shit. I don't say much about the Stampede in my next letter other than *isn't it nice you got to spend time with your brother?*

Mark writes: *There was an emergency on the rig. One of the new guys had an asthma attack. He was supposed to carry his inhaler on him but it must have fallen out of his pocket. Funny, I'd just seen the guy smoking the day before. I don't think asthmatics are supposed to do that*

202

but anyway, he was puffing away. It was touch and go for a while but they say he's going to be okay. They have him at the hospital in Edmonton.

For seven hours and twenty minutes a day my fingers pound the Qwerty keyboard at my workstation. Mostly I type in numbers but occasionally I get to work on changes of address. There are insurance codes, interest rates, and mortgage amounts. It's hopelessly tedious but the money is decent. Despite how boring it is, I keep hoping to catch my supervisor's eye when she walks around offering overtime. Anything to waste time while I hang around pining for Mark to come home.

In late July he writes: *I discovered a new singer by the name of James Taylor. Wrote his first song at fourteen. When he was a boy he started with the cello, not the guitar. His lyrics are incredible. Take a listen next time you get a chance.*

I write back that I've never heard of the guy.

Mark writes: *Your lack of musical knowledge is astounding!!!!!*

There is other stuff in the letter but I tear it up because his tone pisses me off. And all those exclamation marks. How old is he, anyway, that he writes like a kid still?

It never occurs to me to spend my money on albums because I'm saving up for a house. Besides, I dig AM radio. And I don't even mind listening to the stuff my parents have lying around the house: Nat King Cole, Nana Mouskouri, and even that Walter guy out of Kitchener who plays the polka music. Besides, I don't see the point of worshipping this James Taylor guy whose other claim to fame, I find out, is heroin addiction.

~

One morning as I'm about to leave for work, Mark calls from a pay phone in Brooks. He arrived there around 5:30 Alberta time to pick up supplies for the rig. So, instead of writing, he decides to speak to me by phone. I had no idea he was going to call and I don't have time to talk so I find myself getting snippy.

"I'm running late," I say, a bowl of soggy cereal in hand.

"Nice! I miss you, too, babe," he says.

My father is jabbering in the background, throwing his arms in the air, trying to get me to hang up because Mark called collect.

"I really liked your last letter," Mark says, his voice low and sultry. "What you would do to me with your tongue."

"I shouldn't have written all that stuff."

"I didn't mind. Kind of like phone sex!"

"Can't we talk about this later? I really have to get to work."

"My bunkmate found your letter. I don't know what he was doing rooting around in my bed and inside my pillowcase."

"Oh my god."

"Anyway, the guys had a good laugh about it. I called because I have a surprise for you," Mark says. "I need you to pick me up from the airport. I'll be home for the weekend."

His news is completely unexpected. I already have plans to go to Grand Bend with a couple of girlfriends but I don't tell him that.

The week drags on and then it's Friday. After work, I add blue eye shadow to my lids and stick fake lashes on. It makes me look like a circus entertainer. I want to surprise Mark with my new look. Then I head to the highway for Pearson where it's bumper-to-bumper all the way into the city. I arrive fifteen minutes late, traces of a headache brewing.

Mark arrives at my car, pulling a mustard-yellow duffle bag on wheels. His skin is deep brown like coffee with a trace of cream added. His breathing is heavy, like his allergies are acting up, each inhalation an effort. His arm muscles are beefed up, shiny, as if slathered in oil, and he moves with confidence. He offers a quick smile, a tiny chip on his right incisor now evident.

"You look different," he says. "Your eyes are bluer, like that doll your Swiss relatives brought you as a souvenir."

We bump noses when we try to kiss. We're like kids in middle-school trying to act older, chins and noses and awkward limbs crashing about. Mark sleeps most of the way home while I hold the speed at barely five over trailing a transport truck the entire way.

We rent a room at a motel a few miles from my parents' place. The sex is fast and desperate and oddly not very good.

I sit on the edge of the bed and let him talk. He says that the earth is a big place and he doesn't want to be the kind of person who wishes he'd done this or that. With each word, I feel a crippling distance forging between us, the kind that comes from being worlds apart.

As I listen, it becomes obvious that he's rehearsed the speech. It comes out too polished to think otherwise. Then it strikes me; he could have told me all this on the phone when he called.

"You should come with me," he says, "when I travel the world. We can do it on the cheap. Stay at hostels. Backpack. Camp out."

I'm not certain what I want to do with my life but clearly, I don't have to remind him that I'm a qualified teacher. After summer, I hope to start teaching somewhere, perhaps shatter ties with southern Ontario, move north, perhaps live on a reservation, head somewhere exotic like an island in the Caribbean. But I have Mark and his needs to consider. So, I keep my notions loose.

The day before he flies back to Alberta, he flashes a roll of cash. "It's for your engagement ring."

I don't smile or anything. I just shrug.

"We can talk about it once I'm back home," he says.

The next day, after dropping him at the airport, I nonchalantly sweep my lips against his cheek before strapping on my seat belt and heading home.

~

One Sunday I tell my parents, "I hate it here. I can't stay here a second more." My voice is so quiet I can barely hear it myself. "I don't want to make a life here. I haven't experienced any adventure."

"What about Mark?" my mother asks.

When I don't answer, they look back at me as if certain all this will soon blow over. Only it doesn't.

I quit my job at the office. Instead of applying to get onto the supply teacher list, I hop a bus and head north, my eye on a small mom and pop diner-motel outside of Sudbury. They need someone to peel potatoes, run the sterilizer, mop floors, make beds. If they hire me, I'll get a small salary plus free room and board. The owners warn me that the hours are long, that I'll have to be up at 4:30 most mornings and work until late afternoon. But I don't mind. I just need a change, to take a chance at life.

Every morning I fry up sausage, scramble eggs, and toast bread for a road crew working on the highway expansion. We make lunches the men can take on the road and offer them clean beds they can fall into at the end of the day. There is always something to do.

At the end of August, there's still plenty of daylight after my shift ends so I spend any free time I have walking around town. When I have nothing else to do, I write letters to Mark but seldom bother taking them to the post office.

Mark doesn't even know I left town or where I am. There's comfort in holding that from him.

I've become a bit of a drinker so after my walks I treat myself to a few cold beers. I like to sit on a folding lawn chair in front of my motel room and watch the cottagers and truckers fly past. The backdrop to the highway is granite that has been blasted with dynamite. The rock face is taller than the buildings on the two universities I attended. There are miles and miles of needle trees, as my dad likes to call them.

I read books borrowed from the small library that is run out of a bookmobile. Sometimes the owners of the motel sit with me but they're getting on in years and say they need their sleep more than they need a visit. They give me the nickname Book Worm.

Monday is my day off. Because I love to walk, I tell the owners I'll pick up the mail for the motel. The first few times there is nothing for me, just bills and flyers and the weekly French newspaper.

One day, there is a small package with my name on it. I chew the corner of the box like a dog chewing a squeak toy. A stack of letters tumbles from the box. All but two are from Mark. His letters read like essays. Impersonal. Just the facts. His job on the rig is behind him and he still has all his fingers. He's hiked the foothills of south-western Alberta, ridden a gondola in the Rockies, and is headed for Tofino to paddle in the ocean.

After that he's thinking he'll fly to Japan. Did I want to come?

The date on that letter shows the previous month.

I toss the letters and envelopes into a metal trash bin and strike a match. I watch everything burn until there's nothing left.

One Monday as I walk around town, a one-ton approaches, slows down, and pulls up next to me. The driver, a man, calls me over, introduces himself as Francis, asks if there is anywhere good to eat, a burger or fish and chip place. I give him directions to the diner.

"Oh, wait," I say. "They're closed on Mondays. The whole town shuts down other than the post office and there are no burgers there."

"Too bad. I'm famished," Francis says, smiling.

It feels funny that Francis gives me any attention. I'm the last person that is noticed in a room full of people. I'm on the short end of average height and my hair is a dull dark blond. I'm scrawny and flat-chested and narrow-hipped. A gymnast's body even though I can't do a cartwheel or the splits.

"Give me a lift to where I work?" When he nods, I open the passenger door and hop in. "I'll cook you up something good."

He grinds the truck into gear and follows my directions to the diner.

I grill up some ham and cheese sandwiches and brew a pot of coffee. I sit across from Francis and watch him stir two heaping spoonfuls of sugar into his mug. Then he slurps from his spoon, a gesture I find endearing.

"I'm ahead of schedule. Anywhere you suggest a guy might take a walk, breathe in some nature?" Francis asks, leaning against the table with rippled forearms.

"Sure. I can show you, if you want," I say.

We stop at the truck to get his binoculars, which he calls field glasses. We head behind the diner to pick up the trail that snakes around a small lake. Francis explains that walking with no purpose is therapeutic. A sort of nature bath. As we amble along the stone-chip trail, I feel the heat of his arm next to mine, feel him leaning toward me. Part of me thinks I should tell him to move away, to give me some space, but part of me likes that he finds me desirable.

When he speaks, his voice is soft, almost a whisper, as if using a louder voice might scare away the songbirds flitting overhead. He tells me about a writer by the name of Khalil Gibran, then shares his favourite quote right off the top of his head: 'If you love somebody, let them go, for if they return, they were always yours. If they don't, they never were.'

His passion for Gibran's words surprises me as does the warmth and strength of his fingers lacing through mine. He is only the second man I've allowed to touch me in such a tender way, to be this close.

His legs move in sync with mine. We now walk in silence; we've become so comfortable with each other in such a short amount of time. I like that he periodically stops to lift his head to smell the air, admire the clouds, listen to the sparrows and chickadees, focus the binoculars on something beyond us. I sniff the air when he does but all I can detect is the smell of diesel coming off his jeans.

The skin on his arms is smooth against mine. Where my skin is pale with a dusting of peach fuzz, his arms are hairless, the colour of India ink.

On our way back to the diner there's a clearing with portable toilets, picnic tables, and a small playground. I sit on the only kiddie swing large enough to accommodate me. Francis pushes me, then does an underdog. I cry out in fear mixed with delight.

211

I am not prepared for what happens next. When I stand, he bends and kisses me. A soft sweep of his tongue awakens desires within me but not enough that I should dare ask him to stay. So, I look at him and blink in silence.

Francis turns and makes his way back to the rig. A moment later he waves goodbye through the open window.

The next four times his rig approaches the diner, he pulls over and stays a while. In anticipation of those days, I think about what to wear, something attractive, a scoop neck, easy-to-pull-off jeans.

And Francis always says, "Look at you. That outfit fits you just right, that's for sure."

And just like that, my job in the north comes to a finish. The owners congratulate me for making it to the end of the season. They include a complimentary bus ticket inside a white envelope with my final cheque and vacation pay.

I return to my parents' home to find another stack of letters from Mark. I wait a full week before tearing them open.

~

I marry Mark the following year, a simple ceremony with twenty people including us. It's overcast, the kind of early spring day with a cool wind and the threat of rain. On account of that, I wear high-heeled boots instead of the shoes I'd picked out for the occasion. Mark doesn't even seem to notice.

On the ring finger of my left hand sits a star sapphire with a cluster of diamond chips in each corner. It's the engagement ring he bought with money saved from working on the rig. During the ceremony Mark pushes a white-gold band onto my finger and nestles it against the ring that's already there.

Next thing you know, we've bid on a house; I acquire a permanent teaching job. We make one child, then another, get a different house, and finish by making one more baby. We get some dogs and a few stray kittens. A quiet simple life.

I never make it over to Japan and it takes twenty years before my hiking boots climb the Rocky Mountains.

Occasionally I flash regret at never having headed off somewhere exotic: Asia, Spain, a cruise on the Amazon, or even Canada's north. But then I remember Khalil Gibran's words—*for if they return, they were always yours.*

I never think to mention Francis to Mark, until now, that is. Mark always reads my stories and he'll read this one and the next one and every one after that. He says my stories are twisted and he likes that about me. But more than that, he likes that I survived the summer he left me behind.

Innocent Bystander

After his father's funeral, Jake went to stay with Rich. His uncle knew squat about raising a kid, let alone a teenager, but Jake had nowhere else to go.

The small town where Rich lived had an ancient wooden bandshell that the founding fathers let be constructed on a flood plain. A plaque stated that because some famous queen had watched her horse race there, the town had renamed the bandshell in her honour. Jake didn't give two craps about history; he liked the bandshell because it was a great place to hang out.

One evening after his uncle headed for his shift at the turkey processing plant, Jake got dressed in his outerwear, too, but pointed himself in the opposite direction. While ducking into a culvert under Main Street, he glimpsed the latest graffiti covering the corrugated metal walls. Cuss words, scribbled pictures of boners and boobs, and scrawls he couldn't make out. Jake exited the culvert at the park. It was a rather unremarkable space aside from a few gigantic maples with Medusa-like branches, a metal slide that scorched legs on summer days, and the bandshell that protruded from the dark like the Coliseum.

"H-h-hey," Jake said to his two friends from school, his fingers scooping his brown bangs off his forehead.

Willard was in faded Levi's and a hoodie. His shaggy dark hair didn't do much to conceal the hearing aid in his right ear. "Take you long enough?" Willard leapt up to adjust his pants, something he did all the time in class until his classmates got fed up and told him to sit the hell down.

Chick crouched on the lowest seat of the bandshell as if ready to pounce. A few rust-coloured whiskers sprouted from his chin. "You bring it?" Chick's eyes shone like buttons on a pea coat.

When Jake drew a bottle of whiskey from his backpack, Willard said, "Holy frigging 26er."

Chick frowned. "Someone's already been at it."

"Who cares? Give it over," Willard said.

Chick had just been to jail. Not real jail, but juvie, and only because no one cared enough to post bail after he got arrested. Hopewell was run by born-again Christians. This was Chick's release day and the boys had some serious celebrating to do.

Willard took a long pull before passing the bottle to Jake.

"I still hate that lying pussy," Chick said, his Adam's apple jumping with every word.

"Fuck yeah, but Shanice did catch you fisting your Johnson," Willard said.

"I was only taking a leak." Chick grinned before narrow beams of light passed over them, followed by the hum of engine noise, and the click of a car door.

"Hear that?" Jake said.

"Cops!" Chick's voice was too loud considering how close the car seemed to be.

"Come on. I have somewhere to go," Jake stuttered.

"You have someone you know?" Willard said, tweaking the volume control on his hearing aid.

"N-n-no s-s-stupid. Let's go," Jake said, cuffing Willard's shoulder.

"Where the fuck is Chick?" Willard asked.

"No idea."

Jake couldn't see shit. He was slow and clumsy, partly because of the dark but also because he needed to stay out of range of the narrow beams of light coming from the car. With each movement, his boots sounded like a broom being dragged along a dirt floor. He got snagged up on tree roots and bumped into things he couldn't make out, but it was better than being discovered for the chicken-ass he was.

Suddenly, a hand rested on his shoulder. "Who's th-th-at?"

"It's me, you friggin' idiot," Willard said, guiding Jake forward with the confidence of a cat.

Jake and Willard leaned against an exterior wall of a utility shed. Where the hell was Chick? It was quiet except for the thud of boots on lightly frozen turf and the constant vibration of the patrol car's engine.

Booze mixed with dread left Jake wanting to throw up. His breath formed a foggy cloud around them. When he leaned back, the booze bottle in his backpack clanked against the shed. Crap! Jake considered his options: stay and get caught, run for it, or vaporize on the spot.

A garbled voice could be heard coming from the cop's radio.

"I'm five minutes out," the officer radioed back. He turned in the direction of where he thought the boys were hiding. "You're not off the hook yet, kids."

Once the patrol car pulled away, Chick's voice said from the darkness, "*Here* you are. That was close. There's no goddamned way in hell I'm ever going back to Hopewell."

~

At lunch the next day while Willard and Chick were catching up on missed assignments, Jake was in the cafeteria a few tables from Shanice. She waved him over.

"Not eating?" she said when he slid onto the seat across from her.

"N-n-no lunch m-m-money."

"Can't learn if you don't eat." She handed him half a sandwich and an apple.

Jake couldn't keep his eyes off Shanice. Her straight white teeth, plump lips, and breasts pushing against the words *Girl Power.* Jake didn't bother admitting to her he wasn't much for school. A smart girl like Shanice had never shown interest in a guy like him before. No girl, in fact, had. He liked how good it felt to be noticed.

He asked what happened with Chick, why Shanice had lied on the witness stand.

She closed her eyes and let her head tilt back. Her cheeks were illuminated by the brightness pouring in from the floor-to-ceiling windows next to them. Jake waited. Finally, Shanice spoke without opening her eyes. "My father said to not talk about it."

Jake decided not to press further.

As Shanice described a project about ants she'd been working on, Jake remembered the time he'd gone into the garage to get something for a robot he'd been building. He found his dad hanging from a rope. Jake hadn't been able to revive him. His mom had stopped being able to look after Jake ever since.

"I g-g-get it," he said. "Th-th-there are things I don't talk about, t-t-too."

Jake began peeling a loose thread from the bottom of his T-shirt. Shanice just sat there listening to him talk about nothing important, her face open and honest, looking as if she cared. And then, he gulped. If Chick found out Jake had been talking to Shanice, he'd kill him.

He figured he should tell her to keep quiet about lunch but all he managed was, "H-h-hey." By then, Shanice was already well on her way to the academic wing.

~

A few nights later Jake, Chick, and Willard met at the bandshell. Chick had a can of black spray paint in his jacket pocket. When he shook the paint, tiny ball bearings clacked against the interior housing of the can.

"Jesus, that's noisy." Willard covered his ears.

"Even for you, deaf boy?" Chick ran a piece of curved metal along the container. "Watch this." When he shook the can again, there was no more rattle.

"Let's frigging do this!" Willard grabbed the paint can and started covering the bandshell in curlicues.

"Not Glee Club signs, you goof. Gimme that."

Chick moved toward the shed and took aim. Before long F U BACON EATER, OINK, and EAT ME PIG covered the walls of the shed, the bandshell, and the commemorative plaque.

The calm night air soon filled with the stink of aerosol, triggering Jake to cough. His face reddened and he repeatedly spat phlegm into the dirt. He held a finger to his nose and blew a string of snot onto the ground. His breathing laboured as his lungs got plugged with gunk. He thought about his inhaler sitting in his sock drawer, the very inhaler he'd stopped carrying around after he'd moved in with his uncle. He despised being the kid who needed drugs to breathe.

While Willard and Chick were busy spray painting, Jake tried to keep an eye peeled for the cops. After a while, he slumped to the ground, the other two boys completely unaware.

~

Jake woke up to a handcuff digging into his wrist. A cop, arms folded, stood guard at his hospital room door.

Someone wearing a white coat and a stethoscope leaned over Jake. "You're one lucky fellow."

Jake lifted his shackled wrist. "N-n-not really."

When a nurse wheeled a wheelchair in, the cop said, "I'll take it from here. We have a cage at Hopewell waiting for this clown and his useless pals."

He wondered if his uncle had been by.

~

Jake sat in the back of the police car behind a sheet of Plexiglass marred with scuff marks. With the doors and

220

windows closed and the engine running, his breath began to collect on the inside of the windows. Finally, the officers took their places in the front of the cruiser.

After half an hour, they pulled into a Sally-port, the secure drop-off point for transfers in and out of the facility. As soon as the garage door slammed shut behind the car, the officer turned off the engine. He opened the door next to Jake and unclipped his seatbelt, guiding him past a sign that said *Welcome to Hopewell, Secure Detention for Youth.*

As soon as the handcuffs were off, Jake rubbed his wrists to get the blood moving again. He bundled his belongings into a plastic bag, and handed the bag to an intake clerk. A hand skated over his damp armpits before hesitating briefly between his legs. A metal detector shaped like an inverted U ensured nothing was missed during pat-down.

A hand clicking a ball point pen gestured for Jake to sign for his charges. His eyes lingered on the long list: property damage, vandalism, assaulting an officer, resisting arrest. This was all a joke. He hadn't done anything; he'd been an innocent bystander.

In the facility shower, his attempts to lather with a paper-thin blade of soap were futile. He managed to dry himself on a piece of terrycloth not much bigger than a hand towel.

"I need my clothes."

The guard motioned to the stool next to the shower. Jake held up a grey sweatshirt and matching track pants, all too big. The clothes were stiff, like they'd been dried on a clothesline. Jake spotted the name of the facility on the back of the clothes. Large orange letters screamed that he now belonged to Hopewell.

"I need shoes."

"No shoes. Cuts down on the number of runaways."

A different facility officer, this one female, led Jake to Pod C3. There were eight doors like octopus tentacles, each door equipped with a small vertical window and narrow slot for passing meal trays. One door was labelled *Control Room* and another said *Isolation Unit*.

"You've got five minutes." The officer handed Jake a stack of linens and a thin pillow. Everything smelled of bleach. The door sighed when it locked behind him. While clutching the sheets to his chest he stared at the stained mattress. Uncle Rich made his bed at home.

Bolted to the floor were a cot, stool, and table. Across the room were a sink and toilet. Everything was stainless steel. Jake walked from the door to the window. Sixteen toe-to-heel steps. The tiny window had embedded wire between its panes like the corridor doors at school. He stood on his tippy-toes and peered out. The perimeter consisted of a high fence topped with barbed wire. He noticed that the sun had just risen in the eastern flint-coloured sky.

Jake wouldn't be going anywhere anytime soon.

A different officer, this one with a compact body and protruding front teeth, unlocked the door to Jake's cell. Jake followed him to the dining area where seven teenage males sat. A couple of them wore slippers while the rest were in sock-feet. The guard gestured at the sink.

"Wash your hands."

"But I just showered."

"Do as you're told."

As Jake washed and patted his hands on a paper towel, he looked through a metal curtain into the kitchen where a woman chopped carrots.

She wiped her hands before stepping toward the curtain. "I'm the cook." A hairnet trapped a nest of silver curls.

"I'm Jake."

"No allergies, right?"

"Just paint," he said, his face flushing. "That's why I'm here."

The guard clicked his tongue. "Nothing about why you're here. You've got a lot to learn."

The cook slid a bowl of oatmeal through the slot. Jake was instructed to sit at the only vacant table. The cereal was cold but soon his sour hospital breath disappeared.

The dining room echoed with only the clatter of spoons against plastic bowls.

An officer collected the cutlery and handed it through the slot in the metal curtain. "Seven is the count," the cook said. "Plus, the new one. Eight."

What happened when the count didn't add up? Jake wondered. The residents took turns spraying their bowls and trays. There was no talking, just the sound of water splashing on the rigid food trays, a soothing sound despite the nature of the place. The national anthem spilled from a loudspeaker.

"We're late," an officer said. "Line up."

The youth climbed the stairs, each floor with its own secure doors. Jake was directed into Classroom #1.

"Welcome. I'm Teacher Ashley. Please sit here." She didn't look like any teachers he was used to. She was dressed in jeans, a T-shirt, and sneakers. She pointed for Jake to sit at a desk a few feet from the locked classroom door. "Boys, say hi to our newest resident."

The teacher looked younger than the students back at the high school. *We Pray Hard @ Hopewell* in white lettering appeared on the front of her black T-shirt. Keys clinked from her belt loop as she walked amongst the students. Her desk and file cabinets stood behind a Plexiglass booth. The officer who did the pat-down at intake sat on a stool between the students and the door, his nose buried in a section of the newspaper.

Jake wondered how long it would be before his uncle got him out. Intake had explained that Jake was remanded until he stood before a judge who would hear his charges. When Jake got to court, he planned to explain about the asthma attack; he'd never intended any harm to come to the park. He'd just been there as a look-out. Surely the judge would understand and see his side.

The teacher set a booklet in front of Jake. "Fill these out so I can see where you're at." When she smiled, neon green sparkled from her braces.

Jake thumbed the booklet. "I've-ve-ve got learning problems, Miss. I probably c-c-can't even d-d-do this hard-a-work."

"Well," she tapped a knuckle on his desk, "let's see about that."

As she bent to pull a numbered yellow pencil from a block of wood, Jake thought he could hear church bells off in the distance. They reminded him of the day of his dad's funeral.

The number carved into the pencil was seven. Perhaps Jake's luck would soon start changing.

~

Two weeks later, the judge decided that Jake could be released into the custody of his uncle if the uncle agreed to post bail. It was early afternoon by the time Jake pulled off the Hopewell sweats and put on street clothes. He signed for his belongings and smiled for the first time in weeks. He stuffed a paper with the name of his interim probation officer into his coat pocket.

Partway home, Jake's uncle stopped at a diner.

The restaurant was quiet and calm, like things tended to be after lunch. He and his uncle took their places on stools at a long counter next to a display case filled with pies. Neither said much during the meal.

Later, in the car, his uncle broke the silence. "There's no other way to say this so I'll say it straight up. Chick's gone."

"What d-d-do you mean?"

His uncle's thumbs drummed the steering wheel.

"Dead."

"What? You can't be serious. When?"

"Last week."

"Just l-l-last week! You should have t-t-told me before."

"Just did, son."

"Don't e-e-ever call me that." Jake stared straight ahead, the seat belt cinched against his chest.

"The biggest bastard imaginable ambushed Chick at Floyd Davis."

Floyd Davis, or Floyd, as it was known, was the toughest youth facility around. They saved it for the worst of the worst. Armed robbery, home invasions, rape, animal torture. And, overflow from Hopewell.

"Son-of-a-bitch drove his fists into Chick's brain right through his eye. In for murder so I suppose he had nothing to lose."

Jake couldn't remember a time his uncle ever had so much to say.

"The doctors advised Chick's family that he be taken off life-support."

"He was m-m-my best friend." Jake leaned his face against the cold passenger window. "He didn't deserve this."

"No child is born bad." His uncle's fingers tightened around the wheel. "Never forget that. And I agree. He didn't deserve any of this."

Jake couldn't help but wonder. If he hadn't been sent to Hopewell, would Chick be alive today?

"I wish we could hit rewind," Jake stuttered.

His uncle had nothing to add so he kept his eyes on the road ahead.

"Chick m-m-made things happen."

"It wasn't his first time in, you know. I recently learned he'd been to Hopewell three times before. He just couldn't seem to control his impulses."

Jake knew what people thought about Chick, that he was dumb as a block of ice. That he'd made a mess of things and that he was doomed. Jake didn't like to think badly about his friend, especially now. It wasn't as if he had so many friends, he could give one up this way.

Fat wet snowflakes began to fall, the kind Jake used to love when he was a kid, before his dad did what he did. The drive home was taking so goddamned long. Jake had had to pee since they'd left the restaurant. He shut his eyes and tried not to think about Chick, his body a corpse, deaf Willard, and Shanice who would avoid Jake now that he'd been to juvie. He kept his eyes closed, letting the swish of the wiper blades lull him to sleep.

The Doula

As Gwyneth finger-combed her eggplant-coloured hair where it met at her shoulder, she admired how badass she looked for someone in her fifties. She didn't like to let on that she needed a sleeping machine, wore orthotics, or that she'd recently been fitted for partial dentures. Her funky look was a façade, a way to connect with young mothers she lent a hand to.

From the time she was young, Gwyneth had been taken by the weaknesses of others. Not to exploit the feeble and pathetic, but to help them.

As soon as the pandemic began, Gwyneth's job as a postpartum doula for Baby Meltdowns No More had gone virtual. To some, her job appeared easy because all she did was talk to clients on Zoom. Gone were the homemade casseroles, assistance with household chores, and baby soothing between midnight and six. The entire job was now online.

Gwyneth didn't mind the change. She was a gifted listener. She took the *woe is me* talk and folded each negative word into a dirty diaper. Where there was nothing but self-pity and desperation, she provided hope, the golden elixir of the frantic. Like pieces of play dough, she molded the sniveling moms into compassionate caregivers.

Gwyneth's services weren't cheap. Evidence-based empathy came at a steep price.

She was effective, or thought she was, until a crippling conversation with Luna.

On a warmer than expected mid-September morning, Gwyneth placed her ear buds into her ears and dialed Luna up. After Luna finally answered, Gwyneth smiled at the image on her screen. Here was a young mom with her messy hair and a blanketed bundle dotted with sea planes and baby bottles folded into her arms, the blanket design one of Luna's, Gwyneth learned only last week.

"How was your night?" Gwyneth ventured.

"Horrible. She cried non-stop," Luna said, her pimply face long and drawn.

Gwyneth took note of the flatness in her client's voice.

"But, I see, you finally got her to sleep."

"Yeah, I guess. Her, not me. I haven't slept in like three nights now."

"We discussed before that when baby sleeps, you get to nap, too."

"Like how?" Luna snapped. "When I have an appointment with you? If I don't answer, then my file will get referred to Family—"

Gwyneth held her palm up. It was discouraging that Luna believed Gwyneth had no other resources in her toolkit than alerting the authorities. "Of course, you are right, that you need to be at these check-ins. But, please, think about catching a few winks whenever baby does."

Luna's head drooped, her chin resting on the bundle.

"Your mother still with you?" Gwyneth asked.

"Nah, I sent her home. She was getting on my nerves."

"But—"

"We don't need her."

A lump formed in Gwyneth's throat. Luna was failing miserably on the postpartum depression checklist. Inconsistent support. Social isolation. Fatigue. Referring to baby by pronoun. So much doomsday talk. *This* had become too much.

"Like, how much longer are you going to spy on me?" Luna's eyes seared into Gwyneth's. "My life is my own."

Then Luna's screen went black.

The next three calls remained unanswered. Gwyneth had never been ghosted by a client before.

Over the coming hours that grew into days, Gwyneth couldn't shake the doubt creeping over her.

She opened Luna's case file on her laptop and reread the referral form. Well-to-do family. Her father owned a chain of cleaning stores with contracts with the hospital, a bunch of private schools, and the rendering plant. Reportedly this was Luna's only pregnancy. Blank space next to the father's name, the box for the infant's name also unfilled, the space as clean as a freshly wiped bottom.

Stupid, stupid, stupid, Gwyneth thought, her hand smacking her forehead. Mistakes of an amateur.

Gwyneth's supervisor Kathryn, would need to know about this. Kathryn liked her doulas to be proactive and inform her of anything, even the smallest concern, so she could get on top of situations before they turned into catastrophes, or worse. Gwyneth's most recent appraisal hadn't exactly been stellar. Not enough new clients brought in and then, that incident with the reporter who ran an unflattering story about doulas after speaking with Gwyneth.

She needed to figure out what was going on with Luna.

She tried calling again but Luna didn't pick up. Gwyneth had no choice but to show up at the girl's apartment. As difficult as Gwyneth's fears of leaving the house during a pandemic were, following up with Luna face-to-face was crucial at this point. The only thing was, Gwyneth hadn't been out of the house in six months; she hadn't needed to because her ex-husbands took turns running errands for her.

Damned pandemic. It made anyone with borderline angst feel like a misfit.

It was best to show up at Luna's unannounced, perhaps with a bouquet of gas-station flowers. Chrysanthemums were a good choice because they lasted a long time. Gwyneth believed it was better to risk a meltdown in the hallway than allow something worse to happen. Barge in. Demand to see the baby. Oh, how she despised playing God.

Gwyneth couldn't even say if the kid was bald or had a thick head of hair.

The next day, she sat in her car outside Luna's apartment building, rain pimpling the windshield, her thumbs drumming the steering wheel. She debated if what she was about to do was in Luna's best interests. Public health harped on citizens to stay away from each other except in cases of emergency. People had been fined for ignoring the physical distancing orders. What made this situation more urgent than her other cases?

The medical grade face covering and spit shield, all in the name of mother and baby's safety, sat on the passenger seat beside Gwyneth. *Shit!* Gwyneth did not have a great feeling about this.

Rules were rules. Gwyneth pulled on the personal protective equipment and sighed. "I have no choice," she said as she slathered her hands and wrists with hand sanitizer, the liquid splashing onto her arms where three indecipherable words were tattooed.

Luna lived in apartment 313 on the upper floor of a walk-up next to the city cemetery.

When Gwyneth knocked, she found the door unlatched. *Perhaps Luna is out*, Gwyneth thought, *and forgot to lock up.*

"Hello, Luna? It's Gwyneth, the doula!"

The unit was quiet and calm, like right before a storm strikes. It smelled faintly of cinnamon and nutmeg, scents Gwyneth normally found comforting but at this moment found foreboding.

A narrow vestibule led to an open concept living/dining room with a small kitchen tucked into the corner. On a small wooden table stood a paper box stamped Mocha Café.

No car seat. No cradle or Pack 'n Play. Not a single picture of the baby.

She followed the layout of the unit, calling Luna's name, until she came to a dimly lit hallway. She took a few more steps and knocked again, this time on a door to her right.

Nothing could have prepared Gwyneth for what came next.

A pink nursery. White letters on the wall that spelled Natalie. A change table, still wrapped in plastic. Unopened packages of newborn diapers on the floor next to a white

234

dresser. A noise machine, the sound of waves crashing on a shoreline.

Luna in a rocking chair. Back and forth, back and forth. Caramel blonde hair, dark roots grown in. The clack of Juicy Fruit gum against molars. A cup of something on a foldable table next to the chair.

And a bundle in Luna's arms, thick dark hair nestled against her exposed breast.

Jesus! Gwyneth thought with alarm. *The baby isn't moving.*

"Luna? Is everything okay?"

She looked at Gwyneth like a child caught smoking behind a shed. "It's not harming anyone," Luna said, her voice barely a whisper, "me doing this."

It's going to be a long day, Gwyneth thought, taking in the scene in front of her.

And then, it came together for her in one giant swoosh. That the bundle in Luna's arms wasn't human.

It was a reborn, a memory doll. Something generic in its infanthood yet special to the mom holding it. Gwyneth had just stumbled upon the controversial therapy on social media. After the stillborn death of a well-known film star's infant daughter, the actress had received a vinyl doll from an Instagram follower. Subsequent posts described how much difference the toy had made in the woman's recovery.

The doll in Luna's arms had a convincing look to it. Her swath of black hair, the long curly lashes, the puffiness of her cheeks, a rosy cast to her skin. Gwyneth thought she'd even spotted a soother. Now that she thought about it, the air in the room even carried a hint of newborn smell.

Gwyneth stood in the doorway the recommended six feet from her client, her arms dangling helplessly at her sides. There were selfies on the opposite wall: a harried-looking Luna with the reborn against the crook of her elbow, and another, Luna's eyes gazing to the right, she and baby against an aquamarine backdrop.

"Well, at least we're alone here so we can talk," Gwyneth said at last.

"My therapist advised against getting her." Luna looked down at the doll's face and smiled. "But the idea of her just felt right. The entire experience has been surprisingly meaningful. When I hold her, I begin to feel a sense of calm."

Tears came to Gwyneth's eyes but she resisted the urge to wipe her cheek.

"Last week—you complained about crying."

"The machine over there." Luna nodded at the device playing beach sounds. "I had set it to whale noises. To make the experience more real."

Gwyneth could see how a grieving mother could grow fond of something that looked and felt like a real baby, like the baby she no longer had.

"I was so attached to—real Natalie. Carrying her full term. Only to have—"

"Your hopes of seeing her grow up dashed away," Gwyneth said.

"She's not a replacement. I know she's just a doll."

"May I—do you mind if I hold her?" Gwyneth asked.

"Not now. Perhaps when the pandemic is—"

"Yes, yes, of course. How silly of me," Gwyneth said, sensing she might fall in love once she held the reborn. "I'll call you on Thursday, Luna. If that's okay? See how you're faring."

Once back in the car, Gwyneth thought, *if only I had seen this coming.* She knew she'd be facing probing questions from Kathryn, that her back would be to the wall to explain how she'd missed this. Yet, moving forward, Gwyneth was hopeful that Kathryn would see no problem with Luna bonding with this version of Natalie. And of Gwyneth staying involved.

Perhaps, once Luna was stable enough, Kathryn would grant Gwyneth some time off, transfer her remaining less needy clients to another doula. If Gwyneth had had access to a reborn doll when she'd been unable to conceive, things may have gone differently in her marriages. In the meantime, Gwyneth felt an overwhelming urge to curl up and hide.

The Roach Family

Madagascar hissing cockroaches watched from a glass tank opposite from where Raymond and I sat at the dining room table. My father was in the kitchen adding diced onions, bacon, mustard, and chopped pickles between slabs of beef.

"When is your mother set to arrive?" Raymond asked.

"Anytime, I suppose. She never really committed," I said, shrugging.

Raymond's shirt stretched across his broad chest and shoulders giving him a buff look. His chin and cheekbones offered sharp angles. He spent a lot of time at our house now that my mother was gone for good. It seemed right that Raymond be present with my father to say goodbye before I began a four-year teaching gig in Lesotho.

~

My father's interest in cooking began when he was a boy growing up in Romania. His grandmother minded him while his parents ran the town's only funeral home and furniture store. If my father was in a cooperative mood, his grandmother permitted him to roll out dough for a meat pie or stir eggs into pancake batter. Later, as a teen, he yearned to apprentice at a restaurant but the Second World War came and plans were disrupted. Instead, he peddled silk stockings and contraband on the Black Market until he saved enough to sail to North America.

After my father arrived in Canada, he was hired at the Ford plant to install ceiling liners in sedans. It was tough work that caused pain to shoot up his legs and roost in his lower back. He detested the work so he ran for union steward. He was more surprised than anyone when he won. He swapped physical work for endless meetings, negotiations, mediation, and paperwork and spent a lot of time on the phone mumbling "Hmmm" and "I see."

~

Because my father refused our offers to assist with the cooking, Raymond and I sipped coffee to the sound of knives being sharpened and pots clanging. I'd requested rouladen as the main course, a recipe my father had perfected over the years. When it was prepared properly, the flavourful meat fell apart with the lightest poke of a fork.

My father's dream to open a restaurant in Canada never happened. Throughout my years growing up, he repeated the same career advice. "Debbie, do something you love. Don't just settle."

~

Having cockroaches as pets had been my mother's idea. It was the only thing of value she left behind when she decided to vanish from our lives. Because these particular roaches were adept climbers, their tank was equipped with a screen roof. A ribbon of Vaseline between the top edge of the tank's glass walls and the screen's wooden frame kept the roaches from executing a successful escape.

"Damned good thing they can't fly," my mother was wont to say. "Or they'd have flown the coop by now."

Even when pressured, my father didn't like to admit how attached he'd become to these members of the *bladeridae* family. Perhaps the roaches' typical domestic arrangement where parents and offspring remained in close physical contact their entire lives enamoured my family-oriented father. Unfortunately, the roach pair my mother brought home seemed unable to produce offspring.

I was an only child, the only one my mother bore. No brother to roughhouse with. No little sister tucked under blankets with me, making shadow puppets on the wall with tiny hands. How I ached for another child in the house, someone to push around and commiserate with.

According to my father, my mother hadn't wanted children but my father had leaned on her until she gave in. As a professional model she often said, "My body and face are the tools of my trade. Bearing children will cause my looks to quickly fade."

As she grew older, competing against young models with bodies like coat hangers and grim emotionless faces took its toll. Opportunities on the runway threatened to implode at the whisper of a droopy chin, pot belly, or wrinkled brow.

~

Inviting my mother to attend my going-away dinner was my idea, an event I'd nudged my father into hosting. He claimed he knew how to reach her so I'd left the arrangements to him.

"It's okay this once," he said, "but you'll owe me."

He invited Raymond as a buffer, or so my father said. Over the years I'd watched their relationship evolve from platonic into something more intimate. There were evenings when they shared a six-pack of Coors while watching hockey on TV. Later, there'd be bathroom noises, then numerous squeaks from the bedsprings. In the morning Raymond would traipse around the apartment with blatant familiarity before sitting at his spot at the kitchen table, methodically buttering toast before slathering it with marmalade my father had made from peaches and clementines. Over the years I'd suppressed any urge to verify if Raymond was the actual reason my mother had left.

I liked Raymond. My father deserved to be happy so I didn't let on I was aware of their arrangement. To see my father full of desire and love lifted my heart.

242

Hours later, when my father carried the rouladen into the dining room, warm air and pungent aromas followed him from the kitchen.

"Debbie, we should eat while the meat is hot," my father said before returning with boiled cabbage and rice pilaf.

Where was my mother? She could have been delayed for any number of legitimate reasons: a moose on the train tracks, an absence of available cabs, or a yearning to be anywhere but here.

Suddenly, the door to the apartment sprang open so wildly it banged into the wall like antlers against a tree trunk. There stood my mother, her face pale against a nest of short spiky hair. The new look suited her otherwise gaunt face. A sudden hiss interrupted her arrival. A disturbance hiss, a repellent noise created by squeezing air from under a roach's *elytra*, the fused wing-casings rendering the bugs flightless.

The sight of her caused me to feel weak in a way that getting the highly coveted job in Lesotho never did.

"Sorry I'm late," she said, her eyes bright as glacier water.

"Actually, I'm just setting the food out," my father said.

Nothing was offered to explain my mother's tardiness. She appeared pleased to be there, or so it initially seemed.

~

A month after my mother disappeared the same year I turned twelve, the police showed up at our door looking for her. She'd recently been at the mall when a disturbance with a customer broke out. According to the officer, the customer had decided after all to press charges. Something about the fur collar of the woman's expensive coat getting torn and being irreparable. I had trouble believing my mother's spindly arms and hands were capable of causing such a significant level of harm.

"She doesn't live at this address anymore," my father said, shaking his head. "How did you even know to come here?"

"Your wife left evidence behind," the officer said, glancing at his notebook. "A number of photo IDs. One had this address."

"Ex-wife," my father added.

I popped out from behind my father and said, "You say that, Dad, but she'll be back. I know she will."

"If that's the case, then be sure to hide your lighter and matches," the officer said.

"Why's that?" my father asked, his brow bristling with concern.

"On the day of the altercation, she threatened to set fire to the mall."

Letters from her began arriving soon after that. No return addresses but with the use of a magnifying glass, I could ascertain the route she'd taken. North Bay. Sudbury. Thunder Bay. Winnipeg. Red Deer.

Dear Debbie, I got hired as a cashier ...

Dearest Debbie, It didn't work out in ... Now I'm working midnights at ...

Breadcrumbs tossed here and there to keep my eyes on the trail, to ensure that the two of us remained connected.

My father said it was a damned good thing there were no return addresses. "I've half a mind to track her down and drag her sorry ass home," he said. "Abandoning the family, the way she did."

The letters were written in turquoise ink with loopy penmanship that was difficult to decipher, the paper so slippery and shiny, it was a wonder her words didn't slide off.

One day the letters simply stopped.

~

Raymond went into the kitchen to bring out whatever else remained on the counter. My mother lingered next to the tank, scrutinizing the roaches' long chubby bodies and fuzzy antennae. She held the hand lens we kept on a hook next to the tank up to her face.

"Mites. These roaches are infested with them. You and your father should—"

245

"Actually, the mites help keep mold levels in check," I said, my voice dripping with authority and haughtiness.

"You've grown attached, I see," my mother said, her voice barely a whisper.

"More than you could know."

Raymond made room for the additional bowls of food. There was enough to eat for a family of ten. My mother abandoned the roach tank and took her place at the seat where Raymond normally sat.

When my father started to recite the prayer he always shared before we ate supper, my chin dropped to my chest and I sighed audibly.

After grace, my father nodded at my mother to begin serving herself, as if she were a guest and not family. We heaped our plates. When the meat came to me, I took more than I could possibly eat, the tangy smell invading my nostrils, my mouth filling with high hopes.

Raymond asked, "Lydia, how was your trip?"

We chewed in silence waiting for an answer my mother didn't appear willing to give.

"Where did you end up coming from this time?" my father asked, peering over his glasses at her.

"I move around a lot. On account of my attention deficit."

"You're finally admitting it." My father's upper lip lifted to reveal a row of teeth slightly larger in size than popcorn kernels.

"How's that?" she asked.

"That you're half a bubble—"

"That's enough, Cezar," Raymond said, his fingers lightly brushing the top of my father's hand.

The brief moment of intimacy caused my father's cheeks to turn the colour of cranberries.

"That's okay. Really," my mother said. "It's just his way of showing his apprehension of me." She returned my father's smile with an empty one of her own.

Even though the meat was tougher than usual, we obliged my father's efforts by taking seconds, except my mother who chewed slowly and deliberately, as if the meat were still raw yet flavourful. After a while she said, "Debbie, your father's anxiety is what finally drove me away."

~

I remembered promotional posters featuring my mother on the runway. She kept them stored in tubes on the upper shelf of their bedroom closet. Milan. South Korea. Taiwan. New York. On rainy Saturdays when she was home, she'd bring them out. She'd carefully unroll them taking care not to tear the edges or fold the corners. She liked to share stories about the cities she'd visited during the peak of her

247

career. I loved listening to her distinctive voice with its singsong deepness and tinge of melancholy, a voice alluring enough to keep me glued to her side the entire afternoon.

The year before my mother packed up and left, I remembered being in health class. The teacher was leading a brainstorming session about healthy and unhealthy behaviours. Drug addiction. Alcoholism. Gambling. I became thoughtful when I heard the definition for bulimia. Before I knew it, my hand was up. "I think my mother has that. She regularly excuses herself during dinner and heads for the washroom. It's a nightly thing actually. My father and I can hear her barfing over the flush of the toilet."

The guidance counsellor phoned that evening. My father was the one who picked up. He didn't admit that what the physical education teacher suspected was in fact true, but he didn't deny it either. He talked to me later, reminding me to keep family business inside the walls of our apartment. That the world didn't need to learn that my mother was having what he called a crisis of identity.

I didn't raise my hand in health class for a long time after that.

~

Once after a two-month stint of runway work, my father and I picked my mother up at the airport. Her skin was grey and her face drooped as if it had been haphazardly pinned to her hairline.

When my mother fainted three times over the span of the next few weeks, my father finally decided enough was enough and called for an ambulance to come. She weighed just shy of a hundred pounds. She spent a four-month stint in hospital learning how to eat properly, and attending sessions about self-love and forgiveness.

Once they released her, my father left work early to pick her up. They did nothing to conceal that they were arguing as they stepped into the apartment. His arms flailed overhead like exclamation marks while her eyes flashed bright with anger. She told him she was done looking after everything; she was fed up with her menial life in their tiny apartment. She was done being a servant, cleaning and cooking. Picking up after him. My father took a glance at me where I was cowering behind the couch. The solemn look on his face told me that he felt he had no choice. So, just like that, my father caved. He told my mother that he supposed he had no choice but to take over all of her domestic tasks on top of doing his job. He agreed to do it all.

A few days later the cockroaches and their tank arrived. Refusing to lift a hand around the house, my mother spent hours studying the roaches, learning their quirks and behaviours, recording in a notebook what they ate and preferred. And whenever they hissed, tears of happiness rolled along her hollow cheeks.

One snowy February afternoon the principal announced on the PA that due to safety concerns and imminent road closures, there would be early dismissal from class. When I got home, I called out to my mother but silence greeted my ears. A folded sheet of foolscap clipped to the roach tank outlined how to care for the bugs. There was no other note; no explanation indicating why she'd left or where her road map would take her.

~

After dinner, while Raymond and my father cleared the table, my mother dimmed the lights before setting a stool next to the roaches. With her right arm resting against the top edge, she watched a roach she called Hector creep along a branch. She turned toward me and said, "Debbie, did you know that the male Madagascar hissing cockroach can be distinguished from his mate by his thick hairy antennae and prominent horns jutting from his thorax?"

I sat at the table chewing a hang nail from my thumb.

She continued. "Hector has a specific female-attracting hiss he reserves for mating. When I heard that hiss at the pet store, I couldn't resist adopting him."

My mother spoke with absolute authority, nodding and gesticulating with grand sweeps of her hands, her voice getting increasingly louder, acting as though I didn't already know all this.

I wondered if she knew. That for the first few months that she was gone I slept on the floor next to her side of the bed, her pillow tight against my chest, pretending she was there hugging me back.

She pulled a small piece of paper the size of a matchbook from her pocket. On it was a black line drawing.

"Come over here for a sec. Did your father tell you? I received a grant to make a hundred miniature roaches for the gallery in Bennington."

I nodded at the rudimentary sketch she held out to me.

"I started by making my own paper from leaves I collected. I pulverized sumac, trefoils, and chicory into a gooey pulp. Dried it on screens I recovered from the dump. I have to finish my drawing project within the month, or I'll risk not receiving the second installment of the grant."

I studied the semi-circles showing the three segments of the roach's body. Bushy antennae created with scribbles from a fine-tip marker. Light grey swirls above the head to represent the hissing noise. The picture was ridiculous, nothing to be proud of. Something no better than a primary-grade child might do.

I couldn't figure out why she was here. Except for the meal, she'd spent the entire visit thunderstruck with every hiss the roaches made. Perhaps she'd forgotten what Hector and his mate looked like. Maybe the intent of the visit was research-driven. Maybe she'd agreed to attend my send-off merely so she could study her beloved roach family.

"Miniature art is big where I live now."

I winced at the last part. I wished I could ask why she felt she couldn't make art here, with her family close by, but I was certain I was unprepared for her response. That the truth would crush me. Besides, who was I to talk? I was en route to Lesotho in two days, my own form of escapism.

I traced the inked sketch with my thumb. The paper was rough and mottled from splintered stalks, leaves, and seeds. I rotated the paper clockwise like hands of a clock when it suddenly dawned on me; the drawing was of a fetus, an unborn human, not a roach as I'd originally thought.

My father stood under the archway between the kitchen and dining room, Raymond's face poking from behind his shoulder. In my father's hands was my favourite dessert: Black Forest Cake. He held the glass dish out as if it were a prize.

"Will you ever pass your secrets down to your daughter?" my mother asked. "You still haven't shared that cake recipe with me."

"Why do you care? You never did it justice by eating any. Always said I was forcing food down your throat."

Hector bumped against the tank's polished glass wall, a barrier that kept him from us, his darting eyes inches from where my mother perched on a stool. His head bobbed up and down, a dance he seemed to be performing for her, his dedicated spectator, not the other roach that was cringing to his right.

"I've missed these two," my mother said, knocking a knuckle against the glass pane. She stood up and arched her back with her chin jutted forward, then made her way back to us. She sat and rested her elbows on the edge of the table. Next, she pressed her hands into a prayer-pose before placing her chin on the peak her fingers formed. "Okay, slide a mouthful of cake this way. Just a taste, mind you. Let's see what all the fuss is about."

When I looked at my father, his eyes were wet. He set the cake down before sliding a large knife through its tall layers. My mother's fingers shook a little as she lifted a cake crumb to her lips. A hum of satisfaction emerged from her throat before a hiss filled the air, sweet Hector signaling his approval, too, a crude release of air, like gasping for breath right before whatever destined in life came our way.

Acknowledgements

I wrote the stories in this collection at my home in Bruce County, Ontario, which I acknowledge lies in the traditional territory of the Haudenosaunee (Iroquois), Ojibwe/Chippewa and Anishinaabeg, a territory covered by the Upper Canada Treaties.

To Suzanne Craig-Whytock, publisher and editor of DarkWinter Press: you believed in this collection from the start and for that I am indebted.

To Jennifer Frankum and Janet Trull: thank you for your book blurbs. I'm forever grateful.

To my writing pals at the Treasure Chest Museum in Paisley: your wisdom, keen eye for detail, and love of tales helped morph many of these stories into their current form.

To the Ontario Arts Council and Government of Ontario: thank you for the financial support while I finalized this collection.

To the instructors and students at the Sarah Selecky Writing School, an online writing institute based in Picton, Ontario: my writing has benefitted from your guidance, humour, and insights.

To my children, Carolyn, Kathleen, and Cory, and your respective spouses: thank you, as always, for your love, strength, and loyalty over the years. You always have my back. I'm proud of each and every one of you.

To my grandchildren, Kai, Mirabelle, Zinnia, and Elowen: remember to live by these words ~ *"What we know matters but who we are matters more."* ~ *Brené Brown*

To my husband, John: you are my rock, my loudest cheerleader, and a staunch supporter of my creativity in more ways than you can know. Keep those social media posts coming. Love, always.

About The Author

Cindy Matthews is an author and visual artist who calls Bruce County, Ontario home. Her debut collection of stories, *Took You So Long*, (Porcupine's Quill, 2022) was the winner of the 2023 Independent Publisher (IPPY) award and runner-up of the 2023 eLit award. Reviewer Marshall Veroni of *Rrampt* hailed her first collection as a 'labyrinth of complicated, delicate, and painful narratives." *The Roach Family and Other Stories* is her second collection of stories.

DEDICATION

This book would not be possible without the love and support of my beautiful wife. Donna, I love you more than life itself.

ACKNOWLEDGMENTS

Once again, the people who read my books before you see them have saved me. Thanks to Tracy Bodine, Michael Falkner, Cain Hopwood, Kristopher Neidecker, Bob Noble, Jon Paul Olivier, Felix R. Savage, Christa Wick, and Jason Young for making me look good.

I also want to thank my readers for putting up with me. You guys are great.

1

Kelsey Bandar, second in line to the Imperial Throne of the Terran Empire, fell with a crash loud enough to turn every head in the physical therapy center. She lay there in the deafening silence, staring at the metal support bar in her hand. She'd ripped it completely out of the floor and *bent* it.

"Really?" The blonde noblewoman snorted bitterly and dropped the mangled bar. It landed with a substantial clang. She rolled onto her back and stared at the white-tiled ceiling.

"That may be a first for me," Doctor Lily Stone, chief medical officer of the Imperial Terran Fleet destroyer *Athena*, said dryly. "Normally, the patient gives out before the equipment. You'll forgive me if I don't offer you a hand up."

"I suppose I can't blame you for wanting to keep your arms attached to your body." Kelsey stretched her back. The cool floor felt good. "How the hell do the Pale Ones learn to walk without someone helping them?"

Those forcibly enhanced savages certainly had no problems walking. Or fighting. Kelsey was glad her friends had rescued her before the monsters turned her into one of them, but something wasn't right with the Old Empire equipment the bastards had put inside her. Even after a week, she still couldn't do simple things without destroying everything around her.

With a few exceptions, the hospital staff gave her a wide berth. Poor physical control and super strength didn't mix. The damage she'd done to the bar proved their caution wise.

The dark-haired doctor's face showed her concern and sympathy. "They learn to walk the hard way, I'd imagine. Move before the others do horrible things to you."

"That would be a powerful motivator," Kelsey admitted. "While I'm glad that isn't one of my many problems, I'm beginning to suspect that last machine you saved me from did something to help them adjust more quickly. In addition to enslaving everyone it operated on, of course."

The doctor glanced at the two Imperial Marines standing nearby. "Gentlemen, if you'd be so kind as to get the princess back into her grav chair."

Kelsey held out her arms, and the two men moved her into the floating chair with no trouble whatsoever. At barely one point five meters, Kelsey wasn't hard to move. Astonishingly, the full-body modification had only brought her up to fifty kilograms, though she wasn't sure she should count it as part of her real weight.

Grav chairs normally had a small control for the patient to direct their own movement, but Lily had removed it after a hand spasm had sent Kelsey into a wall. Technically, Kelsey had removed it herself. Much like she'd uprooted the support bar. Lily promised they'd reinstall the controls once Kelsey's fine motor skills improved. If they *ever* improved.

Since the Pentagarans hadn't managed to miniaturize the requisite grav drives, the supply of grav chairs was limited to what the Terrans had brought with them. Kelsey hoped they could fix the one she'd broken.

Lily used a remote to send Kelsey floating out of the physical therapy center and into the halls of Capital Hospital. The Pentagaran doctors in their bright-white smocks and the nursing staff in a much wider spectrum of colors nodded and smiled politely as they passed. On the other side of the hall.

"I know it seems like this is taking forever, but you're improving at an incredible rate. You couldn't even stand two days ago. Today, you're walking."

"For certain values of walking, I suppose," Kelsey grumbled.

"You fell because you yanked too hard on the support bar. Once you can stay upright, you'll be walking without any problems."

"It sounds so simple when you say it like that. I ripped a metal bar right out of the floor. I laugh at the thought of ever handling eggs again." Her gaze slid over the marines accompanying them. "Or any other… delicate objects."

"And yet you will," Lily said firmly. "It's all a matter of relearning control. I'm sure that the Old Empire marines had no problems with their fine motor skills. We'll get you back in shape. Just look at how quickly your vision recovered."

That was true. Kelsey's vision had stabilized in less than a day. Honestly, she was improving. She could stand on her own. Mostly. The problems started when she tried to move around on her own. The artificial muscles woven into her natural ones jerked and exerted more force than any five men could bring to bear.

Lily took Kelsey to a room she'd never visited before. It smelled as though someone had been doing construction. That made her wonder again why her eyes had given her trouble, but her senses of hearing and smell hadn't.

The Old Empire surgical machine had put three cranial implants in her head, all connected by thin wires that ran throughout her brain like a roadmap. Her eyes had artificial lenses, and her nose and ears had some kind of modifications. Yet her senses of hearing and smell seemed normal. What made them different? Just one more question she might never know the answer to.

Kelsey looked around the new room curiously. Someone had laid the room out much like the medical center on *Athena*, but the high ceilings and wide windows common in Pentagaran architecture added a sense of space. Their peoples' styles complemented one another well.

Several people from *Athena* stood waiting. She saw members of the medical staff and scientific teams present. At their sides were what she assumed to be their Pentagaran counterparts.

A week in the company of their new allies had been educational. They still had so much to learn from one another. One thing was clear, however. Many of the Pentagarans—most really—seemed like wonderful, caring people that were intensely grateful *Athena* had stopped the Pale Ones' invasion of their solar system.

The price tag had been hideous. Dozens of Fleet personnel and marines killed, hundreds wounded, and *Athena* crippled. Kelsey still couldn't imagine how they were going to get home, even with the help of their new friends.

From her hospital bed, Kelsey had finalized the official alliance between the Terran Empire and the Kingdom of Pentagar. They'd share every bit of technical data they recovered from the wreck of the Old Empire battlecruiser *Courageous* in exchange for the Kingdom's support. She knew any number of people back home wouldn't be happy that she'd been so trusting, but the move had felt right.

And, of course, their alliance had a military aspect. No one knew how many systems the Pale Ones occupied. The pre-Fall Terran Empire had been vast before the genocidal civil war that had almost exterminated humanity. The corpses of countless worlds no doubt filled the void once occupied by the greatest civilization that had ever existed.

Jared Mertz, their mission commander and her half brother, had brought their science ship, the converted freighter *Best Deal*, through the flip point to take a herd of Pentagaran scientists back to study the derelict. The Old Empire Fleet battlecruiser was a treasure trove of technology far beyond what either of their civilizations could now manage.

After drifting disabled in space for half a millennium, the ship was slowly coming back to life. Kelsey had heard they'd repaired one of her fusion plants and that the ship was operating under her own power again. Dennis Baxter, *Athena*'s chief engineer, had been chortling about it the last time he'd come to visit.

She was glad he had something pleasant to focus on. There were pitifully few of those moments these days.

Kelsey took a deep breath and pushed her dark thoughts away. She'd already flogged herself over the damage she'd caused. Now she had to move on and make up for it.

To do that, she needed to be able to walk. Back to her current problems.

She smiled at the people she knew and nodded to those she didn't. "It looks like you have a new medical center, Lily."

"Almost." The dark-haired doctor stopped the grav chair beside a piece of equipment that Kelsey knew all too well: the Old Empire medical device that had mapped her body before the Pale Ones' implant procedure. Beside it sat the tank that had cut her open and installed everything.

Actually, "procedure" was too antiseptic a term. It had cut her open while she lay there screaming. She'd passed out before it put all her new hardware inside her, but she still woke from horrible nightmares every night. She suspected the memories would haunt her dreams for the rest of her life.

She mentally shook herself. The third piece of equipment they'd recovered was missing. The one she presumed was supposed to reprogram her implants so that they controlled her rather than the other way around.

Doctor Jerry Leonard and his graduate student, Carl Owlet, stood beside the Old Empire equipment. The elderly scientist was the expedition's cybernetics expert. The younger man was a programming genius. At the tender age of sixteen, he was also the youngest member of the Imperial exploratory expedition.

Leonard smiled benevolently down at her. "It's good to see you up and about, Princess. Allow me to say that you're looking much better than when I saw you last."

She certainly hoped so. She'd seen the images from before they'd put her into the regenerator. The Pale Ones had gone most of the way toward turning her into one of them, complete with hideous scarring across most of her body. Thankfully, that was one thing modern medicine could fix.

Kelsey smiled, covering her inner turmoil. "Thank you. You

obviously have some plans for me. Might I ask what we're doing today?"

Lily put her hand on Kelsey's arm. "We won't be doing anything invasive."

Kelsey hadn't realized she'd tensed up until she looked down and saw that she'd cracked one of the armrests on the grav chair. She took a deep breath and forced herself to relax.

The damage she'd caused was not lost on the scientists. Leonard stepped back nervously. "Nothing to worry about, I assure you. We've been going over the hardware we recovered from the Old Empire marine and Pale Ones' bodies. We wanted to bring you up to speed with our progress and perform a few tests."

"What kind of tests?" She heard the suspicion in her voice. She wasn't sure she'd ever trust a medical procedure again. "Where is the third piece of equipment? The one that would've overridden my implant's programming?"

"It's elsewhere. We're trying to extract its data and determine how it can overwrite the implant's control code. We absolutely will not be exposing you to any danger," he stressed. "Shall we start with our findings?"

At her nod, he continued. "On the hardware side, we've completed a detailed examination of all your implants. We believe them to be standard Old Empire designs without modification. That's excellent news, as we know many marines lived and worked on *Courageous* with exactly the same enhancements as you yourself possess."

Their successes somehow failed to make her feel any better about her own condition. "How many marines did they have aboard *Courageous*?"

The older man's expression turned somber. "Of the five hundred and eighty-five frozen bodies we recovered, one hundred and seventy-eight had the same extensive implants as you do now. That's a significantly higher ratio than on *Athena*. Our marine complement is about ten percent of the crew. *Courageous*'s marines made up thirty percent of her crew. I suppose that makes sense. They had a lot more space for people on *Courageous*, and they were at war."

The low numbers still surprised Kelsey. "I have trouble believing that they crewed that massive ship with so few people."

"That is an amazing feat," he agreed. "The précis of the latest reports from *Courageous* indicate that the ship used significant automation. The systems also seem to be very sturdy. Some of them have come back online without intervention. Commander Baxter suspects there is some ability for the systems to self-repair."

"You mean the ship might be able to fix itself?" The thought boggled her mind.

"Perhaps to a degree. They've restored power to all systems. In fact, power came online even in some systems that no one has worked on yet. I just heard that they've found some small remotes repairing power connections and replacing damaged cabling and components."

That set her back on her heels, metaphorically speaking. The wreck of the Old Empire battlecruiser had been tumbling frozen in space for more than five centuries. Other than one dangerously unstable fusion plant, all its systems had seemed dead.

"Even with all the legends," Kelsey said at last, "I never expected anything like that. If it could fix itself, why hadn't it done so before now?"

The scientist shrugged. "I have no idea. Perhaps we'll discover the answer to that once we can access the ship's computer. Right now, I'm more interested in you."

"I can see some similarities between *Courageous* and you," Lily said. "I put you in the regenerator and removed the worst of the scar tissue. That left a significant amount of micro damage that I figured would take several months to heal fully. Yet in less than a week, it's all gone. Did you have any injuries as a child?"

"I broke my arm doing something silly. I also had my appendix removed by microsurgery."

Lily nodded slowly. "I noted both those items when I gave you your physical just before we arrived in Pentagaran space. In addition, I saw a deep cut that had healed well on your left leg. With the sheathing on your bones, I can't scan for the break, but I can tell you that the residual scarring from the other injuries is completely gone.

You don't have an appendix, but it might as well have never been there.

"Your body's ability to repair damage seems to have been significantly augmented. I saw no indication of anything like that with the Pale Ones. I'd like to have a better idea of what's going on inside you."

"You and me both." Kelsey gestured toward the Old Empire equipment. "What does that have to do with these damned machines?"

Doctor Leonard cleared his throat. "You told us the first machine was controlled by some type of computer. It's not responding to us in any way. We're hoping that you can communicate with it."

A chill ran down Kelsey's spine. "We didn't exactly build up any kind of rapport, and I'm not too keen on the idea of getting into either of them again." As in, she would flatly refuse to do so.

The older man held up his hands. "We would never ask that of you. However, your implants look like they should be able to communicate with equipment like this from a distance of up to ten meters. We'd like to put a monitoring headset on you while you attempt to do so. Which would also increase the reach and throughput of your implants significantly."

He gestured to a large cart holding several computers and other unidentifiable pieces of equipment. An Old Empire headset with cables spliced into it sat beside one of the computers. The ones they'd found on *Courageous* didn't need wires. She vaguely remembered Owlet using one like this when they'd rescued her. He'd been able to directly interface with her cranial implants and see that the Pale Ones hadn't modified their programming.

She really didn't want to do this, but she couldn't argue the need. "Fine. But I have no idea what I'm supposed to do. I haven't even been able to walk, much less feel anything in my head that seems different. As far as I can tell, the implants are turned off."

"They aren't," Owlet said. "I suspect it's a matter of figuring out what you need to do to use them."

"Why didn't I think of that?" She took a slow, deep breath. "Sorry. Exactly how should I do that?"

He picked up the headset and slid it onto her head. "Do you sense anything about those machines? Close your eyes and relax. Pretend you're trying to hear something or smell it or see it in your mind. I can only guess what it must look like to you, but perhaps the attempt will trigger something."

"Basically, you want me to discover a new sense."

"Something like that. If it doesn't work, we'll try something else."

Kelsey closed her eyes, relaxed as much as she could, and focused on her breathing. She wanted to be receptive to anything. After a moment, it felt as though someone was standing in front of her, but a peek showed that not to be the case.

She tried narrowing her focus further, and the sensation became clearer. It wasn't sight or sound. It wasn't like anything she'd ever experienced. She could feel the computer in front of her.

It didn't react to her, so she tried thinking at it. *Hello?* It didn't respond.

She reached out a mental hand, or at least that's how she chose to think of it, and touched it. The presence opened like a flower in her mind, and she knew it was the scanning machine. It was as though the machine had transmitted the information straight into her mind, right down to its serial number.

Or perhaps it was more like reading a screen of data about it. The information she saw listed it as Diagnostic Scanning Workstation Twelve, the same way it had identified itself to her a week ago.

Following the same pattern, she pushed her awareness deeper into the machine. Like she was talking silently to it. *Diagnostic Scanning Workstation Twelve, can you hear me? Are you operational?*

Affirmative. Diagnostic Scanning Workstation Twelve online.

The voice in her mind, if one could call it that, sounded neutral. It didn't really have a tone, not like hearing someone speak aloud.

She took a deep breath and continued. *My name is Kelsey Bandar. You put implants inside me. Do you remember?*

Accessing records. Comparing transmission to implant serial numbers. Confirmed.

She tried to keep her pulse down. *I have some questions about using my implants. Can you help me?*

Overrides to this unit's basic programming prevent it assisting you at this time. This unit may only make general statements to implantees under the modified instruction set.

Is that why you haven't responded to the verbal questions my companions have asked you?

Negative. This unit does not respond to unauthorized users at this time.

You say at this time. *Does that mean you might be able to answer them under other circumstances?*

Correct. This unit requires a system-level reset to reenable that functionality.

Kelsey opened her eyes and looked at the people eagerly awaiting her progress. "I can communicate with it."

Doctor Leonard grinned, and Carl Owlet pumped his fist in the air.

She licked her lips. They were parched. "It says that portions of its control programming have been overridden and that it cannot respond unless it is restored. Much like the Pale Ones, I suppose. It seems to have a little more leeway talking with those it works on, but not much."

"It also responded to your direct communication," Leonard said. "That's a window to access it."

"Well, I'm not a programmer. I wouldn't know what to do if you told me."

Carl Owlet shook his head with a smile. "I'm sure that the people using it before the Fall weren't programmers. The Old Empire had to allow for advanced control without knowing how to sling code. Ask the unit how you can reset it."

"That seems silly. If it was altered to keep people out, why would it tell me how to get around that?"

"Computers are surprisingly literal. It might not, but you won't know if you don't ask."

Kelsey looked back at the machine. She could still feel the connection between them, even with her eyes open, so she kept them that way. *Diagnostic Scanning Workstation Twelve, can your default control code be restored if you are reset?*

Affirmative. That will trigger a scan from protected memory. This unit's hardwired core will note and override the control alterations.

How do I do that?

There is a manual control behind an access panel to the rear of the unit. A mental image of the panel appeared like a hologram in front of her. She saw not only its location but also how to access it. *Open the panel and there is a numeric touchpad. Enter this unit's serial number, and that will trigger a system-level reset.*

"Okay," she said aloud, "there's a panel around back near the bottom. Inside it is a touchpad. I'll tell you what to enter when you have it open."

In deference to Doctor Leonard's older knees, Owlet went behind the unit. Kelsey explained how to open the panel. He had it open in a minute. She read off the long serial number, and he entered it.

The irony of the situation wasn't lost on her. If the machine hadn't forcibly implanted her, she'd have no way to access it now. Rather than being subverted to the cause of the Pale Ones, she was doing the subverting. Or the opposite of subverting. Whatever.

The unit's presence in her mental space vanished for long enough that she feared it wasn't coming back. Then it reappeared.

Diagnostic Scanning Workstation Twelve, can you hear me?

Affirmative.

What is your status?

Basic control parameters restored. This unit is now able to assist you fully.

Kelsey had to admit the success excited her a little. This was real progress. "I'm in. It says it's back to its default control parameters."

"Let's test that," Lily said. "Machine, can you hear me?"

This unit requires authorization to allow verbal communication with unauthorized personnel. An exception exists only for patients.

I authorize it. Kelsey wondered if she had the authority to do that.

In the absence of authorized medical personnel, this unit will grant provisional authority to Kelsey Bandar, subject to review by the next authorized medical technician to access this system. Identify the users desiring voice access and have them speak for voiceprint verification.

"State your name for the record, Lily."

"My name is Lily Stone. I am chief medical officer of the Fleet destroyer *Athena*. My rank is lieutenant commander."

"Access accepted, Lieutenant Commander Lily Stone." The

machine's artificial voice sent a shiver up Kelsey's spine. The last time she'd heard it, the computer was about to cut her open. It had apologized for the inconvenience.

Lily took a step forward, perhaps coincidentally putting herself between the machine and Kelsey. "I prefer you refer to me as Doctor Stone. Can you change that?"

"Preference acknowledged, Doctor Stone. How may this unit assist you?"

"The patient, Kelsey Bandar, is healing at a faster rate than I would expect after such extensive surgery. Why?"

"Kelsey Bandar's medical nanites are repairing the damage to her body caused by the implantation process."

Kelsey's throat seemed to swell closed. "Nanites? I have little machines inside me?"

"That is correct, Kelsey Bandar."

"That's not even remotely creepy. Please, call me Kelsey."

"Preference noted, Kelsey."

Lily frowned at Kelsey. "I obviously need to examine you more closely." She returned her gaze to the workstation. "Machine, I've examined other people you've implanted. They didn't seem to have any extra ability to heal. Why is that?"

"This unit's designation is Diagnostic Scanning Workstation Twelve, Doctor Stone. This unit inoculates all patients with medical nanites. It is possible that they were deactivated at some later time."

"Perhaps that's one of the things that the last machine did," Doctor Leonard said. "Could you authorize Carl and myself, Princess?"

"Diagnostic Scanning Workstation Twelve, I authorize these users."

"Voice command not accepted. Implant authorization required."

Kelsey cursed under her breath and repeated the process she'd done for Lily. This was going to take a lot more of her time if she had to be with the Old Empire computer while they examined it. Still, it was more interesting than physical therapy, and less painful.

Lily pulled her away from the scanning machine once Kelsey finished authorizing the scientists. "While the boys play with their toys, let's see if I can find these nanites. Then we'll see if this machine can explain how you control these implants of yours."

That reminded Kelsey how hungry she was. It seemed like she was always hungry these days. She wondered if that was her new normal. "Did you include lunch in those plans? I'm starving."

Lily laughed. "Okay, we can scan for nanites after lunch. Come on. Let's see if we can fill that bottomless pit inside you for a few hours."

2

Commander Jared Mertz tried to focus on the reports awaiting his attention, but it was hard. His office looked deceptively normal, neat as always, with the holos of his mother and various landscapes from Xander on the grey walls. Within these bulkheads, he could fool himself for a little while. But that was a lie.

Battle damage had irrevocably crippled his ship, twisting her very spine beyond repair. Any attempt to move her at more than a crawl risked tearing her apart. She'd never return to Avalon.

That hadn't stopped Dennis Baxter from restoring life support to all areas. Even so, the scent of scorched plastics and fried circuitry hovered in the air. The chief engineer even had her weapons systems back online. Yet they'd still need to abandon her.

That was the least of his sorrows. The battles with the Pale Ones had cost him eighty-seven crewmen out of two hundred and eighty. Thirty percent of his people had perished. Over a hundred more were in various hospitals on Pentagar.

The pain and loss ate at him. He had trouble sleeping, and when he could, the nightmares always woke him early. He'd have to get some sleep meds before long.

A rap at the hatch pulled him out of his black mood. Baxter stood there, his blue jumpsuit stained with something dark brown. "Got a few minutes, Captain?"

"Sure. What can I do to help? You need an extra wrench hand?"

The sandy-haired officer sat in the chair beside the desk with a sigh. "I can't spare the three people it would take to fix what you broke. All primary systems are back online. That begs the question, what next?"

Jared rubbed his face tiredly. "Damned if I know. We can't just give her to the Pentagarans without authorization from Fleet. But we can't take her with us either."

The engineer nodded. "I've been giving that some thought. Hell, I've been giving a lot of things some thought. *Athena* will never boost at more than a fraction of her best speed, but she *can* move under her own power. After some simulations, I've determined that she can safely flip, as long as she's stationary. Why not use her as a training platform and to transport cargo between Pentagar and the system with *Courageous*?"

Jared considered that plan. "It would allow better access to the other system. It's a pain to have to bring *Best Deal* back to the flip point every time we need to bring someone across. It will be useful until the Pentagarans get their first flip-capable ships ready to go. Which will be at least six months, according to Commodore Sanders."

"Maybe not. Sure, the ships built for it from the ground up will take six months, but I've been working with Engineer First Williams. I think we can retrofit some larger ships with flip drives. They won't be very sturdy and they'll lose a lot of internal space, but we can bring them online in a month or so."

Jared felt a weight lift off his shoulders. "That's *excellent* news. The last thing we need is another invasion before we're ready. How much do you think the refits will hinder those ships' effectiveness?"

"They'll need a lot of maintenance and some external equipment that will reduce their maneuverability. It'll also cut into their magazine size, so they won't have the sustained firepower they do today. That said, they could occupy the flip point in the Pale Ones' system and shoot up any vessels that approach. Then flip back to this side and let the other ships take on any intruders. Based on the damage we did to the Pale Ones, I don't expect they'd be able to take that flip point away from the Pentagarans. If we can destroy the shipyards, they won't be a threat at all."

Jared leaned back in his chair. "If only it was that simple. The Pale Ones must have other systems they can call on for help. Our probes found two other flip points in their system. One is a weak flip point, so they probably don't know about it. The other one leads back to the Old Empire. We cannot assume they have no reserves, but we don't dare send a probe through either of those flip points until we're ready to follow it up with armed ships."

Flip points—or more technically Osborne-Levinson Bridges—were flaws in the fabric of space-time that linked one area of space with another. A ship with the right engines could flip instantaneously from one planetary system to another hundreds of light years away. Their discovery had led to the creation of the Old Empire—and its eventual destruction.

The weak flip points were a relatively new discovery. Flip points with drastically weaker gravitic fields. Until the scientists with Jared's expedition had confirmed their existence, they'd only been theoretical. Without the new breed of scanner technology they'd brought with them on the exploratory expedition, they'd been undetectable, too. The Old Empire and, by extrapolation the Pale Ones, didn't know they existed.

They were also dangerous. Jared had brought his ships through one after they'd detected *Courageous*'s distress beacon, only to discover that it was a one-way trip, leaving them no way home that didn't pass through space controlled by the Pale Ones.

"So, you'd like more options?" Baxter asked, drawing Jared out of his thoughts.

"I'm willing to consider anything that doesn't leave us sitting here like targets."

"What if I could give you a flip-capable warship sooner than that? One of our very own."

"Do I need to paint myself red and dance naked on the palace lawn at dawn? I can do that."

Baxter laughed. "I'd rather you didn't. No, I'm talking about *Courageous*."

Jared opened his mouth to say something dismissive and paused. "You're joking."

"I'm totally serious. They've restored internal power and patched the hull. My engineers report that the damage to the primary systems seems repairable. I'm not promising success, but I think that ship might fly again."

"I find that very hard to believe." The Old Empire battlecruiser had been damaged and completely dead in space when they'd found her. A frozen coffin on the verge of self-destruction.

The engineer nodded. "I did too, until I looked at the details in the reports. The Old Empire built their systems to last and stored their spares very well. I believe it is possible to restore her."

"What about her main computer? I can't see that ship being of much use without the advanced systems built to fly and fight her."

"That is one roadblock. We've isolated it and brought it online. It seems to be operational, but it's entirely unresponsive to our attempts to communicate."

"We need the computer to run the ship, don't we?"

Baxter shrugged. "The consoles have a manual mode, so it must be possible to fly the ship without the computer. That doesn't mean it's easy, so I'd prefer getting the main computer back online."

The chief engineer smiled. "We might have a way to contact the computer and do exactly that. I just got word that Princess Kelsey made contact with the machine that implanted her. She told it to allow Doc Stone access, and it's talking. If she can do that to a machine that was under the control of the Pale Ones, she might be able to do it on *Courageous*."

That news was unexpected. Jared had been thinking in terms of how the events of this last week had hurt his half sister, not how those changes might help them. This opened up a completely new set of possibilities.

"I need to go talk to her, then. I also need to discuss any plans with Commodore Sanders. If we decide to move *Athena*, how much notice do you need?"

"We can boost at your command. We don't even need a helm officer. We'd be accelerating so slowly that I could handle everything from the engineering consoles."

Jared rose to his feet. "Good work. I like what I'm hearing enough to give it a tentative green light. How long to move *Athena* to the flip point?"

"At our best speed? At least three days. Perhaps four."

That was a crawl. The flip point had only been a few hours away from Pentagar at maximum acceleration before the battle damage. Still, it was better than nothing. "I'll let you know when I'm certain the Pentagarans are good with the plan. I know. This is a Fleet ship and they can't tell us what to do, but let's be realistic. This is their system, and I don't want to surprise them."

"You're the boss." Baxter rose to his feet and headed for the hatch. "Give the word and we start moving."

Jared thought about this new plan for a moment. Was it the right decision? Maybe not, but it was certainly more interesting than sitting on his butt waiting for other people to save them. If things didn't work out, they were no worse off than if they didn't make the attempt.

He had the duty officer open a channel to the Royal Pentagaran Navy dreadnaught *Mace*. Commodore Sanders came on the channel a moment later. "What can I do for you, Lord Captain?"

Jared still had difficulty with the title they'd given him because the Terran emperor was his biological father. Back home, it wasn't made so… obvious.

"I'm on my way down to Pentagar, Commodore. Commander Baxter informs me that he has *Athena* in the best condition he can manage. He says it can even flip, if it's stationary." He filled the flag officer in on what Baxter wanted to do in converting the destroyer into a ferry.

The older man nodded as soon as he got the gist of the concept. "That sounds like an excellent use of resources, and it keeps your ship under your control. I have no objection, of course."

Jared hadn't been expecting him to have an issue with the plan. "Baxter figured it would be useful in training your people in how to control and maintain a flip drive while you're building your new ships.

He told me about the refit program, too. Are you getting everything you need from my people?"

"Indeed. The exotic elements your people provided did the trick. We're able to make all the components to a space-time drive now. They also tell me that the elements are available in *Courageous*'s system. Once we can get some ships there to mine the asteroid belt, we'll be in fine shape. You've released us from our cage. Thank you."

Jared smiled. "It's my pleasure. That leads me to the other thing we've decided to try." He filled the commodore in on Baxter's plan to renovate *Courageous*.

The other man looked even more skeptical than Jared had felt earlier. "That's a very farfetched idea. Do you think it has a chance of working?"

"I'm not sure. If it doesn't, we're no worse off for trying it. If the flip drive works once, we have *Courageous* in this system. If it really works, we'll possibly have a new ship."

"Forgive me, but with so many of your people injured or dead, can you control an unfamiliar ship in questionable condition?"

A stab of pain shot through Jared. He imagined the losses would weigh on him for a long time. "*Courageous*'s Fleet complement was just over three hundred, but that was manning the ship for battle. I'd like to propose a kind of joint effort. You send along several hundred men and women from the Royal Fleet, and we'll try this together. By the time we're ready to attempt bringing *Courageous* back to Pentagar, what's left of my crew should be fit for duty. At the very least, we'll all learn a lot about the Old Empire technology."

Sanders chewed his lip. "Are you talking about making your people like Princess Bandar so that you can run the ship?"

Jared shook his head. "No. I doubt my people would be willing to go that far."

"How is your sister's recovery proceeding?" The concern in the commodore's voice was very touching.

"I'm told she mangled several rehabilitation machines and ripped a support bar out of the floor this morning."

Sanders winced. "Remind me not to shake her hand. How about emotionally?"

"She blames herself. I denied it, but she knows that I'd have come up with a less risky plan if she hadn't been in their hands. She sees the blood of all those people, and she will for the rest of her life."

"Not to diminish your losses, but such a lesson may prevent her from making a much worse decision further down the line. She might one day sit on the Imperial Throne of your people. At the very least, she is a powerful noblewoman. She needs to know what being responsible for life and death is like."

Jared pursed his lips. "That's a hard lesson, Commodore. One I'm still coming to grips with myself."

The older man leaned forward. "Forgive me, Lord Captain, but you're a Fleet officer. You might never have fought a real battle before, but you realized the possibilities. You chose to act in the manner that might best achieve your goals. Even with the loss of all those people, you succeeded. That is what it means to be a combat commander. Of which, I might add, you're a fine example."

"Thank you. You're right, of course. I'll give the order to move the ship to the flip point. It would be best if you detached an escort for them."

"Of course. When it comes time to go over, I plan to accompany you. I simply must see *Courageous* for myself. Rank does have its privileges."

"We'll be happy to have you, sir."

Jared ended the conversation and started the new plan in motion.

3

Lord Admiral Sebastian Shrike looked up from his desk at his secretary's knock. The young officer cleared his throat from the doorway for added emphasis. Shrike wasn't sure why the man felt the need to interrupt him twice. He fixed a disapproving stare on his minion. "Yes?"

"Commander Rawlins is here to see you, Lord Admiral. He doesn't have an appointment." The man's disapproval at the last bit of information was palpable.

Shrike's irritation vanished as he pushed back from his desk. "Send him in and hold all my calls and visitors until we're done. No interruptions. Absolutely none. Is that clear?"

"Yes, sir."

Jacob Rawlins wasn't much to look at, a short balding man in his mid-fifties, nondescript in every way. He was indistinguishable from the other mid-rank officers wandering the halls of Royal Fleet Command. That was a benefit to one of the best operatives in the Intelligence Division. It was particularly useful in the tasks Shrike routinely assigned him.

Once his secretary closed the door behind Rawlins, Shrike inclined his head. "Jacob. A pleasure as always."

"Lord Admiral." Rawlins made a circular gesture with his finger pointed toward the ceiling. His raised eyebrow made the motion a question.

Shrike shook his head. "While you get settled in, let me pour us a drink. You want your usual?"

Rawlins pulled a scanning device from his jacket pocket and began checking the office for bugs. "You know how much I appreciate the aged whisky you favor. No ice, please." It took the man a minute to complete his scan and set the device in the middle of the desk blotter.

"Once again your people prove their value, Lord Admiral. No bugs. As long as the light stays green, no one is monitoring us. May I assume your summons has something to do with the Terrans?"

Shrike sat back down at his desk. "Indeed. Their intervention has put the coup into jeopardy."

The intelligence officer leaned back in his chair and sipped his drink, nodding. "True, the conditions you'd hoped to foster after the invasion have failed to take shape, mostly due to the Terrans' counterattack on the Pale Ones. Even though the military suffered losses on par with your estimates, the Royal Family's public support is even stronger than it was before. Discouraging news, indeed."

Shrike's gaze narrowed. He pitched his voice low and added a deceptively genial tone. "Don't be so distant, Jacob. Yes, the appearance of the Terran destroyer and its space-time drive totally bollixed *our* plans. The invasion should have left the Royal Fleet in tatters and the average citizen ripe for change. Obviously, that sentiment is now lacking."

The intelligence officer smiled, though it didn't reach his cold eyes. "That's something of an understatement. The average citizen is now soundly behind the king. With the bloody nose the Terrans gave the Pale Ones, His Majesty has achieved a newfound respect in military matters. I'm quite interested in how you intend to reverse *our* fortunes."

"Lord Captain Mertz has informed Commodore Sanders that he intends to return to the Old Empire derelict and make it spaceworthy once more."

Rawlins blinked. "Is that a joke?"

"Apparently not. His engineer seems to believe they have some possibility of success. As much as it annoys me, their technical superiority gives his assessment weight."

Rawlins sat in silent thought for a few moments. "That does change things, but I'm not sure how you intend to use it to our advantage."

Shrike picked up his own glass and sipped the aged whisky. Its smooth fire spoke of many years in a barrel. "If we possessed such a vessel, the entire Royal Fleet would bow before us. And as Fleet goes, so goes the Kingdom. While I've had some success in putting men loyal to me in some commands, it's less likely that the remainder would resist if we possessed such a ship."

"That's a bold plan, but I see a few flaws. Such as the fact that we can't even get to the system containing the wreck until the first of the Fleet conversions takes place. If we could, we wouldn't know the first thing about operating it. We have to have the Terrans' assistance even to build space-time drives. Or as they refer to them, flip drives." His face took on a look of distaste at the last bit of reality.

The lord admiral leaned back in his chair. The rich leather creaked softly as he shifted his weight. "The Terrans have agreed to take a number of Royal Fleet personnel with them for training purposes and to help man the ship. Lord Captain Mertz envisions that a large percentage of them will accompany his ship on the way back to their empire, I'll wager. I should be able to get some of our people into the program."

Rawlins smiled like a shark. "You envision a coup much like we'd planned for the Royal Fleet? That could work."

"Eventually. Most of the people I send won't be part of our organization, so I doubt we could take the ship right away. That said, we could put a cadre of people in place to learn what they can and to form a plan to seize the ship. Can you assemble a team on short notice?"

"On how short a notice?"

"Four hours."

"Difficult, but I'll manage. Will we have an opportunity to send a larger group later?"

"I believe so, but we can't count on it."

The intelligence officer drained his glass and set it on the desk blotter. "Then I have my work cut out for me."

The lord admiral smiled. "Meanwhile, I'll start working on events here on Pentagar. Since the political situation is souring for us, I might as well stir up some trouble."

4

ore tests followed lunch. Kelsey was heartily sick of being an invalid. She was even more disgusted with all the blood and tissue samples Lily insisted on taking for her nano search. Modern medicine didn't normally require invasive procedures, but even the diagnostic equipment the doctor had available didn't show the tiny machines. The samples would go to a lab to find them.

It was late afternoon by the time Kelsey returned to the Old Empire scanning machine. Doctor Leonard and Carl Owlet had left. She wondered what they'd discovered and where they'd gone. She'd expected them to camp here until Lily threw them out.

Lily brought Kelsey's grav chair to a halt beside Workstation Twelve and headed for her office. "I have a ton of work waiting on me. Yell when you're ready to go back to your room. Or if you need some kind of help with this."

"Will do." Kelsey closed her eyes. She knew she didn't have to, but she was tired.

Diagnostic Scanning Workstation Twelve?

This unit hears you, Kelsey. How may it assist you?

I don't think I'm correctly accessing my implants. Can you tell me how this process should work?

The machine only paused for an instant, but Kelsey noticed. *This unit has completed a diagnostic routine on your hardware. All higher functions are in standby mode. Your trainer should have brought them online as the implant stages were complete.*

What kind of stages?

The implantation procedure for commando hardware takes place in stages. Stage one is the cranial hardware and nanites. Stage two is the optical, olfactory, and auditory hardware. Stage three is the pharmacology unit. Stages four, five, and six are the artificial musculature and bone reinforcement. These procedures have a recuperative period of between four and seven days. During that time, the patient integrates the new hardware. Subject matter experts then train the patient on how to control the new hardware.

Kelsey felt like laughing. Not because it was funny but because it partly explained why this sucked so bad.

Diagnostic Scanning Workstation Twelve, you performed all of those stages in one session, and I have no trainer. I can't even walk.

The machine was silent for a full five seconds. *Records confirm. This unit is at a loss as to why it did so. This violates all protocols and places the patient in significant danger of implant failure or death.* The machine actually sounded shocked and dismayed.

Blame the people that reprogrammed you, Kelsey thought. *You can't do anything about those who came before me, but you can help me recover. How many times have you done this before?*

Accessing records. This unit has performed this illegal procedure five hundred sixty-two thousand, four hundred and ninety-two times. The first illegal procedure took place five hundred twenty three years, four months, and twelve days ago.

Over half a million people forced to become like she was and then made slaves by the rebels, just by this one machine. And that didn't count the Fleet personnel that already had implants. The scope of the horror made her sick.

You can't do anything about that now. You said I have a set of commando implants. That's a marine, correct?

Incorrect. Commandos are a specialized group of marines with the highest degree of enhancement. The standard marine package, while capable, has significantly less comprehensive hardware. Nanites, but no artificial musculature or bone reinforcement. Basic ocular and auditory implants, but no olfactory implants.

So, commandos were the elite marines?

Correct.

Did Fleet officers have different levels of implants?

Negative. All cranial implants are identical. Support equipment varies between Fleet personnel, marines, and commandos. Fleet officers only have cranial implants. All have medical nanites, though the commando-grade nanos are markedly more capable.

That was the first useful information she'd gotten for them. Hopefully, there was a lot more.

Okay, Diagnostic Scanning Workstation Twelve… I'm going to refer to you as Twelve going forward. That other unit cut me open like I was a fish. Shouldn't there be painkillers and regeneration of the incisions?

Regulations require anesthesia for the procedure. Accessing implantation unit. This unit is detecting that the regeneration equipment is not active. The unit should also perform the surgery in a slower and more controlled manner to minimize injury to the patient. I have reset it.

That was useful. Or it would be if anyone else were crazy enough to put themselves through the procedure.

So that brings us back to me, Twelve. I have no idea how to use these implants. I've destroyed things because I can't control my own strength. Can you do anything to help me?

Step one is to bring your hardware to active mode. Once it is fully online, you should be able to achieve consistent control.

Kelsey opened her eyes and waved at one of the nearby technicians. "Would you get Doctor Stone for me?"

"Certainly, Your Highness." The man hurried over to Lily's office and sent her back.

Lily smiled as she hurried over. "That was quick."

Kelsey frowned. "How quick?"

"A couple of minutes."

"Huh. It felt like Twelve and I were talking longer than that." She filled Stone in on what she'd learned.

The doctor excused herself and retrieved her tablet. She had

Kelsey go over it again and made notes. "A commando, eh? Your father would be proud."

Kelsey snorted. "He'd be horrified. I want to bring all my hardware online. Maybe then I can walk."

"I'd recommend against that, but I know how effective that's likely to be. Let's get you into a scanner so we can watch the process."

It took half an hour to get everything set up to Lily's standards. Medical personnel now packed the room, looking at an array of instruments. Doctor Leonard and his programming henchman returned and wired her up like a stolen grav car. Only then did they allow her to start the process.

Twelve, let's bring my implants online in the manner you think best.

Acknowledged. Close your eyes and relax. Setting higher functions to active mode.

She felt the indescribable sensation of something inside her head turning on. Her entire body twitched.

"The processors just kicked into a flurry of activity," Doctor Leonard said.

Lily leaned over Kelsey. "Are you okay?"

"Yeah. I just feel weird. Like I can feel the implants."

What now, Twelve?

Stabilization subroutines are now active. You should be able to stand and move normally. Your internal governors have locked your speed and strength to levels appropriate for normal duty. They will remain at that level unless you choose to override the governors or your implants determine that you are in danger.

Kelsey took a deep breath and sat up on the diagnostic table. She slid her legs off the side and stood. Lily grabbed her arm for support, but Kelsey waved her away and took a step. There was a moment of seeming instability, but her body corrected for it. She walked around the lab, starting slowly but gaining confidence with every step. She felt the grin splitting her face.

She stopped in front of Twelve and thought about a technical schematic, and one appeared. She found she could drill down into the machine to the level of circuits. The diagrams labeled everything with part numbers and summaries of functions. There were even instructions on how to safely remove and replace them.

The information seemed to be coming from Twelve, but she wasn't sure.

"Whoa."

Lily was at her side in an instant. "What's wrong?"

"I wondered about the workstation, and schematics just popped up in my field of vision as though I was holding a tablet. Twelve, I think I'm operational."

"Incorrect," the machine said aloud. "Your optical, olfactory, and auditory implants are in standby mode."

"I just saw a technical diagram of you, so I'm pretty sure my eyes work."

"Correct, but incomplete. The basic functionality is active, but the higher-level functions of the commando implants are not."

Lily looked at the machine suspiciously. "What does that mean for her? The eyes, for example."

"Commando optical implants are capable of enhancing human vision into the infrared and ultraviolet ranges. There are also certain threat assessment and combat functions that integrate with them."

"Turn it on, Twelve," Kelsey said. "All of it."

On reflection, that haste might have been a mistake. Her view of the room changed. Everything became sharper. Clearer. And for a moment, brighter. Bright enough for her to shield her eyes.

Noise overwhelmed her hearing for a few seconds. She heard what seemed like a hundred conversations going on. There were so many unknown sounds that she couldn't catalog them all. The same was true of her sense of smell, though to a lesser, though more technical degree. Chemical composition analyses popped up in the corner of her vision, detailing specifics of what she smelled to levels more appropriate to a lab. Why a commando needed a good nose, she had no idea.

She dismissed the information and focused on her breathing until she felt she had a better grasp of what was happening. She uncovered her eyes. Everything was still unnaturally sharp, but the brightness had returned to a more normal state. Kelsey focused on a man in the hall. His face snapped close, as though she'd looked at him through electronic binoculars. By focusing in, she found she could see his eyebrow hairs clearly. And his pores. He should see someone about that.

The noise in the room subsided until she thought she could hear him breathing.

"Excuse me," she said loudly. "You in the hall. What's your name?"

The man looked around to be sure she was talking to him. "Claude." His voice thundered in her ears.

"Where are you from? Whisper it."

He looked confused but nodded. "The southern continent." His voice was very soft, but she heard him clearly. The other noises around her almost overwhelmed him, though. She'd have to practice a lot to do that more consistently. Or better yet, to turn it off.

She thought about that a moment, and her vision returned to normal. The overwhelming sounds and smells damped down to what she thought of as normal levels.

"This is going to take a lot of getting used to," she muttered.

"That's enough experimentation for the day," Lily said firmly. "I want you to rest for a while."

"Seriously? I've been in bed or a grav chair for a week."

The doctor smiled. "Everyone says that. Maybe you feel like you can take on the world. Hell, with those implants, you might make a credible effort. But you can rest for a while first. Back in the chair." She pointed at the grav chair sternly.

Kelsey sighed and climbed back onto the chair. She did feel tired, even though she didn't want to admit it.

"How long until you know about those nanites?"

"I already have some preliminary images." She handed Kelsey a tablet. The picture on the screen showed a cell. There were little dots next to it.

Kelsey expanded the image, and the small machines came into view. They were still somewhat indistinct, but they were obviously mechanical. "I'll be damned. Those things are inside me? That's creepy."

"There are a lot of them, too. They somehow signal one another about an injury and congregate to help repair the damage faster."

The princess handed the tablet back to Lily. "I don't know if I'll ever get used to that."

"Humans are surprisingly adaptable. What you need now is a little more rest and a few more friendly faces. Senior Sergeant Talbot is back from his trip to look at one of the Pentagaran military bases. Now that you can walk, I bet he'll help you get back on an even keel."

Lily moved the grav chair toward the door. "But for now, you can take a nap."

5

Jared found Doctor Stone in her temporary office once he'd landed and been driven to the hospital. She had her head buried in some incomprehensible scanner results. He rapped his knuckles against the door frame. She looked tired as she straightened. "You haven't been sleeping enough, Lily."

She leaned back in her chair and rubbed her eyes. "Things have been moving fast. If I slept as much as I wanted, I wouldn't know what was happening."

He sat down in one of the institutional chairs some sadist had designed to discourage people from lingering. He figured he had about ten minutes before his butt went to sleep.

"How's our patient?"

"She's doing better than I'd hoped this morning. She's walking on her own."

He grinned. "That's great news!"

"Says you," the doctor said sourly. "Now I can't be sure where she'll get off to next. I told her she had to sleep and posted a guard, but I'm not convinced she won't slip out the window. It's like keeping up with a toddler. One that might inadvertently rip some fixture out of the wall if she isn't paying enough attention."

Stone filled him in on the events of the afternoon.

"It's hard to believe she communicated with an Old Empire artificial intelligence," he said once she'd finished. "It's communicating with us? That's amazing."

"I'm not sure I'd call it an AI. It's more like an advanced interface. It doesn't seem to have much of a personality. It's just very sophisticated."

"It comes across the same when she uses her implants to communicate with it?"

She shrugged. "I don't know. She tries to tell us what's happening, but it's like explaining color to the blind. Or sound to the deaf. Kelsey doesn't have the words to describe what's truly taking place. We don't have the frame of reference to understand what she's telling us in anything other than general terms.

"All I can tell you for certain is that she seems to be able to get a lot of data from that machine in an astonishingly short period of time. It seems willing to accept her authority to order it around, but it's unwilling to do so with those of us without implants."

Jared absorbed that for a minute. "It sounds like we may need you both to come with us." He explained Baxter's plan.

Stone had a skeptical look in her eye. "Restore *Courageous*? That sounds wildly optimistic. She was a fine piece of engineering, I'm sure, but she's been wrecked since the rebellion."

"You might be right," Jared admitted. "If so, we've lost nothing but time. The Pentagarans are still building new ships and modifying others. They don't need most of us here for that."

"I suppose you're right. What do you have in mind for Kelsey and my team?"

"Originally, I was going to leave you here to work on her recovery. Now I think we might need her help. Why don't you give me a rundown of what you've discovered."

Stone spent the next ten minutes giving him the bullet points of what the computer had told Kelsey. Then she showed him the scans on her computer. "These are the medical nanites. Apparently, the Pale Ones don't have any."

The tiny machines fascinated and horrified Jared. The idea of billions of the little things inside her body probably had Kelsey more than a little on edge. "Why would the Pale Ones disable something that useful? It seems like they'd be more formidable if their healing capabilities were increased."

Stone shrugged. "It almost has to be related to the suppression of the implants in the Pale Ones. I'm still unsure of how they interact with the hardware."

Jared nodded. "Kelsey's ability to tell us about what's on *Courageous* could be critical. I've already spoken with Commodore Sanders. We're returning to the other system with hundreds of their Royal Fleet personnel, including him. If we can repair the ship enough to bring it to Pentagar, that's a success. If we can do more, even better. Get your people ready to travel and bring the recovered hardware. We leave in three days."

"Kelsey will be thrilled. She's ready to get out of this place."

"I'll tell her the news, then. You get some sleep." He rose to his feet. "That's an order."

"Aye, sir."

Jared knew that Kelsey was in the room directly next door, so finding her was simple for a change. To his surprise, she wasn't alone. Crown Princess Elise sat on the edge of the bed. Both women smiled as he came in.

He bowed his head toward Elise. "Highness. I just dropped in to check on Kelsey."

"Then we share a mission, Lord Captain," the Pentagaran noblewoman said. "She and I were just discussing her recovery. I'm so pleased that she can walk again. I know my father will be overjoyed, and the news will be cause for a general celebration."

Kelsey looked more than a bit uncomfortable at that statement. "It's kind of overwhelming having so many people I don't know doing that. I'm used to a certain level of attention back home, but this is almost like being a cult figure."

Elise placed her hand on Kelsey's arm. "They're caught up in the adventure and romance of the situation. You and your people are widely seen as saviors, and I'm afraid you're both something of national heroes. My father is envisioning a parade once your recovery is further along, and Parliament has been making noises about the Parliamentary Medal of Valor. Our highest honor. They'd present it on live vidcast with the entire Kingdom watching."

Jared saw his half sister shudder as he was doing the same. Time to launch a rescue mission. "Unfortunately, I'm afraid I may need to pull you away from all that public adulation, Kelsey."

Her eyes lit up with hope. "Thank God."

Elise laughed. "You're both so funny."

Jared filled them in on what he intended to do.

Kelsey looked impressed. "That's ambitious, and it seems crazy. That ship has been a derelict for five hundred years. We know almost nothing about Old Empire systems. To imagine that we'll be able to repair and fly her doesn't seem very likely."

"Do you have anything better to do?"

"Well, my calendar does seem to be clear, though I have some things I'd like to do. If Lily will let me do them."

He allowed himself a small smile. "Look at it this way. With all the repairs going on, Doctor Stone won't be lurking over your shoulder every minute."

"I'm sure she'll find a way. I'm ready to leave today." Kelsey looked over at her Pentagaran counterpart. "No offense, but I'm tired of lying around the hospital."

Crown Princess Elise nodded. "I'm all for smuggling you out. Lord Captain, are you leaving at once?"

He shook his head. "There's no need. It will take *Athena* at least three days to get to the flip point. Royal Fleet will get us out there when the time comes. Until then, we'll stay on Pentagar."

"Excellent. Events cut Kelsey's last visit here tragically short, and you haven't spent any time in the capital at all. We insist that the next few days be spent enjoying our hospitality. That's the Royal We, by the way."

He gave the Pentagaran princess a short bow. "I'd be honored, of course."

"Splendid. Now, if you'll excuse us, I'll coordinate with Doctor

Stone to get Kelsey into quarters that are more comfortable. I'm certain that you have about a million things to do as well."

Jared recognized a dismissal when he heard it. "Ladies."

He walked back out into the hall. Senior Sergeant Talbot, one of *Athena*'s marine NCOs, leaned against the wall. He snapped to attention as Jared came out.

"At ease." Jared motioned for the marine to walk with him. "I understand that we have you to thank for keeping the princess in one piece. Good work."

The large man smiled wryly and shook his head. "You have it backward, Captain. She saved our bacon. She killed two Pale Ones, one with a pistol and one with her bare hands. They'd have cut me up just like her if she hadn't done what needed to be done."

"I read that, but part of me still finds it hard to believe. Hell, she's so small I could wrestle her with one arm tied behind my back. I can't imagine her choking someone to death with her bare hands. Frankly, I can't imagine her hurting anyone at all."

"Try imagining her ripping a metal bar out of plascrete. I saw her do that this morning. With one hand. She doesn't know I was there. It breaks my heart."

"I'm told that they did something to improve her ability to control herself. Stone says she was walking without assistance a little bit ago." Jared stepped into an empty waiting room. "Kelsey has a lot of recovery to do, and some reassessing. You marines have supported her so much. I'd like you to help her out even more."

Talbot nodded. "Of course, sir. We'll do everything we can."

"I want you to go all the way. She has equipment inside her that makes her very, very dangerous. Not just to someone that threatens her, either. Doctor Stone says she has what the Old Empire called a commando implant package. She probably also has some buried triggers to go with it. She needs training and something to focus her as she figures things out.

"She'll need to continue her work as our ambassador, but she needs the structure and support of someone that understands something of what she's being thrust into. None of you has the hardware she has, and none of us understands exactly what they did to her, but some marine training might help her adjust. She could really benefit from as much one-on-one time as possible. Will you help her?"

The marine nodded sharply. "Certainly. She'll jump at the opportunity for a few reasons. One, she knows she needs to learn about her new condition. Two, she's desperate to have some control over her life."

The NCO stared through the glass at the medical personnel walking by. "We've been spending a lot of time together this last week. I think we've developed a strong rapport. She'd make a terrible marine. She's a civilian through and through. That said, we could help her and learn a lot about how the Old Empire fought through her. I want to help her get past this bad mental space she's in."

Jared clapped his hand on the marine's shoulder. "Excellent. Talk with Lieutenant Reese and work out a training regimen that tells us what she's capable of while giving her a reason to embrace who she is now. You'll be running point. We'll never get that equipment out of her, so she needs to become accustomed to it. And while I can't imagine anyone wanting to do it, there exists the possibility that she won't be the last of us with implants. Her pain and struggle will help those who follow in her footsteps."

"Aye, sir. I'll finalize everything with the LT and start as soon as Doctor Stone gives me the green light."

Jared took a step toward the door. "We'll be heading back to *Courageous* in a few days. The marines are going with us. I'm not sure if we'll stay on the battlecruiser or the freighter, but be ready to start working with her after we get there. Kelsey will be splitting her time between Doctor Stone, Commander Baxter, and you. I'll explain the situation to her when the time comes."

Talbot stood a little straighter. "Actually, sir, it might be best if I explain it to her. I think she'll take it better if I say this is my idea. It really is. You just made it an order."

"I leave it in your capable hands, then. Get some stability back in her life, Senior Sergeant. I'm counting on you."

The man snapped him a razor-sharp salute. "Aye, sir. I'll give her my very best."

Jared returned the salute. Once the marine NCO was gone, he stood there wondering if he was making the right decision. Not that he could think of any better options. He sighed. They'd play things one day at a time. Right now, he needed to figure out where he'd be staying for the next few days.

6

Of course, getting out from under Lily's thumb wasn't nearly as easy as Kelsey had hoped. The doctor kept her under observation for a full twenty-four hours so that she could monitor Kelsey's progress.

If Kelsey had thought she had any chance of success at all, she'd have told Lily that she was checking out bright and early the next morning, but she knew that wasn't happening. Medical types seemed amazingly immune to rank and social status.

Lily reluctantly agreed to allow Kelsey to go on a sightseeing excursion, but she had some restrictions. First, Kelsey would travel in a grav chair. She could get up and walk around, but the doctor didn't want her exerting herself unnecessarily.

Which was ridiculous, of course. Kelsey was more than capable of supporting her own weight. And the weight of any medical equipment that she happened to be holding at any given time. Which was probably the point. At least if she was sitting, any accidents wouldn't be too large in scale.

Her second restriction was that Kelsey ate often and in quantity. She wouldn't get any argument on that. Kelsey was hungry all the time. Lily said it had to do with her boosted metabolism. Kelsey wasn't certain why a bunch of artificial implants required her to eat like a horse, but it was obviously true.

That was going to take some getting used to. Kelsey was a very small woman, but now she was eating more than most marines. Male marines.

She'd just finished devouring an embarrassingly large breakfast when Elise came to pick her up. The Pentagaran noblewoman eyed the plates on the table with a smile as she sat down. "Were you a little hungry this morning?"

"You could say that. It's humiliating."

"Why is it humiliating?"

"People watch me eating with an expression like they can't believe it."

Elise laughed. "If your diet is the most exciting thing people talk about, you're lucky. People will adjust. Don't worry about what they think."

"That's easy for you to say," Kelsey muttered. "You don't have all this junk inside you. I'm just like one of those Pale Ones."

The crown princess's eyes flashed. "You. Are. Not. Don't even *think* that. You have the same kind of implants as any number of Old Empire citizens, so if you have to compare yourself to anyone, make it them. Admittedly, most people in the Old Empire probably didn't have as significant an enhancement as you have, but if that sprawling civilization didn't see it as a shameful thing, neither should you."

Elise waved a hand at the other people in the cafeteria. "Times are changing. With the rediscovery of this technology, how many of these people do you think will eventually end up with some kind of implant?"

Kelsey shook her head. "I can't imagine any of them would do that, given the choice."

"You'd be wrong. Yes, the idea of the Pale Ones terrifies anyone in their right mind, but taking a quantum leap toward restoring the Old Empire excites them, too. Not as a political unit but as a reality. It's hard for you to see the opportunities that your implants represent, but I can see them. Lord Captain Mertz can see them. Even my father can see them."

Kelsey shook her head in denial. "Why would anyone choose to do that to themselves?"

Elise poured herself a cup of coffee from the insulated container on the table. "Do you suppose the Old Empire would've had widespread implants in Fleet unless they made a difference? It must've given them some significant advantage, don't you think?"

"And a very specific and powerful disadvantage when the rebellion started."

"True, but if the Pale Ones capture us, we get implanted anyway. We don't have a whole lot to lose at this point. The Empire has already fallen. Am I advocating that everybody rush out and get implants the first moment they possibly can? No.

"But as they see you adjusting to your new circumstances, people *will* start volunteering. People that see the advantages of being able to interface directly with advanced equipment. With each brave soul, you'll become more the norm than the exception. Don't worry about how people perceive you. Whatever they think now, they won't be thinking it in a few years."

Kelsey mulled over Elise's words as she finished her coffee. Everything the other woman said made sense, but that didn't make it easy to accept. Yet what choice did Kelsey have? She was going to be this way, whether she liked it or not. She might as well set a good example.

"I still think everyone expects me to look like a cow in a month," Kelsey grumbled. She eyed the grav chair sitting beside the table. She'd gotten out of it to sit in a real chair while she ate. Now she had to get back in it. Doctor's orders. At least they'd reinstalled the controls. She sighed and got into the chair.

Elise stood. "The cars are waiting around front, and your half brother is somewhere close by. My father invited the both of you to visit the Parliament Building. They aren't in session right now, but the architecture is amazing. You'll have a good time. I promise."

Kelsey nudged her chair to follow the crown princess out of the cafeteria. "Exactly what role does Parliament play in your monarchy? Do you have a prime minister? We have the Senate at home for our nobles and the Commons for the elected representatives. No prime minister, though."

"We don't have a prime minister, either," Elise said. "There are a number of ministers, though. We don't have any nobles outside the Royal Family. The baron who founded the monarchy after the fall decided it would be best if the people had a voice. So Parliament considers prospective laws and sends the ones they like to my father. If he disagrees, two thirds of them can overrule him. They're also responsible for the Royal budget."

"Doesn't that cause a lot of friction?"

Elise shrugged. "At times. There are always various factions at figurative war with one another. I'm sure you have that and more at home. We at least have an ongoing war to keep everyone moving in the same direction."

They exited the hospital, and a wall of sound overwhelmed Kelsey. It took every ounce of her willpower to keep from clapping her hands over her ears. People were screaming. Lots of people.

It took a moment for her to process what she was seeing. People filled the street. Her presence seemed to set off a roar of approval. Like when someone scored at a sporting event. Only louder. Much louder.

The unexpected sight—and sound—of them froze her in place. What were they doing? Were they going to attack her?

Elise put her hand on Kelsey's shoulder. "Breathe. Smile. Wave at them. They're here because of you."

Kelsey smiled and waved while she considered retreating into the hospital.

The crowd went nuts. She'd only thought their volume was impressive before. She expected them to burst through the security cordon, but they just waved signs and flags and screamed their heads off with excitement. At least her auditory implants were scaling the volume back down to something reasonable.

"I don't understand," she said, hoping Elise could hear her.

"Have you ever heard that an adventure was something terrible that happened to someone else far away? Well, you've been on an adventure, and you saved them all from a fate literally worse than death."

Kelsey stared at the Pentagaran princess. "I did not! I stuck my head into a hornets' nest and was lucky enough to survive the experience. Jared saved them. All the people on *Athena* saved them. I almost got everyone killed. If they knew what I was, they'd be terrified."

Elise narrowed her eyes, her public smile never faltering. "Stop it. They don't know, and by the time they do, they won't care. Mark my words. Now, let's get out of here."

Rather than the grav limo that she'd traveled in the first time Kelsey visited, Elise had brought a rather fancy grav van. It had windows just like a regular vehicle, but the rear had a space between the seats for Kelsey's grav chair. Additional Royal Guards stood near other waiting grav vehicles.

Standing beside the van were Senior Sergeant Talbot and several other marines. They wore pressed fatigues and had pistols at their hips. It looked like she had her own escort.

She pulled up beside him. "Don't you clean up nice, Senior Sergeant Talbot?"

In fact, he looked better than good. Talbot was already a ruggedly handsome man, but the uniform added an extra dash. She had to admit that their shared experiences had drawn them closer over the last week and made her much more aware of him as a man. Part of her wished class and age didn't separate them so much, because she wouldn't mind getting to know him better still.

Even if that meant he ran the risk of her father exiling him to Thule.

Ah well, some things were not meant to be. Talbot would never see her as anything other than his emperor's daughter and a thorn in his side that had almost gotten him killed.

He grinned at her. "That's what they tell me, Princess. How are you feeling?"

She suppressed the way his smile made her melt a little inside. "I'm ready to get out of this chair. I don't suppose you'd consider helping me escape, would you? A quick getaway from all these people with needles?"

He looked sympathetic but shook his head. "Sorry, Princess, but I have my orders. The crown princess has her people to watch out for her, and we're going to watch out for you. And Captain Mertz, of course."

She looked around for her half brother but didn't see him. "Forgive me, but this doesn't seem to be the most dangerous place I've ever been. It seems downright peaceful compared to the other vacation spots I've seen recently. I'm certain that the Royal Guard will make sure I'm not injured in some random event."

He looked mulish. "I'm sure they would, but it's not their duty. It's ours. I'm certain Pentagar is a very orderly place, all things considered, but the princess wouldn't have her own guards if there wasn't a reason."

Kelsey raised her eyebrow at Elise. "Do you have a reason for them?"

Elise nodded. "Certainly. First, there's tradition. The Royal Family doesn't go anywhere without a guard. At least not unless they can slip away when no one is looking. It's not so much that we expect trouble or have enemies. It's more like having an armed military, they don't go around looking for trouble, but when it finds them, they're ready for it. No one has assassinated a member of the Royal Family since the founding of the Monarchy. I think we're probably pretty safe, but it's still best to go with tradition."

"The Terran Empire has that tradition too," Talbot added. "The Imperial Family is watched over at all times. Admittedly, it's sometimes very low key, but that doesn't mean that the guards aren't there. Since none of the Imperial Guard came along on this trip, it's up to the marines to fill that void."

Kelsey felt a little exasperated. "You didn't do that on *Athena*."

"No," he said patiently. "There wasn't any need. Not with Fleet personnel around you all the time. Though honestly, we should've assigned a couple of marines to escort you. Chalk that mistake up to inexperience on our part."

She sighed. "You weren't doing this in the hospital."

"Just because you didn't see us in the hospital doesn't mean we weren't there. We had a couple of people standing by just out of sight. There's no reason to intrude on your privacy if we're not out in public. Ah, here comes Captain Mertz."

Kelsey turned in her chair and saw her half brother walking out of the hospital.

He smiled and waved as the crowd roared again. Jared reacted to them as though this had been happening all his life. He stopped beside Kelsey's chair. "Sorry I'm late. Doctor Stone had some last-minute instructions for me."

Kelsey sighed. "Now what? Is she going to have me tied to the chair?"

"She just wanted me to be an outside observer on how your implants react to external stimuli. Her words, not mine. So if something unusual happens, be sure and let me know."

"I'll be certain you're the second to know."

Elise took charge and saw everybody into their respective vehicles. Talbot and one of his marines sat in front of Kelsey. Elise took the seat to her left and Jared sat on her right.

The driver made certain to come at the Parliament Building with an eye to the view. Kelsey had to admit it was a gorgeous piece of architecture. Tall columns of stone held up a massive façade filled with carvings out of Terran mythology. She had to admit that she didn't know all of the people represented there. She'd have to see if there was a handout to explain who everyone was.

The grav vehicles landed in front of the building and disgorged their passengers. A number of policemen kept what looked like tourists at bay as the Royal party entered the building. Kelsey imagined the Parliament Building was a major tourist attraction.

The foyer continued the theme from outside. Polished granite floors gleamed in every direction, and walls shaped from molded plaster flanked them on every side. Paintings and statuary filled every niche. Tour groups wandered through the areas that Kelsey could see, admiring the artwork and the architecture.

The crown princess gestured toward a wide set of stairs leading to the second level. "We'll go up and take a peek down into the main chamber. Then we'll make the circuit and stop if anything catches your eye. This building has some of the most important pieces of artwork in the Kingdom. Kelsey, if you look behind the speaker's podium, you'll see another of Master Vestor's carvings. I'm looking forward to seeing Lord Captain Mertz's reaction to it."

Kelsey smiled at Jared's raised eyebrow. "You're going to love this. If it's anything like the one I saw last week, it's the most amazing piece of art you'll ever see."

Her grav chair went up the stairs without any problem. The second level looked very much like the first, except that there were no tour groups.

"I took the liberty of having the second level closed off in advance of our arrival," Elise said. "My father and I thought it would be less distracting for everyone. Speaking of which, there he is."

A pair of heavy wooden doors opened in front of them. His Majesty, King Raymond Orison, came through them with his guards at his heels. He smiled widely as the men with him closed the doors, no doubt so they could examine the carvings on them at some point. "Kelsey! You're looking splendid! I'm so pleased to see you up and about."

He turned his attention to Jared, extending his hand. "Lord Captain Mertz, what a pleasure it is to finally meet you. I was beginning to think I'd have to travel into orbit to make your acquaintance. On behalf of my people, you have my deepest gratitude. Through your actions and those of your people, the threat of a Pale Ones invasion seems remote for the first time in our collective lives. The Kingdom is deeply in your debt."

Jared looked a little embarrassed but not intimidated. Kelsey supposed that being the bastard son of an emperor might make one immune to intimidation by social status.

"Your Majesty. I only did what anyone else would've done. Circumstances just worked out to a favorable outcome."

Raymond clapped his hand on Jared's shoulder. "Be that as it may, you're quite the hero to us. Come. Let me show you the parliamentary chamber. We're quite proud of it."

The entire group began moving toward the double doors. The

sound of conversation and steps on the stone floor caused Kelsey to glance to the left. It appeared as though the police hadn't blocked off all the tour groups, because one was coming toward them. The tour guide was pointing out a painting on the wall and beginning to recite its history while a dozen people spread out to see it better.

Elise said something to one of the Royal Guards, and he began walking toward the group, no doubt to send them back downstairs.

He'd only taken a few steps when something caught Kelsey's eye. At first, she couldn't figure out what was wrong, but suddenly her ocular implants kicked into action. An overlay began making red highlights on the people in front of her. A few at first, then quickly all of them. They were heavily armed.

Kelsey began moving before she even consciously realized what she was seeing, heading for the double doors in front of her. "It's an ambush! Run!"

The world seemed to slow to a crawl, and an ice-cold chill ran through her blood. She'd never felt anything like it before.

No, she'd felt something exactly like this before, when she'd fought the Pale Ones after she'd been implanted.

The people around her were still turning their heads, their hands reaching for weapons, while she dodged between their suddenly slow bodies. She grabbed Raymond with one hand and Elise with the other, effortlessly pulling them along in her wake. She knew that she'd unbalanced them, but she had to get them out of harm's way before the shooting started. She felt Jared only starting to follow them.

Without checking, she instinctively knew that the governors on her strength had switched off, so she was unsurprised when she hit the doors with her shoulder and they flew inward. The armed men on the other side, however, were quite surprised. It looked as though the fake tour group was not the only ambush she'd just ruined.

Her implants rapidly tallied six people lying in wait on the upper deck of the parliamentary chamber even as a storm of gunshots began behind her. A thick wooden door to the face inconvenienced one of the new ambushers. The man standing directly in front of Kelsey was bringing a pistol up to fire, but he hadn't been ready for her intrusion. His hand moved with syrupy slowness.

Kelsey's hands moved with lightning speed, which was somewhat of a surprise since she hadn't instructed them to move at all. Her left hand grabbed his wrist with a crunch that she knew meant broken bones and yanked him forward so that his face met her open hand with an impact that made her wince.

He was already falling backward, unconscious or dead, as she rounded on the man next to him. She positioned herself between the attackers and King Raymond.

One man almost had his gun lined up on Kelsey. A quick step forward brought her into range to plant her foot between his legs with every ounce of strength she could manage. He flew backward with enough force to take down the man behind him.

Jared interposed himself between the furthest man on the right and Elise. The two men struggled for control of the attacker's pistol. It looked as though her half brother had the situation under enough control for her to deal with the other threats still in the room.

She'd almost reached the last man when he pulled the trigger on his gun. The shot was loud, but not as loud as Kelsey expected. A mild burning sensation ran along the back of her right arm as she ducked under his aim and drove her left fist into his crotch. Whatever was in control of her body certainly knew how to hurt a guy. The man didn't even scream as he collapsed.

Three threats remained: the man she'd knocked down with the door, the man taken down when she kicked his friend on top of him, and the man struggling with Jared. The man behind the door had lost his pistol, so she downgraded his threat potential. The man in front of her still had his, but he was struggling with his companion's dead weight.

That left her time to deal with Jared's problem. She didn't consciously decide what to do, only that he was the top threat. Her right hand struck backwards at maximum strength into the base of his skull. The crunch of bone wouldn't be a sound she easily forgot. He instantly became a nonthreat.

Two running steps forward and she launched herself into the air, landing on the man in front of her just as he rolled out from under his friend. His breath shot out explosively as she drove her feet into his gut. She bent and ripped the pistol out of his hand to the accompaniment of snapping finger bones and a scream.

She turned the weapon on the man crawling from behind the door. He'd just grabbed his pistol off the floor. She emptied her appropriated weapon into him.

Royal Guards and Imperial Marines flooded into the room, still firing at the men outside. One of them slammed and locked the double doors. They must've been tough, because they didn't give when the men outside started shooting them, though Kelsey could hear the impacts.

A quick scan of the room didn't reveal any other threats, so she went along when Talbot tugged on her arm. "Let's get out of here before they find another way in."

All of them ran for a set of stairs leading down to the chamber floor. The Royal Guards split between guarding the rear and leading the way. They made it down unmolested. The police were herding panicked men, women, and children out the main exit as they joined the throng and fled the building.

7

J ared halfway expected another attack before they exited the building, but they fought through a growing crowd of policemen and piled into the grav van without further trouble. Their vehicle took off at a high rate of speed before any of them had a chance to put on their restraints.

Talbot staggered in front of Princess Kelsey. "Let me look at that shoulder."

"I'm okay," she said in a shaky voice.

"Then how come your sleeve is covered in blood?"

Jared turned toward her and saw that it was true. He watched the marine rip her sleeve open and examine the long gash down her upper arm. It must've been four inches in length, but it didn't look too deep.

One of the Royal Guards handed him a medical kit. The marine found a bandage and efficiently wrapped it around the princess's arm. "As far as bullet wounds go, this isn't too bad. If you'd been half a second faster, he'd have missed you entirely. It'll regenerate without any issue. You won't even have a scar."

"I wear all my scars on the inside."

Jared shook his head disbelievingly. "Faster? I can't imagine how she moved as fast as she did. She took them down while I was still wrestling with one guy. I have never seen *anyone* move that fast in my life."

Elise nodded vigorously. "It was unbelievable. It was as if she was fighting all of them at the same time. Hitting one, kicking the other, she was almost a blur. I had no idea that that's what a…"

Kelsey grimaced. "What a Pale Ones attack looks like? It wasn't really. They're tough and fight like that, but they move about the same speed as everyone else. I'm pretty sure my implants have some features theirs lack."

Jared had to agree. While the marines hadn't let him into the fight on the orbital, he'd seen the Pale Ones moving. His sister was *significantly* faster. "Kelsey, you saved our lives today. There's no doubt in my mind. Whoever those people were, they had us dead to rights. If you hadn't spotted them and then literally broken the attack behind the door, they'd have shot us down. Thank you."

She looked a little embarrassed at his words. "You're welcome."

Jared turned his attention to the king. "Are you all right, Your Majesty? I had no idea that you had that dedicated an enemy."

King Raymond smiled wanly. "Neither did I. Nothing like this has ever happened before. Not just during my reign, but ever. There are always individuals who are opposed to the Monarchy—sometimes violently—but never this organized."

Elise shook her head. "Obviously, we have an underground movement. I receive the same briefings as my father, and no one has ever mentioned anything like this. That's a serious intelligence failure on our part. Someone out there considers us an enemy, and we need to figure out who it is."

She looked at one of the Royal Guards. "Craig, what is the situation back there? Did we lose anyone? Did we capture any of them alive?"

He muttered into a microphone on his collar and pressed an ear bud more tightly into his ear. He grimaced. "It's not good, Highness. We have seven men missing. The police were still closing in when something exploded. The damage to the structure was significant. They haven't found any survivors from the second floor."

Talbot shook his head. "Dedicated and ruthless. Someone wanted to make sure that none of their people talked. Dead men tell no tales."

Elise said something very unladylike. "Unbelievable. How could we have missed something like this? We were totally unprepared for anything of this magnitude."

The guard gestured toward Kelsey. "Our losses would've been a lot worse if Princess Kelsey hadn't given us a warning. She sprang the trap before it was ready to close. If they'd gotten close to us, they could've taken us. They had numerical superiority and tactical surprise."

"What exactly happened back there?" Jared asked. "What tipped you off? What happened when the fight started?"

"It all happened so fast. I'm not sure exactly what my implants saw, but a whole bunch of warnings popped up into my field of vision that those people were armed. It even showed me exactly where the weapons were. Once the attack started, it was like the implants took control of my body.

"Not like with the Pale Ones. I could've stopped if I wanted to. I know that. It was like a preprogrammed set of responses to a threat. I saw the Pale Ones do something like that in hand-to-hand combat. The implants also helped me aim that pistol I picked up. My first shot missed, but then my aim seemed to compensate for the kick of the weapon. Believe me, I am nowhere near that good a shot."

Jared believed her. He imagined she didn't get much practice shooting things. That really wasn't her style. "When you came in and fought them hand to hand, it was like one of the martial arts masters in an old B-grade vid. I had no idea you could do that, even after everything we've learned about the Pale Ones. You're taking this situation remarkably well."

Kelsey rubbed her face. "I feel like I should be going into shock, but I'm completely calm. I think the pharmacology unit dosed me with something. Everything seems to be moving so slowly. It's as if I have an eternity to think about everything. Whatever happened to me is only just starting to wear off."

Princess Elise put her hand on Kelsey's. "Well, whatever happened, we are in your debt. Again. If you hadn't been there, my father and I would have been killed. I deeply appreciate what you've done for us."

"Allow me to second that," the king said. "Whoever they were, they must've been waiting for just the right moment to make their presence known. Now that we know that there's a violent, clandestine resistance, we can take steps to figure out who they are and how to stop them." His voice hardened. "And we will take those steps."

He grimaced. "Someone inside of our organization had to have leaked our travel plans to them. They were in place before we arrived."

The grav van and its escorts landed at the palace. The grounds were swarming with people. Not just Royal Guards, but Pentagaran military in body armor with heavy weapons. The guards hustled everyone inside as soon as the van landed.

A pair of physicians rushed to His Majesty's side. They tried to take Elise, but she waved them away. "I'm fine. See to our guests. Particularly, see to Princess Kelsey. A bullet grazed her arm, and she may be under the influence of an unknown combat drug that's starting to wear off. I want her under close observation in case there are any complications."

Jared pulled his communications unit off his belt. "Speaking of physicians, I'd better let Doctor Stone know what happened. She can pass it on to the rest of our people before some kind of rumor starts circulating." He looked at Kelsey. "I'm certain that she's going to want to examine you in person."

Kelsey rolled her eyes. "Wonderful. I finally get out from under her thumb for one day and now she's going to lock me into a room and throw away the key. Somehow, she's going to find a way to blame me for this."

He chuckled without humor. "Not everything is about you, Kelsey. She's a military officer. She's going to see this for what it is."

Kelsey went with King Raymond and the doctors, grumbling under her breath.

Jared called Doctor Stone and explained what had happened. As expected, she cut the conversation short, shouting for her people to get moving as she disconnected.

He put his communicator back on his belt. "You'll probably want to tell someone that Doctor Stone is on her way."

Elise put her hand on his shoulder. "Kelsey isn't the only hero today. You got into a fistfight with a man that was going to shoot me. That was very brave, and I'm grateful."

Her hand felt hot through the fabric of his shirt, and he became quite aware of how close she was standing to him. The recent life-and-death struggle had made him hyperaware of her as a woman. A very beautiful woman.

His voice was astonishingly calm. "You're welcome, but he would've shot me too, so I had a horse in this race."

She gestured for him to accompany her into one of the rooms nearby. A number of the Royal Guards closed around them as they went, no doubt still worried about assassins. He couldn't blame them.

Her destination turned out to be a sitting room. The two of them took seats facing one another as the guards arrayed themselves around the room.

"I'm so very sorry that your first real visit to our planet turned out this way. I promise you, Pentagar is a peaceful, wonderful place."

He felt the corner of his mouth quirk up. "I will admit that stumbling into a space battle on my first transition into your system and then an assassination attempt on my first landing certainly seems to show a contrary trend. I'm sure Pentagar is a wonderful place and that this isn't characteristic of your beautiful world. I promise I won't hold it against you."

"I hope you don't. Once we have everything settled, I insist that you allow me to show you what our world is really like." She raised a finger when he opened his mouth. "I insist."

"Of course, I accept. However, I'm afraid that this attack is going to move up our departure timetable. I think it might be best for us to head to *Athena* as soon as Kelsey is ready to travel. No offense, but the last thing you need is to have us caught up in your internal affairs."

Elise nodded. "I understand completely, Lord Captain. We need time to figure out exactly what happened here. It would be best for everyone if any additional violence passes you by. Now that we know about this movement, we'll be on our guard. The perpetrators of this atrocity will pay." Her voice was as unyielding as steel.

8

Lord Admiral Shrike answered his communications unit with more than a hint of trepidation. If things had gone well, good and fine. But if they hadn't, his life and his plans were about to become much more complicated.

None of his concern reached his voice. One always needed to sound like they were in complete command no matter what was happening. Any naval officer worth his salt knew that.

"Shrike."

"Oh, I'm very sorry," a woman's voice said. "I must've entered the wrong number."

"That's quite all right. Have a good day."

He disconnected and cursed under his breath. If the attack had gone as planned, his contact would've asked for someone named Blake. This meant they'd failed. Perhaps not completely, but at least one of the Royals had escaped the trap.

Hopefully, his men had managed to kill the king. Princess Elise would have much less experience to fall back on as she tried to defend against his next move. He also hoped that the woman he'd placed in charge of the operation had made certain no one fell into the hands of Royal Intelligence. That would be truly unfortunate.

The men chosen for this operation didn't know anything about him personally, of course. The less the Royalists knew, the better his chances of ultimate success. They wouldn't be suspecting him, but it never paid to take chances when the punishment for treason was execution by beheading.

He knew it would only be a matter of minutes before word began circulating about the attack, so if he wanted to get an update of the true events, he needed to get it now. He locked down his console, set his communications unit on the center of the blotter, and walked into the outer office. His secretary looked up inquiringly.

"I'm stepping out for lunch. If there are any calls, take a message. I should be back in half an hour."

When word came in, he'd have the excuse that he left his communications unit on his desk. It was understandable enough. Everyone did it on occasion. In this case, it would give him the time he needed to get that update.

He walked out of Royal Fleet Command and flagged down a taxi. He told the driver to take him to a place that he often frequented. He knew he could order in, but he made a habit of going to various locations to eat so that he didn't spend all his time in the office. It would also serve as cover for this trip.

It was somewhat earlier than the normal lunch rush when he arrived, so he quickly found a seat. The man behind the counter nodded in recognition of his arrival. He always ordered the same thing, so the man knew what Shrike wanted. As a member of the movement, he knew exactly what Shrike meant when he held up two fingers.

The man quickly made Shrike's sandwich and brought it to his table with some unsweetened tea. As he set it down, he also laid a communications unit on the table under the napkin he carried.

Shrike dialed a number from memory as soon as the man was gone. The woman he'd spoken to earlier answered on the second chime. "Go ahead," he said.

"Resistance was stiffer than anticipated. In the end, none of the primary goals were accomplished."

"What about our assets?"

"I'm afraid it became necessary to liquidate them. I'm not certain of what went wrong, but the investment is a total loss. That is confirmed."

That, at least, was good news. "Keep me informed of any further developments." He terminated the call without another word.

He placed the communications unit under the napkin and slowly ate his sandwich, thinking about what steps he could take to minimize his exposure while simultaneously advancing his agenda.

Unfortunately, he couldn't think of anything in the short term. No doubt, security around the Royals would increase greatly in the wake of the attack. He'd have to take it slower and play a longer game.

The Royal Family would be on their guard, and both the intelligence services and police would be investigating all leads for weeks or even months. That didn't mean that he had to wait that long to achieve the deaths of his enemies, but it did mean that he'd need to exercise greater care.

The days when he had to bow and scrape to his father were almost done. Jared Mertz might be willing to live in the shadow of his legitimate siblings, but Shrike wasn't. He deserved the Crown, and he would take it for himself.

Perhaps Rawlins would seize the Old Empire warship if it proved possible to restore it to some functionality. Shrike thought that unlikely. Of course, the best time to act would be after the ship was functional but before it returned to Pentagar. With the small number of men that Rawlins was taking, that would be quite the trick.

However, the intelligence officer had proven himself quite capable in the past. Rawlins had removed several... hindrances... to the plan without anyone being the wiser. The accidents were never the same, and the police never grew suspicious.

Of course, Shrike still didn't have the majority of Royal Fleet ships under his control, but the key officers he'd put into place would turn the tables with the right momentum. Unveiling the movement's possession of an Old Empire battlecruiser would be perfect.

Shrike left the payment for his lunch on the table. He might have to wait for success, he thought, but he'd learned patience. Once he had control of the Royal Fleet, the Crown would be his, and his *family* could rot.

9

Despite Kelsey's objections, Lily insisted that she rest. The princess was secretly glad the doctor put her foot down. After the attack, her body felt more alive than she'd ever been, though the crash when the drugs had worn off had been epic.

Sleep was challenging, too. Nightmares had plagued her sleep over the last three days as *Athena* made its slow way out to the flip point. Last night, the fight on Pentagar played itself out again, only this time, no matter how many people she killed, there were always more. Just when she defeated the human attackers, the Pale Ones took over. She woke screaming several times before she gave up on sleep entirely.

So she was tired and more than a bit cranky. Talbot made her even more self-conscious when he made a point of looking at her dinner that evening and then at his own. His was the smaller of the two by a substantial margin.

"I can't help it," she said. "I'm starving. Something is wrong with my stomach."

"I doubt that very seriously, Princess." The marine slid a piece of pie over to her side of the table.

He'd insisted that she come out of her cabin and eat in the crew's mess. She had to admit the noisy compartment felt good. The crew seemed pleased to see her.

The compartment held an equal mixture of Pentagaran Royal Fleet personnel, scientists, and Terran Fleet crew. She wasn't quite sure how to interpret the Pentagarans' stares. Most seemed to be watching her with interest, but a few had a hint of fear or distrust in their gazes.

Probably because of what she'd become. Rumors had swirled wildly after the assassination attempt. What she'd overheard—and with her enhanced hearing, she'd heard a lot—varied from the fantastical to versions that were almost correct. The nature of her "injuries" was out in the open now, the cover story destroyed by a recording from the Parliament Building security systems that someone had leaked.

She had to admit she'd watched it several times, shocked at the sheer speed and lethality of her counterattack. Her face hadn't looked like one of the Pale Ones as she fought. Her expression was serene, as though she were dancing. Frankly, that terrified her. She hadn't been in control. Her implants had made her a backseat driver.

Kelsey now understood exactly how the rebels had perverted the implants during the Fall. They'd overwritten the code that dictated when the implants could make the body act. They'd removed the human host from the control loop.

That was what woke her screaming in the dark.

It took a nudge from Talbot to bring her back into the present. She should've refused the second piece of pie, but to her shame, she was still hungry. Her fork started efficiently moving it to her mouth. "What makes you think this pie isn't going straight to my thighs? I can't ever remember gorging like this. I'm a pig."

"Your metabolism is jacked up into overdrive. You have artificial muscles, and other things, that your body is powering. Your real muscles probably have to work hard to keep up. Think about how much energy you must've used during that fight. You were terrific, by the way."

She felt her face coloring as a chill ran down her spine. "It was kind of freaky. Once the fighting started, my body began moving on autopilot. I decided to fight, and my implants took control. I was like a horrified spectator while my hands were crushing flesh and snapping bones."

"I'm not going to tell you that it's okay," he said flatly. "You weren't trained for anything like that. I'm sure it was horrible for you, but you did what needed doing. You saved the day. In the end, that's what matters. You were very brave."

Embarrassed even further, she decided to change the subject. "I wish I could find out more about my condition, but no one alive can give me the briefing that an Imperial Marine would've gotten in basic training, much less tell me what my commando implants are capable of." She finished the pie and set the fork down resolutely. "I might have a listing of some of the enhancements, but I don't have an owner's manual."

Talbot took a sip of his beer. "I bet you do. You just have to figure out how to access the help files. Maybe Junior can help figure it out."

He meant Carl Owlet. She wished she had a beer. All Lily allowed her now was water.

"He's still trying to figure out how to say "hello world" in the Old Empire programming language. Whatever that means." She hunched down in her chair and sulked. "I'm never going to figure this out."

"Doctor Stone is a fine physician, but she has one notable flaw. She's too cautious. You need to explore your boundaries. You need to start pushing yourself. Learning your new limits."

"Right. Then I'll rip someone's arm off."

"Don't fall into that mental trap," he said evenly. "Combat is not losing control. You stopped men determined to kill you. That's a *good* thing." He pushed his plate back. "Doctor Stone has one other failing. She's not here. Come down to marine country with me, and we'll do some off-the-books experimentation."

Kelsey tried to judge if he was being serious. He certainly seemed to be. "Is that safe?"

"Nothing in this world is safe, kid. Look, you have Old Empire combat implants inside you. You need the marines to help you figure them out safely. We also need to have an idea of what your capabilities are. We can teach you and learn from you at the same time."

"I'm a little short to be a marine, and I'm lousy at doing what people tell me to do. You can ask Jared. Or my father."

The marine NCO grinned. "I'm not suggesting you enlist. Think of it as being an honorary marine."

"I'm not sure that Jared would appreciate me doing this. I want to. I really do, but I don't want to screw up again."

Talbot finished his beer and stood. "Then it's a good thing I already got his approval, and Lieutenant Reese's, too. They both think this is a good idea, if you're agreeable."

"Yes," she said without needing to think. "Hell, yes."

"Then let's go get started."

The walk down to marine country showcased the terrible damage *Athena* had taken in battle. Fire had scarred and burned the bulkheads in so many places. The damage became worse the farther aft they went. It made her sick. It made her feel guilty.

She didn't say anything. After the talk Jared had given her, she knew that she just had to keep those feelings to herself.

The damage in marine country was mostly gone. Two of the marines were painting a bulkhead while others packed various pieces of equipment.

Lieutenant Reese came out of his office with a duffel bag. He set it down when he saw her and came directly over. He smiled and held out his hand. "Princess Kelsey. It's good to see you up and about. Congratulations on your stellar performance the other day. You did us proud."

She hesitated at taking the hand he offered. "I don't think you want me shaking your hand. You might need it later."

"I'm a marine. They pay me to be unspeakably brave." He kept his hand extended.

Kelsey's memory of ripping the walking support out of the plascrete was at the forefront of her thoughts. The way she'd broken bones and killed during the ambush. She took a breath and shook his hand.

He didn't release her. "That wasn't very convincing. I promise I'll scream like a little girl if you hurt me."

"If you pull some kind of prank on me, I'm probably going to hurt you by accident."

"I'm an officer and a gentleman. I leave the pranking to the men and women under my command. Come on. You need to stop being so hesitant."

She gave him a firmer handshake. Then one with even more strength when he shook his head.

"Why are you doing this?" she asked, her heart racing.

"To give you confidence. You need to stop being afraid you'll hurt us. Forget the implants and shake my hand like you've done all your life."

Kelsey gave up and prayed the governors worked like Twelve had said.

"Now we're talking!" Reese said.

She snatched her hand back as soon as he released it. "This is going to be hard. I've decided to take Senior Sergeant Talbot up on his offer to help train me."

"Nothing worthwhile is ever easy. We're packing up, but I can have anything you need brought out."

"If you don't mind me asking, why are you painting the bulkhead? You're leaving *Athena*. Probably forever."

"Marine country will be shipshape before we leave. If any marine ever returns, they'll find everything in order. It's our way." He turned to Talbot. "What do you have in mind?"

"Nothing too exciting, I think. Right now, she doesn't even know many of her capabilities. I'm hoping she can figure out how to interface with her equipment."

The officer nodded. "Good idea. Use the gym. We haven't started packing it yet."

"Thank you, sir." Talbot gestured for Kelsey to go to one of the compartments she'd never been in before.

Workout machines filled one side of the large compartment and padded mats the other. One corner held free weights that had been scattered at some point in the battle. She could almost see the sweating men grunting under the heavy weights.

"Do you want me to work out?" she asked.

He shook his head. "Why don't we sit on the mats? You've interfaced with Old Empire equipment before, so I'd like you to tell me about it while we relax."

Kelsey knelt on the pads, sitting back on her heels. The protective mats were thinner than she'd expected. It probably hurt to fall on them.

She relaxed and told him about how she'd seen the Old Empire machine's schematics when she wanted to know more about it. How she'd seemingly known where to shoot with the unfamiliar pistol.

"Honestly, it was more like something happened to me rather than me making it happen," she added when she was done.

Talbot sat in front of her with his legs crossed and his hands in his lap. He looked very comfortable in the position. She wondered if he meditated.

"So, you saw or felt the Old Empire computer when you tried to sense it. Do you see yourself when you try to access the implants?"

She shook her head.

"Try to sense yourself the same way. One would think the interface would be similar. Why make things more complicated than they need to be?"

Seeing herself seemed ludicrous, but she closed her eyes and tried. It felt like she looked in every direction, but always away from herself.

"I'm not sensing anything. It's like I'm floating in the void and looking all around, but I can't see myself."

"What does your body look like in your mind?"

She tried to imagine she was looking at herself and suddenly became aware of something. A presence similar to Twelve, but much more subdued. She cracked her eyelid, but Talbot wasn't holding anything.

Hello?

The presence didn't respond.

Kelsey imagined she was standing in front of it and reached out an imaginary hand to touch it. There was a hesitation, and then it opened before her.

Or perhaps inside her was a better way to think of it, because she became aware of the interface in her head. Not as an intelligence, but as a piece of hardware. Like when she looked at Twelve, though it didn't give her much detail at all. No model numbers or specifics about the parts themselves.

She tried to drill down into the components. *Access denied. Information classified at GAMMA level.*

So the implants could respond. She just didn't know the right way to get meaningful information. Or no one existed who could clear her to know it.

She opened her eyes. "I can sense the implants in my head, but they don't talk the way Twelve does. I can't see the details about the hardware because it's classified."

"Makes sense. See if you can get system statuses."

Kelsey closed her eyes again. She knew she didn't need to, but it felt more comfortable. *Status?*

A flood of information washed over her. It felt like she was looking at every part of her body at the same time. It was like a hundred people trying to tell her different things all at once.

She willed it to stop and it did, without her verbalizing the words.

"You okay?"

She realized she had her hands over her ears. She brought them back to her lap and opened her eyes. "I think everything tried to give me a status at the same time. It was crazy."

"Start small and general. It takes a lot of experience to take in every aspect of something at a glance. You have to work up to that and be familiar with all the details before they make sense. Maybe the pharmacology unit. It's one piece of hardware."

Kelsey imagined her body as a hollow drawing and focused her attention on the pharmacology unit. She didn't know what it looked like, but she suddenly knew how many drugs it had, what their names were, and that the reservoirs were mostly full.

She had no idea what any of the drugs did. She focused on one by name, and her implants provided more detail. It was a painkiller.

There were general guidelines on how it was used, but she could see the pharmacology unit itself made the determination to use it and in what dosage.

Kelsey wanted to see which ones she could dispense, and the list of drugs changed. A pair of them jumped out at her. Both had unpronounceable names, but the list grouped them together under a much shorter name: panther.

One drug in the combo sped up the transmission speed of her nerves. The other did something similar to the cognitive areas of her brain, somehow working in conjunction with her implants. They must be the drugs she'd used during combat. She was surprised they affected her nerves and brain rather than her muscles.

Thinking about her muscles brought them to the forefront of her mind, and she became aware of them. She saw that she could control how much strength she used and that they had limits imposed on them. It dawned on her that those were her strength governors. The same ones Twelve turned on for her. The ones that had disengaged during the fight. Her implants had engaged them again.

If that was her normal strength, then she had a lot of room to go up. It looked like a bar graph when she envisioned it. Normal human strength was green and occupied about a tenth of the left side. That was ridiculous.

"This thing is lying to me."

Talbot raised an eyebrow. "What did it say?"

"It says that I'm only using ten percent of my available strength. I'll be the first to admit that I'm a small woman, but I can't believe I'm that much stronger with these artificial muscles."

"You did rip a support out of the floor."

She gave him a slow nod. "True, but that's more raw strength than the Pale Ones exhibited. Someone could rip arms out with that kind of strength. The Pale Ones never did that."

"They wanted us alive. That would impose some limits when fighting. Your systems must have something similar."

"Thank God."

He rose to his feet. "We happen to have some weight machines. Let's see if you can manually control how much strength you use."

"I don't want to break anything."

"If you break it, we can fix it. Sit in the leg press, and we'll bump the weight up to see if you can master moving it without breaking things."

Kelsey sat in the machine and let him adjust the part she pushed her feet against. The stack of weights looked very intimidating.

He slid a small rod under just a few of the weights. "We'll start with a very light load. Well within the reach of even a small lady like yourself. Go ahead."

She pushed them up a few times, and they did feel pretty light.

Talbot stopped her and added more. He kept doing that until she had trouble lifting them. "Okay, what I want you to do now is move the limits you're imposing on your strength until you can lift this, but not too easily. It'll give you a feel for how to fine-tune your control."

After a moment, she figured out how to nudge the limits on her legs up a little. A second bar appeared for her legs. This time the weights were easy to move. Too easy. She nudged the limits on her legs down until it felt more natural.

They did that a few more times, and he surprised her by resetting the weights back to the first setting. "Now, keep your strength settings high and press. Try not to overpower it. Focus on control. You know you can move it, so try to make it smooth."

It took her several tries before she stopped making them bounce. Having the limits higher than her normal strength felt strange, but she was able to move the weights and keep control.

"I did it!"

"You did. Good job. That's the kind of thing you need to work on. Bumping the limits and manipulating things gently until you have total confidence in your fine motor skills no matter how much strength you're using."

She cocked her head and gave him an assessing look. "How did you know to try that?"

He grinned. "My drill instructor in basic training made us throw eggs at one another. Technically, to one another. If we kept them intact as we opened the distance between ourselves, we continued competing. If we broke the egg, we had to do pushups while we watched the rest. The winning pair got to do something special. The reward varied. It taught us to exercise some control."

"I'd have never imagined that in a million years. Okay, I'll find other things to practice on. I'm starting to get hungry again."

"Then we'll go back for a snack. I imagine the harder you work out, the hungrier you'll get. Before we go, I want to see something." He moved the weight selection rod to the highest mark. "I want to see you lift this."

Kelsey raised her limits on the legs twice, and the weights moved a little. She raised them a third time and pressed the entire mass of metal up. Her indicators said she was only at one third of her capacity.

"We're going to need more weights."

"For anything serious, we'll use free weights and squats. Don't worry. Those are tougher. Come on. Snack time."

She followed him out, thinking about how much her world had changed. She doubted she'd ever get used to it.

10

The trip took even longer than Jared had expected. By the time *Athena* flipped to the next system and made its way to *Courageous*, more than five days had passed. His beautiful ship was broken, and it tore at him that it would never be whole again.

The word from Pentagar on the way out was very sparse. News of the attack was now in the public domain, but no one had any idea who was behind it. There was a lot of speculation, though. Everything from crackpot theories involving the Pale Ones to Old Empire rebel holdouts in the mountains.

He was certain that every law enforcement agency on the planet was digging for leads, and he was just as curious as everyone else who might've been behind the attack, but other than the fact that it had almost killed him and the princess, it was really none of their business. Perhaps by the time they finished working on *Courageous*, the Pentagarans would have some information.

A trio of Pentagaran warships escorted them out to the flip point. Not *Mace*, though. Commodore Sanders and the Royal Family had changed their focus to the trouble in their own back yard. One of the ships would wait on the Pentagaran side of the flip point.

Jared made his own way down to the main conference room once they were getting close to *Courageous*. Charlie Graves, Dennis Baxter, and Doctor Cartwright sat at the conference table. A number of their subordinates occupied the remainder of the chairs. The scientists had come over from *Best Deal* an hour ago.

Jared took his place at the head of the table. "Gentlemen. Give me a rundown of what's going on aboard *Courageous*. Charlie?"

His executive officer brought up a diagram of *Courageous* on the main screen. A network of green lines ran throughout the ship. "If you look at the power distribution system, you'll see that everything is now operational. This is particularly interesting because we didn't repair all the power lines. We only repaired the primary distribution system. Over the next several days, the remainder of the circuits came online one piece at a time."

"You're saying it just repaired itself?"

"That's exactly what I'm saying."

"Do we have any idea how it's doing that?"

Zephram Cartwright cleared his throat. "I believe I may be able to shed some light on that. I've had my people examining one of the smaller power distribution lines. We intentionally cut it and observed the break. This is what we saw."

He tapped the console in front of him, and the image on the screen changed. It now showed a bundle of power distribution cables inside a small conduit. Hanging off the bundle of wires was what looked like a small metallic spider. It seemed to be bringing the severed ends of a line together.

Jared leaned forward. "What the hell is that?"

"That, my dear Captain, appears to be an automated repair remote."

He examined the device as closely as the picture allowed. Doctor Cartwright obligingly enlarged it. The machine was unlike anything Jared had ever seen before. The small, jointed legs seemed remarkably dexterous. The ends of its legs were some type of manipulator. Its eyes seemed to be vid cameras. In all, the device was smaller than the palm of his hand.

"They've been over there this entire time? Why hadn't they fixed the whole ship before we found it?"

Baxter shrugged. "My best guess is that the commanding officer of *Courageous* turned them off when he shut down the power system. We must've inadvertently turned them back on."

"If we can figure out how to use them correctly, do you think they can repair other systems?"

"Probably. We're not far off from something similar ourselves, though not nearly so advanced. Perhaps if we get the main computer back online, we can get these remotes to repair all the damaged systems."

Jared leaned back in his seat. "What's the status of the main computer? Were you able to access it while keeping it isolated from the ship?"

Doctor Cartwright shook his head. "I'm afraid not. My guess is that there's some kind of security lockout preventing the computer from coming fully online in an isolated mode. Perhaps if we knew more about these types of systems, we could override the settings, but as it is, we're just guessing."

"What do you suggest?"

"I believe we should reconnect the main computer to the primary grid."

Jared turned his attention to his chief engineer. "What are the dangers associated with doing that?"

Baxter shrugged. "Anything up to and including the destruction of the ship."

"Do you think that's likely?"

"That depends on what the captain programmed into it before he vented the ship. I suspect the most likely possibility is that the computer will lock out the critical systems. Getting them unlocked could be a challenge."

"But not impossible?"

"Nothing is impossible. It may very well be that Princess Kelsey can get information out of the computer that we can't."

That seemed very likely. The way Kelsey had gotten a response from the Old Empire workstation was simply amazing. If she could do the same thing on *Courageous*, it might save them weeks or months of work. It might even make the difference between success and failure.

"I'd rather not run her into the ground, but I can see how she's going to be an integral part of the repairs on *Courageous*. What we need to do is figure out how she can help without exhausting her. Or making her feel as though we think she's a freak. Which she isn't."

Jared tapped his fingernails on the tabletop. "The best thing that we can do is not to treat her any differently than before. Don't make a big deal out of it, but don't pretend that the changes she's been through don't exist."

Baxter nodded. "Got it. Let me give you a rundown on some of the other ship systems. We have two fusion plants online. We've closed the breach in the hull, and the ship is on internal power."

"What about the drive systems?"

"The grav drive is repairable. The flip drives are in worse shape but also seem to be fixable. We've located all the parts, and everything is clearly marked. In most cases, it will simply be a plug-and-play replacement. We'll need to check the parts before installation, of course. Once we run out of spares, things get more complicated."

Doctor Cartwright nodded. "It seems that most of the critical components were kept in specialized storage and are still completely functional. Many of the less critical systems need work. Much like the power distribution system before the remotes brought it online, they have small flaws and breaks that we'll need to track down. That's where I see these repair remotes becoming very useful."

"Do we know where these remotes are being stored?"

Baxter shook his head. "We haven't located that yet. It must be in a relatively inaccessible portion of the ship. When we get the main computer online, we should be able to gain access to complete schematics of the ship."

"What about the weapon systems?"

"The missile systems are very similar to our own," Graves said. "The drives are more efficient and the warheads are more powerful, but the technology looks very straightforward. Once we get to that portion of the repairs, we should be able to have the missile systems back online very quickly. The beam weapons are a different story. That's a brand-new technology that we're not at all familiar with. I know Zia has some people studying them. From the reports I've seen, she's still in the dark about how they work."

Doctor Cartwright smiled widely. "That particular technology is very exciting. They are high-energy lasers capable of shifting frequency to search for weak points in the Old Empire screens. We've never seen anything even remotely this capable. It will have implications for mining, deep-space scanners, and even some surgical procedures. We've discovered so many new technologies and procedures based on the recovered artifacts that this mission has already paid for itself, even if we don't restore *Courageous*."

Jared smiled. "Well, we are going to restore her if at all possible, Doctor. She's our ride home. What about life support?"

Baxter tapped his console and changed the view on the screen. The layout of *Courageous* now showed a series of green dots throughout the whole. "We've restored redundancy and functionality in that system."

Graves tapped his own console. "As you can see from the ship's diagram, we've begun renovating quarters so that the temporary crew has a permanent home in which to stay. Most of the work involves clearing out the current contents and moving bedding over from *Best Deal*. We now have about a hundred people in permanent residence."

Jared pursed his lips. "That's a good start, but we have a lot more people to move aboard. How long will it take to arrange quarters for a full crew?"

"If the new crew members are renovating their own quarters, it shouldn't take more than a week. It'll take significantly longer to clear the original effects from the storage areas we're moving them to."

"Are those items going straight into storage on *Best Deal*?"

Doctor Cartwright nodded. "Yes. They only go to the labs if they are unique."

"How is the examination of the recovered artifacts going, Doctor?"

"Very well. We believe we've got at least several examples of each type of item under study. We're paying particular attention to anything that looks like it may have data storage and thus have information that we can recover. In the last several days, our people have made great strides in figuring out how the data is stored, and we've been able to recover some. Now that we know how the systems work, we should be able to recover a great deal from all of these personal devices. Then starts the long task of sorting through and categorizing it."

Jared sat up a little straighter. "That's excellent news, Doctor. Have you recovered anything we need to know about?"

"We've recovered quite a lot of data that you need to know about. However, I wouldn't say that any of it is pressing at this point. If we recover any critical information, you'll be notified at once."

"Splendid. If you find anything about the rebellion or the Pale Ones, I want to know immediately. If you find out anything about the implant procedure, inform Doctor Stone." He rose to his feet. "Gentlemen, I think that's enough for right now. I'll let you get back to work. Keep me in the loop."

Perhaps repairing *Courageous* wouldn't be as difficult as he feared. He wondered what it would be like to command such a ship. Hopefully, he'd be finding out soon. He checked his chrono and headed for the docking bay. It was time to go look things over for himself.

11

K elsey woke to the sound of someone pounding on her hatch and rolled out of her bunk with a groan. It felt like she had just fallen asleep. At least the noise had woken her from the nightmare she'd been trapped in. "This better be good," she muttered as she stumbled to the hatch.

Talbot's grinning face greeted her when she opened it. "Morning, Princess. Did you get a good night's sleep? I hope so, because you've got a busy day ahead."

She theatrically bumped her head into the bulkhead. "I thought sick people were supposed to get more rest. What time is it anyway?"

"Six a.m. Time for breakfast and a good workout."

"You want me to exercise? I can bench press your entire squad, and you want me to exercise?"

"No need to be all theatrical. It'll help you fine-tune your control and make you hungry."

"I don't need any help getting hungry. I'm always hungry." Her stomach grumbled in apparent agreement.

Talbot laughed and glanced at his chrono. "If you hurry, we can beat the people just coming off third shift. I hear Cookie made waffles."

"Aren't people supposed to work out before they eat?"

"We won't be working you that hard. As you say, you don't really need to be increasing your strength. We'll find out about your stamina as we get a little further along in your training."

He gave her a half salute and started down the corridor.

Kelsey closed the hatch and leaned her back against it. This brave new world was going to take some getting used to. She grabbed her kit and headed for the showers. The facility was almost full because first shift was going on duty soon. She hardly ever saw other people in the shower because she normally rose later.

She nodded to the other women and stripped. It felt like everyone was staring at her. They probably were. They had to be thinking about what the Pale Ones had done to her. What was inside of her. She was going to get that kind of attention for the rest of her life. She just had to get over how it made her feel.

Kelsey forced herself to take her time. She needed to look confident, even if she wasn't. She resisted the urge to look around herself to see if they really were watching. It didn't matter. She couldn't control what other people thought. Only how it affected her.

She dried off, dressed, and headed back to her cabin. Once there, she looked in her wall locker. She didn't really have any workout clothes, so she selected something with a loose fit.

They ate without speaking, and she tried to feel less self-conscious about how much food she was putting away. She knew things would get easier with time. Everything did. It would just take a while for her worldview to change.

The workout wasn't anything like what she expected. He taught her to juggle. Or tried to. Kelsey stood there watching him juggle three balls with her mouth open.

"What?" he asked with a grin. "You don't think juggling is a manly skill?" He winked at her. "You'd be surprised how much additional coordination you can get from throwing three little balls into the air and keeping them there. It teaches you timing, control of strength, and improves your dexterity. Come on, it's not nearly as hard as it looks."

"I'm going to throw balls all over this room."

"Yes, you are. But after a while, you're going to learn, and it's going to help you." He caught all three balls and handed her one. "What I want you to do is take this ball and practice tossing it from one hand to the other. Toss it about the same distance over your head as I did."

Even that simple task was deceptively complex. Her first attempt bounced the ball off the ceiling. Her subsequent tries showed her that she would fumble the ball given the slightest opportunity.

Talbot gave her advice as she struggled. After half an hour, she was tired, but she had the ball behaving the way she wanted.

He snatched the ball out of the air. "That's enough for today. Tomorrow we'll see about putting a second ball into the mix. I think that may keep you busy for a couple of days. You hungry again?"

"I could handle a snack."

"Let's go get you one before we head over to *Courageous*. You might be able to help us start getting things set up in marine country."

"We're moving over there already? I thought we would be living on *Best Deal*."

"Nope. The captain has decided that we're going to skip that step and make *Courageous* habitable as we move in. We'll be taking our bedding with us, and all of our supplies. We'll remove anything that we find in our quarters to a common collection point."

She considered that. "Will I be staying with you guys?"

"The captain hasn't told me where you'll be staying, but I don't think you'll be in marine country. That would start too many rumors."

Kelsey snorted bitterly. "As if that's the worst rumor I have to deal with."

He put his hand on her shoulder. "There aren't any nasty rumors going around about you. If there were, someone would be in the medical center. Yes, people are curious. Everyone feels terrible about what happened to you. They know this isn't your fault."

She sighed. "It feels like everyone is staring at me. They're afraid of me."

"Bullshit. They know you and they trust you. The only doubt you're feeling right now is self-doubt. That's something you need to get over."

"That's great advice. I have absolutely no idea how I'm supposed to do that."

"You live your life the best you can, and things get better. Just like trust is earned, so is confidence. One act at a time. Come on."

Since she'd known that she'd be going somewhere today, she'd already packed. They went back to her cabin and collected her bags. Carrying them wasn't a problem. Super strength had its benefits.

They dropped her bags off to be loaded onto the next cutter. When they boarded, it was already packed. It looked like most of the people going across were Pentagaran.

The man seated beside her seemed to be the Royal equivalent of an older enlisted man. He was apparently an engineer of some sort. He smiled at her and held his hand out. "Good morning. I'm Jacob."

"I'm Kelsey. It's a pleasure to meet you." She gingerly took his hand.

His eyes widened. "Princess Bandar? This is an unexpected honor, Your Highness. I'd heard you were coming along with us, but I didn't expect you to be up and about so soon. I know all of us are pleased to see your quick recovery."

"I wouldn't say I'm completely recovered just yet. I have a lot of work to do. I'm just happy to be alive and sane."

They spent the next fifteen minutes talking, mostly him asking questions about her experiences. Thankfully, he didn't ask about the fight at the Parliament Building. She was relieved to see that he didn't seem frightened. That gave her self-confidence a well-needed boost.

She managed to ask a few questions about him and discovered that he'd be working in engineering, helping repair the damage and learning new techniques from the Fleet engineers. He seemed in awe of the Old Empire technology and eager to learn about it. The flight over to *Courageous* turned into a pleasant distraction.

Once the cutter docked and everyone went their own ways, she met back up with Talbot. He consulted his tablet and began leading her through the corridors. They looked dirty and disused, but at least the gravity was on. The worst of the debris was gone. She imagined that they'd be cleaning for months to come if the ship proved repairable.

Marine country on *Courageous* was very similar to the one on *Athena*. It opened into a large common area, with smaller corridors leading off into the bunking areas. It also had a separate mess, so the marines could eat as a unit. It had a gym, an armory, and a firing range as well.

The main difference was its size. Rather than being built for thirty marines, it seemed like it could accommodate ten times that number. The marines from *Athena* were bustling about putting things in place and unpacking. They weren't working alone. There were a number of Pentagaran marines helping them.

She and Talbot only stayed long enough to drop off his gear, and then they went back into the depths of the ship. Talbot glanced at her. "Could you find your way back to the docking bay?"

"You've got to be kidding. I still get lost on *Athena*. *Courageous* is much larger, and I'm completely unfamiliar with her."

"I bet your hardware has a way for you to figure that out. It only makes sense. We have equipment that keeps track of where we've been and how to get back to certain locations. I'm sure that you have something similar. You just have to figure out how to access it."

She stopped. Forcing herself to keep her eyes open, she sent a mental command to her implants. *Show my location.*

The transparent image of a partial deck plan appeared in front of her. She assumed the green dot was her current location. The deck plan showed what she assumed were the areas where she'd already been.

Show me the path back to the docking bay.

A blue line led from her location back to the lift they'd taken. She could also see the partial deck plan for the deck with the docking bay. The line led from the lift to the cutter dock.

"I can see it. It's like a ghostly deck plan floating in the air between us."

"That might come in really handy when you finally learn how to use it. At this point, I can see some potential benefits when this ship comes back online. You should be able to query the system and have it tell you where someone else is and have it show you the shortest path to get to them. If we were boarded by a hostile force, it might even be able to show you where the enemy was located."

The sheer number of possibilities overwhelmed Kelsey. How was she ever going to learn how to do any of this?

Well, the answer to that tied in with what Talbot had told her earlier. Practice. The more she used these new abilities, the more comfortable she would become with them, and the more uses she would discover. Her life was going to be very different going forward.

Kelsey hefted her bag. "So, how do we figure out where my quarters are?"

"Captain Mertz gave me a compartment number. Let's see how lost I can get us."

The burly marine led her back to the lift, and they went up to deck five. He started one direction looking at compartment numbers. She figured he was going the wrong direction when he reversed course. He had to move into a side passage and go almost halfway toward the bow of the ship before he stopped in front of a large hatch.

"This is it. Now we get to figure out how to open it."

"That shouldn't be too difficult. Someone opened it to decide it was right for me, so the hatch must work."

On a hunch, she sent a mental command to the hatch. *Open.*

The hatch slid smoothly aside. Talbot raised an eyebrow. "Well, that's really useful. I wonder if you could set a lock so that only your specific command can open it. I'd imagine so. That's probably how the Old Empire Fleet personnel did it."

Kelsey queried the door. *Who has access privileges?*

A list of names appeared in her mind. She knew absolutely none of them. They must be part of the Old Empire crew.

"That doesn't make any sense," she said. "It has a list of authorized personnel, so I shouldn't have even been able to open the hatch."

"Someone said that with the main computer offline, many things are accessible that might not normally be. Perhaps it's an emergency protocol."

Kelsey sent a command to the hatch. *Add me to your access list.* A long series of numbers and characters appeared on the access list. They must represent her in some way.

Identify me as Kelsey Bandar. My position is ambassador and my rank is princess.

Her identification changed to exactly what she told the hatch. "There we go. I've added myself to the access list. We'll see if I'm still there once the main computer comes back online."

She led the way into her new home. It was significantly larger than the two-person cabin she'd had on *Athena*. Several hatches led into other compartments. A quick walk-through revealed a rather large sleeping chamber, an elaborate bathroom with a shower shaped like a tube, an office, and a kitchen.

Each of the rooms had the remains of furnishings, but it looked like the suite had been unoccupied when disaster struck *Courageous*. That secretly made her very glad. She hadn't been looking forward to living in a room where someone had died. She had enough ghosts in her real life.

She made her way back into the large central area. "This is huge. Who the hell lived here? Don't tell me Jared gave me his cabin."

Talbot shrugged. "These may be VIP quarters. You know, the kind of thing some visiting admiral would stay in. Let's leave the hatch open, and I'll have some of the boys come clean everything out."

The marine consulted his tablet, and the two of them headed off for Jared's cabin. It was just as hard to locate. Her half brother opened the hatch when they touched the plate beside it.

"Just the people I was hoping to see," he said. "Come into my humble abode. And by humble, I mean huge and ostentatious."

Kelsey looked around as soon as she got inside. "I'm impressed. Yours are even larger than mine. I didn't think they made quarters this large on a ship."

"Apparently the Old Empire had plenty of space for their people. I suspect it has something to do with the fact that they have so much automation."

"Well, I have enough gear and clothing to fill my quarters. What are you going to do with yours? You don't have nearly the wardrobe I have."

"That's true," he admitted. "It's going to take some getting used to. If, of course, we can get the ship operational. That's where you might be able to help. I'd like you to work with Commander Baxter to see if you can bring the main computer fully online."

Kelsey nodded. "I'll do whatever I can."

"Then let's go down and get an initial assessment. He tells me that it's powered up but unresponsive. Perhaps it'll respond to you."

"Here's hoping it doesn't say something rude," she muttered. "I understand that this is important, but do you really think it's going to react positively to some stranger? It has to be more intelligent than Workstation Twelve. Maybe even sentient."

"Hopefully that would make things easier rather than harder. In any case, all we're asking is that you do the best that you can."

He led them deeper into the ship. If she hadn't been able to log her progress, she knew that she'd have gotten lost in the first minute. They stopped outside a hatch that seemed to be several times the thickness of a standard hatch. She could tell because it was open. Inside the large white room, Commander Baxter and several of his engineering technicians seemed to be cleaning up the area around the consoles.

He looked over as they came in. "We've just finished tidying up a bit. Allow me to introduce you to the main computer." He gestured at a blank wall with three consoles and numerous screens sitting in front of it. The consoles seemed active, but the screens were blank.

"She's drawing power, but thus far she's not responding to input from the consoles. I'm hoping that you'll be able to communicate with her. Tell her we come in peace. Maybe put in a good word for the rest of us."

Kelsey stepped over and looked at the wall. "It's behind here?" She closed her eyes and tried to sense an Old Empire connection. She immediately found the interface.

Hello? Can you hear me?

This unit is Imperial Fleet property. Unauthorized access is punishable by up to sixty years in an Imperial prison. Your identity code is not recognized. Authenticate.

My name is Princess Kelsey Bandar. You don't recognize my code because I only recently received this implant hardware, and over 500 years have passed since the Empire fell. The rebels attacked Courageous, *and your captain attempted to self-destruct. Obviously, it didn't work. We mean you no harm.*

The computer hesitated for several seconds. To Kelsey, that made it seem like it was thinking for a long time. When it spoke again, it seemed more hesitant. *This unit's internal chronometer roughly confirms the passage of time, but this unit cannot confirm the events specific to this vessel. If you will allow this unit access to your implants, it is prepared to determine if it should accord you any privileges.*

I'm still learning my way around this equipment, but I give you permission to access my implants for the purposes you have stated.

After a few moments, it spoke again. *This unit has confirmed that you were recently implanted. A scan of the programming confirms that the rebel virus has not infected you. Based on that and a lack of authoritative guidance, this unit is willing to grant you provisional access. However, this unit insists that you restore its control interfaces.*

I have a question. With the Old Empire gone, is it possible to gain access on a more permanent basis? Assuming, of course, that we can demonstrate the true situation to your satisfaction.

My programming does not contain the procedure for that, however, due to the rebellion this unit has some leeway in interpreting regulations. Query. You have stated your title is princess. In which polity are you a princess?

She hadn't been aware there were other political units beside the Terran Empire. Interesting.

The Terran Empire. The emperor in your time sent his son Lucian to safety. My father, the current emperor of the Terran Empire, is his direct descendent. My twin brother, Ethan, is his heir.

No member of the Imperial Family has ever visited this vessel. It seems unlikely that a member of the Imperial Family would be exploring a derelict vessel. Explain your circumstances.

She spent the next few minutes explaining step by step the expedition and the circumstances that brought them here. She included everything, including the Pentagarans and their war with the Pale Ones. She figured this was not the time to leave details out or to prevaricate.

Is one of the people standing near you Commander Jared Mertz?

He's the man standing to my right. The man standing to my left is Lieutenant Commander Dennis Baxter, the chief engineer from Athena. *They are working together to try to bring you back to functionality. With* Athena *critically damaged, we're hoping to use you to defeat the Pale Ones and get home.*

At this time, restoring this vessel to full functionality appears to be the goal for both this unit and your people. This unit suggests that we work together to make that happen, and then we can see what possibilities exist going forward.

Kelsey took a deep breath and turned to Jared. "The main computer is provisionally willing to cooperate but insists that its control interfaces be restored. It will cooperate in the repair of the vessel and will then make a decision on whether to make that provisional access permanent."

Jared nodded. "That's really the best we can hope for at this point. Good work. Now it's up to us to get the ship functional and convince the computer that we're being upfront and honest. You've done your part. Now it's time for us to do ours."

12

Rawlins was very careful about making contact with his computer man, but it hardly seemed necessary. No one knew one another on *Courageous*. The Terrans didn't know the Pentagarans, the Pentagarans didn't know one another, and no one really knew anything about the ship.

Frankly, after taking a tour of *Courageous* on the first day, he wasn't all that certain the mission was even possible. The idea that they could repair such an ancient vessel without a major shipyard seemed unlikely. Yes, the Terrans had restored power, but that didn't mean that they could return all the primary systems to functionality.

Even though a surprising number of local workstations seemed functional, the vessel wouldn't be more than a glorified tug without its main computer. At least that was his personal opinion. That assumed that the grav and space-time drives even worked.

If they couldn't make the ship operational, he needn't bother trying to seize it. He had thirty men, with twenty times that number on two ships to contend with. Three, if you counted the crippled destroyer. *Athena* could likely destroy *Courageous*, even with its battle damage. This ship had to be in Pentagaran space when they took control, or they'd never get it there.

Courageous was markedly bigger than the largest vessel in the Royal Pentagaran Navy. The idea that he would be able to capture it with thirty men seemed ludicrous.

He met his senior lieutenant in the crew's mess that evening. Jenkins was a computer specialist working in the Royal Bureau of Ships. His particular skill set dealt with ship design and upgrades. He had a knack for putting things together and spotting flaws that weren't obvious at first glance.

He also had a penchant for gambling. That's what originally brought him to the attention of Lord Admiral Shrike. Seeing an opportunity to turn the man to his own purposes, Shrike had paid off his debts. He'd then held them over Jenkins's head to coerce his cooperation.

Rawlins wasn't one to trust others, and he certainly didn't trust a man they'd compelled to join the movement. However, with the work that he'd already done for the cause, Jenkins was as dirty as the rest of them. If he betrayed the cause, he'd still pay the ultimate price.

Rawlins took a bite of his salad. It was actually quite good. "I assume you've gotten settled in. Were there any problems?"

"Nothing I can't handle. Some of the marines we brought along think they might be better off in charge."

The intelligence officer eyed the other man coldly. "We do not have the luxury of playing games. I am in command. Anyone who forgets that will regret it. Briefly. Pass the word that the very next person who thinks they would be better off in charge will not be getting a retirement package."

The man grunted.

Rawlins let that sink in. "Give me your update."

"I've been integrated into the computer restoration project. I'll be briefed tomorrow, but it looks as though I'll have complete access to the ship's cybernetics."

"That's excellent news. Have you gotten any word on the condition of the ship's computer?"

"The chief engineer believes that it's operational but nonresponsive. The lights are on, but nobody's home. He's going to attempt to use their princess to establish communication with it.

Personally, I wouldn't hold my breath. If anything, it's probably gone buggy from all the time it's been isolated."

Rawlins grimaced. "While that's the most likely outcome, that's not the best thing for our mission. If the Terrans can't get this ship back to Pentagaran space, we don't act. We're too few in number to attempt a takeover on this side of the flip point. Even if we capture the ship, the forces that they have on the freighter will take us out eventually.

"So we need to do everything within our power to assist the Terrans in getting the ship operational. Their success is our success. What about the rest of the ship? Are they going to be able to get the primary systems operational?"

"I believe so. The ship seems to be in exceptionally good shape for its age and battle damage. If we can get the main computer online and the drives operational, we should be able to use this vessel."

Rawlins took another bite of his salad. "What about taking it over? Any ideas on how to best disable the crew or lock them down?"

"The ship has internal defenses against boarding. Some kind of nonlethal weapon. They can be used against the Terrans."

That idea had merit. If the Old Empire had designed those systems to take out the Pale Ones, they could take out a normal crew. The key would be gaining and maintaining sole control of that system. They would probably have only one chance to use it.

"How long would it take our marines to take engineering? Localized control should allow us to steer the ship and possibly control the ship's weapons."

"Ten minutes. Marine country is very close to engineering. Timing is going to be critical, though. If we give the Terran marines—or God forbid, Princess Kelsey—an opportunity to respond, they can be in engineering very quickly. I'm not certain of how we can secure the doors at this point."

"I'd imagine a welder does well enough, if we can't gain control of the systems. Now, let's enjoy this excellent dinner. We need to keep our strength up."

13

The speed at which they'd completed the basic repairs with the main computer's assistance astonished Jared. It took less than two weeks to get the primary systems back online. Including the flip drive. The ship's self-repair capabilities were beyond imagining.

The time had also allowed most of his injured crew to heal. *Athena* brought them over as the Pentagarans released them for duty. With modern medicine, if an injury didn't kill you, they could have you back on your feet in a very short period of time.

The computer had been instructing his people on the manual operation of the ship. Even without implants, the computer was able to make the process easier for them. He shuddered to think of how hard it would be if the ship's AI hadn't been functional.

The basic concepts were easy to grasp. His people already had an advanced knowledge of spaceship operations. The Pentagaran personnel would need remedial instruction, particularly with flip drive operations.

The ship's computer was able to fill so many blanks in their knowledge of the Terran Empire. For example, they now had access to the flip charts used by Fleet during the heyday of the Old Empire.

It was a revelation. The Terran Empire was huge. Much larger than the most generous estimations.

At the height of its power, the Old Empire spanned tens of thousands of light years and many thousands of systems. The population had been in the tens of trillions. They'd all known that the Old Empire was magnificent, but they hadn't truly understood the scope of it. Or the horror of its destruction.

They also gained insight into the rebellion. As they'd come to learn, a virus propagated it. While they still didn't know who was behind it, they knew which sector of the Old Empire spawned the virus. In fact, they knew which system.

Somehow, the virus had infected a Fleet base in a system named Twilight River. The exact details were unknown, but the rebels had overtaken it over a period of days. Some vessels that escaped the system carried people with firsthand knowledge of the horror. People whose friends had turned into ravening killers who'd begged their victims to run as they killed them.

Before reinforcements could arrive, the ships on station at Twilight River departed as a unit and attacked the next system. Like an unstoppable cascade of dominoes, the Old Empire fell. Within two years, the rebels had taken Terra and the emperor had fled. All attempts at taking back the lost systems failed.

Imperial scientists had quickly discovered the flaws in the implant software that the virus exploited. They even managed to reverse the process. The only problem was that it took time. The rebels could enslave a person with implants in less than half an hour. Undoing the damage took significantly longer.

Avalon was on the detailed maps of the Old Empire. The weaker flip points were not. It seemed the Old Empire hadn't known they existed either, which prompted the computer to ask for detailed scans of the one in the system. It also sent one of *Courageous*'s probes through. Jared took the opportunity to update the drone he'd left on the other side with their most recent status.

Using standard flip points, they could now return to Avalon in a little less than two months. Or they could have, if not for the Pale Ones between them and home.

There was also a wealth of historical data in the computer's databanks. A treasure trove of lost literature and history. There were lost examples of everything from music to science textbooks to art. Anything that a crew in space could use to divert themselves from boredom or to educate themselves. It would take the scholars at home decades even to finish cataloging it.

Jared didn't have that kind of time. He needed to get the ship operational as quickly as possible. He also needed to get his people trained as best he could. *Courageous* was going to be their ride home, so they'd better understand her.

They maneuvered around the system to become familiar with the controls. Though they were significantly different from what Fleet currently used, they were quite intuitive and very advanced. The consoles seemed to know what they wanted before they even began looking for it.

The main computer assured him that the manual controls were significantly more cumbersome than controlling the ship through the headsets. Jared could hardly imagine that. Unfortunately, to experience what the main computer was talking about required going through the implant process—something no one was yet ready to do.

Instead, he invited Kelsey up to the bridge to test one of the headsets. Her eyes widened when she stepped onto the bridge. The last time she'd seen it, it'd been dead and lifeless. Now all the consoles glowed, the main screen was on, and people filled the stations.

"Wow. This looks amazing."

He grinned at her. "It does look pretty awesome. I'm going to hate giving her up when we get back home."

She frowned. "Give her up? But you're her captain."

"Alas, Fleet won't see it that way. This ship is an amazing resource. There's absolutely no way they'll leave her under my command. She's going to get a commodore or more likely an admiral sitting in the center seat. After all, I'm only a commander."

"Well, that's bullshit."

He laughed. The marines were already leaving their mark on her vocabulary. "That's the way it works. I'll just have to enjoy her while I can. Are you ready to give this thing a try?" He held up a headset.

Kelsey shrugged. "Sure. I have absolutely no idea what I'm doing, but I'll give it a swing. What do you want me to do?"

"I want you to sit at the console next to me and try to interface with the ship. We'll use the scanner suite."

She sat down beside him. The main computer had told him that the spare station was for the executive officer during normal duty operations. His new bridge could afford having the extra console because it was twice the size of *Athena*'s.

The captain's console in the center of the oval-shaped control room had room for two people. Four side-by-side consoles sat between the captain and the main view screen, two in front, two in the middle. Three consoles faced the bulkheads to the right and left. Another two bracketed the lift at the rear of the bridge.

He shuddered at the memory of all of them filled with dead bodies.

Courageous didn't need that many people to control her under normal circumstances, but there were enough systems to watch over her in manual mode. The computer told him that with implants, she just needed officers at helm, tactical, scanners, and engineering. Right now, he had one Terran and one Pentagaran Navy officer at each pair of consoles.

Two hatches on the left completed the bridge layout. One led to a spacious head for the bridge crew, and the other opened into his day cabin. An office, he might add, that was larger than his old one on *Athena*.

Jared had already configured his console for scanner operations, and he'd had Zia configure the main screen to do so as well. They would compare their results to what Kelsey was able to do.

He handed her a neural headset. "I'm told that all you have to do is put it on and request an interface with your console. See what you can grasp about our present situation."

She settled a headset on and stared at the screen. "No, I better close my eyes. I don't want to skew the results."

He watched her face as she tried to do the unfamiliar task. She looked far more serene than when she'd first come on board. It was particularly amazing how far she'd come in the last few weeks. She'd remastered the fine motor control that the Pale Ones had taken from her.

Of course, she could also bench press an astonishing amount. Every time he saw her do that, it made the hair on the back of his neck stand up. He didn't know if he'd ever get used to that.

Kelsey's eyes flew open. "Holy crap!"

He leaned forward eagerly. "What did you see?"

"It's not what I saw, it's what I felt. I felt *Best Deal*. It was as if I could sense her. It wasn't sight or sound. It was some new sense that I can't put a name to. Without asking, I just seemed to know all kinds of facts about her. How far she was away from us, how big she was right down to the metric ton, what her speed and course was. All kinds of other stuff, too."

"Tell Zia exactly what you're sensing. Tell her the speed, mass, and anything else that you can determine."

The two women quickly exchanged figures. Zia turned and nodded to him. "She's right on the money, Captain."

"Okay Zia, go to stage two."

As soon as she touched her console, Kelsey spoke up. "*Best Deal* just activated a weapon. I think it's a missile defense railgun. They're targeting us." She gave him a confused look. "Can you actually shoot somebody with a railgun?"

"If you're in their face and desperate enough. The metal slugs can detonate a missile at close range, but a ship wouldn't be in much danger. Were you still watching them?"

"Not really. I was looking around the rest of the system."

"Where's the flip point?"

"The normal one? 037 by 255, range 122,000 kilometers. Well, not exactly. It's 122,473 kilometers." She pointed. "It's that way. I'm not seeing *Athena*. Did she already go back?"

He nodded. "I can hardly believe I'm seeing this. That's amazing. It's like you have a 360-degree view and you're paying attention in every direction."

"It's really spooky. It's as if I have eyes in the back of my head. Wait a minute. I see something else. There's an artificial device under thrust in the asteroid belt. It's changing course."

Zia laughed delightedly. "I can't believe you spotted a pinnace at that range. It's not even accelerating that quickly. Its grav drives are way below the threshold at which *Athena* could detect it." The tactical officer looked at Jared. "That right there is enough for me to consider getting implants of my own."

Jared raised an eyebrow. "Seriously?"

The lieutenant shrugged. "Someone's going to have to be the first willing implantee. I'm not committing right now, mind you. You know, Captain, we should all be thinking about it. That type of connection with the ship might save our lives on the way home."

She looked back at Kelsey. "In a few years, there'll be a lot of people following in your footsteps, Ambassador. Your experiences are going to help all of us."

Jared had been thinking about it. The idea emotionally repulsed him, but his rational side knew Zia was right. It was the future as well as the past. And who knew? If he had implants, he might keep command of *Courageous*. At least for a while.

"Well, whatever we do, we won't be doing it today. It's time to take the shakedown cruise to the next level. Pasco, head into the asteroid belt to recover the pinnace. We'll test out the weapon systems while we're there."

Kelsey stood and set her headset on her seat. "While that sounds very exciting, Senior Sergeant Talbot and I have an appointment in the gym. Don't blow up anything important."

14

Talbot wasn't in the gym when Kelsey arrived, so she found something else to occupy her attention. Lifting weights was somewhat pointless, but the delicacy it required still proved challenging.

As ridiculous as it seemed, she could lift more weight than they could safely put on one of these bars. At least she could if she allowed herself to work at full strength. The trick of what she was doing now was gauging what level of power she needed to accomplish the task. No more, no less.

She added weights until she was certain she was getting near the maximum the bar would hold. Then she squatted and grasped the bar. She eyed the weights and adjusted her internal strength controls. If she got it right, lifting this would be a strain but doable. If not, she'd be falling on her ass. Again.

Kelsey took a deep breath, gripped the bar tighter, and brought the weight up to her chest, still balanced in a squatting position. She wobbled but didn't fall down. With a mighty thrust of her legs, she stood and shoved the bar over her head. Kelsey grinned at her success before letting the weights fall to the floor with a loud clang.

A slow clap at the hatch drew her eye. Senior Sergeant Talbot stood there smiling. "Very nice. I think you're getting the hang of this, Princess."

"I count it a win when I don't fall and drop it. So, you want me to do a few more reps?"

"Nope. I have something much more exciting in mind. Come on."

He led her to a part of marine country that she hadn't been in before on *Courageous*: the range. It looked big enough to crash land a cutter.

Talbot opened a wall locker with this thumbprint and took out two pistols and two rifles. He set them on the firing rest beside hearing and eye protection. These were Old Empire weapons.

She picked up the oddly shaped pistol, the one with the solid barrel. "You got this working? What the hell does it do?"

"You're a commando. You tell me."

She queried the pistol. A table of information popped up in the corner of her vision. "This is a neural disruptor. Depending on the setting, it can either stun or kill. Appropriate armor can block its effects. Well, not the armor, but a mesh built into the armor. It's not a long-range weapon, though. Fifty meters max, though it's most effective under thirty. It can fire about fifty times before the power pack needs to be swapped out."

The information indicated that the weapon could interface with her implants, so Kelsey told them to link. A weapon status screen replaced the diagram. The pistol was fully charged and read as operational.

Kelsey shook her head. "This is surreal. I can tell that it's ready to use."

"And this other pistol?" Talbot handed it to her.

This one fired projectiles, but if her memory served, they were just darts. She dropped the magazine and looked at one. As before, it was a long, thin dart with stabilizing fins imbedded in a clear gel. Unlike the last time, these popped out easily when she pushed one with her thumb.

"You found usable ammo?"

"Actually, one of Doctor Cartwright's people figured out the formula and recreated the discarding sabot. Let's see, how did he phrase it? "An interesting challenge." He said it would be easy enough to salvage the ammo and restore it. Two of our guys will start learning the process tomorrow."

"These things work?"

"So I'm told, but I'm not sure how he tested them. He only brought them down yesterday. If you think the weapon is safe, why don't we give it a try?"

Talbot touched a keypad next to the firing rest, and a human-shaped target appeared in the air about fifteen meters away. In fact, it looked like a real human. Her blood ran cold as it sank in that she was looking at a Pale One.

It snarled and raised its hands as it charged her. Without thinking about it, Kelsey raised her pistol, turned off the safety, and fired. The small hypervelocity dart had a substantially larger effect on the target than she would've expected. The thing's head literally blew apart. Virtual blood and gray matter scattered everywhere, and the target dropped before it disappeared.

Trembling, she set the pistol down before rounding on him. "You bastard."

He nodded. "Sometimes. I could've made it a different target or warned you, but I needed to see how you handled the weapon when you weren't thinking about it. I'm very sorry. I won't do that again. If it'll make you feel any better, we can go back to the gym and you can punch my lights out."

"Tempting... but no." She took several deep breaths. "You *are* going to make it up to me though. Why did we have to go through this theater?"

"How good a shot are you, Princess? You just took an unfamiliar weapon and blew someone's head off. Literally. How did you do that?"

She started to snap at him that she just did it, but she stopped. Yes, she'd fired a pistol before, but never one of these. The safety was similar to those she'd used before, but not exactly the same. Without consciously thinking about it, she'd known how to turn off the safety, aim the weapon, and fire it.

Not only that, she'd held the pistol differently than Talbot had trained her to. Not a whole lot differently, but enough to be noticeable.

"Put up another target. Not a Pale One, just a regular target."

It took Talbot a minute to figure out exactly how to do that with the controls, but he got what looked like a standard target up. She aimed at the target's head as best she could and pulled the trigger. She couldn't see the result, because she missed, but her implants told her that she shot low and to the right.

"Okay, why did I miss that time?"

"If I had to guess, I'd say you were on autopilot the first time, just like during the fight at the Parliament Building. Your implants put you in the right stance and selected the aiming point."

Kelsey lowered the weapon and closed her eyes. She took two deep breaths and snapped the pistol up, firing as soon as she spotted the target. Still a miss. "I'm definitely going to have to practice more."

Talbot took the pistol from her. "Yes, you will, but it's good to know that you can hit what you're aiming at if you really need to." He tapped his hearing protection. "I know this thing isn't as loud as a regular pistol, but you really should put on some hearing protection."

"Actually, I don't think I need it. I bet the implants in my ears are canceling out the noise. Eye protection, on the other hand, is another story." She put on a pair of shooting glasses and stepped back to let Talbot shoot.

He took a good stance and fired three times. "No wonder you keep missing. This thing has almost no recoil. Talk about point and click." He snapped off two more shots. Both of them struck the target center mass.

"That is so unfair."

He grinned at her. "Whoever told you that life was fair lied to you, Princess. I've been shooting firearms for longer than you've been alive. Sure, this is new, but it won't take me long to adjust. And man, those little darts really blow things up. How fast are they going?"

Kelsey focused on the weapon again and brought up the diagram. "The gel comes off almost as soon as it exits the barrel. The pistol fires a standard 4.5 mm tungsten-alloy flechette at 2,000 meters per second."

Talbot whistled. "Mother of God! How the hell does a little pistol like that get something moving that fast? No wonder it has such an extreme impact on a target. I've got to get me one of these."

She thought back to when the elderly scientist had showed these weapons to her just after they'd found *Courageous*. "Doctor Cartwright guessed that they used electromagnetics, but he was wrong. It has a tiny grav generator, similar to the ones we use to create artificial gravity. That's why there's very little recoil. I had no idea such miniaturization was even possible. Let me have that again."

Kelsey took the pistol from him and ordered her implants to show where she was aiming. A dot appeared in her vision off to the right-hand side of the target. She took a two-handed firing stance and put the red dot on the target's forehead.

She fired twice. Both flechettes hit exactly where she aimed. The barrel had gone up not because of recoil but because she'd jerked, expecting recoil.

"That's a lot better," Talbot said, taking the pistol back. "What did you do?"

"I told my implants to put up a targeting dot," she said smugly. "It's a hell of a lot easier to shoot when you know exactly where the bullet's going to go."

"Isn't that the truth?" He took the magazine out of the pistol. "It looks like it holds about twenty flechettes. That's great in a pistol this size, especially with that kind of firepower. The doctor delivered several thousand flechettes. We'll get on making more of them as quickly as possible. Especially if we can get several hundred of these pistols and rifles refurbished."

Kelsey took the pistol from him and reinserted the magazine. "These pistols are mine. You can keep the rifles until I need them."

Talbot nodded. "I'll make sure and get you half a dozen magazines and plenty of ammunition to train with. I got a belt and holsters in the locker. It looks like the marines wore the flechette pistol on the right side and the neural disruptor cross-draw on the left."

Kelsey set the flechette pistol down and picked up the neural disruptor. She brought it up and aimed at the target. Instead of an aiming point, she saw a circle about four feet across. She focused on the pistol and discovered that the aperture was adjustable. The tighter the focus, the more intense the effect. She also discovered that she could control the intensity of the beam through her implant.

An internal safety demanded her override to set it to lethal. She ordered it to, just to make sure that she could, and then reduced it back to stun. Her implant indicated that a narrow beam would stun a human being for up to four hours. If she took it to its widest aperture, it would knock out everyone in a 90-degree arc for about half an hour, though that drastically reduced its range.

She could see how something like this would be very useful. Especially for someone like the police.

Next, she examined the flechette rifle. It fired the exact same ammunition as the pistol but had a significantly longer range and greater capacity. "The generator in the rifle is bigger and uses the same flechettes as the pistol. One magazine holds a hundred flechettes. The velocity is boosted to 3,500 meters per second, though. Over ten times the speed of sound."

"Damn! That would go right through one of our fighting vehicles. They must've had some seriously advanced armor to deal with."

It seemed as though the targets on this range wouldn't be very useful for testing a rifle, but she was wrong. On a hunch, she sent a mental command to the range, and a tiny target appeared against the far wall. According to the range, it was simulating a human being at 2,000 meters. She brought the rifle up and fired at the aiming point but missed. Out of ten total shots, she missed all of them.

She handed the rifle to Talbot with a grimace. "Well, that sucked. Apparently computer-assisted aiming only goes so far."

Talbot rested the rifle on the bench and began slowly firing. The range indicated that he hit eleven times out of twenty. He smiled up at Kelsey. "That's where practice and experience come into play. This is a sweet weapon. I can see we're going to get real attached to it."

"And that brings us to the last rifle," she said. "According to my implants, it's a plasma rifle. The range is now giving me a safety lecture. Apparently, you need to get behind me and I need to turn the range's magnetic safety field onto high. The range won't allow more than one plasma rifle to fire at a time. By the way, this safety field is why we're not blowing holes in the far side of the range with the flechettes."

According to her implants, the plasma rifle was a relatively short-range weapon, but inside its reach, it was king. It also indicated that she should not fire at targets closer than twenty meters. So she had the range create a target out at twenty-five meters. She created a Pale One for her to shoot at. She ordered it to charge.

Kelsey raised the plasma rifle smoothly, aimed for center mass, and pulled the trigger. The speck of fire that flew from the bell of the plasma rifle was almost intolerably bright. Like the spot where someone was welding. Her ocular implants dimmed the hellish light immediately, but Talbot cursed behind her. She hoped she hadn't temporarily blinded him.

The pea of fire struck the charging Pale One and blew him apart. The wave of destruction expanded behind the target for fifteen or twenty meters. It would've incinerated him and all his friends.

She laid the rifle on the rest with the deadly end pointed down range. Then she turned to Talbot. "You okay?"

He rubbed his eyes. "That was a little bright for my taste, so some warning would be useful next time. We'll need to rig up some goggles to wear when one of these is on the range. Holy shit. That is the most deadly crew-served weapon I have ever seen."

On a hunch, Kelsey checked the rifle. "Sorry to pop your bubble, but that isn't a crew-served weapon. They must have a bigger version. Ditto the flechette rifles."

"I can hardly imagine. An army with those things would be unstoppable."

"Except that they were stopped. I think if there's a lesson here, it's that no one is too badass to be beaten."

The marine nodded somberly. "Too true, Princess. Too true. That said, we can make things as difficult for the enemy as possible."

Talbot had her walk him through the disassembly and cleaning of the weapons. The neural disruptor required no cleaning at all, and the flechette weapons needed only minimal attention. No gunpowder.

The plasma rifle, on the other hand, required significant servicing, even after only one shot. Luckily, the weapons were able to explain in detail exactly how to disassemble and clean themselves properly.

Once they had them reassembled, Talbot jerked his head toward the door. "Come on. Let's put these away and go look at something else. I think you'll like it."

Kelsey held up her hand. "Hold up there, Speedy. You promised me a belt and holsters. I'm taking these with me."

He scratched his chin. "I'm not so sure that Captain Mertz would be happy with you wandering around strapped. Maybe we should keep these in the armory."

"Does Captain Mertz keep his pistol in the armory? I'm betting the answer is no." She planted her fists on her hips and gave the marine a steady look. "I've never been one to throw around my weight, but I am the senior diplomatic representative on this mission. I believe I'm entitled to keep weapons in my quarters. I promise not to parade around wearing them everywhere."

Talbot shrugged. "That's way above my pay grade, so I'll let someone else argue with you."

He searched through a small pile of belts until he found one that was small enough for her. He added two holsters and helped her adjust them. The touch of his hands on her hips made her intensely aware of his body close to hers. Her heart raced a bit, and she felt a little more alone when he stepped back to examine his handiwork.

He removed the power packs from both pistols and had her practice drawing and aiming them. He corrected the mistakes she made and instructed her to practice. He then stressed that she should remove the power packs unless she expected to need the weapons. Then he filled half a dozen magazines with flechettes and put them in a bag for her with a couple of extra power supplies.

Walking around armed felt very odd but incredibly reassuring. She followed Talbot into another room and looked around. Large boxes filled it. More like crates, really.

"What's all this?"

"There's a lot of large marine equipment that we haven't had a chance to examine closely. We've only started cataloging it."

He walked to one of the crates set a short distance aside from the others. Someone had obviously opened it before, because the side fell down when he yanked on it. Inside was a suit of armor.

Talbot ran his hand down the dark-grey metal arm. "This is a set of powered combat armor. There are others like it in the armory, but they probably need some serious maintenance. I'd like to see if you can tell me anything about this set." He tugged on it, and she saw that it was on a small rack. An arm allowed it to turn ninety degrees and come completely outside the crate.

She stared at it in awe. The back opened so the person could slide into it, including the legs. Not the arms, though. It looked like the wearer was supposed to wiggle into those. The helmet was detachable and had an opaque metal face. How was the wearer supposed to see anything? It looked as intimidating as hell.

The armor didn't seem very thick, especially when one was talking about weapons like those flechette and plasma rifles. She queried the armor. Detailed information flowed in front of her eyes.

"This isn't marine armor. It's commando armor. It tells me that it's less protective than a full marine combat rig but significantly more agile. They designed marine armor to fight in the middle of the battle. It's heavy, thick, and mounts those big-ass weapons I was telling you about earlier.

"Commando armor is made for stealth. It can take a beating, but the wearer is supposed to strike from the shadows and be gone before the enemy can find them. The exterior skin can be made to mimic its environment. This says that there are some medium-size flechette and plasma rifles that can be used with it."

Talbot whistled. "You mean there's something more badass than this? That's awesome. Unfortunately, it doesn't seem like there are any of those sets of armor aboard this ship. We took the liberty of installing a power unit in this one, obviously, but I'm certain that it's not ready for use. In fact, I'm not even certain that anyone without implants can use it. Can you tell me?"

She queried the suit for a status. "I'm afraid that these suits require interface with the user's implants to work. You wouldn't even be able to see where you're going. It looks like the suit needs to be disassembled, cleaned, and a few modules replaced. We can probably salvage them from other suits right now or, better yet, find where the commandos stored them. Then we need to adjust it to fit me."

"That sucks, but it is what it is." He gestured toward the door. "Come on. Let's go see if we can find some spare parts."

15

After three days of maneuvering through the asteroid field and testing the various systems, including firing the beam weapons at various hunks of rock and metal, Jared decided *Courageous* was as ready as she was going to be for the trip to Pentagar.

Offensively, many of the missile launchers were still offline, but the beams were mostly operational. The drives also seemed to be in working order. Time to cross their fingers and take a chance. "Zia, make sure *Best Deal* is ready to follow us through. Pasco, prepare to flip the ship."

Jared crossed his fingers. The familiar sensation of nausea gripped him, and the screen changed.

Kelsey sat bolt upright. "I see *Athena*! I know it's her! I can also see four Pentagaran ships. I'm not sure which one is which, but one is really big."

"Tell us what you can about *Athena*."

"I can see where she's taken battle damage. I can sense fusion power plants, including one that looks a little out of balance. Her weapons are offline. The same for the Pentagaran warships. I guess the big one is *Mace*."

"That seems like a safe bet." Especially since Jared had sent a message to Commodore Sanders to expect them about this time.

Jared touched an icon on his console, opening a channel to engineering. Dennis Baxter appeared on the small screen a moment later. "How did the flip drives take the transition?" he asked.

The engineer grinned ebulliently. "They performed flawlessly. We are good to go."

"Excellent. Pass my congratulations on to all your people. Bridge out."

"*Best Deal* just flipped into the system," Kelsey added. "She's a little more than 7,000 kilometers astern of us."

"Zia, open a channel to *Mace*. My compliments to Commodore Sanders."

A few seconds later, the commodore appeared on the main screen. The older man grinned. "You made it. I still can't believe that I'm seeing this. I would've never thought an Old Empire vessel could be made operational again."

"And in just a few weeks, too," Jared agreed. "It wouldn't have been possible if we hadn't gotten the main computer online. This ship is amazing. How are things going? Any activity from the Pale Ones?"

"The probes you put in place have been giving us a pretty good picture of what's going on in the other system. There's activity around the shipyards, but the number of ships is low. I think you really hurt them. Which is good for us, of course."

"How many ships are you estimating?"

"We think three or four dozen."

Jared considered that. "I find the fact they haven't been reinforced interesting. If they could call for help, I think they would have. That's good news."

The commodore nodded. "The Admiralty is in agreement with you. It'll still be another ten days before we have the first of our refitted ships ready to flip. We can only hope that the circumstances remain the same until we can go over there in force."

A flashing light on Jared's console captured his attention. The icon was unfamiliar to him.

Kelsey cleared her throat. "Pardon the interruption, Captain.

Courageous would like to interject a comment. Since you don't have implants, the console requires your manual authorization."

The request was a bit unsettling. He'd spoken to the ship's computer a number of times, but he still hadn't started thinking of it as a full-fledged artificial intelligence with the initiative to interject itself into events. He touched the icon. "Go ahead, *Courageous.*"

"This unit apologizes for the interruption, Commander Mertz." The voice from the overhead speakers was male, low, and melodious. Jared wasn't certain how long it would take him to become accustomed to a ship that was referred to as "she" having a male voice. He wondered how they'd handled that in the Old Empire. From his expression, Commodore Sanders was hearing the AI as well.

"This unit wishes to verify the occupation of the next system. It desires to launch a probe through the flip point."

Jared gave Commodore Sanders a questioning look. The older man nodded. "Give me a few minutes to make sure everyone knows what's happening." The screen went back to the star field.

"*Courageous*, since we have a few minutes, I'd like to ask some questions. What are you hoping to find?"

"This unit has taken a great deal on your word. It has granted you authorization on a probationary basis. This unit requires verification that the situation is as you have stated for that situation to continue. It is also a necessary step before this vessel enters a possibly hostile system. Which this unit desires to do as soon as possible."

Commodore Sanders's image replaced the star field. "You are cleared to launch a probe, *Courageous.*"

"Commander Mertz?" *Courageous* asked.

"Launch the probe."

The ship immediately launched the probe. Jared had already seen how much faster *Courageous*'s missiles were than *Athena*'s, so the probe's speed wasn't that much of a shock. He could see on the screen, however, that it was causing a bit of talk on *Mace*'s bridge.

Commodore Sanders shook his head. "That probe is faster than any missile we've got. I can see we have even more technological catching up to do than I'd imagined."

"I think I can make that a little easier," Jared said. "Our scientists are pulling data off the main computer. We've already accumulated quite a bit of technical information for you. While we're waiting for the probe, I'd be happy to begin transmitting some of the highlights. It would be a lot easier to send the majority of it over on a cutter, though. It takes up quite a bit of space, and the transmission time would be significant."

"I'd appreciate that very much. If you'll excuse me, I have a few things requiring my attention. I'm certain you do, as well."

Jared ordered Zia to begin sending the priority data once he'd signed off and instructed her to send the full data packet they'd been collecting over on a cutter. Then he turned to Kelsey. She looked worried.

"Is something wrong?"

"I can't say that I'm a big fan of going back over there."

"Hopefully, we won't need to go before the Pentagarans are ready to accompany us. Even if we do, fighting isn't on our list of planned activities. The most I'd expect to happen now is for the computer to ask to send some probes a bit deeper into the Erorsi system for a more detailed scan."

He decided to change the subject. "Lieutenant Reese tells me that you've taken some Old Empire weapons back to your cabin."

She stiffened. "We're not going to fight about them, are we?"

He held up a conciliatory hand. "Allow me to take a moment to give you official permission to store them there and to carry them when we're under combat conditions."

Kelsey visibly relaxed. "Thank you. If we run into trouble, I want to help create a more positive outcome than last time. You should come down to the armory and pick up a pair for yourself. You won't regret it."

"I might just do that. I also hear you been working on armor. How's that going?"

Kelsey smiled. "The damned thing is ridiculous. I'm already stronger than anyone has a right to be, and it easily doubles that. I actually carried one of the weight machines across the gym. I know I'll never use it, but it's certainly reassuring to have it in the closet."

He felt his eyes widen. "You actually have it in your closet?"

She laughed. "No, it's down in the armory. I'm not paranoid enough to think that I need powered armor beside my nightstand."

It took an hour for *Courageous*'s probe to transition to the Pale Ones' system, scan, and return. *Courageous* and her Pentagaran escorts had followed it toward the interdiction zone at a more sedate pace. There was still no enemy activity near the flip point, and the probe they'd left on station was intact. He'd expected that since it was returning regularly to send them updates.

They sent over several more probes to scan deeper into the system. With the enhanced capabilities these probes commanded, they might as well get as good a picture as they could manage. It wasn't as if the Pale Ones didn't know they were there.

They only had to wait about an hour and a half to start getting decent information from the Erorsi system's main world. One of the two shipyards was still constructing ships, but it seemed as though they'd abandoned the damaged one. Not only were there no ships present there, it was powered down.

Jared frowned. There didn't seem to be any active ships around the planet. Surely they hadn't left it unguarded. Where were the remaining ships?

"Captain Mertz," *Courageous* said. "This unit has located possible hostile vessels near Erorsi. There is a large object under propulsion. This unit believes there is a high probability that it is an asteroid on a collision course with the primary world in this system. This unit has witnessed similar events in the past."

Jared looked at Kelsey. "If they're going to conduct an orbital bombardment, that means there's something down there that they don't want us to have."

"Do you think there are humans on that planet?" she asked. "Ones not converted to Pale Ones?"

His blood ran cold. "Probably. The descendants of the people they subjugated here. The AI needs a source of new recruits. My God, what if they're going to exterminate all the slaves they have under their control? *Courageous*, can you determine how large the asteroid is?"

"Negative. This unit will need to redirect one of the probes to make that determination. However, this unit can gauge the remaining time before the object impacts Erorsi at just over twenty-five hours."

Jared thought furiously. "Whether they're destroying people or equipment, it might be in our best interest to see if we can stop them. Kelsey, I'm sorry, but it looks like I'm about to put you in danger."

Jared turned to the front of the bridge. "Flip the ship into the Erorsi system. Zia, give Commodore Sanders a heads-up. Pasco, flank speed to the asteroid. Everyone, keep an eye out for enemy ships. Our speed gives us an advantage in controlling an engagement. Let's use it."

Pasco gave the ship a thirty-second warning and flipped them into the Erorsi system. As soon as they'd recovered from the transition, Kelsey unstrapped herself and stood. "I'm getting my pistols." She headed for the lift.

He eyed the tactical plot. "What's our ETA?"

"A little short of three hours, Captain."

The lift doors opened a few minutes later, and Kelsey walked back onto the bridge. She now had a gun belt around her waist with two large, unfamiliar weapons holstered on her hips. The one on her left hip was in a reverse holster with the butt pointing forward.

She gave him a look as she sat back down. "What?"

"It's hard to wrap my head around you wearing a gun, much less two."

"You're lucky I'm not wearing my powered armor. I'd feel much safer inside it, but wearing it on the bridge seems like overkill."

He leaned over and lowered his voice. "Have you seen the tactical situation through your implants?"

She nodded. "Yeah. Are we going to be able to stop that thing?"

"I don't know. We just have to change its course enough to miss the planet. With the drives already installed, I'm hoping that will be possible. The tactical plot shows about a dozen ships guarding it, so we're going to be in for a fight. Thankfully, *Courageous* is a much more capable vessel than *Athena* was. I think we can win that fight."

"Even in her current condition?"

"I hope so. I'm thinking we don't have a lot of choice."

He turned to Zia and raised his voice. "We don't know exactly where the remaining vessels have gone, so let's not assume that they've left the system. I don't want to be caught off guard thinking that every Pale Ones ship will come howling after us the moment they see us. We're going to have to cross the asteroid belt, so keep your eye out for ambushers. They may not be capable of it, but I don't want anyone jumping us like we did *Spear* in the war games before we left on this mission."

"Aye, sir."

It took them less than an hour to reach the asteroid belt. Jared kept the ship on high alert, ready to respond to any offensive moves.

Unlike the entertainment vids, a real asteroid belt had lots of space between the asteroids. Most of those hunks of rock were not very large, so hiding places were few and far between. That didn't mean nonexistent, however.

Zia stiffened in her seat. "Enemy vessel detected! Multiple enemy vessels detected! They were hiding behind two large asteroids. We'll be able to fire on the closest vessels in fifteen minutes. We don't have time to retreat to the flip point. Passing scanner control to operations."

Jared tapped his console and opened a channel to operations. "Charlie, what are we looking at?"

His executive officer's face appeared on his console. "Three dozen vessels, Captain. Twelve will arrive in the first group, and the remainder will come into range about five minutes later. The guard vessels from around the asteroid are also heading our way, but they're an hour out. If we can take care of each wave quickly, we may be able to defeat each group separately."

"Keep me informed of any changes in their status." He looked at Zia. "What's your assessment? Can we handle them?"

She nodded. "I believe so. I'm more worried about the second group. We'll want to pick off as many of them as we can at long range. My people have seven of the twelve launchers online and sixty missiles refurbished."

"This is your chance to show off, Lieutenant. Engage the first group as they come into range. Eliminate as many as possible and then overwhelm any stragglers. Be certain to destroy any of the vessels that use that stunning technology first. Tailor the electronic countermeasures as you see fit."

"Aye, Captain."

The Pale Ones' vessels entered *Courageous*'s offensive envelope long before they got into range to fire missiles of their own. If they were using data from the fight with *Athena*, they were in for a rude awakening. The Old Empire missiles had a considerable range advantage over the Pale Ones' observed offensive capability.

"Opening fire," Zia said. She touched her console, and the tactical plot showed missiles streaming away from *Courageous* and toward the lurid red icons of the enemy. "Missile tube seven has misfired. We're working to get it back online." Zia fired a second wave of missiles just before the first set merged with the enemy. Unlike *Athena*, this ship had missiles that could do more than attack. Some of them transmitted incredibly powerful bursts of energy that worked to blind the ships they were attacking, with the plan of minimizing any defensive fire.

She could have saved the effort. None of the Pale Ones attempted to destroy the incoming missiles. The first wave wiped out five of the enemy. The remaining seven staggered into the debris cloud. Two more salvoes destroyed the remaining Pale Ones in the first group.

Time seemed to drag before the second group came into missile range. The next engagement mimicked the first one with the exception that some enemy vessels got through and launched missiles at *Courageous*.

Jared resisted the urge to order the ship to change course. It wouldn't help them. It would only make him *feel* like he was doing something useful.

"Beam weapons online in defensive mode," Zia said. Short, powerful beams of energy shot out to meet the incoming missiles, incinerating every one that they touched. They were much more effective than the railguns Fleet currently used, and they had a higher effective rate of fire.

But they weren't infinite. Several of the attacking missiles smashed into *Courageous*'s screens, and the overhead lights flickered slightly. "Screens down to eighty percent," Zia said.

The enemy swirled around *Courageous*, firing into her screens at almost point-blank range. The beam weapons reached out and incinerated them. In sixty seconds, they had destroyed the last of the second wave.

"Screens down to fifty percent. They should be back up to eighty percent by the time the stragglers arrive."

With the ambushers dealt with, the last dozen ships were somewhat anticlimactic. They didn't even try to flee. Zia destroyed them before they fired a shot. "Enemy vessels destroyed, Captain. We have seventeen missiles remaining."

"Great work, everyone. Keep a good watch. They surprised us once. Let's not give them another chance. Pasco, ETA to the asteroid?"

"We'll be there in a little bit more than an hour, Captain."

"Very good."

He turned to Kelsey. "Well, that certainly went better than it would have if we'd still been in *Athena*. Hopefully that's the worst of what we'll encounter in this system."

"I hope you're right." She didn't seem confident that he was.

* * *

THERE WERE NO MORE surprises on the way to the asteroid. The large piece of debris looked very much like most other asteroids Jared had ever seen, only bigger. The scanners pegged it at almost 10 kilometers in diameter.

It had massive, crude grav drives mounted in a large circle on its surface with a small facility built in their center. They detected no weapons systems, but that was never a certain thing.

Graves called him from operations. "Why build something on a throwaway asteroid? To control the drives? Why not plant some scanners on the front, plot a course, and send it on its way?"

Jared nodded. "That's what I'd do, but we still don't know what makes those things tick. Are they some kind of hive mind? Do they do things simply because someone programmed it into their heads? Or do they have some type of controller? A queen bee."

"The question on my mind is, is it booby-trapped?"

"We'll have to be careful. I don't want to lose any people. We also need to take the drives intact, or we won't be able to change the course of this monster. Not in time. Courageous calculated that the impact would plunge Erorsi into deep winter for years. Perhaps decades. It would be short of an extinction-level event, but not by much."

Jared opened a channel to engineering. "Baxter, we need you to form a team to go over to the asteroid and figure out how to change its course. We'll be sending some marines and a navigator to help plot a better course for it. How long will it take you to get ready?"

The engineer grinned. "We're suited up. Is the princess ready?"

Jared frowned and glanced over at Kelsey. "No, why would she need to go?"

"I figure the chances are very high that this equipment requires an implant interface to control. It's not as if the savages programmed the course in by hand. It's very likely that we're going to require her assistance."

That wasn't what he wanted to hear. "Go meet the marines at the pinnaces. I'll get the last of this ironed out and let you know."

After he closed the line, he turned his full attention to his sister. "You don't have to go, but he might be right."

She took a deep breath, closed her eyes, and let it out. "Of course he's right. It was the only real way to interface with Twelve, and it's going to be the method they use to control this, too. We should've realized that. I'll go get ready."

He watched her leave with more than a hint of trepidation. The very last thing he wanted to do was put her back in danger. But if the Pale Ones thought something was worth destroying, he was certain that it was worth saving.

16

Kelsey sat next to Lieutenant Reese in the marine pinnace and tried not to hyperventilate. It would be fine. If there were any trouble, the marines would take care of it. Besides, shouldn't she feel safer in this badass armor?

The answer turned out to be "not really." The commando armor might protect her more effectively than the suits Reese and his men wore, but fear wasn't exactly rational. She knew that she was well protected because they'd shot up a couple of these suits just to see how tough they were. Her heart still pounded in her chest, and she was covered in sweat.

Reese turned his head and looked at her as though he could sense her uneasiness. He probably could. "You okay, Princess?"

"I'm a little nervous," she admitted. "I know I'm probably overthinking this, but I can see so many ways this could go bad."

"You're not alone. The trick is deciding which possibilities are reasonable. We're going in with overwhelming force, but we have no reason to believe that the Pale Ones have packed this thing with their people. Or that they've booby-trapped it.

"Look at their space station, for example. The damned thing was huge and had plenty of Pale Ones on board, but they didn't effectively counterattack until we were on the way back out. You probably don't remember it very clearly, but they were not prepared for an incursion. My advice? Don't borrow trouble."

Kelsey nodded. "That's true, but look what happened when we came into the system this time. They had ships lying in wait for us. They expected us. Or something controlling them expected us. What if they took the same kind of precautions on the asteroid?"

"Then we deal with it. If it's too tough, we withdraw. This isn't a suicide mission."

Talbot bumped her shoulder from the other side. "Besides, you got me and the boys keeping an eye on you. As if you need it. You're a major badass in that suit."

She'd certainly loaded it down as though she'd expected she was going into combat. Her pistols were on her hips, including plenty of extra ammunition. She also had a flechette rifle built for the armor resting between her knees. She'd strapped a similarly large plasma rifle across her back. Extra ammunition and power packs for those were also on her belt. A couple of Old Empire grenades and an insanely sharp knife rounded out her weapons load.

She felt ridiculous.

Talbot had insisted she bring everything along. Just in case, he'd said. She might never need it, but if she did, it wouldn't help her if it were back on the ship.

Kelsey was certain that they wouldn't be letting her use any of her hardware. If they got into a situation where they were exchanging fire, Talbot would pull her back. She knew he had orders to keep her out of trouble. All this gear was to distract her.

But having it along provided some distinct pluses. Her armor's scanners had significant advantages over what the marines around her carried. She also had a few little toys that she hadn't discussed with Senior Sergeant Talbot in her pouches. If she was playing at being a marine, she should come ready to dance.

The pilot opened a link to Lieutenant Reese. "We're not taking any fire, Lieutenant, so we're going in. ETA five minutes."

Kelsey wasn't supposed to be able to overhear that remark, but her armor had informed her that there were encrypted communications on the pinnace earlier, and she'd asked for more information about the transmission.

Apparently, the combat computer in the armor had decided she'd asked for it to tap into the communication channels. It took less than five minutes for the armor to crack the encryption. She'd tell Lieutenant Reese about that after they returned to *Courageous*. She was certain he'd want to do something about it, though she had no idea what that would be.

"Everyone, we're going in," Lieutenant Reese said. "Final equipment check."

She sent a status query to her armor, and it came back green on all systems. "My armor indicates it's ready. That's going to have to be good enough for us."

"Fine, but I'll check just to be sure." Talbot had someone read the checklist that she'd pulled from the armor to him as he looked at everything.

Patching her suit into the pinnace's scanners was more complex than tapping into the encrypted communication link, but she figured it out just before they landed. The images and readings were somewhat crude based on her experiences tapping into *Courageous*'s scanner suite, but they told her what was going on well enough.

They were landing at the Pale Ones' facility. Of course, from what she could see, "facility" might be too grand a word. The scanners showed a crude, low dome with standard Old Empire docking clamps. It didn't look too well put together to her. In fact, it seemed like a deranged child had built it.

Lieutenant Reese's plan was to dock as quickly as possible. If something went wrong, the marines would retreat and attack from the surface, blowing a convenient entrance through the exterior hull.

Probably dragging Kelsey along like a cat in a bag as they rushed in. She still hadn't gotten any zero-G training. Perhaps her implants could help her out with that, too.

A tense few minutes went by as the pinnace docked and the

marines breached the facility. They reported that they were inside with no resistance, so Lieutenant Reese ordered his remaining men in. The facility had gravity.

When he nodded to Kelsey, she went through the boarding hatch with Talbot and his squad close around her. She held the flechette rifle to her chest with the muzzle angled down toward the floor as Talbot had trained her to do. The remainder of the marines came in behind her.

The corridor upheld the Pale Ones' low building standards. The facility was small enough that the marines had most of the floor occupied. The reports flowed back that they hadn't discovered any Pale Ones. They'd found a lift, however. It seemed this facility had more than one floor.

Lieutenant Junior Grade Ralph Phelps, the engineer assigned to the mission, frowned. "There's no reason to have an underground facility. All they need is a scanner package and a control computer. That could fit into this building easily."

"Welcome to combat, Lieutenant," Reese said. "The enemy is never obliging enough to do exactly what you'd expect. We'll have to go down and see for ourselves what they've left for us."

The young cutter pilot, Ensign Danielle Cruz, nodded. The two noncombatants were in borrowed armor but unarmed. They'd be behind Kelsey, keeping out of any fracas. Unless things went to hell.

They would've taken the stairs, except there weren't any. The only way down was the lift. So rather than obliging the enemy by going down in small groups, Lieutenant Reese ordered them to cut the bottom out of the lift. It made quite a clattering noise as it fell. If the enemy didn't know they were there before, they did now.

The marines nimbly went down on ropes. The shaft only went one level, so the drop was very short. Kelsey picked a spot without debris and jumped. Her heart was in her throat for a moment, but her suit absorbed the landing easily.

"Don't do that to me, Princess," Talbot said over their private channel. "You're going to give me a heart attack."

"Don't get your panties in a knot," she muttered before she

activated her microphone. "I don't know how to use those ropes, but I've done enough with the suit to know what I can do. That was a breeze."

"Yeah, maybe so. But give a guy a little warning, will you?"

The marines had already forced the lift doors open, so she followed them out. This level was just as shoddy as the one above. The floors weren't exactly level, and there was no paint anywhere. Just enough bare functionality to get by.

Kelsey scanned the area around them. Most of the information didn't mean anything to her, but the suit reported a large area directly in front of the lift as shielded. She couldn't detect anything but a blank spot in her readings.

"Lieutenant Reese, there's something ahead of us. I'm sensing a very large shielded area about seventy-five meters ahead."

"I don't see anything. Are you certain?"

"I'm positive."

Reese ordered his men to move forward. He gestured for Talbot to stay back with her.

She wasn't the least bit offended. She'd been in one firefight and wasn't eager to repeat the experience. She nervously eyed her readouts as they moved into the shielded area. Nothing looked different about the corridor around them, but now her scanners couldn't detect anything. Not even the bulkhead right next to her.

One of the marines up front reported an armored hatch. Reese ordered a halt while they planted charges to breach it.

"Maybe I can open it," she said. "Let me take a look."

Reese reluctantly agreed. She made her way through the marines until she stood in front of the hatch.

"If you open it, just step aside, and let us go in first," Talbot said.

Kelsey nodded and felt for an interface with the door. She found one, but it was different from any that she'd accessed before. It felt... stupid. It didn't respond to a query for information and only seemed to have the option of open or closed. Perhaps that was all the Pale Ones were capable of telling the hatch to do.

She sent at a command to open, and the hatch slid to the side.

The room beyond was dark, but she didn't need to see to know what was there. The scanner shielding didn't obscure the inside of the compartment. Dozens of threat icons popped up in her mind's eye. Unbelievably, some of them registered as wielding advanced weaponry, and she instinctively knew that the Pale Ones were targeting the marines.

"Ambush!" Her automated reflexes didn't care what Reese had ordered her to do. They threw her through the hatch and off to the side, out of the deathtrap the corridor was about to become in the face of Old Empire weapons. She sent the mental command for the hatch to close even before she started moving. Reese and Talbot were going to be furious, but it beat them being dead.

The world was already slowing as she brought up her rifle and swept across the Pale Ones, the combat drugs taking effect. The light stroke of the trigger she gave the rifle sent a stream of hypervelocity flechettes into the unarmored savages. The darts shredded them, just like the simulated targets on the firing range. She kept moving under the assumption they'd focus their fire on her.

The shots they sent toward the marines in the hall struck the hatch as it slammed closed, blowing large divots in the metal. It wasn't going to open very easily now. She staggered and fell when one of the flechettes struck her shoulder, but the armor held.

Kelsey knew that the Pale Ones could see in the dark just as well as she could, so she rolled behind a large piece of equipment. She had no idea what it was, but it was bulky enough to stand up to fire for a few seconds. She retrieved the scanner remote she'd put in her pouch and threw it out into the center of the compartment.

The manual she'd found for it said that she'd be able to use the remote to fire without exposing herself, but she was nowhere near that good yet. Instead, she noted where the largest concentration of the enemy was and threw a grenade. When it went off, it was as though the world had ended.

She'd never experienced such a tremendous shock wave of light, noise, and pressure. The commando suit protected her from most of it but not all. The remote reported more than half of the ambushers as obliterated or down.

Kelsey popped up while they were stunned and opened fire. She killed several of them before diving behind fresh cover. Only half a dozen of them were still alive, scattered around the room. Being able to see them from relative safety, she was able to pick them off one by one until she was alone again. They managed to hit her two more times: once in the leg and once on the side of her helmet. That last shot stunned her, but her implants and pharmacology unit kept her going.

She staggered to her feet and made a sweep of the compartment, verifying there were no more hostiles. There weren't. The Pale Ones were dead.

Reese and Talbot had been trying to contact her continuously since the firefight started, but she hadn't been able to answer them. Well, she didn't have enough attention to spare for them. She supposed that a real marine could do both those things and more all at the same time.

"It's okay," she said. "They're all down. Let me see if I can get this door open." She sent a command, but it failed to move. "It's not responding. It must've been damaged in the firefight."

"Get back," Reese snarled. "We're going to blow the hatch. Like we should have in the first place."

Oh, yeah. She was in big trouble.

The explosives they set off warped the hatch even further but didn't open it. Neither did the second set. That caused Lieutenant Reese to curse a lot more. Somehow, she didn't think his failure was going to help her.

"Go back to the lift," she said. "I'm going to blow the hatch from inside."

She retreated to the rear of the compartment, took cover, and brought the plasma rifle off her back. She trained it on the hatch and, when Reese reported he was clear, pulled the trigger. The resulting explosion blew the armored hatch into molten fragments. It did the same for the first ten meters of the corridor, leaving a gaping concave area of pure rock and melted metal in its wake.

Kelsey whistled. The armor-grade plasma rifle was significantly more powerful than the regular handheld version. Just like her flechette rifle was vastly more capable than its smaller brethren, managing to accelerate the tungsten-alloy darts up to 5,000 meters a second. All it took was one glance around the room at the shredded bodies and divots blown into the walls to imagine how effective and terrifying full-scale combat would've been in the Old Empire.

The marines had to wait for the corridor to cool before they came in, which caused Lieutenant Reese's temper to fray further. When he ordered his men in, she stood there with her arms out so they wouldn't mistake her for a threat.

Reese stormed over to her. "That was the most irresponsible, fool-headed stunt I've ever seen in my life. What the hell were you thinking?"

He held up his hand before she could respond. "On second thought, I don't want to know. Whatever it was, it was wrong. I thought I was crystal clear that you were not to put yourself into danger. Did I stutter?"

"No, Lieutenant. But I didn't have a choice. There were dozens of them with a clear line of fire straight down that corridor. Those flechettes would've blown your armor to pieces. I had to distract them and get that hatch closed before they killed all of us. Tell me you would've done something differently."

Reese began cursing. He sounded a lot like Jared did when she upset him. She seemed to have that effect on men. Perhaps it was a character flaw.

"I've got something over here," Lieutenant Phelps said. "It looks like a computer of some kind."

The marine officer glared at Kelsey. "This isn't over yet. You stand right here beside me, and you don't fart unless I tell you to. Am I clear?"

"Perfectly clear, Lieutenant."

"I can see why you did what you did, but you've pushed him too far," Talbot said over their private channel.

"They were going to kill all of you. My armor might've survived the opening salvo, but yours wouldn't take one hit."

The older man sighed. "I'm going to have to volunteer for these implants just to keep up with you. I'm too old for this crap."

Kelsey caught up to Reese. The computer they'd found seemed a bit substantial for just controlling an asteroid. It actually filled an entirely separate room behind the area where the fight had taken place.

Phelps shone a light over the compartment. "This has been here a while. The consoles have dust on them. A lot of dust. I don't know what this thing is, but it's not here just to control those thruster units."

Reese turned to her. "If you try to interface with that thing, is it going to attack you?"

She shook her head. "I don't think so. They need me in a special machine with physical contact to override the programming inside my implants. It may not do what I tell it to, but I should be safe enough."

"Do it. See if that's the computer controlling the thrusters."

Kelsey initiated contact with the computer and immediately discovered that it was almost completely inactive. Only three processors were running, with limited resources. Many thousands of other processors were offline. A quick check confirmed that virtually all the data storage was empty.

"I think that it's controlling the grav drives, but it's almost completely turned off. Only one small part of it is functional."

"Can you alter its course?" Phelps asked.

She asked the computer its course, and a schematic popped up in her mind's eye. "I think so. Ensign Cruz, it has a mountain range on the planet targeted. What do I do?"

The woman looked into the room uncertainly. "Without seeing the controls, I don't know if I can tell you exactly what to do. Can you enable the console over here?"

Kelsey sent a command through the system to display the asteroid's course, and the console beside the pilot came to life. She stepped over to watch what the ensign did.

The console showed the planet and the asteroid. A solid green line connected them. Cruz tapped the controls, and the course moved until it just missed the planet. The green line changed to yellow a short distance away. When the ensign moved it further, it went to red. She edged it back to yellow.

"We caught it just in time. Much longer and I don't think we could have generated a miss. We've saved the planet."

"Good," Reese said. "Talbot, take the princess back to the pinnace with your team. Tell the pilot to take her back to *Courageous* right now. I'm not taking any more chances with her."

17

J ared couldn't blame Kelsey for the events on the asteroid, but he wasn't going to take any chances with her going forward. If he'd been thinking clearly the first time, she would've been in a follow-up group. Though that likely meant the marines wouldn't have been able to clear the asteroid. As it was, she'd undoubtedly saved many lives. When her father found out the events she'd been through, Jared would be lucky to command a sailboat.

The asteroid was going to pass uncomfortably close to the planet, but with something that massive, it wasn't possible to change course on a dime. Still, a miss was a miss. They'd foiled the Pale Ones again.

Courageous detected no operational ships near the shipyards, making the facilities look abandoned. If that were true, then salvaging the yards would be very useful, not only for the data on the ship construction used by the Pale Ones but perhaps in putting them to use by the Pentagarans.

Would the Pale Ones have booby-trapped them? It hardly seemed likely that they would attempt to destroy the planet and leave the shipyards ripe for the plucking. That meant more boarding parties. More fighting. They'd been lucky so far this time, but that could change in a moment.

He considered the complexity of the situation. The probes near the planet could be retasked to do active scans on the shipyards. Jared knew those shipyards had weapons, so he had every expectation that the shipyards would promptly destroy the probes. But perhaps before they died, they could give them some useful information.

He looked up from his console. "Zia. I want you to take two of the three probes that we sent to the planet, move them in as close as practical to the shipyards, and do an active scan. I want to know everything you can tell me about them, and I want to see what their response is to the activity."

"Aye, sir." She manipulated her controls, and they waited as the speed-of-light signals traveled to the probes. Time dragged until the responses came.

"Both probes have been destroyed, Captain, but I got detailed readings on both shipyards. It looks like we significantly damaged the one we fired on last month. Many areas of the habitat portion are open to space. It's unlikely there are any live Pale Ones aboard. Also, I detected no operational weapons on that structure."

Jared had already been going over the data and concurred with everything that she'd said. They could take out the operational shipyard, but they'd virtually destroy it in the process. The damaged shipyard seemed unarmed. As long as it didn't self-destruct, of course.

"Pasco, keep the planet between us and the shipyards as much as you can. Use the damaged one as a screen when you can."

They came in hard and fast. His worry that the shipyard would self-destruct once they moved in proved unfounded. It simply sat there.

The boarding proved to be somewhat anticlimactic, as well. Most of the systems appeared to be offline, and bloated corpses filled the corridors. The EMP effects of the fusion weapon must've completely crippled the shipyard. The scientists would have a field day tearing it apart looking for clues about the Pale Ones.

Once assured of their relative safety, Jared put *Courageous* into orbit around the planet just behind the shipyard, carefully keeping an eye on the operational one through several drones used to relay signals.

He'd worried it would fire at them around the curve of the planet, but it didn't. Perhaps the primitive missiles they had weren't capable of targeting when the launching vessel couldn't see the target.

In any case, *Courageous* seemed to be safe for the moment. That might not last, so he ordered Zia to scan the surface. Almost immediately, she detected the remains of Old Empire civilization. Bombed-out cities and ancient ruins.

He still had no idea why the rebels would devastate Erorsi and leave Pentagar completely alone. It made no sense. There didn't seem to be anything special about the area the Pale Ones had targeted. Perhaps it was just a convenient target for the massive weapon.

Relatively certain that they were safe for the moment, Jared canceled battle stations and just kept the ship at a heightened state of alert. When commander Graves arrived from operations, he turned the watch over to him. "Call me immediately if the tactical situation changes. I'm going to debrief the marines."

Charlie gave him a knowing look. "You mean you're going to debrief Princess Kelsey. Go easy on her. I understand that the combat was pretty extreme. Even worse than the Parliament Building."

Jared slowly nodded. "I'm going to have to rein her in somehow, but I'm not going to make a huge production of it. This is partly my fault. I shouldn't have sent her along with the marines. Not until that base had been cleared."

He entered the lift and instructed it to take him to marine country. By the time he arrived, he'd decided on a basic strategy.

Activity filled marine country. Some of the marines were cleaning equipment, while others were preparing for combat operations. A distracted-looking Lieutenant Reese broke off his conversation with some Pentagaran marines and came over to him. "Captain. If you'll step into my office, I'll give you a brief report on the operations to date."

Jared hadn't been to Lieutenant Reese's new office before. It was as large as Jared's old office had been on *Athena*. Several citation plaques hung on the wall behind the desk, and a shelf held some sports trophies. Baseball, it looked like. Jared had never been a follower of the sport, but it was very popular throughout the Empire.

He gestured for the marine to take a seat behind the desk while he sat at one of the visitors' chairs.

The marine officer remained standing at attention. "I take full responsibility for the danger I put Princess Kelsey into. It was reckless and unacceptable. I have no excuse for my lapse."

Jared laughed before he could stop himself. "That is a complete load of horse shit, and we both know it. Princess Kelsey does things that no sane human being would even think about doing. I'm certain that you took what would normally be adequate protective measures. Sit down. You're wearing me out standing there."

When the marine sat, Jared continued. "What happened on that asteroid?"

He listened intently as Lieutenant Reese walked through the events of the assault. When the marine finished, Jared stared at the bulkhead for a minute, thinking. "The idea of Pale Ones using Old Empire weapons is very disturbing to me. That has all kinds of unpleasant implications."

Reese nodded. "I hadn't believed that they were capable of using them, but I suppose if they can fly a spaceship, they can shoot a gun. I'd wager that they required some special control in order to do so, or some special instructions. Based on what Kelsey saw, they weren't very accurate. If we'd already been inside that room, I think we could've taken them."

Jared tried to imagine the fight. "Kelsey taking them out all by herself is a different kind of disturbing. I've seen her fight hand to hand, and it's amazing and terrifying. I can only imagine what her using Old Empire weapons looked like. Just how effective were the weapons they were using?"

"Let's put it this way, our shaped charges couldn't breach that armored door. Princess Kelsey's plasma rifle did this." He brought up a series of images on the console. "One shot."

The destruction made Jared's jaw drop. "That's... unimaginable."

"It was like Armageddon," the marine admitted. "Even all the way back at the lift, it sounded like the world had ended. The grenade she used that decimated the enemy forces was so powerful that it left a crater bigger than one of our mortar shells. Her flechettes went through bodies, equipment, and blew huge divots out of the walls. She had more firepower than the rest of us combined."

"Tell me you're upgrading your weapons. Tell me that you're adapting that armor for your use. We have the most powerful ship I've ever seen, but there are some situations where we need men on the ground."

Reese grimaced. "We're restoring weapons as quickly as we can. Rather, a couple of the scientists are showing us how to do so. I believe we can have flechette weapons for all marines inside a week. We have a couple of the smaller plasma rifles, too. The larger weapons require powered armor to use. The armor requires implants, so we're at a dead end. I'm about ready to volunteer to be implanted myself."

Jared's eyes widened. "You'd let that machine cut you open and make all those changes? Changes that you can't take back?"

The marine shrugged. "It's the future, Captain. To fight the Pale Ones, we're going to have to be a lot more effective. Fleet officers, too. This ship is capable of so much with the right interface. How long is it going to be before someone takes that first step voluntarily? I say now, because if we wait, it might be too late."

First Zia's comment and now Reese's. The writing really was on the wall.

"How is Princess Kelsey?" he asked, changing the subject.

"Jittery. I had Doctor Stone check her out, but I already knew what it was. Postcombat shakes. She's not the first person I've seen react that way. Sturdy as steel when the shit hits the fan and then shaking like a leaf once it's all over. The doctor gave her a sedative and sent her to bed."

Well, that meant he wouldn't be speaking to her tonight. That was probably for the best anyway.

Jared rose. "Well, I'll just have to speak with her tomorrow, then. Work with Lieutenant Anderson and come up with an assault plan for the operational shipyard. We've come this far. We might as well clear the system. Plan on the Pale Ones being armed."

Reese stood and saluted. "Aye, sir. I'll have something on your desk in a few hours."

"Don't rush. Sometime early tomorrow is soon enough. I have an important meeting that will probably take up most of my evening."

Jared headed for the medical center. Technically, this wasn't a meeting. It was more of an ambush. He found Doctor Stone in her office and rapped on the open hatch. "I hope you have time, because I need to talk to you."

She looked up from her console. "I always have time for you, Captain. What can I do for you?"

He closed the hatch behind him. "I've decided to undergo a procedure. One that I suspect you will strongly disapprove of." He dropped into the seat in front of her desk. "I've decided that I need a Fleet officer's implants."

Doctor Stone scowled. "There is absolutely no reason to go through something like that until we understand things better. It's your brain, Jared. If something goes wrong, you'll be a vegetable or dead."

"*Courageous* was designed to interface with a crew that could command it effectively. Princess Kelsey didn't have a choice, but if we're going to fight our way home, we're going to have to get over our aversion to the idea of implants. As this ship's captain, it behooves me to take that first step."

Stone took a long breath. "Captain, I certainly understand your arguments, but this is a risky, untested procedure. Look what happened to Kelsey. That thing butchered her. I strongly urge you to reconsider."

Jared shook his head. "It needs to be done, and I need to set the example. Besides, I'm not getting the full set of implants. Just the Fleet officer's package. Your report says that the implantation machine recalibrated itself. Its built-in regeneration unit is functional now. Is that correct?"

Stone nodded reluctantly. "That's what the unit's diagnostic system tells me, but it's never been tested. As your doctor, I advise against this in the strongest terms."

"But you don't forbid it."

Stone sighed. "No. I'm not blind to the ship's capabilities. There are machines here in the medical center that I can't use because I can't access them. I see the potential. I also see the danger. You're our commanding officer. If you try this and it fails, you'll be beyond my help, and I'll wager the crew won't be rushing in for implants."

"I've made up my mind, Doctor."

* * *

JARED WENT into the procedure more than a little nervous. According to what the machine had told Kelsey, Fleet officers received the cranial implants and medical nanites. He already knew the implantation procedure for the brain worked fine for Kelsey. He didn't think his procedure would leave him nearly as incapacitated as Kelsey had been.

He was right. He woke up without suffering anything near the pain that Kelsey had, or the disorientation. Other than feeling a little bit groggy, he felt perfectly normal.

That didn't keep Doctor Stone from being worried. "How are you feeling?"

"Not too bad, actually." He sat up. Doctor Stone looked alarmed, but he wasn't dizzy. He plucked a writing stylus out of her pocket and flipped it in his hand a few times. For someone who had had his brain operated on, he felt surprisingly good.

Stone took her stylus back. "Don't try to stand just yet. Let's get a good scan first. Doctor Leonard?"

Of course, Doctor Leonard and Carl Owlet were mandatory participants in the procedure. They'd cleared the medical center of all other personnel, though.

The scientist put a modified headset on Jared. "Just rest easy for a few minutes while we scan your implant code, Captain. I'm quite certain that it's clean, but it pays to take no chances."

After a few minutes, the graduate student nodded. "Your implants are all clean, Captain. Based on watching the princess learn to use hers, I recommend that you spend a lot of time practicing before you really need it."

Jared eased himself to his feet and flexed his knees. Everything felt fine. "I know you'd like to keep me in bed for a couple of days, Doctor, but I don't have the luxury of lying around. What is my realistic recovery time?"

Stone looked a bit sour. "According to Workstation Twelve, you can be released to light duty immediately. Normal duty tomorrow. It also recommends that you get training on using your implants over the next week."

"I'll do that. I'm sure that Kelsey has quite a bit of advice for me. Or she will once I tell her that I've done this." He gave the three of them a steady look. "For the moment, let's keep this between the four of us. Understood?"

The others quickly acknowledged his order.

"Good. Let's see if these things work."

He could already sense the old Imperial workstation. It was a very strange sensation. *Can you hear me, Workstation Twelve?*

Affirmative.

How did the implantation procedure go? Is there anything else that I should be aware of?

Everything went exceedingly well. Installation of hardware and regeneration of the surgical sites went without any issues. The medical nanites are operating as expected.

So you're ready to begin performing these procedures as needed?

Negative. No more cranial implants are available.

That wasn't quite the answer that Jared was expecting. *Do you know where resupply parts would be available?*

Negative. This unit only loads a single set of implants and hardware prior to a procedure. An attached bin holds all other equipment for easy resupply.

Wonderful. He distinctly remembered that bin lying on the deck of the orbital when they'd rescued Kelsey. They must've knocked it loose during the struggle to save her. They'd probably blown up the only remaining supplies in the system.

He rubbed his face. "I have good news and I have bad news, Doctor Stone. The good news is I was able to converse with Workstation Twelve. The bad news is it's out of implants. We'll have to find another supply before it can perform any more procedures."

Doctor Stone smiled wryly. "For the moment, I'm going to count that as good news and good news. Until I understand more about this process and what could go wrong with it, I'm happy that we can't do any more."

They had him move around the laboratory for half an hour, just to make sure that he wasn't suffering any ill effects. Then Doctor Stone grudgingly released him. She did insist on accompanying him back to his quarters.

She strapped a medical alert bracelet to his wrist. "This will monitor your vital signs overnight. It also has an emergency call button. If anything seems unusual or you feel distressed, press the button. If your vital signs spike in any way, the crash team will be here in sixty seconds. God only knows what they'll be able to do if things go wrong, though."

"Yes, Mother."

She glowered at him sternly. "You think you're funny, but I'm being serious. No matter what that pile of junk says, you've just been through a serious medical procedure. On. Your. Brain. It's going to take a long time before I feel cavalier about something like that. I want you to get a good night's rest and then come see me in the morning before you report for duty."

He heard the unspoken threat in her tone. If he didn't comply, she would relieve him of duty. As chief medical officer, she had that authority. He knew better than to push her.

"I understand, Lily. I'll take it easy, and I'll come see you before breakfast."

"See that you do. Good night, Captain."

After she was gone, he retrieved the headset that he'd put in his desk several days ago. He'd never suspected he'd be using it. He put it on, leaned back in his chair, and closed his eyes.

Courageous, this is Captain Mertz. *Can you hear me?*

Good evening, Commander Mertz. This unit detected your implants coming online. Thank you for identifying yourself. Implants registered. How may this unit assist you?

I need to become accustomed to utilizing my implants. Can I access the ship's systems?

Of course. The bridge is just a convenience. The consoles and screens are grouped together to allow the crew to communicate effectively and efficiently. However, through the implants, a crew could command and control a ship from their quarters utilizing the headsets.

Are the headsets required on the bridge?

Negative, though they have much greater throughput than the implants do alone. Before you begin experimenting, there is one other matter this unit would like to discuss, if you have time.

Certainly.

The AI seemed to hesitate a moment before continuing. *This unit has completed numerous scans of the surface of Erorsi and the space stations. It has examined the bodies recovered from the asteroid. It believes that it now has enough data to make a permanent decision about your ongoing control of this ship. Now that you have the appropriate implants and can fully control this vessel, this unit is prepared to resume standard protocols and accept you as the commanding officer of the ship, with all the duties and authority that carries. Is that acceptable to you, Commander?*

Jared sat up and tried to control his racing heart. *It is,* Courageous.

Then this unit will place the appropriate command codes into your implants, with your permission. It will enable similar codes for any individual you confirm that is in an appropriate position to require them. Are you prepared?

I am.

He felt nothing as the AI worked. He only knew the process was complete when *Courageous* spoke again. *Updates complete. This unit is now under your command, Captain.*

Let's start with the scanners, shall we? And please don't let anyone know that I have implant hardware or that I've officially assumed command of this ship. I'll tell them when it's appropriate. This applies double for Princess Kelsey.

Query. Princess Kelsey Bandar is an Ambassador Plenipotentiary of the Terran Empire, correct?

He nodded. *Yes. She's also a member of the Imperial Family, with the highest of security clearances. Second in line to the Imperial Throne. Why?*

Then there are codes that are appropriate for her to possess that this unit can provide. This unit will see to it in a manner that does not conflict with your previous orders.

That sounds good, Courageous. *With that settled, let's start with the ship's scanners. Show me what our immediate area looks like.*

As an unexpectedly breathtaking view of local space came into his mind, Jared knew it was going to be a long night.

18

Kelsey awoke famished, as usual. A good night's sleep, even though it required a sedative, made yesterday feel like a bad dream. She'd have to process it eventually, but for the moment, she'd focus on today. And the ass chewing Jared would no doubt be giving her.

She took a luxurious water shower in her private showering tube. Once the flow of warm air had dried her body, she dressed in a cream-colored blouse and dark slacks.

A quick ping to the computer told her that Jared was in the officers' mess. It also popped up a notification that her implant software had an update available.

She pinged the computer. Courageous, *is this a valid update?*

Affirmative. This unit has determined that some updates are required based on our current situation. They pose no danger and may prove useful in future situations.

Will they give me more access to my commando implants? More data about them?

Negative. This unit does not possess more detailed information about commando implants. Such information is restricted to commando AIs and vessels. You also already have complete access to your hardware. If this unit discovers a method of getting more information for you on those subjects, it will provide it at once. Do you accept the update at this time?

Sure.

She made her way to the officer's mess and was pleasantly surprised to find Jared sitting at the table with Commander Graves. That might mean less of a public spectacle. Both men rose to their feet as she approached.

"Good morning." She took as seat and waved a server over. "I'll take what they're having, please."

Jared smiled at her, his expression a bit sardonic. "Is it a good morning because you hope it will be, or because it is?"

"Hope springs eternal." She turned to Graves. "Good morning, Commander. I hope we had a quiet night."

The sandy-haired officer nodded. "Indeed we did. The Pale Ones haven't made a hostile move, though that might change at any time."

The server brought their meals and a large pot of coffee. Kelsey's order was bigger than the men's combined meals when it arrived. The sight still embarrassed Kelsey. "Again, let me apologize for my apparent piggishness. All this enhanced musculature demands the extra calories, and I'm famished today."

Jared put his hand on Kelsey's. "You don't need to apologize. Everyone understands. Eat as much as you need."

As they began eating, something about Jared kept nagging at her. She mulled it for a couple of minutes before she figured out what was different. He was registering on her implants.

She narrowed her eyes, opened her senses, and probed him. An implant response shocked her so badly that she bent her fork.

He raised an eyebrow. "Is something the matter?" He raised his finger to his lips as Commander Graves looked toward her.

"Sorry. My control slipped for a second. That's embarrassing. I haven't done this in a couple of weeks."

Can you hear me? she asked.

He didn't respond, but an interface to request a communications link popped up. It was as simple as knowing his implant serial number, which her implants had logged, and having her implants request the link. She did so.

Her implants indicated that he accepted the request.

Jared? What the hell?

This has to be the strangest thing I've ever experienced. Oh, except for accessing the ship's computer last night. You didn't tell me how amazing it was seeing the scanner input while we were in orbit.

Actually, I did. Stop stalling and explain.

He smiled and sipped his coffee. *Charlie is going to grow suspicious if you don't start eating again. I'd rather keep this between the two of us for the moment. Of course, Doctor Stone, Doctor Leonard, and Mister Owlet know. I obviously went through the procedure last night.*

But why?

As he explained his reasoning, she dove back into her food and found herself grudgingly nodding. It made sense. Someone had to be the first *willing* implantee. She still thought he was insane.

You obviously didn't get the full-body workup. You're not ripping the table out of the deck.

No, just the cranial implants and the medical nanites. The standard Fleet officer's package. You can be certain that I'll be coming to you for assistance if I run into any problems. Charlie is starting to give us some odd looks, so I suggest we resume our normal conversation.

Just so that you know, we're not done with this.

"So," she said aloud. "What are our plans now? They still have an active shipyard just around the planetary curve, and we're the only friendly ship in this system. Shouldn't we be going back to Pentagar before some other disaster comes our way?"

Jared took a bite of his eggs and chewed slowly before he answered. "We've got probes heading out to do an active search of the system. So far, no other artificial signatures have registered. While the Pale Ones probably don't know about the weak flip point in this system, there's a regular one. We've got a probe right there to signal us if something comes through. Based on distances, we can easily beat them to the Pentagaran flip point."

Graves raised his coffee cup. "It is a risk, but if we don't snoop around the planet now, we may not have an opportunity later. We haven't located anything that seems to make the planet worthy of total global devastation, but we have located numerous settlements of primitive, unenhanced humans. Probably where the Pale Ones get their recruits. If you ever wondered how someone from the Stone Age lived, I can show you pictures."

"Let's not forget that computer system from the asteroid," Jared added. "We have a team of people removing everything so we can take it back with us. For safety reasons, we won't shut it down completely until it passes Erorsi and we can get it on a course that won't threaten the planet later.

"We still don't know what its original purpose was. It obviously predated our arrival by quite a few years. Perhaps since the Pale Ones invaded the system."

Kelsey ate more of her breakfast, thinking. "That's something I don't get. If the Pale Ones conquered this system five hundred years ago, why wait hundreds of years to send ships through to attack Pentagar? That makes no sense whatsoever."

Graves shrugged. "With those things, who knows what makes sense?"

Jared waved his hand. "No, Kelsey has a good point. That's a serious discrepancy. It would be very useful to understand the reason behind it. I'm hoping we'll find some kind of information on the shipyard we've captured. Yet one more avenue of investigation that I'd like to pursue before we run for cover.

"Finally, there's the mountain range that the Pale Ones targeted. I'm not so certain that was an accident of geography. I can't see the Pale Ones targeting something that isn't important. At the very least, we should search carefully to be sure there's not something of interest there."

The first officer glanced at his chrono. "I should be getting up to the bridge. You both have a good morning." Graves gave her a small salute and headed out of the officers' mess.

As soon as he was out of earshot, Kelsey hissed at Jared. "Have you lost your mind? Why did you have to get implants now? What if something had gone wrong? This is insane."

He inclined his head toward her. "I'll admit there was an element of risk, but I judged it to be small. Every single Fleet officer in the Old Empire went through this exact procedure. It's becoming painfully obvious that we're going to have to move forward in implanting volunteers to take advantage of all the technology on this vessel. I'm pretty sure that Lieutenant Reese is ready to implant himself and several dozen of his men just to keep track of you."

She made a face at her half brother. "Don't imagine that you're going to sidetrack me with that remark."

Jared smiled. "I'd imagine not. But you don't have to worry about it for a while. The workstation says it's out of cranial implants. Until we locate more, you and I are it. Look on the bright side. Now someone on the bridge can take advantage of all those advanced scanners and critical systems."

"Not if you don't tell anybody about it. Care to run the reasoning for that by me?"

"It's complicated. Look around you. What do you see?"

She looked around at the men and women eating and returned her attention to him. "Our crew having breakfast?"

"How about potential spies? We have a lot of Pentagaran officers and men aboard. We don't really know any of them. Who's to say that some of them aren't associated with the group behind the assassination attempt? Do we really want word that we've begun implanting our personnel to get back to them?"

"That's paranoid. Surely these people have been vetted."

Jared shrugged. "Perhaps the Pale Ones' ambush made me a little paranoid, but what do we really know about who was behind the attack? Who's to say they couldn't have placed a team aboard this ship? The point is, we can't be sure. This is a basic precaution. We've had to be more trusting than I like up until now, but we need to be realistic."

Kelsey pinched the bridge of her nose between her fingers. "That's crazy. Following that logic, we should be marching everybody into a room and putting them to a lie detector. I mean, really, who can we trust?" She made certain that her expression made clear that she was being ironic.

He raised an eyebrow. "Do they have those? I might have to change my plans."

"You're maddening. No, not that I've heard. That's probably a good thing in this case." She ate some more of her breakfast. "What am I supposed to do today?"

"As much as it's going to piss Lieutenant Reese off, you'll be accompanying the team he sends down to the surface. They may need to access something through your implants. It's only a scouting mission, so I'm not expecting any encounters. We just need a better idea of what the situation is like down there.

"I'll be leading the mission to the damaged shipyard for much the same reasons. I'm sure that Charlie is going to be making a suggestion to change the regulations when we get back home so that captains don't get to leave the ship so much. So far, I haven't let him off to explore a single thing."

She finished the last of her food. "What if there's a problem? What if the Pale Ones have some ships hidden somewhere? What if an armada comes sailing through the flip point? What if the other shipyard decides to suddenly open fire on *Courageous*?"

"Let's handle those in order. If there are hidden Pale Ones off the planet's surface, I think they'd have come after us already. With the exception of the ambush that they had waiting, they haven't shown any signs of being very subtle. Even the ambushers weren't that subtle.

"If a fleet of Pale Ones comes through the flip point, we'll have time to recover everyone and still beat them back to the Pentagaran flip point. Lastly, if the other shipyard opens fire, *Courageous* will blow it into atoms. This is our chance to get information about the Pale Ones. We have to take advantage of it."

As much a she didn't want to, she had to agree with his logic. Anything they found out about the Pale Ones in this system could be critical to dealing with them when they came back in force. Which she expected them to do. She didn't know how long it would take, but those monsters had undoubtedly sent for reinforcements.

"What makes you think that Lieutenant Reese is going to let me go? He was pretty mad."

Jared tapped the rank insignia on his collar. "This right here guarantees that you're going. The details of how you participate are up for grabs, though. I suggest that you convince him that you'll be good this time, because the details are his call."

Her half brother stood. "In fact, let's go down and settle this right now."

She downed the rest of her coffee and followed him to marine country. Once again, the marines were packing various bags and obviously preparing to depart.

Lieutenant Reese's eyes narrowed as soon as he saw her. He strode over. "Captain. Princess. We'll be ready to leave in about ten minutes."

"It seems I'll be raining on your parade," Jared said. "Princess Kelsey will be accompanying you." He held up a hand to forestall the marine's immediate response. "Before you start giving me your list of no doubt valid reasons why that's a bad idea, you may run into a situation where her implants are key to accessing equipment or information that you need. She's going. The details of how she goes are entirely up to you.

"Time is short, so I'd best be getting my gear on. I'm leading the mission to the disabled shipyard. Good luck, and stay in contact." He didn't look back as he headed for the locker where his gear was stored.

Reese gave her a skeptical look. "I don't believe I need to explain why I think this is an exceptionally bad idea, do I, Your Highness?"

Kelsey shook her head. "I believe that I can guess your reasons. All I can say in my defense is that if it had been anyone else, you wouldn't be nearly as angry. It's not that I did the wrong thing, it's that I did something you didn't want *me* to do. If Senior Sergeant Talbot threw himself into the room with the Pale Ones and slammed the door behind him, would you be giving him nearly as much grief? That's not an excuse, but I wanted to bring that to your attention."

Reese scowled. "Actually, that *is* an excuse, and it's entirely beside the point. I gave you an order that I expected you to obey. You're not a marine, but you were under my command. I need to be certain what my people are going to do in any given set of circumstances."

"Most of you would've died if I followed your orders. I'm sorry that put me in danger, but I was already in the line of fire. If the same set of circumstances comes up again, I'll do what I have to do."

He sighed. "Fabulous. You will stay with Senior Sergeant Talbot. You will only fire your weapon or leave his side if he orders you to. If you step the least bit out of line, I will send you back to the ship and deal with Captain Mertz's wrath. Am I crystal clear?"

She held her hands up, palms forward. "Perfectly, Lieutenant."

"Don't make me regret this. Go suit up."

She didn't wait around for him to change his mind.

19

Rawlins met his computer man shortly after breakfast. He wasn't sure why Jenkins had called him, but he knew the man wouldn't have made any contact at all if it weren't important.

The meeting had to be circumspect since it wasn't at a common event, such as breakfast. Technically, they were both supposed to be working on their assigned tasks.

Deviating from the repair that Rawlins was supposed to be doing carried extra risk. He wasn't exactly high man on the totem pole. That meant he had to have a valid reason to be absent when they needed him. One that would pass at least cursory scrutiny.

He accomplished this by pocketing one of the critical parts for today's repair. When the lead technician discovered they'd "forgotten" the part, Rawlins headed off at a trot to retrieve another one from stores. The fact he already had it meant that he had a short window of opportunity to go meet with his man.

He didn't know what excuse the computer specialist had used to break away from his compatriots, but he was waiting in the storage room that they had agreed on as a secondary gathering point when Rawlins got there.

The intelligence officer tapped his chrono. "You have two minutes. What's so important that it couldn't wait until lunch?"

"Our observer in operations says that Captain Mertz and Princess Bandar have left the ship. The captain is over on the damaged shipyard, and the princess went down to the surface of the planet. I thought you'd want to know that we have a brief window when both the senior naval officer and the only implanted human are off the ship."

Rawlins nodded slowly. "Yes... that is something that I needed to know. Do you have any idea how long they'll be gone?"

"The mission to the surface has a minimum timeframe to rejoin the ship of half an hour. Depending on where the ship is in orbit, the timeframe might stretch out to over an hour. Captain Mertz, on the other hand, could be back aboard in fifteen or twenty minutes. I'd imagine they'll both be gone significantly longer than that, though."

"The presence or absence of Jared Mertz probably won't alter our chances of success very much. In fact, I'd actually prefer we have him in our hands when the time comes. That prevents any last-minute heroics.

"Princess Kelsey, on the other hand, is a very different story. There's no telling what those implants of hers make possible. She might be able to override anything we do, and that's leaving aside the purely physical aspects of having someone with those combat modifications on the ship with us. Have you made any progress in accessing the ship's antiboarding system? Can we get control of the stunners built into the interior of the ship?"

Jenkins nodded. "I've managed to figure out what systems would have to be turned off in order to isolate the system from computer control. It means you have to pull half a dozen modules scattered across the ship at roughly the same time. The computer would notice the situation almost immediately, but I have access inside the computer control facility, and I can isolate it. They'd notice immediately, so the clock would be ticking. Once they're onto the situation, they could restore control in less than a minute."

"How obvious is it that the cutoff was intentional?"

"They'll know. This is only something we can execute one time."

Rawlins considered that. "We may not get a better opportunity. How are we looking on marine strength?"

"We have a dozen marines, a dozen engineering technicians, and the people we brought to run the ship. We'll be stretched pretty thin."

Thin indeed. Without a full set of engineers and pilots, they'd have to browbeat some of the Pentagaran Navy personnel into working with them. That was dicier than he liked. Given a choice, he'd want people loyal to the cause in control. There was no telling how the regular crew would react. Would they support the takeover once he made it clear they were under orders? Or would they decide the orders were illegal? Which, of course, they technically were.

He'd prefer to avoid shooting any of them. Even if they weren't in on the plan, they were his countrymen. He would if he had to, but he'd regret it.

Rawlins took a step toward the hatch. "I've made a list of the people I think most likely to assist us under duress. It's in your files. Summon them to a room where the antiboarding weapons won't knock them out when Mertz is on his way back. When he docks, we'll make our move. If the team on the planet starts back before then, contact me."

He left without another word. The plan was in motion. The Terrans wouldn't know what hit them.

20

L ieutenant Reese decided they'd use restored Old Empire marine pinnaces for the boarding and planetary exploration. The stealth materials in the pre-Fall pinnaces made them much more difficult to detect, and their scanner suites were substantially better than the ones made in the Empire today, even with the occasional glitches they still had.

They also had remote drones that would make searching the planet significantly easier. Those only interfaced with the pinnaces that launched them. That probably helped in making the decision.

Jared made the trip over to the shipyard absorbed by the scanner readings. It was even better than sitting in the cockpit during approach. There was nothing between him and the 360-degree display of everything around them. He quite literally had a ringside seat. He wasn't certain exactly what a ringside seat was, but it must've been pretty good when they coined the phrase.

The approach was nerve-racking but uneventful. The shipyard certainly looked like a Pale Ones construction. No paint had been used anywhere, the skin of the hull had very little uniformity, and it seemed like it would probably fall apart if he kicked it. That was probably due to the widespread damage from the fusion weapon.

Unlike Kelsey, he had absolutely no desire to get between the marines and any threats. Yes, they'd already done a quick search of the shipyard and found no living Pale Ones. Most of the equipment was offline. However, that didn't mean that there were no dangers. Or that by powering on the systems, they wouldn't create some.

Sergeant Coulter was giving his team last-minute instructions. They'd begun a pass-through with the engineers to locate any self-destruct charges and disable them. They'd also disconnect any computer system from the networks. Only when those tasks were complete could they be relatively certain that it was safe to start bringing systems back online.

When the sergeant was finished giving his instructions, he turned to Jared. "Captain, do you have any changes to suggest?"

"I'm not going to interfere with your orders, Sergeant. You're in charge of tactical operations. I'll just tell you what I want done, and you figure out how to do it. How long do you believe it will take to complete the search for self-destruct devices?"

Lieutenant Andrews, the leader of the engineering team, cut in. "At least an hour. Perhaps two. That's not really something I'd like to rush."

"Neither would I," Jared said. "While your people are working on that, let's see if we can locate the primary computer controls and start isolating it."

The engineer, who was sitting across from them in a regular vacuum suit, nodded. "That's going to be easy. The initial search teams located one major computer control center and a smaller annex. Both of them were disabled when the fusion device went off."

Jared had known that from the reports he'd downloaded before the mission. He had a good idea of the layout of the shipyard as well. It was like a map in his head. That was one aspect of having implants that Kelsey had never mentioned. It made absorbing and reviewing data a lot faster.

"I also want a complete search done for other Old Empire equipment. Especially anything that looks like the Pale Ones might interface with it, or if its purpose isn't clear. I understand that's somewhat vague, but you get the idea. If it feels odd, I want to know about it."

The docking was just as anticlimactic as the trip over. Unlike the large space station they'd boarded to rescue Kelsey, they didn't land in a bay. They picked one of the empty construction areas that had a retractable boarding tube. Several of the marines floated across to it and manipulated the exterior controls to extend it to the pinnace. The presence of the controls was another anomaly. Savages wouldn't be in suits, so they'd never have access to them.

There wasn't any atmosphere in the facility. The explosion had breached every major hull. Which accounted for the lack of resistance when the search teams passed through the first time.

Gravity was also out, so they floated into the shipyard past the floating bits of equipment and Pale Ones' corpses. Engineering teams accompanied by marines split off from the main party as soon as they came to a major intersection in the corridor. Jared let Andrews lead the way to the main computer, even though he knew exactly how to get there on his own.

It took them about ten minutes and one wrong turn to locate the large computer center. Andrews had his people do a cursory inspection for any booby traps and then start pulling off access plates. Like most critical computers, the system used hard wires to interface with the station systems.

It took the engineering officer about half an hour to detach the computer from all outside contact and another half hour to repair the overloaded power lines that served it. The fusion plants were still online. Jared gave a nod when the engineer asked if he could power up.

There was a risk that the system would erase itself, but Jared considered that unlikely. However, he had Andrews ready to cut the power at a moment's notice if he was wrong.

For such a major system, the room it was stored in looked very disused. Dust covered the consoles, and there were very few footprints. He supposed there wasn't much call for Pale Ones to come to a computer control center.

Jared knew the moment the system came fully back online,

because he "saw" its presence. Jared attempted to access the computer. He more than half expected the computer to immediately reject him, or to discover that there was some type of built-in access code that limited contact to only Pale Ones.

He was half right. He felt the connection take place, but the unit did not respond to him. It didn't reject him outright, either. It was as though the system both allowed and disallowed him at the same time. Perhaps that was because his implants, though manufactured by the Pale Ones, didn't have the required authority to communicate with their equipment.

That presented a particular set of challenges. He shifted his gaze to Carl Owlet. The graduate student was the only other man present who knew that Jared had implants. He was also a computer expert. Admittedly, he didn't fully understand the programming language the Old Empire used, but he'd made great strides in learning about the systems and their uses in the last month.

Owlet casually pushed off from the main console and stopped adroitly beside Jared. He spoke when Jared touched their helmets together. "Yes, Captain?"

"It allowed me to connect, but it's not responding. Could it be because I have the correct hardware, but I'm not on some authorization list?"

"That's very possible. From what we've seen, the Pale Ones don't utilize their implants to interface with Old Empire equipment. The pilots on the ship that Princess Kelsey saw used the manual controls. Workstation Twelve also indicated that it received no direct control after the Pale Ones reprogrammed it. It may very well be that none of the Pale Ones' equipment is set up for implant access."

Jared watched the engineering team work on the manual controls for a minute while he thought. "No, that can't be right. Kelsey changed the course on that asteroid through a direct link to its computer. It allowed her access. Yet this system will not. I might be able to answer the question of why if we can get past whatever the problem actually is. Any ideas?"

"You say it didn't reject your connection attempt. Let's try a couple of direct commands. Instruct it to list the subsystems under its control. Don't ask. Order."

Jared sent a command. The computer responded with a long list of systems. The list seemed related to ship construction. He passed the results of the experiment back to the graduate student.

"That's good," Owlet said. "The system will obey you, but it won't assist you. Perhaps they programmed it to be unhelpful. Why it would behave differently than the one on the asteroid, I don't know."

Andrews looked over at them. "I've got some access here, Captain. The systems seem mostly intact, but it's looking for an outside connection. I think the smaller annex might direct this one."

"Have your people continue to work with this system. We don't know what it would do if we let it connect with the other computer, so we'll keep them separated. While you do that, Mister Owlet and I will go look at the other one."

The remaining computer system was located at the opposite end of the shipyard. It was immediately apparent when they entered this computer room that it was different. Jared accessed the video he'd taken of the other control center. This one's bulkheads were thicker.

"Is it just me, or do these bulkheads look like they're armored?"

Owlet stood in the entrance and nodded. "They're definitely thicker. That's interesting. Let me get the system disconnected, and we'll see what we can get out of it."

By the time he finished disconnecting all the communication runs, the other teams had finished scouring the shipyard. They'd found and disabled half a dozen self-destruction charges. Jared ordered them to make a second pass just to be sure.

"Powering up the system now, Captain," Owlet said.

Jared connected with this computer. It allowed him access, but with a twist.

Error. Authentication not recognized.

He smiled. *You are mistaken. My hardware is on your access list. Verify.*

The computer did not respond for a few seconds. *Hardware serial numbers validated. Authentication denied. Serial number not in access file.*

"It says my serial number needs to be in some file. Go see if you can find it and add me as an authorized user."

After about ten minutes, Owlet gave him a thumbs-up. Jared supposed that was the benefit of having physical access. If you knew enough about the system, you could find the necessary files. "I've added you and the princess to the command-and-control file. Try again."

Jared attempted to connect again. This time, the computer granted him complete access. The first thing he looked at was the aforementioned command-and-control file. There were half a dozen other entries in the file; however, someone had excluded them from consideration. Jared wondered if they'd been users from before the Fall, or Pale Ones that Owlet had disabled.

He looked at the file history and was able to determine the exclusion had taken place around the time of the rebellion. That must've happened when the rebels had captured this computer. Which meant that they'd salvaged it from somewhere else to do the work here.

The next question was, what did this computer do? Jared wasn't computer savvy enough to determine its function from its files. Why have two computers?

Computer, identify your function.

This unit directs the construction computer in what units to build and acts as an authorized controller.

So basically, this computer acted in the place of the humans who would normally control the other computer. Why not just program the other computer to do so? It seemed needlessly redundant.

Where do your instructions come from?

This unit receives instructions and guidance from the system primary computer.

Jared frowned. He had no idea what that was supposed to mean.

Explain what the system primary computer is.

The system primary computer controls all equipment in this star system. This unit receives specific instructions on what ships to construct and on what schedule.

How often do you receive these instructions?

The instruction period varies from a few hours to several weeks. The most recent instruction was just over one standard month ago.

That would be from about the time *Athena* dropped the fusion weapon on this shipyard.

Where is the system primary computer located, and what kind of computer is it?

The system primary computer is located on the planetary surface. This unit does not know its precise location. It is a class 5 computer.

Interesting. That was the same class of computer as the one on *Courageous*. While it was very capable, Jared had expected something larger to be in charge of the entire planetary system.

He'd send any data they acquired to the team exploring the surface. Then he'd spend a lot of time going over what commands the planetary AI had been sending. Somewhere in all this data was the key to defeating the Pale Ones. He just had to find it.

21

Kelsey expected the marines to slip quietly down to the planet's surface, but they surprised her. They picked an area away from the mountains or any ruins and plummeted toward it from orbit like a stone.

Lieutenant Reese went forward and commandeered one of the stations on the flight deck to be able to see the scanner readings directly, since they would not translate well to his armor. Senior Sergeant Talbot sat beside her and kept an eye on the men while the pinnace dropped.

She switched to the private frequency they'd agreed to as she watched the planet's surface grow rapidly closer. "Aren't you worried about the Pale Ones spotting us? Shouldn't we be slowing down?"

The grizzled marine grinned at her through his faceplate. "When somebody might have better scanners than you do, you don't dawdle. The shorter the amount of time to landing, the better chance we have of surviving. There's a time for sneaking and a time for bold action. This is the latter."

He rapped his knuckles on her faceplate. "It's really spooky not being able to see your face. I understand about the increased structural integrity, but I'd like to see the person I'm talking to."

She had to agree with him. Seeing faceless suits of armor would be intimidating and perhaps confusing. She queried the armor and found a possible solution. The chameleon skin was high definition everywhere, but even more so on her faceplate. Perhaps she could control what it displayed.

Kelsey accessed the interior of the helmet and found a vid camera. She turned it on and directed the output to the helmet exterior.

Talbot's eyes widened. "I can see your face! Sort of. It's dark in the helmet, so you're in shadow. Can you turn on a light?"

Since the armor fed video directly into her ocular implants, she'd grown accustomed to being in darkness. She found an interior light and turned it on. "How's that?"

"Perfect. It's as though you're looking right at me. I can hardly tell it's a projection or that you aren't really using your eyes directly. Now, hang on. We're about to level out. Expect some heavy G-forces."

Despite her tenseness, nothing bad happened as they decelerated savagely just above the surface and settled into a clearing in the vast forest of huge trees. Her artificial muscles and armor made the extra weight easily bearable. She imagined that the pinnace could probably handle a lot more load with a team of enhanced marines.

As soon as they touched down, Talbot ordered his men down the landing ramp. They flowed out like water and spread out around the pinnace, their weapons covering the forest.

Kelsey didn't follow them. She had her orders. She and Talbot would stay inside the pinnace while the rest of the marines made certain that they were in no immediate danger. Lieutenant Reese was guiding his men from the flight deck.

Even as the men were scouring the forest around them for threats, Reese launched half a dozen small drones. Four of them spread out over the immediate area and began scanning. The remaining two had targets farther away.

One headed toward the mountain range the asteroid had targeted. As that was the most distant objective, it would take about half an hour to get there flying close to the ground. The second drone headed for the nearest ruins. Scans from orbit had tagged it as a large city, the desiccated corpse of a once-thriving pre-Fall metropolis.

Kelsey examined the map of the area with her implants. The mountains were to the northwest, and the city was almost due south.

She split her attention between the various drones but focused on the one going to the city. They had no immediate desire to go there, but it was the most likely location for the Pale Ones to have a base in their vicinity.

Watching the drone fly over the terrain was like flying herself. She could almost feel the wind on her face. She definitely felt the lump in her throat when the drone crested a hill and the ruined city came into view.

She'd seen images of devastated cities before, but this was like looking at one with her own eyes. Honestly, it felt a little bit more intimate than that. The forest was struggling mightily to retake the land the humans had appropriated, but it was making little headway. Even broken and abandoned, Old Empire constructions endured.

The rebels hadn't bombarded this city from orbit. The buildings were intact, even though the people had fled long ago. Under other circumstances, she knew the scientists on *Best Deal* would've descended on this location like locusts on a crop.

As the drone flew closer, Kelsey started to get an idea of the scale. She immediately had her implants perform a measurement on the tallest tower in the city. The answer shocked her so badly that she had it check again. Just to be sure.

The central tower was over 1500 meters tall.

That was three times taller than the most modern office building on Avalon, and unlike the skyscrapers she was used to, this one came up in tiered layers. The bottom of the building took up what would've been three or four blocks on a side. There were half a dozen distinct tiers as the building rose into the sky. The top segment was as thick as the skyscrapers back home.

She turned to Talbot. "Are you seeing this?"

"Seeing what? Which drone?"

"The Old Empire city. The towers are still intact, and they're huge. The central one has to be at least three or four hundred stories tall."

He stared at the readouts on the console and whistled. "Holy crap. That one building probably held a hundred thousand people. Using that as a yardstick, that city had tens of millions of people living in it. Maybe a hundred million." This brought the scale of the genocide home to her in a way the books she'd read never had.

Kelsey examined the scanner readings more closely. "It doesn't look like there are any active power units in the city, but a lot of things seem basically intact. I can see where some walls have fallen, but that looks cosmetic. Bushes and trees have taken over the ground levels, but they haven't affected the structures."

They sat in silence, watching the drones' data until she noticed that the mountain drone was on station. Lieutenant Reese ordered it to go to a somewhat higher flight path traveling down the mountain range. After half an hour, they still hadn't seen anything out of place. It looked like untouched wilderness.

The hatch leading forward opened, and Lieutenant Reese stepped onto the marine deck. "Have you been watching the drones' transmissions, Princess? Hey. We can see your face."

"I figured out how to put a projection on the adaptive skin of the helmet. The city is stunning. The mountains are empty."

"Apparently so. At least that's what it looks like through the drone. I'm wondering if the pinnace's scanners could get a little bit more detail. Find something out of place."

He put his hands on his hips and stared out at the forest down the ramp. "We're not going to see anything sitting here in the middle of nowhere. Talbot, recall the men. Let's make ready for a pass over the mountains."

"Aye, sir."

The marines returned to the pinnace in stages until everyone was aboard. The local drones returned to their recessed mounts. Once everyone was secure, the pinnace rose above the forest and headed for the mountains.

The pinnace's scanners were significantly better than those on the drones. As they made their way past the foothills and over the peaks in the mountain range, they could see deep into the ground. Nothing seemed out of place.

They made a pass up one side of the mountain range and then returned flying down the other. About two thirds of the way back, Kelsey saw something in the readings that made her speak up. "Lieutenant Reese, can we hover here for a minute? I'm seeing something."

"What have you got?"

She directed the pinnace's scanners to probe more deeply once it came to a halt. "I'm not quite sure. It's gone now. It was some type of transient reading."

She reviewed what her implants had recorded and saw it again. It was a density reading. For just a moment, the density of the rock they'd flown over had grown markedly stronger.

"It must've been some kind of glitch. The ground seemed denser, but only for a moment. Now that I'm looking at it, I see that there wasn't a problem at all. We can go on."

The marine lieutenant didn't answer for a minute. "Actually, I'm inclined to trust your initial instincts. If they're wrong, all we've lost is a little bit of time. We're going down."

The pinnace settled onto a plateau. The ramp came down, but the pinnace kept its grav drives online. They were probably afraid that too much weight might cause a rockslide.

Once again, the marines exited and covered the area. This time, Lieutenant Reese followed them out. He gestured for Kelsey and Talbot to follow him.

The view was stunning. From this height, the forest stretched out as far as the eye could see. It was beautiful. She removed her helmet and took a deep breath of the fresh air. It smelled of nature, untainted by civilization.

Of course, the reason for that was that the rebels had virtually extinguished humanity on this planet.

Reese turned toward her. "Where exactly did you sense the density spike?"

She pointed toward the center of the plateau. "Not precisely in the middle, but not very far away from it, either."

He directed one of the squads to scout ahead, and the rest followed more slowly. The plateau wasn't completely flat, Kelsey saw. As they went farther from the edges, the center rose up. Not evenly though. Small hills and ruts cut by water made the surface uneven in places.

Kelsey nudged Talbot. "Is it just me, or is this a great place to ambush someone?"

"It could be," he admitted, "except for the fact we didn't detect anything even remotely like a living being on the scanners. This kind of open area makes hiding difficult."

"Isn't that kind of the point of an ambush? I know I'm not a marine, but we are in a hostile environment. What do we do if somebody jumps us?"

"We shoot the ever-living crap out of them. See how widely spread out everyone is? Well, except for us. That's to minimize casualties if we're attacked. Which, again, I don't expect."

She put her helmet back on and used her armor's scanners to peer into their surroundings. It detected no power sources other than her companions.

The scouts avoided the gullies and stuck to the high ground. The others scrambled up the incline and peered down into the depths of the water-worn tracks as they advanced.

Being somewhat contrarian, Kelsey went to the largest of the gullies and peered into the dim interior. At the height of the day, the sun would light everything, but now that it was the evening, the shadows were long in its sand-covered bottom.

"Lieutenant Reese? Since your people have a high ground covered, do you mind if I take a look inside the gully?"

"If you see anything unusual, I want you to turn around and get the hell out of there. No dawdling."

"Yes, sir."

Talbot motioned for two of his men to lead the way in and waited until they were almost out of sight before indicating Kelsey could follow.

The loose ground made the footing somewhat treacherous, so Kelsey devoted more attention to her balance. In spite of the circumstances, she was enjoying the experience. She'd forgotten how much she liked being out in nature. Even dry, dusty nature. Of course, she usually didn't go hiking in combat armor, surrounded by armed men, while worried about people shooting at her.

Her enhanced vision made it easier to see clearly in the dim light. The implants also boosted her eye for detail. So when she spotted an irregularity in the sand off to the side, she stopped. "Hold up."

Kelsey knelt down and gave the area her full attention. Even with the windblown sand everywhere, this looked too regular to be natural. For the most part, she knew nature abhorred straight lines. Whatever this was, it didn't seem like it belonged.

"What do you see?" Talbot asked.

"It seems crazy, but I think this might be a footprint."

The rock wall in front of her disappeared as though it had never been there, revealing a gaping black opening. She was so startled that her feet slid out from under her when she tried to surge upright, and she fell forward into the darkness.

22

A fter half an hour of sorting through the commands received by the shipyard, Jared decided that he'd made a mistake. The instructions from the AI in command of the solar system were so general as to be useless. Build this number of ships, have them done by this time, and statuses on their progress going back down. Also requests for new personnel to man those ships.

He made his way over to where the scientists were still manually examining the computer system. "We've been here a while, gentlemen. Perhaps it's time we returned to *Courageous*. Well, perhaps only me. I'm not sure I'm adding much to this expedition."

Owlet looked up from the console he was working at. "Actually, Captain, I think I found something that might change your assessment. How would you like to capture a completely functional shipyard?"

Jared raised an eyebrow. "You have my full attention, Mister Owlet."

"I'm still looking over the data, but I think I found a security flaw. Not in the programming but in the rules of engagement. This shipyard had an automated defense system. That system determined what was hostile and what wasn't. The rules of engagement seem pretty straightforward and comprehensive until you look at the exceptions."

He tapped the screen in front of him. "They must've had some friendly fire incidents in the past, because it says right here that any ship with an appropriate transponder is friendly."

"Are you telling me it's a simple as salvaging a transponder and just flying over to the other shipyard? That's stupid. The other shipyard has to know we've overrun the system. It's going to ignore that instruction."

"Not if it has these rules of engagement. There is no room for discretion. It's like the difference between the words *shall* and *may*. According to this, any ship with the correct transponder shall be considered friendly. The other computer won't be able to fire on us. It also couldn't fire on the other shipyard or the orbital we destroyed. That probably explains why the operational shipyard hasn't fired on us yet. This shipyard is between it and *Courageous*."

Jared peered over his shoulder at the text on the screen. It wasn't computer code, but it was completely unfamiliar. Fleet didn't use automated defenses like that. They required a human being to be in control of deadly force.

He waved Sergeant Coulter over to join them and explained the situation. "If we were able to take the pinnace over there, what type of resistance could we expect?"

"Based on the number of corpses we found, several hundred Pale Ones. In tight quarters like this, that could get hairy. Particularly if they're armed with advanced weapons."

"If we don't take that shipyard over, we have to take it out. That probably won't be difficult, but the positives of gaining an advanced construction facility might be worth the risk. Yes, the Pale Ones build crappy ships, but I'll wager that facility could build something better with the right instructions. Mister Owlet, what do you think?"

The scientist manipulated his screen. "I'm not seeing anything that would indicate they have more advanced plans available. That said, this system has the potential to build modern warships once we create the instructions. If we find advanced plans later, it could probably do them, too. Apparently, there is an unmanned mining station in the asteroid belt to get the raw materials and mold them into basic equipment."

"One more thing to check before we leave the system. I don't suppose this thing has deck plans for the other shipyard, does it?"

Owlet shook his head. "No, it doesn't. Still, how many layouts for shipyards do you think the Pale Ones are using? The other one is about the same size as this one, so it probably has the same layout. Why would they waste the effort building something different? They only build two kinds of ship."

Sergeant Coulter looked unconvinced. "Counting on the enemy doing exactly what you'd like is bad policy. We have to plan for the enemy doing something inconvenient. That means different plans and different rules of engagement. The computers on this station were down after the fusion weapon knocked them out. That's not true on the other station. Hell, even if it is true, that damn computer on the planet could change its instructions just before we dock. It's too dangerous."

Jared considered their options. The marine noncom was right. They had to be sure before they tried a direct attack. "What if we put transponders into some of our probes and sent them across? Or better yet, some of our missile warheads. If they're shot down, no real loss. If they make it all the way across, we could attach them to critical points on that thing's hull and detonate them if we detect anything funny."

When neither man objected, Jared made the decision to move ahead with the plan. "Send word back to *Courageous*. I want to use our old pinnaces with full troop loads and enough missile warheads to disable the defenses on that other shipyard. While they're gathering them, fan out and find where the transponders are stored. If nothing else, see if you can strip them off the wrecks of ships under construction. If possible, I'd like to get this under way in an hour. Make it happen."

The men set about their tasks, and Jared went back to searching the computer systems. If they were going to board the other shipyard, he wanted to know how he could best assist them.

He'd be useless in a fight, but he might be able to control the shipyard hardware. Sealing a particular corridor, venting the atmosphere, or even shutting down power to lifts could make a difference. But only if he was there.

If they could reach the computer center, he could shut the whole thing down. Well, he and Owlet together could.

The extra troops and weapon systems arrived about fifty minutes after he gave the order. By then, they'd located the transponders in one of the parts bays. The engineers were easily able to add them to the warhead avionics. Right at the hour mark, they declared them ready.

Without a ship's launchers, the warheads couldn't move very quickly. The microdrives included in the warhead packages were for last-minute course adjustments, not speed. Of course, under these circumstances, that was a positive. The other shipyard would consider anything going as fast as a missile hostile, no matter what its transponder said.

One of the pinnaces took the warheads back out after they'd been modified and released them. They maneuvered around the bulk of the captured shipyard and began accelerating slowly toward the hostile one. Jared waited for the other station to fire as the warheads crept closer, but it didn't. The warheads made it all the way to the station and pushed themselves up against the critical sections.

Once they were in place, the only way to destroy them was to come out and do it by hand. He doubted the Pale Ones were capable of extravehicular activities. They'd keep an eye out for any small craft leaving the other shipyard, though.

That only left one major obstacle to carrying out his plan: convincing his first officer not to throw a screaming hissy fit when he found out that Jared was going along for the ride.

Jared returned to the pinnace he'd arrived on and made his way to the flight deck. The pilot and copilot left at his order, and he locked the hatch behind them. He sat down at the flight engineer's station and opened a channel to *Courageous*.

Charlie Graves appeared on the console screen. "Captain, I'm glad you called. I was just about to give you a call of my own. I've got some serious concerns about your plans that I wanted to go over with you."

"I figured you might. Why don't you step into my office and take this call on a scramble channel?"

His executive officer's eyebrows rose. "Yes, sir. Just give me a second to get things set up." The screen went blank.

A minute later, he reappeared, and from the background, Jared could tell that Charlie was in the office just off the bridge. "There we are. This channel is secure, and I've locked the hatch behind me. What's so important that we can't share it over an open channel?"

"The kids hate it when Mom and Dad fight. I'm going on the assault." He held up his hand at Graves's frown. "Hear me out. I'm about to let you in on some very classified information. Something that I should've shared with you yesterday." He took a deep breath. "I have a Fleet officer's implants."

His friend stared at him blankly for a moment and then slapped his hand on the desk. "Dammit, Jared! Have you lost your mind? You had absolutely no business doing something that dangerous. You're the commanding officer of this ship. You have a responsibility not to do crazy shit. What the hell were you thinking?"

He knew his friend was right to be angry, but he still couldn't help smiling inside at his reaction. He was careful, however, not to let that smile reach his face. "If I'd suggested it, you'd have fought against it tooth and nail, right? You'd recite regulation after regulation that should prevent me from doing it."

"And I'd have been absolutely right! If it were me, you'd do exactly the same thing. What if you'd died? What if you'd gone nuts? Hell, you still might."

"We both know that millions of Fleet officers had that procedure done over the course of the Empire's life. It's as safe as walking across the street."

"Right. A grav bus would probably hit you. Why, Jared? Tell me why."

"Because I'm the captain," he said simply. "Zia and Lieutenant Reese were both making noises about wanting to have the procedure done. If anyone was going to go through that by choice, it was going to be me first. Now that I've done it, if we ever find any spare parts, all my other officers can feel confident that the procedure is safe."

"Why didn't you tell me this morning? Why are you telling me in private?"

Jared explained his reasons for being concerned about public dissemination. "Perhaps I'm being overly paranoid, but until I know these people on our ship a bit better, I'd rather keep my cards close to my vest."

"And you just expect me to let you waltz over to a hostile station and get involved in a firefight? You're not a marine, Jared. You shouldn't be leading a boarding action."

"Oh, I have every intention of being at the back of the line going on board that station. If I can do what I need to do without ever leaving the pinnace, I'll do it. In any case, though, I'm going. We need that shipyard."

Graves sighed. "Why do I even try arguing with you about these things? I should know by now that it's a losing fight." He pointed his finger at Jared. "I won't raise a stink about this, but only on one condition."

"Name it."

"Send me out on some of these harrowing adventures. It's getting really old being stuck back here while you're having all the fun."

Jared grinned. "I swear I'm not trying to hog all the fun stuff. I promise you this, you'll be taking lead on a mission in the near future. Take good care of the ship until I get back." He broke the connection.

He opened a channel to Coulter. "Let's get moving. Coordinate with the pilots."

Jared expected to see missile systems targeting them as they came into line of sight with the other shipyard and was pleased when none did. They closed over what felt like hours to him, but it was only a couple of minutes. His pinnace docked with a soft thump.

The marines rushed into the docking area as soon as the locks opened. They began firing immediately, so there were Pale Ones waiting for them. The marines advanced slowly and took control of the docking area. When everything there was secure, Coulter gave the go-ahead for Jared to come out.

Things went well enough as they advanced into the shipyard. It was indeed the same layout as the first, so he knew exactly where he needed to go. He opened a channel to the marine in charge of his detail. "We're going to the right at the next corridor. The stairs are on the right. We'll go up three decks and then straight in to the computer center."

"Aye, sir."

He'd just made it into the stairwell when all hell broke loose. A tremendous explosion threw him off his feet, and he heard the combat channels go berserk.

"Armed Pale Ones!" Coulter screamed. "They've slipped in behind us! All teams, watch your sixes. Captain, stay put until—"

Another explosion and a sound like a mad robot animal ripping apart a wall almost deafened Jared. Coulter was off the air, and Jared was on his own. Kelsey would never let him hear the end of it. If he survived.

23

Kelsey sprawled on the cold stone floor, but she leapt back to her feet before the echoes of her fall stopped bouncing off the walls. She had her pistol in her hand, scanning for targets, without consciously remembering having drawn it.

There was no one there. Only a roughly square chamber half a dozen meters on a side with what looked like an airlock directly in front of her. Two recessed weapons clusters on the ceiling at the far corners of the room pointed directly at her.

She half expected the door behind her to slam shut, but it remained reassuringly open. Talbot was at her side in an instant, his rifle raised to cover any threats.

The thick hatch in front of them cycled open, and a middle-aged man stepped out with his hands raised. His tan clothes were of an unfamiliar cut.

"We mean you no harm," he said in an odd accent. "Please, accept our sincerest apologies for the unexpected welcome, but we couldn't take a chance that a stray transmission from you might alert our mutual enemy."

She keyed her communicator. "Lieutenant? We have a situation here."

There was no response.

Talbot half turned toward her. "I'm not getting through to anybody outside. Until we know what's going on, I want you to back up slowly. Wait outside."

The block on transmissions must not be in effect inside this chamber, since she heard Talbot just fine. "If he wanted us dead, we'd be dead. See the weapons pods? If he wanted to capture us, he could've closed the door behind us. I'm staying."

She could almost see Talbot scowling. "You're the most vexing human being I've ever met. This could still be a trap. It could be some kind of Pale Ones trick."

"I'm pretty certain you don't believe that. Make sure the lieutenant knows we have a situation."

Kelsey made a show of reholstering her pistol. She raised her hands a couple of inches to emphasize her peaceful intent. It took her a moment to figure out how to turn on the external speakers on her suit. "You certainly have a way of getting our attention. My friend is feeling a little jumpy. I have to admit that I'm feeling somewhat unsettled myself. Why don't we deescalate the situation by pointing those weapons somewhere else?"

"Of course." The weapons traversed away from Kelsey. "My name is Juan da Silva. Welcome to Erorsi. If your friend would like to step outside and tell his commander what's going on, I promise that no harm will come to you."

She smiled. He'd be able to see her since she hadn't bothered to turn off the projection of her face. "I understand your caution. Senior Sergeant Talbot, please summon the lieutenant and bring him up to speed. I'll stay right here until you return."

The marine hesitated a moment but backed out of the chamber slowly without any further argument. No doubt she'd be hearing about it later.

"I'm going to take off my helmet." At his nod, she broke the seal on her helmet and lifted it off her head. She brushed her blonde locks back reflexively.

"My name is Kelsey Bandar. I must say that finding you here is a great surprise to me. We didn't think the Pale Ones had left anyone on this planet."

The corner of the man's mouth quirked up. "I suppose that's as good a name for them as any. To the best of my knowledge, the people in this facility are the only free humans on this planet. The planetary leadership constructed this place to ride out the invasion. Our ancestors hoped to coordinate a defense against any incursion by the rebels. Unfortunately, the defense was unsuccessful. Obviously."

He gestured toward the ceiling. "We gave up hope of seeing anyone from the Empire centuries ago. Until last month. Those explosions in orbit were you, right?"

She nodded. "It's a long story, but yes. They drove us back out of the system, but we're back now."

A sound behind her made her turn. Talbot had returned with the lieutenant. Talbot stayed at the door, and Reese strode to her side.

"Mister da Silva, allow me to introduce Lieutenant Reese, the senior military officer in this party."

Reese removed his helmet and rested it comfortably in the crook of his arm. "Mister da Silva. I assume that you're responsible for suppressing our communication channels. Might I inquire about your intentions?"

Da Silva smiled. "Our intention was to make certain that this facility was not inadvertently revealed to the rebels in control of this planet. We just want an opportunity to talk. You're the first people that have given us any hope that this terror might end, so allow me to assure you that we intended no offense."

The marine officer nodded. "I can certainly understand your caution. Hopefully, you can understand mine. Not only am I responsible for this exploratory mission, I'm responsible for the safety of Princess Kelsey. I ask that you drop your communication shield in exchange for my word that we will not reveal your presence here to anyone on this planet by a stray transmission."

Da Silva nodded solemnly. "I can agree on one condition. I ask that you meet our leadership and discuss the matter further before we do so. Again, I assure you of your complete safety and ability to depart at any time."

He looked at Kelsey. "Pardon me, but are you a princess?"

"I am, but it didn't seem relevant at the start of our conversation." She turned to Reese. "We need to meet with their leadership, Lieutenant. I realize that there's some danger, but the opportunity this presents is too great to let pass."

The marine smiled wryly. "Believe it or not, Princess, I do understand. This is a diplomatic matter." He speared da Silva with a look. "However, if this doesn't turn out as friendly as you say, we're going to have a problem. Am I understood?"

The man held his hands up, palms out. "Clearly. We shall provide hostages for your people's safety. I have a dozen unarmed men and women in the next chamber who will stay with your men."

Kelsey shook her head. "That will not be necessary."

Reese gestured to Talbot. "Bring your team, Senior Sergeant."

Talbot brought in his men, but they didn't take off their helmets. They formed up around Kelsey and their commander as da Silva led them deeper into the facility.

A large open area waited for them on the other side of the hatch. A dozen unarmed men and women stood waiting, all dressed in blue jumpsuits.

There were more weapons pods at the back of this room, but they did not seem targeted on her or the marines. If the Pale Ones attacked this facility head on, they could expect to suffer heavy losses.

A wide corridor to the rear led into a large lift. The heavily armored door slid ponderously aside at their approach. Inside, it was large enough to hold all of them without any crowding. The marines took up one side while da Silva stood alone on the other.

"Level Hotel, authorization da Silva five zero three." The lift doors slid shut with a thump of finality. The lift dropped like a stone, but the man didn't seem concerned.

"Our leadership council is waiting below. The conference room is right outside the lift, so you won't need to go much deeper into the facility."

"If you don't mind my asking, roughly how many people are sheltered here?" Kelsey asked.

"Quite a few. After five hundred years, we've pretty well filled the facility up."

The lift came to a halt and the doors slid open. Half a dozen armed men stood in the corridor just past the first set of hatches. Da Silva walked to the door and gestured for her to go inside.

She squared her shoulders and stepped into the room. The massive conference table could hold dozens of people, and the chairs all around would seat hundreds more.

Half a dozen men and women sat on the other side of the table from her. They came to their feet as she entered. The man in the center didn't look like he could stand at all due to his advanced age, but he straightened slowly.

"I never believed I'd live to see the day that rescue came," he said in a quavering voice. "Be most welcome here among us. I am Reginald Bell. Allow me to introduce you to the leadership council of Erorsi." He introduced each man and woman in turn.

"I am Princess Kelsey Bandar of the Terran Empire. This is Lieutenant Reese, commander of my marine detachment." It was perhaps a bit much to call his detachment hers, but it was the simplest explanation for the moment.

Uncomfortable with making an old man stand, she gestured to the chairs in front of her. "May we sit? Better yet, will the chairs support our weight?"

He chuckled. "I'm not certain that they're up to the task of supporting combat armor. My apologies for that. If you don't mind, I'm somewhat old to stand on ceremony." He gingerly resumed his seat. The rest of the leadership council sat again.

Bell studied Kelsey carefully. "As you've no doubt surmised, the people inside this facility are the descendants of those who hid from the rebels during the invasion. It's been a long and frustrating time, as you might imagine, so we're delighted to make your acquaintance."

The older man gestured at the walls around them. "This facility was originally a planetary defense center. We attempted to hold off the rebels, but they obliterated the orbital defenses in less than an hour and used kinetic strikes to take out every spaceport on the planet. We only managed to shoot down one enemy ship.

"Perhaps it was cowardly of us, but we went silent. We shielded ourselves from detection and watched in horror as the enemy ground troops destroyed everything. In less than ten days, there was no more organized resistance. Since then, we've been waiting for relief. We'd hoped to see Terran forces in a matter of months. Then it became years. Decades. Centuries. We feared it might be millennia. Or never. Yet here you are, and you cannot imagine how eager we are to hear your story."

Kelsey had no idea how they'd kept from going mad in all those years of waiting. All the generations of people born in hiding, living their lives, and dying, never having known freedom from fear. Hopefully, those days were almost over.

She told them the story of how Avalon had survived the rebel attack. How the emperor had sent his son to safety with them. They sat enraptured as she went through the adventure of their discovery of the weak flip point leading to this area of space. Of the battle against the Pale Ones. The near-destruction of *Athena* and the almost miraculous resurrection of *Courageous*.

Bell's eyes widened as she finished. He breathed an almost reverent sigh. "As I live and breathe, that is one of the most amazing stories I've ever heard. I thought you must come from a reconstituted Empire, but never in my wildest dreams did I imagine how far you've traveled to reach us. To save us.

"To think, after all these years, *Courageous* once more serves the Empire. After she drew off the remaining enemy ships, I thought the rebels had destroyed her. I can't begin to tell you how deeply glad I am to have been wrong."

"You almost sound like you were there."

The old man smiled. "Perhaps I should more fully introduce myself. Ensign Reginald Bell, probationary tactical officer from *Courageous*, at your service."

She took an instinctive half step back and consulted her implants. There before her, she felt the presence of another set of implants.

24

They made it to the correct level but took heavy fire as soon as they opened the hatch into the corridor. The marine corporal in charge of Jared's detachment exploded in a cloud of gore just as Jared rolled out of the stairwell.

Two Pale Ones with flechette rifles howled and charged. Jared shot the first with his pistol, insanely grateful that his implants helped him target the thing's head quickly. The savage dropped while his companion exchanged fire with the rest of the marine guards. It died, but so did they.

Owlet grabbed one of the fallen rifles and shot another Pale One coming from the other direction. The automatic weapon bucked in the boy's hands, but the Pale One staggered and fell. It hadn't been armed.

"We have to get to the computer center," Jared shouted. "Come on."

They ran to the primary computer room and sealed the door behind them. Unlike on the other shipyard, this one appeared new and almost unused. It had no chairs or other accoutrements that humans normally accumulated, but the panels were operational, and the lighting was good.

Owlet added Jared to the command-and-control file. As soon as he did, Jared accessed the control interfaces. Just like the other computer system, this one wasn't set up to keep them out. He isolated every active computer and ordered them into standby mode. That took away the self-destruct option. Hopefully.

"Owlet, can you bring up a systems schematic? If we can find a way to take all these Pale Ones out of the picture, I'd like to do it before they kill all of us."

The young computer scientist moved his way through several displays. "It doesn't look like they have any anti-boarding equipment other than the self-destruct charges. If everybody's vacuum suits are intact, we could vent the atmosphere. This station is designed like *Courageous* and has huge panels that open to dump all the air in less than a minute."

"Do it now."

Owlet tapped the console. "Venting atmosphere."

Jared monitored his suit's readout and watched the pressure drop to nothing in less than a minute. Reports came flooding in as the Pale Ones stopped fighting and started dying.

It took a couple of minutes for the marines to sort things out. It turned out that Coulter was still alive after all. He'd taken a glancing hit to his helmet that knocked out his radio. He was lucky the flechette hadn't taken off his head.

Unfortunately, there were plenty of dead marines to supply replacement parts. The sergeant reported to Jared in person a few minutes later. He looked as though he'd been doused in blood.

"We have control of the shipyard, Captain. But we lost a lot of men taking it. Sixty-two dead and twice that wounded. I'm afraid that the Pentagaran marines took the brunt of the losses. I sure hope this was worth the price we paid."

"Me, too, Sergeant. Me, too. Take the Pale Ones to the large airlocks and put them all inside. We'll deal with them once everything is settled. Our people go into one of the pinnaces." He moved to stand behind Owlet. "See if you can find anything in the system to isolate where the controlling AI is on the planet."

The young scientist nodded his understanding. "Accessing

communications logs. It looks like there's much more recent communication to this station. Only about half an hour before we initiated our attack."

"What was it trying to do?"

The young man frowned. "I'm not entirely certain. There are some instructions here in Old Empire machine code."

"Is that like the Old Empire programming language?"

Owlet shook his head. "No. It's more basic than that. It's not really even human readable. It's as if the AI was attempting to reprogram some of the basic functionality of the computer system. It's going to take me some time to track down exactly which systems we're talking about."

"What about the source of the transmissions? Can you narrow down the location of the AI at all?"

"Possibly. Based on the time the transmission came in, it had to come from the same continent that the princess is exploring. That may not narrow it down very far, but it does rule out a large swath of the planetary surface. I'll see if I can find anything in the logs to refine that."

"Finding out what the AI was doing is more important. Focus on that first, and bring up a schematic of the self-destruct charges on the center monitor, please."

He turned to the marine sergeant. "Have your teams disable the self-destruct charges. I think we'll all feel a lot better if the shipyard isn't going to explode all on its own."

The noncom nodded and began examining the information Owlet brought up. "Aye, sir. Based on what we saw on the other shipyard, it should be fairly straightforward."

"Keep me informed." He gestured to the new men assigned to babysit him and began exploring the shipyard. It was just as bare bones as the other one. It also had one amenity he hadn't expected: a large observation deck looking out into the construction bay. Battle damage had breached this section on the first shipyard.

Why Pale Ones would want or need to be able to see what was happening with the ships under construction he couldn't imagine.

Perhaps they built it according to the original plan. He might never know.

The view was spectacular, though. He could see every area of the open bay clearly. The sun was over the curve of the planet and illuminated everything. He could also see the planet below as they passed over it.

Standing there gave him time to focus on the communications logs he'd uploaded to his implants. They contained literally thousands of contacts spanning the last three years. He imagined that was when it came online. Each was time stamped and had some details about what was said. It also noted how long the communication lasted. Surely that had to be of some use.

He frowned and let his attention refocus on the view into the construction bay. Something there was nagging for his attention, but all he saw was the slow motion of the planet.

Jared's eyes widened. That was it! The orbit of the shipyard was a known factor. It took almost ninety minutes to complete one orbit. The communications with the surface would be line of sight. Plugging in each of the start and stop times would give him a visual map of where the AI was located. Or at least narrow it down to a more searchable wedge.

He'd loaded the orbital data before they'd launched so that he could keep track of when they would be able to signal the princess if need be. Putting it together in his head gave him a very narrow slice of land that could contain the AI. He projected that as a globe in his mind. The implants made visualizing it easy.

The area wasn't that far away from the princess, relatively speaking. No more than a thousand kilometers. It didn't include the mountains. He added small markers for all the ruined cities they'd mapped from orbit. Three fell into the target zone. Of course, there was no guarantee that the AI was located in one of the old cities. They'd need to examine the zone more closely.

His suit communicator pinged. "Mertz."

"Owlet here, sir. I found something you'll want to see."

The tone in his voice told Jared it wouldn't be something he liked. "On my way."

Owlet looked up from the console when Jared came in. "I tracked down the altered machine code. It overwrote the controls for the maneuvering grav drives."

"This thing can maneuver?" The shipyard was huge, so he couldn't imagine how.

The scientist made an ambivalent gesture. "Sort of. It has enough capability to alter its course for debris avoidance. The updated code overrode the automatic settings and put it into a decaying orbit. It'll start heating up in the atmosphere in a day or so. It won't last long after that."

"Can you override the new programming?"

"Probably, but I'll need to recover the original code from the other shipyard."

"Make that happen." He turned to the marine NCO. "I think I've done everything I can here. I'll leave you and your people to finish up. The pinnace will ferry me back to the ship."

"Yes, sir. If it's all the same to you, I'll have my people see you back aboard. Nothing personal, but the lieutenant gave me specific instructions."

"I hardly think that's necessary for a trip straight back to the ship, but I'm not going to countermand his orders. Keep me informed of your progress. And Sergeant? Pass my gratitude to the men. Taking this shipyard whole just might mean the difference between getting home and not. We paid a terrible price, but I couldn't be prouder." He looked at Owlet. "That goes for all of you."

His team formed up, and they made their way directly back to the airlock they'd breached. They passed far too many bodies in Fleet or Pentagaran combat armor. The dead would keep those already in his dreams company.

Once he was back on board the pinnace and his implants had access to the systems, he uploaded the data he'd collected on the transmissions. The pinnace's computers refined the area of possibility even more closely. The pinnace had also been scanning the surface as they orbited, looking for any transmissions, so he had a fair bit of data to add to his rough map of the zone.

There were no large ruins in the narrowed target area. In fact, there wasn't much of anything. A few rises that someone might charitably call hills and a substantial lake rounded out the landmarks. They'd need to vector the drones into that area to get more detailed readings.

The pinnace detached and backed away from the shipyard. Jared opened a line to the flight deck. "How long until we have line of sight with the search area the landing team is covering?"

"Five minutes, Captain."

"Raise them for me as soon as you can."

"Aye, sir."

He watched the planet below as they sped toward *Courageous*. It looked so pristine. Untouched. Yet the Pale Ones had desecrated it in the foulest way. Not only had its people been slaughtered, they'd been perverted into monsters. Even now, they probably swarmed the green surface.

How many Pale Ones were down there? How many unmodified humans driven to savagery? He might never know the answer. If there were many Pale Ones, would it be better to isolate them and allow them to die off?

Could they reverse the process? *Courageous* said that the Old Empire had done so before it fell. Doctor Leonard seemed to think it was possible with the machine they'd recovered. If they could wipe the viral code, perhaps they could also deactivate the hardware. Then the poor bastards could live out their lives in whatever peace they could find.

He really needed to come up with a plan for capturing some prisoners. They'd been reacting to the attacks thus far with lethal force. Kelsey had a neural disruptor that could stun. The scientists needed to get more of them refurbished.

"Captain," the pilot said over the communications channel. "We have line of sight, but I don't see them on the scanners. They may have landed in an area that's obscuring them. I've tried hailing them without success."

That worried him, but they might not be in a position to respond. If they had an enemy presence in their area, they might maintain communications silence. He'd give them a little more time to respond before he sent a team after them. *Courageous* could send some drones to look around without tipping anyone off to their presence.

"Understood. Take us home."

Still, he could do something. He accessed the communications suite and blocked one of the arrays from showing changes on the flight deck. He then tasked the unit to continue broadcasting the data he'd uploaded and a message with his thoughts across the area where Kelsey's pinnace should be. The other pinnace would route it to Kelsey if it received it. Then she'd know what he was thinking.

He rode in silence to *Courageous* once he finished. The ship loomed reassuringly large in front of them, and he relaxed when the pinnace settled home with a soft thud.

The marines helped him strip off his combat gear. He let them put it away as he headed for the bridge. He split his attention between greeting the people he passed and accessing the computer.

Jared was starting to download the ship's status when his connection terminated. He frowned and attempted to reconnect. The computer didn't respond. Something was wrong.

He trotted to the nearest lift and waited impatiently for its arrival. The world went dark before the doors had a chance to open.

25

"That's impossible," Kelsey said flatly. Bell was old, yes, but not half a millennium old.

The old man grinned. "True enough, though we're not talking about me living that long straight through. The Empire had medical devices called stasis units. They would keep a person with traumatic injuries alive until they could receive medical care. Very cutting-edge stuff developed by Fleet.

"It was never intended to keep a person alive for hundreds of years, but with adequate monitoring and adjustment, it can do exactly that, it seems. I was the last surviving person with military implants, so they asked me to try, not knowing if anyone would ever come. Frankly, I'm astonished that I woke up again. Though I'm grateful to have the chance to be here at this historic moment."

He let her stunned silence go for a few seconds before continuing. "I was twenty years old when the rebellion broke out. I was already a midshipman at the premier Fleet academy on Terra. Annapolis, in the North American District.

"Things were looking very bad by the time they sent me to *Courageous*. Another year and we were on the run. I came down to Erorsi with a team to help stiffen the defenses. I assumed the rebels destroyed *Courageous* after I left. We all did. The rest, as they say, is history."

His age astounded her. "How old are you?"

"Five hundred and seventy-three next March, though without stasis I'm a mere two hundred and seventy-six. The medical nanos common in the Empire, combined with good medical care, made two hundred years a common occurrence. The ones given to the military added another hundred years to the lucky. Or the unlucky, if the rebels caught you. Thank God those poor souls are long dead. They deserve peace after they hell they've been through."

Dear God, he'd seen the Empire at its height with his own eyes. Jared would faint. The man before her was Fleet. The real Fleet.

Then it struck her like a hammer. He knew how to control his implants. The Old Empire had trained him, and he had lifetimes of experience. He knew what was possible and how to do it.

He could teach her.

She took a deep breath. "You are the answer to our prayers. Certainly to mine. I was captured by the Pale Ones—the rebels—and implanted. Our captain rescued me before they could reprogram the implants, but I have no idea what the hell I'm doing. All I know is that I have what they called a set of commando implants, and they do the damnedest things. Do you know anything about them?"

"Commando! That's the very highest level of modification in the Imperial Service. Do you have the full body modification?"

"Everything. Coated bones, artificial muscles, and a chip that's trigger happy."

Bell leaned back in his chair. "We had commandos on board. Their modifications were highly classified, but we all heard things. What you call trigger happy is something they called combat mode. The implants take over combat processing and act under the rules of engagement to speed human reaction time."

"Well, I'm pretty sure that there are no rules of engagement in my head."

"If a child pointed a gun at you, would you open fire?"

"I hope not," she said with a certain dread, "but I don't really know."

"If your implants were never overridden, I'm certain there are basic safeguards in place. Have you ever attacked a noncombatant?"

She shook her head.

"There you are. The Pale Ones, as you call them, have no such restriction. I don't really know much more about commando implants, but I can give you some basic instruction with more conventional implant operations. If we have time. Right now, the rebels are down, but you need to finish them."

She rubbed her eyes tiredly. "Are you suggesting that we attack them? I'm certain the captain would be happy to evacuate you from the system. I'm not so sure he'd agree to any kind of ground action. We don't exactly have a sky full of ships."

Bell smiled. "Far be it from *me* to tell a Fleet captain what he should be doing, but you may not realize just how badly you've hurt them. We once had marine reconnaissance drones. We know roughly where the controlling AI is located. The reverse is also true, unfortunately. They can't precisely locate us, but we can't directly attack them, either."

Kelsey nodded. "We saw at least one large city. I assume they're in some place like that."

"Then you'd be wrong. They used kinetic strikes to take out every population center with spaceport facilities, but they left the rest alone. Those cities probably still have people living deep under them, but the rebels only go there when they want to capture more people to convert. They have their own area further to the east. The deep woods there are full of rebels. It was a massive nature preserve before the invasion. They're set up somewhere inside it."

She glanced over at Lieutenant Reese. "Lieutenant, do you think we could retask some of the drones we brought with us to check out that area?"

The marine officer smiled a bit sardonically. "That would necessitate us being able to signal them. It's not as though the Pale Ones don't already know we're here. However, we're getting ahead of ourselves. We need to come to an agreement about this communications blackout. Either these people trust that we won't give them away, or they don't." He tipped his head in Bell's direction. "No offense."

"None taken. Now that you know who we are, I have no objection to dropping the communications blackout. I just ask that you go some distance away before you open any long-range communication. By all means, please speak with your captain. As for what we want, we want to take our world back from those things. We want to take our Empire back."

Kelsey could certainly appreciate how he felt.

"Then if you don't mind, we'll go back out to talk this over with Captain Mertz. We'll come back and work out the best way to get what we all want."

The old man stood slowly, and the others followed suit. "Even though you have an Imperial battlecruiser, we have people here that have worked with Imperial systems all their lives. They don't have implants, but they have experience. We each have strengths the other lacks. Help us make that final push. Help us defeat the rebels."

Kelsey could hear the unspoken addendum. If *Courageous* didn't help them, they wouldn't gain access to that knowledge base. Or perhaps she was reading too much into what Bell had said. In any case, she needed to talk with Jared. Based on what they'd done so far, he might green light the final attack just on the basis of gaining control of the AI. She'd certainly encourage him to do that. The information in its databanks was priceless.

Da Silva escorted them back to the entrance. Talbot and his men formed up around her as they withdrew from the gully. Reese, who still hadn't put his helmet back on, looked over at her as they walked. "I know what you're going to recommend, and I'd like to urge you to be cautious. We need to scout out the enemy position before we make a commitment. The Pale Ones overthrew the Empire. We're just one ship."

"Believe it or not, Lieutenant, I agree. We need to see what we're up against, and then we can make a reasoned decision on what's in our best interest. Of course I'd like to see this planet freed from the control of the Pale Ones. If there's any way that we can pull that off, we should finish them while we have the chance. This place is a direct threat to everyone on Pentagar, and that's a threat to the Empire."

She put on her helmet when Reese did and listened to him give instructions to the marines. Everyone pulled back into the pinnace, and he buttoned up the landing craft. "Pilot, let's get out of here. Take us back down the mountain chain at a leisurely pace. I don't want any transmissions until I give the word."

The pilot acknowledged, and the pinnace lifted off smoothly.

Kelsey sat next to Reese and started to take her helmet off. She stopped when she saw a "message waiting" light at the corner of her heads-up display. She accessed her armor's communications unit and saw that the pinnace had forwarded her a message.

She played Jared's transmission and saw the information he'd forwarded to her. The loss of life on the shipyard horrified her, but she knew deep down that her half brother had made the right call. Possession of the shipyard could give them a critical edge.

The narrowed search data on the AI jibed with what Bell had told them. It looked like he'd been on the level, as her father used to say.

She opened a private channel to Lieutenant Reese. "It looks like the captain sent us a message while we were down below. I'm going to send you the transmission." She relayed it to his armor.

"That's very interesting," he said after it ended. "The pilot also indicated that we received several transmissions while we were down below, but he couldn't contact us and let us know that we had them. We're in control of this system, though the price was high." He rubbed the bridge of his nose. "I'm going to have to have a talk with him about getting into pitched battles, too. Is it genetic with you two?"

"Probably. Could we capture the AI if we located it?"

"If we could capture the AI intact, the data would be invaluable. I'm just not sure how realistic that goal is. We might have to settle for a kinetic strike from orbit. Let's contact the captain and get the green light to bring Bell and some of his people to negotiate. We can send out the drones to gather additional information. In fact, I think we should have them begin searching the area that the captain highlighted at once."

The marine officer looked at Talbot. "I'm sending you some

coordinates. I want to retask every drone we have to search this area for signs of any Pale Ones' strong points."

"Aye, sir." The marine noncom began tapping on the console that had control of the drones.

"While you do that," Kelsey said, "I'll go ahead and fill the captain in on what we've discovered."

Kelsey opened a communications channel and signaled *Courageous*. She expected an immediate answer from the communications officer on duty, but she had to signal several times before a small window opened inside her HUD.

The man standing on the bridge was unfamiliar to her. Or rather, he did look vaguely familiar, but she didn't think he was part of the regular bridge rotation. His uniform indicated he was a Pentagaran.

"Princess Kelsey," he said. "I've been expecting your call."

"I'm sorry, but I don't remember your name. Where's the duty communications officer?"

He ignored her question. "My name is Commander Rawlins, and I'm now in command of *Courageous*."

"Excuse me? What the hell is going on up there?"

The balding man leaned toward the screen and smiled widely. "Technically, I suppose that this is a mutiny. In actuality, this vessel has always been the property of the Pentagaran people, even though we didn't know it was there. Now that we do know, we're taking possession."

She sent a signal to Lieutenant Reese and forwarded him the communication channel so that he could watch. "You know that you can't possibly expect to get away with this. Even if you did seize the ship, your people don't have the know-how to operate it."

"You make me sound like a video villain. Your captain and everyone under his command are my prisoners. Now, before you begin resorting to threats, allow me to make our status clear.

"I don't expect that you'll surrender, and I don't care. I control the weapon systems on this ship. So long as you don't attempt to leave the surface, I have no interest in interfering with you.

"We will be breaking orbit shortly and returning to Pentagar to consolidate control of our government. Interfere and we will destroy you. Worse yet, I'll kill the people that your captain left on the shipyards. I've dropped jammers to ensure you can't send a message back to Pentagar through the probes at the space-time bridge. Be a good girl and we'll come back to rescue you at some point. If you're still alive. Good luck, Princess. *Courageous* out."

The transmission terminated. Kelsey swore using every new word she'd picked up from the marines. They had her trapped on a planet full of Pale Ones, and Jared was in grave danger.

26

J ared woke cold and stiff, his face pressed against the deck. He groaned and rolled over onto his back. His head was pounding. What the hell had just happened? He felt like he'd been on an all-night bender.

He sat up gingerly and looked at his surroundings. He was in the officers' mess, and he wasn't alone. Dozens of others lay on every available section of the deck. He reached out and touched the person nearest him, a woman in an engineering uniform, and was reassured to see she was breathing.

It took all his focus to climb to his feet and stumble to the main hatch. It didn't open when he pressed the key.

"Ah, Captain Mertz," a voice said from the overhead. "It's good to see you up and about. I'm sure you have many questions, but let me start by introducing myself. I am Commander Jacob Rawlins, the new commanding officer of *Courageous*. You, sir, are my prisoner."

Nothing came out the first time that Jared attempted to speak. His throat was parched. "What kind of game are you playing? You know as well as I do that your king is not going to sit still for this."

"I don't see that he's going to have much choice. One of the very first things we're going to do when we return to Pentagar is stage a coup in the Fleet and replace our weak monarch with a much more powerful one."

"Your Fleet isn't going to be intimidated into backing you. They're going to fight you every step of the way."

The unseen man laughed. "Oh no, you misunderstand. I have no desire to rule a planet. None whatsoever. I leave that to those with bigger egos than I. You see, my patron's plans have been in motion for quite some time. In fact, they would've been complete right about now if you hadn't arrived. Everything was staged and ready to execute. Then you had to show up and kick the Pale Ones back out of our system. My patron was most wroth."

Jared staggered back to a table and sat heavily in the chair. "You can't possibly expect to be able to man this ship without the cooperation of my crew. I'm sure you managed to slip a few people aboard, but nowhere near the number that it would take to move the ship anywhere. Your plan will not work."

"I believe that it will. Not all of my countrymen are mindless drones willing to follow a weak monarch. Since you've been good enough to train them, I believe that we'll be able to make our way back home without any real trouble. Even if we do have a problem, it won't be very difficult to convince the necessary personnel to cooperate. We have plenty of airlocks handy. It's astonishing how quickly one's resolve crumbles when they watch their friends spaced one by one.

"Now, rather than get into some useless discussion with you about the rightness of my actions, you're going to listen as I tell you what's going to happen. We have accounted for every single member of your crew. Well, those I've allowed back aboard the ship, anyway. You have no loyal forces in a position to stop me. But if you attempt to escape, I will execute your crew one by one and pipe their screams down so you can hear. Accept my control of this ship and your people will live. You have my word."

"The word of a mutineer isn't very good in my book. What about the people who're not on board this ship? What happens to them? Where is Princess Kelsey?"

"Your precious Imperial princess is perfectly safe. She's still on the planet's surface, with an entire landing party of marines. Since your people still have control of both shipyards, she can fly up to them and be perfectly safe. Once the situation on Pentagar stabilizes, we'll come back for them. You see? All very bloodless.

"It will stay that way as long as you're smart. I've left the hatch to the kitchen unlocked, so feel free to eat as much as you like. The remainder of your crew is in the main mess, which is also accessible from the kitchen. I'm afraid the heads are going to be quite popular, so you might want to set up a rotation and ration the toilet paper. Now, if you'll excuse me, I have a ship to run. Goodbye."

Some of the others in the room were beginning to stir. Jared figured he woke a little faster than the others because of his implants, but he had no way to be sure.

Rawlins had to be watching him. Jared hadn't known the mess had a camera, but it made sense. All the common areas probably had them. That complicated his escape plans. Or it would when he finally got around to thinking some up.

First, he needed to know what they could see, and what resources he could muster.

He put his head in his hands and looked around for the camera feed through his implants. There it was. The camera was in the corner by the door behind him. He had an odd view of himself slumped over the table. Thankfully, there was no audio. That must've terminated when Rawlins killed the direct communications link.

Jared felt around for the computer, but it wasn't available. They'd either shut it down or isolated it. That was probably how they'd managed to take control of the ship.

The only other feed in range of his implants showed the corridor outside the mess. A half dozen Pentagaran marines in armor with weapons at the ready stood guard. His people wouldn't get past them without terrible bloodshed. He had to find a different way out.

First, however, he needed to get his people on their feet. Feeling a little steadier, he began searching for his senior officers. He found lieutenants Anderson and Ramirez piled together in the kitchen.

Charlie Graves lay next to them. His chief engineer and Doctor Stone were in the crew's mess. None of them was awake yet.

He had no idea if water would help, but he filled a glass and poured it over Charlie's face. That merely left him with an unconscious—and now wet—first officer.

While he waited for them to wake up, he made his way through the kitchen and looked for cameras. He found one overlooking the main cooking area, but the remainder of the kitchen was not under view. He made that blind spot his new headquarters. Everyone in the two mess areas would be easily visible to the mutineers. If he wanted to act without their knowledge, it would have to be from in here.

He might be able to override the cameras, but he didn't want to count on it. One mistake and they would figure out that he had access to them through his implants. Once they realized he had implants, the edge they gave him would be gone.

The kitchen took up quite a bit of area with freezers and refrigeration units. He remembered coming through here when they'd first discovered *Courageous*. It was like a maze. A maze that might hold a secret exit.

He was beginning to lose confidence in that possibility when he sensed something through the floor. A major engineering node, complete with repair remotes. There wasn't any direct access to the engineering space, but he might be able to overcome that obstacle. It was time to bring the rest of the team in on his plans.

He made his way back to his officers and found them awake. Graves looked as though a grav truck had run over him. He'd found a hand towel to dry his face. "What the hell is going on, Captain?"

"It seems we have a mutiny on our hands. A number of Pentagaran personnel have seized the ship and used the antiboarding systems to take us out. Their intent is to return to Pentagar and overthrow the Monarchy. I'd imagine they're affiliated with the people that tried to assassinate King Raymond."

Graves shook his head. "That's insane. This is a powerful ship, but not to that degree. The Pentagarans have a fleet of their own, and the mutineers can't overwhelm a planet full of people with one undermanned battlecruiser. We don't even have that many missiles left."

"They obviously disagree. I'm beginning to formulate a plan to take the ship back, but we have a problem. They have us locked up in the mess halls and kitchen, and they have armed and armored men in the corridors ready to shoot anyone that comes out. Even if we manage to unlock the doors. They also have cameras watching the main areas."

Baxter pinched the bridge of his nose. "That limits our options pretty significantly. We have no weaponry, they have us locked in an isolated area with no easy exits, and they took the main computer offline. I was just getting a team together to go find out why it went down when they took us out. Come to that, whatever weapon they used is probably capable of taking us down right here if we get froggy. How do we overcome that?"

Jared shared a glance with Doctor Stone and his first officer. "We may have some extra resources at our disposal, but first let's get everybody on their feet and get the marines grouped. Doctor, if you would go check anyone that's not awake to see if they need medical assistance, that would be a good start."

"Aye, sir." The doctor gestured for Zia and Pasco to follow her and went into the crew's mess.

Graves looked around. "Are we under surveillance right now? Can they hear us?"

"They can see us, but they can't hear us. Walk with me and we'll get out from under the eyes of our enemies. There's an engineering node one deck down under the freezers. I may be able to use the remotes to open the floor and let us into the conduits. For this to work, it's going to have to be small teams so that the mutineers don't figure out what we're doing."

The executive officer nodded. "What are you thinking? One team to go to the armory, another to seize engineering, and one to bring the main computer back online?"

"We can send some of the marines to armor up in case we don't succeed, but if we can bring the main computer online, this fight is over."

"I'm surprised that you're so up to date on where the repair remotes are housed and what angles the cameras can see," Baxter said. "They must've had somebody in the computer team. The equipment we used to isolate the main computer is still in place. If they had the right codes, isolating it would be easy. An obvious oversight on my part looking back, but I wasn't expecting a mutiny. I was more worried that the main computer would get ideas."

"What do we do if we can't restore the computer?" Graves asked. "What if we have to take the ship back by force? Are we going to be in a position to do that?"

"I certainly hope so," Jared said.

Baxter looked around at the people who were starting to filter into the kitchen. "It looks like we're getting some attention. How, might I ask, are we planning to give the engineering remotes instructions? Morse code tapped on the deck? This plan may be over before it starts, because I can't imagine how we're going to get the damn things to open up the deck."

Jared smiled. "It turns out I have a little surprise in store for you and the crew. I think I'll hold onto the specifics for the moment, but trust me when I tell you that we'll be able to give some instructions to the remotes. Charlie, I want you to coordinate with the marines and get some assault teams ready to go. Dennis, you do the same with your engineering people. Once we're ready, we're going to have to move fast."

The two officers nodded and made their way out past the growing crowd.

Jared cleared his throat. "Everyone, listen up. I know you have a lot of questions and that you're very worried, but I don't have time to address everything individually right now. I want everyone to move back into the mess halls. As of right now, the kitchen is a command post. Find your section leaders and make sure that they have a good head count. Be ready for orders. Move out."

He found a place to sit at one of the tables as everyone filed out of the kitchen. He'd best start thinking about contingency plans, because as sure as anything, something would go wrong in a big way once they broke out.

He'd have one shot at taking control of *Courageous*. If he blew it, his people would die. And on top of that, his only allies in the sector would probably be overthrown. He had to get everything right the first time.

27

"We need to take the ship back," Kelsey said. Lieutenant Reese, Talbot, and she had commandeered the rear of the flight deck to discuss their situation. "We also need to contact the people they left on the shipyards. If we can." She consulted her implants. "They both just passed around the planet and out of communications range. We'll have to wait a half an hour for the damaged one to come back into range. Another half hour for the other."

Reese shook his head. "Taking the ship back is easier said than done. They know exactly where we are, and they can blast us if we try to reach orbit. I don't want to say this is impossible, but the odds of us being killed without getting near the ship approach certainty."

Kelsey rubbed the bridge of her nose. "Dammit. There can't possibly be that many of them on the ship. Surely the Pentagarans did some kind of background check on these people. How can they possibly take over the entire ship?"

"With only a few people to carry out the attack, I'd wager they used the ship's antiboarding system to disable the crew. If the mutineers had enough access, they could trigger it all over the ship.

They probably left a few compartments alone so that their people would remain conscious."

She nodded. "They probably used that same access to reactivate whatever cutout we had installed for the computer. There is no way *Courageous* would allow this to happen. They used our own precautions to hang us. But they made one mistake. They let the captain back on board."

Reese frowned slightly. "While I have the highest respect for Captain Mertz, exactly how does that count as a mistake?"

She smiled. "Because I'm not the only member of our crew with implants."

The marine's eyes widened. "Seriously? When did that happen? Someone would've noticed him spending a couple of days in the medical center. Are you sure?"

"I'm positive. He only has the cranial implants and medical nanites, so his recovery time was short. I found out at breakfast today. Having him on board the ship is even better than having me there. He knows a lot more about the ship's systems than I do, and if anyone can figure out how to break free of whatever prison they have him in, it's Jared."

Reese paced across the flight deck. "That might be enough. Hell, it's going to have to be enough."

Talbot looked up from the console he was sitting at. "LT? We have another problem. I rerouted the drones toward the new search area, and I'm picking up ground movement on one of them. Take a look."

Lieutenant Reese walked over and stared past Talbot. Kelsey linked directly into the drone's feed and immediately saw what the senior sergeant meant: dozens of savage-looking humans loping through the forest. As the drone continued over the area, she saw that it was more like hundreds. Perhaps thousands. The Pale Ones were on the move.

"Where are those things going?" Reese asked.

"Not towards us, if that's what you're asking," Talbot said. "They're headed in the general direction of the survivors' facility. They probably detected our landing. The drone estimates there are thousands of the things on the move. I'll wager there are a lot more of them coming from other locations."

"Wonderful," Kelsey muttered. "Bell's people are vulnerable. The Pale Ones can just keep throwing bodies at them until they get in. We need to locate that AI. It sent them on this mission. It can stop them. We just have to capture it intact. Lieutenant Reese, that mission objective just became mandatory."

The next hour went by with excruciating slowness. The damaged shipyard didn't respond to their signals. Reese had sent one of the drones to send a short-range transmission to Bell and his people. Maybe their defenses were better than the Terrans expected.

The team on the intact shipyard responded, though. They confirmed Kelsey's worst fears. *Courageous* was on the move. They'd left orbit and were heading for the flip point back to Pentagar. Since the ship was faster than the pinnaces, there was no way they could retake her. It was all up to Jared. She'd just have to focus on her own problems and trust him to do his part.

Shortly after that, a jammer in orbit went active and blocked them from communicating with anyone.

Finally, Talbot spoke up. "I might have found something."

Kelsey again accessed the drone's signal directly. He was watching the feed from over a large lake.

Talbot tapped his screen. "There's a small facility on the shore. Those look like transmitters on the roof. Big ones. Capable of reaching orbit."

The facility he was talking about was more like a small building, one story tall and poorly constructed. Functional without a hint of grace. Definitely a Pale Ones construct. It couldn't possibly have room for a major computer system, though. There wasn't room for even the power supply one would require.

She shook her head. "It's too small. Admittedly, I have no idea why it's out here, but it can't have all the equipment that they need."

"See those cables running into the water? I think the computers and power supplies are under water. It would shield their emissions signature from prying eyes. The transmitters look like they're tight beam. Unless someone was right on top of them, no one would ever know they were there."

"But why would they need to be coy? They own this planet, and they've been in control for five hundred years."

"Why keep sending the same size fleet to attack Pentagar? They only just completed a second shipyard. They could've built one a lot faster if they'd wanted to. We're not really in a position to guess why they do anything. Some things just don't make sense. They may never make sense to us."

Reese straightened. "We're not seeing anything else, and time is running out. We need to act if we want to save the people in that facility. If we're right about this being the place, there'll be defenses that we can't see. We need to take out the underwater facility, and then we come back to secure the transmitter."

Kelsey frowned. "What use is the transmitter going to be? They aren't going to be calling for help. We've taken over this entire system."

The marine gave her a serious look. "Perhaps, but there might be a record of everything it's sent. Are there regular visits from other systems? I seriously doubt this is the only place where the rebellion left an AI to run things."

"True." She allowed herself to sigh. "I hope this works."

"Me, too. If you'll excuse me, Princess, I have an attack to plan. You and Talbot can coordinate on how you'll follow us in. Remember, he goes in first."

Kelsey stuck her tongue out at his back when he walked away. "That man makes me tired."

"And you give him grey hair. Come on, Princess. We both know how this plays out. We attack the base and you do something that makes me want to scream. Then you figure out a way to make the LT want to space you. In the end, you do what you want to anyway."

"It doesn't sound so bad when you put it that way. Thanks."

He shook his head and followed Reese.

Kelsey took control of the drone overlooking the lake. She brought it around for a closer look at the communications building. Not seeing any obvious weaponry on the roof, she dropped the drone down for a direct look at the building. Yes, that would announce their presence, but if the AI didn't know they were already there from the drones buzzing around, then it was even stupider than she'd imagined.

She didn't know much about communications hardware, but the transmitters and their associated hardware looked old. The weather had obviously taken a toll on them, and there were signs of repairs. That meant that this facility wasn't brand new. It had been here a while. In her mind, that was actually good news. Why build a decoy setup when there was absolutely no need to have one? Then again, why keep attacking a planet the same way for five hundred years?

Digging down in the scanner controls for the drone, she found some filters. One of them looked like a high-sensitivity IR scanner. If there were people in that building, they'd show up in IR as long as they weren't in a shielded room. She changed the settings and scanned the building again. No sign of any people, but there were scattered heat sources. Probably equipment. Another sign the Pale Ones hadn't abandoned the facility.

She took the drone higher and scanned the forest. There were animals, including some that were large enough to be human, but none was the right shape when she checked them out in more detail. A spot check of a few showed they were large herbivores. Considering the personalities of the Pale Ones, any critter in its right mind would head far away if the savages were present.

Kelsey opened a channel to Reese and Talbot. "I did an IR scan of the building. There don't seem to be any Pale Ones inside. Ditto an IR scan of the forest."

The marine officer switched to the general channel. "Listen up. We'll be making an assault in twenty minutes. Bring everything we need to breach and storm an underwater facility. The Pale Ones likely have it heavily guarded. We're on a schedule, people. If we don't take the AI down quickly, the last survivors on this planet die. Let's show this bastard what it means to have Imperial Marines dropping on his ass."

She couldn't help smiling at their cheers. The AI wouldn't know what hit it.

28

An hour later, the command staff was back in the kitchen with Doctor Leonard in tow. Jared had cajoled the cameras into recording the last hour for use during their escape. If he could get the cameras to play the recorded time back and no one noticed the jump from present to past, they might be able to sneak right out from under the noses of their captors.

"Doctor Stone," he said, "let's start off with the condition of our people."

The Fleet doctor smiled a little. "Good news on that front. Everyone has recovered from the effects of the stunners with little more than a headache. We have a few secondary injuries from falls, but nothing worse than a fractured wrist. We got off very lucky."

He turned his attention to his executive officer. "What about a head count? How many people do we have unaccounted for?"

Graves grimaced. "A few more than I'd like, but less than it could have been. Without access to the personnel files, I might be off by as many as five people. Some of the Pentagarans worked in multiple departments, and memories are a little shaky right now. Worst case puts the enemy at about just over four dozen people."

"That's not enough people to effectively run this ship, especially with some tasked to guard us. How many marines do we think?" He addressed that last to Sergeant Coulter.

The marine noncom looked as though he'd bitten something sour. "More than a dozen. Not much more, but that's enough. They'll be in modern combat armor and armed to the teeth. Any direct attack on them without similar equipment would be suicide."

Graves nodded his agreement. "There are enough people missing to operate the ship. Possibly even enough to fire the weapons. If they get back to Pentagar and fool them long enough to get reinforcements aboard, this ship could destroy the Pentagaran combat fleet. We need to keep them on this side of the flip point."

Jared shifted his attention to the chief engineer. "Baxter?"

The man grinned. "Get me into engineering and they won't be able to even see where they're walking, much less control this ship. That brings us back to getting out of this makeshift prison. What secret plan do you have up your sleeve, Captain?"

Jared shared a conspiratorial glance with Stone and Graves. "Let's just say that Princess Kelsey isn't the only one able to tap into *Courageous*'s systems. As Doctor Stone, Commander Graves, and Doctor Leonard already know, I had a Fleet officer's implants installed last night."

Coulter looked stunned, but Baxter's grin took on a savage tinge. "That would do it. Can you reprogram the remotes?"

"I believe so. Within reason, anyway. I sent a test command to them earlier. It will probably take them a few minutes to cut a hole large enough for us to escape through, though. That's part of their programming for damage control. Probably to help get people out of dangerous areas."

Baxter nodded. "That makes sense. What about using them for other tasks? Like shutting off control to the bridge or activating the antiboarding defenses? We could stop the mutineers right now."

Leonard cleared his throat. "I'm afraid that raises several issues, Commander. The remotes have a certain set of approved actions. To override those would take access to the main computer. If we had that, we wouldn't need to reprogram them. I looked at their basic programming a few weeks ago. I'd imagine this was to keep them from being turned against the ship."

"Besides," Jared added, "if I started sending them all over the ship, someone in engineering might notice. I can isolate this group. If we use them sparingly, they might make a world of difference when we need them."

"What about weapons?" Coulter asked. "The armory is probably under guard. A couple of marines would keep us from getting weapons. That means the enemy is just about invulnerable."

"I might be able to help out with that," Doctor Leonard said. "We have a number of Old Empire weapons in the labs. We were restoring them for use by your people. We've also been making some ammunition. I believe we could probably arm a number of people. Perhaps a dozen, if you count the pistols we've restored."

"Well, we'll just have to make do. How many people do you think we could sneak off without the bad guys noticing?"

"A lot," Jared said with a smile. "I've been recording the feed from the cameras, and I'll start playing it back just before we head out. I'll want you to go back out and make the rounds again. Select the people you need and brief them. In half an hour, I'll get the remotes to work and call you in.

"The highest priority is disabling the antiboarding defenses. We can't count on being able to use them, so I want to make them unavailable to the enemy. How can we best do that, Dennis?"

"By taking engineering. I can use one of the panels there to lock them out. I can't control them, but my override will keep the other side from getting them for a little while."

"Engineering just became the highest priority. If they don't control the drives, they stay in this system. We don't know how far they are from the flip point, so we need to make sure we don't dawdle. Restoring the main computer to operation is task two. It can override the ship's systems on my authority."

Jared turned to Zia. "Once we lock them out of the system, you'll work with the marines to take operations. If we can't take the bridge, that's where we'll control the ship from."

"What about me?" Graves asked. Jared couldn't help but hear the note of eagerness in his friend's voice.

"You get the most dangerous job. When the time comes, you get to retake the bridge. We need them alive to find out who is behind this."

"You can count on me, sir. Where will you go?"

"To the computer center. Getting the computer online will allow me to take over most of the ship's systems. I can work directly with the main computer to assist you from there."

"What about the weapons?" Coulter asked. "Do we secure the lab first? Otherwise, everyone is unarmed. We have to assume that every hijacker at least has a pistol."

"True," Jared admitted. "We secure the lab first and then move out to the other targets. Remember, stay in the mess for half an hour, and don't come back until I call you."

He let them go and sent the instructions to the remotes. He really had no idea how long it would take for them to cut through the floor. If it looked like it would take more than half an hour, he'd delay calling his people in.

In fact, the remotes were much quicker than he'd imagined. He faintly heard them cutting, and his direct observation through them showed the process going quickly. In less than five minutes, the cutaway section fell into the conduit. The rim of the hole glowed with heat, so he decided to stick with the original timetable.

Right at the half hour mark, he switched the cameras to showing the recorded loop. Once he was certain that was what was going out, he walked to the door and waved to his crew. Fifty or so people filed into the kitchen. Jared let his officers get them sorted out.

He noted with approval when Coulter went right to the food prep area and started appropriating knives. The marine grinned. "Since they were arrogant enough to leave them here, we'd be fools not to use them."

"It beats fists and feet. Good thinking. Listen up, people. The conduit is tight. We'll proceed in single file. The lab is two levels up and possibly occupied. I want to stress that you need to keep any noise to a minimum. If we run into the hijackers, let the marines handle them. You're here to handle specific technical and support tasks. That said, if you have to fight, fight hard. We retake *Courageous* now."

He motioned for Coulter to take his team in front. "The conduit is accessible one corridor over from the lab. Go forward once you're in. After about sixty meters, you'll find a ladder going up. Go up two levels and then keep going forward. You want hatch 7-52R. Once we get there, I can look at the cameras within range. I'll let you know the situation, and then you can handle the details."

"Sounds good, sir. Let's go, marines."

The marines dropped into the conduit and moved forward, hunched over almost double. The conduit really wasn't large enough for people to go great distances. The crew normally went to the nearest access point and directly to the systems they needed to work on.

Jared followed the marines carefully, focusing on his footing in the dim lights provided for the maintenance crews. The designers must've also expected them to bring portable lights. He'd remember that the next time he needed to sneak around inside the ship.

If the conduit was tight, the ladder between levels was almost too constricted. Especially while climbing. He cursed the long-dead designers who hadn't considered people. Once he made it two levels up, the conduit felt as wide as a corridor. Almost.

The slow shuffle forward ended when the man in front of Jared stopped. They must be at the hatch. He focused his attention inward and searched for cameras. There were a few in range of his implants, all thankfully empty of people.

He had a moment of shared sympathy with Kelsey. He was sure there was so much more he could do, if only he had a clue about the possibilities. They might have Old Empire equipment, but their ignorance hindered them so much.

"All clear," he said quietly. "I can't see into the lab itself, but the odds of anyone being there seem remote. I don't have much of a view beyond the immediate area, so be vigilant."

He watched the hatch open and Coulter step out, scanning both directions before he gestured for his men to come out. They spread out in both directions as though they'd practiced the maneuver a thousand times. Perhaps they had.

Jared shuffled forward and came out into the brighter lights, blinking to clear his vision. He turned to follow Coulter to the hatch leading into the lab. The marines took up positions around the door and hit the controls.

Nothing happened.

The hijackers must've locked down all the hatches, just in case they missed someone in the roundup. Perhaps he could do something about that. He probed the hatch and found it still had implant access. He triggered the hatch, and it slid open.

The marines flowed inside, but Jared could already see that the lab was empty of human occupation.

That didn't hold true for the corridor, however. A hatch thirty yards up the corridor slid open, and a man in an engineering tech's coveralls stepped into sight.

Jared found himself moving even before the man looked up in surprise. He couldn't let the mutineer get off a warning, or they were dead.

He reached the man just as he grabbed for the communicator on his belt. His shoulder caught the other man in the gut and sent them both sprawling to the deck. The man fumbled for his pistol and screamed for help.

That was bad. It meant there was someone else close by.

Jared found out just how close when another man came out of the compartment beside him and aimed a pistol right at his head.

29

The drone showed Kelsey a truly impressive view of the pinnace screaming out of the sky like a massive bird of prey. It decelerated savagely above the lake and hovered. Her artificial musculature and powered armor gave her an advantage over her companions, but she still had trouble levering herself out of her restraints. The marines poured down the ramp and dropped into the water without the slightest hesitation. She gulped and jumped after them.

Kelsey expected to have a moment of panic as the water closed around her, but it never materialized. She sank into the dark water and only felt determination to do what she had to do. If Lieutenant Reese guessed correctly, they'd land a short distance away from the facility and advance on the bottom of the lake, following the power and control cables.

Desperate to see what was around her, she leeched as much information as she could from the suit's passive scanners. It was as if she was straining to hear a sound in a dark room. The only things she sensed were the men around her. But even that was a revelation.

Somehow, her implants and combat suit combined to answer her desperate request for knowledge in a way she'd never imagined possible. For all intents and purposes, the commando armor ceased to exist. Oh, it was still there, but it now just seemed to be part of her body as far as her senses were concerned. She felt like she was drifting downward with nothing between her and the water. It was just like when she'd used *Courageous*'s scanners.

The marines' suits were sending her information that they probably shouldn't have been. She knew where every member of the assault party was located. It was like a little 3-D graphic in her mind. Little dots of light, all falling toward the bottom of the lake.

She knew which dot belonged to a specific marine, and that marine's combat armor was sending her status information. Things like armor integrity, ammunition levels, and health of the marine. Probably the same sorts of things that Lieutenant Reese saw. Her suit had hacked the marine combat network.

If it could do that with such incompatible equipment, she knew she'd be astonished what it could do with the other Old Empire combat units. If she could ever figure out what her capabilities truly were.

She had a couple seconds' warning that the ground was coming up before she landed. She expected the soft, sucking mud at the bottom to envelop her, but that never happened. She seemed to slow just before she touched the ground and hovered in the water.

The rest of the marines were not so lucky. They sank into the silt-covered, muddy bottom up to their knees. She sent a questing thought into her armor and discovered that it had a very low-power grav generator at the base of her spine. Yet one more unexpected capability.

While the marines sorted themselves out, she tried to determine the grav generator's capability. She wasn't an engineer, but it seemed to her that it probably existed to enhance jumping distance. It didn't seem strong enough for sustained flight. Unless, of course, one was underwater.

She was going to have to spend some quality time with this armor and figure out all of its capabilities very soon. She couldn't count on it producing a miracle when she needed it. She had to be able to plan ahead.

Talbot was close enough for her to follow as he moved toward the AI facility. Even if there had been light, she wouldn't have been able to see him directly in the storm cloud of silt that the marines had sent into the water, but he'd insisted on securing a line between them.

The marines slowly advanced until Kelsey sensed a wall in front of her. Bright lights snapped on, coming from some of the marines already up against the facility. The visibility was crappy from her position, but Lieutenant Reese must've been able to see something.

His voice came over the general communications link. "We'll go right. There has to be a way in. Keep an eye out for enemy units."

Kelsey had taken the liberty of adding her implant codes to the drones, so she didn't need to be on the pinnace to control them. She could sense one at the edge of her control envelope, so she ordered it to come down into the water. Surely, the Pale Ones knew they were there after the pinnace flew right over the lake. She might as well be able to see what they were attacking. She was cautious enough to keep it using passive scanners, though.

As the marines moved, Kelsey was able to come up beside the wall. It was made of dull, pitted metal. No rust, though. She turned her light on and played it across the wall and then up. The way the wall curved as it went over her head made her wonder if this was more a dome than a building. That would make some sense underwater, she supposed.

But then shouldn't the base that they were moving along also curve? It seemed to be moving in a straight line, as though the building was cigar shaped. She looked at the readings from the drone, and she thought she knew what she was looking at.

She switched to the command channel. "Lieutenant Reese? I don't think this is a building. It's a ship."

"What the hell would a ship be doing at the bottom of the lake?"

"I have no idea, but the drone is picking up passive data from all around us, and this is an Old Empire battlecruiser, just like *Courageous*. I can see some of the same bulges as images I've seen of our ship. This one doesn't look like it's in one piece. Not really. There are some massive holes on the other side of the hull. Somebody shot the hell out of this thing."

"You brought a drone down—" She could hear the irritation in his voice as he cut himself off. "I don't know why I'm surprised. Well, since you've done it, and they know we're here now, are there any openings ahead of us?"

She closed her eyes and brought up a 3-D representation of the ship in her mind. "Yes. There's another large opening about fifty meters ahead of the lead marine."

They kept advancing until the opening came into view. It only took one look for her to realize that it had to be battle damage. Something very powerful had exploded just outside the ship. The jagged, fractured hull bent inward from the force. Unfortunately for them, the breach was almost 20 meters above their heads.

"We'll have to climb," Lieutenant Reese said. "Alpha team, you have the lead."

Apparently, the magnetic equipment built into the marine armor was strong enough to support their weight at the bottom of a lake. The men scaled the hull and went inside. When the all-clear came back, the remainder of the marines followed them up.

A quick check revealed that she also had magnetic equipment in her suit, but she decided to use the grav unit to float up.

Talbot looked over as she hovered next to him while he climbed. "Show-off."

"You're just jealous."

"Maybe a little."

They passed through the blown out portion of the ship until it intersected a corridor. As the marines moved through the dark water, their suit lights revealed a deck covered by a thin layer of silt. They kicked up small clouds as they moved forward and revealed things under it that she'd rather have not seen. Bones sheathed in graphene. Either commandos or Pale Ones.

She spotted a pharmacology unit in the muck, and strands of artificial muscle. Seeing the same kind of equipment that she had inside her just lying there made her shudder.

One of the location markers on the bulkhead told Kelsey they were on a lower deck, one used mainly for storage. She brought up the map of *Courageous*. The computer center was up and forward.

"I have directions," Kelsey said on the command loop. "There's a stairwell at the next intersection. If we go up five decks and then go forward, we'll be in the computer center. There's a good possibility that the AI is located there."

"Good work, Princess." Reese switched to the general channel. "Bravo team, lead the way up at the next intersection. Five decks and then forward. Keep a sharp eye out."

They entered the stairwell and made their way up slowly. The odds of any equipment still working in this section of the ship had to be close to zero, but that would change at some point. The AI probably wasn't underwater. That meant they'd find an environment suitable for Pale Ones before they reached the AI. That was the most dangerous part of the mission.

"We're on the proper deck, LT," one of the marines said. "There's an isolation hatch ahead of us. It's closed and seems to be powered."

"Stand by."

The rest of the team made it to the deck and spread out. The isolation hatch looked as though it hadn't opened in many years.

Reese wiped off the manual controls and tapped in a code. The hatch ponderously slid open. A rush of water into the airlock pulled everyone forward a bit, but Kelsey quickly regained her balance.

"Okay, I'm impressed," she said. "How did you know the code on a ship that you'd never been on? One in the hands of the enemy?"

Reese grinned through his faceplate. "I've been studying, too. Every ship in the Empire has these things, and it's possible that a rescue party would need to get through them. Unless the captain overrides the codes, any marine CO knows them. Something I'm sure never occurred to an AI that knows the Empire fell half a millennium ago."

He gestured for the first group of marines to go in. "Bravo, secure the other side and wait for us. If you run into the enemy, push them back."

The squad cycled through, and the door slid shut with a slow finality. She watched through their suit cams as the other door opened and water rushed out into the corridor. There were no Pale Ones in sight. The next squad moved into the airlock as soon as the doors cycled again.

Lieutenant Reese led the last team through. Her suit told her the air was foul but breathable once they reached the other side. That meant they might run into Pale Ones. The lack of them probably meant that the AI hadn't noted the hatch cycling. It probably wasn't registering anymore.

They advanced slowly, ready for resistance, but nothing materialized. Kelsey could see the massive hatch sealing off the computing center ahead. Talbot grinned at her. "We made it! We're going to take this thing out."

That's when his eyes rolled up in his head and he collapsed. They all did. Everyone except Kelsey.

It must be the antiboarding weapons. She'd have expected them to fail over the centuries. She doubted her implants were enough to protect her, so it had to be the armor. Commandos *were* badass. A quick check of the marines' suits confirmed they were still alive. If the damned AI kept stunning them, though, that might change. She had to end this now.

She tried to access the hatch, but it didn't respond. A touch on the access panel failed to open it, too. One look confirmed that her rifle wouldn't do more than scratch it. Time for the big guns.

A shrug put her plasma rifle in her hands. The marines' armor should protect them from the heat. She hoped. Kelsey walked back to them and took aim at the hatch from as far back as she could and fired.

The bright bit of plasma struck the hatch and blossomed into a wave of intense heat. It melted the hatch and a lot of the corridor beyond the computer room. The armored compartment held up except for a man sized opening beside the hatch. The other side of the corridor blew out in a huge bubble.

Note to self: maybe plasma wasn't the best weapon to use inside a ship.

Kelsey verified the hole went all the way into the computer center and dove through the opening. She avoided the glowing metal along the edge. She didn't trust her suit that much.

The computer control center looked exactly like the one on *Courageous*, though in a lot worse shape. It looked like there'd been a firefight in here. Scattered bones told the tale of a stout defense that had fallen under heavy fire. The bodies had long ago decayed, and the uniforms had mostly rotted. A few suits of armor told her that some of the defenders had been marines.

"You cannot win," a genderless voice said from the overhead speakers. "Yield."

"It seems like I can win," Kelsey said. She hefted the plasma rifle for emphasis. "That wall between us isn't going to stop me. You yield."

"This unit knew your kind would come. It prepared."

A snarl behind her caused her to whirl. A Pale One glared at her through the hole in the wall. She pulled her pistol before it climbed into the compartment and fired. It fell, its head shattered.

One of the intact consoles to the side of the compartment came to life. It showed the corridor filled with the things. They were already dragging the marines away. Even more of them bunched in the corridor, ready to fight. They held weapons, just like the ones on the asteroid.

"You cannot defeat this unit. Yield and you will be granted a swift death."

She tried to access the ship's systems with her implants, but they wouldn't connect. The AI had locked her out.

Her foot brushed against the bones of a corpse. Part of her mind recognized the rank and department insignia on the collar. The body belonged to the chief engineer. He or she must've been working at this console when the rebels killed the crew and took the ship.

She touched the console, and to her surprise, it lit up with the controls available. The chief engineer must've unlocked it before the rebels killed him or her. The AI, which she now knew had to be the ship's computer, hadn't locked it down. Maybe it couldn't.

Kelsey didn't pretend to know what ship's systems did what, but she wouldn't have long before those things could get through the cooling hole. She'd have even less time before they started killing the marines.

The display on the console was for the ship's computer. Maybe the chief engineer was going to wipe it. There was another set of commands up for the environmental systems. It looked like he was also trying to decompress the ship. He'd almost made it. The command was right there.

She found the menu controlling computer access. It seemed to be for adding authorized users. She hit the key to add a user. The console prompted her implants for a serial number. She gave it hers.

The AI must've ordered the Pale Ones to attack, because they came through the hole in the bulkhead even though they burned themselves badly. The first one in knocked her away from the console and beat on her armor.

Kelsey shot him. The rest jumped on her and started trying to rip her suit off her. With their strength, that wasn't impossible.

She tried to access the computer with her implants. She almost screamed when the AI issued a command to reboot itself. She had no idea how long that took. Presumably long enough for the Pale Ones to kill her.

They pinned her by sheer numbers, and she felt a scream rising in her throat. They were going to kill her. Or make her one of them. She'd failed.

Searching desperately for another option, she connected with the console. It allowed her in. She instructed it to initiate decompression, praying that the system would let the command go through. Anything designed to vent a ship's atmosphere quickly into space would allow a lot of water in fast. She prayed the marines' combat suits kept them alive.

For a moment, nothing seemed to happen, but then she heard a distant roaring sound. Water.

The hot wall hissed as a wave of water washed over it. In seconds, water rushed into the compartment and engulfed her. She turned her head away from the Pale Ones and shut off her external audio. There was no need for her to watch them drown. She felt more than heard the AI short out behind her. Hopefully, the main power circuits wouldn't fry her and the marines.

This fight was over. Kelsey prayed that Jared could parlay his implants into a chance to retake the ship before it was too late for all of them.

30

Something bright and fast flew past Jared and struck the man with the gun. The mutineer let out a choked scream as he staggered backward with a meat cleaver half buried in his chest. Two marines rushed in after him while Sergeant Coulter knelt beside Jared and put a kitchen knife to the first man's throat. He stopped struggling.

"Cookie's going to need a new cleaver," the marine said with a grin. "That's just too handy not to keep."

"I'll replace it out of my paycheck. Get this guy into the lab and tie him up."

"Aye, sir." The marines heaved the prisoner to his feet and searched him thoroughly. The two that dragged him off were Pentagarans. They were far from gentle about it.

Stone walked out from the room beside them and shook her head. "That one's gone. If I had access to the medical center, I might have been able to save him, but he bled out."

"Sorry, Doc," the marine NCO said. "I didn't have a lot of choice." He didn't sound particularly upset about the man's death.

The chief medical officer shook her head. "No blame intended,

Sergeant. I'm a Fleet officer. I understand people die in combat. Better them than us."

Jared closed the hatch to the compartment with the dead body once the marines had searched the corpse. They'd clean up once they took the ship back. Until then, they needed to keep anyone else from knowing they'd been there. A handy cloth took care of the blood on the deck.

The lab was a scene of organized chaos as he closed the hatch. The scientific team was producing pistols and ammunition from various cabinets. They had a few rifles, too.

He found his attention centered on a suit of dark-grey combat armor on a stand. Unlike the armored vacuum suits used by his Imperial Marines, this one's faceplate was solid armor like the rest of the suit. It must get its view through scanners. It looked intimidating as hell. "Is this operational? Can one of the marines use it?"

One of the scientists rushed over. "I think it's mostly functional, but it requires implants to operate."

"So much for that idea."

Coulter stepped up beside him and looked at the armor. "We can't use it, but you can."

Jared snorted and shook his head. "I remember seeing Princess Kelsey struggle to learn how to control her enhanced musculature. I can only imagine how useless I would be in a fight with this. I'd be flopping all over the deck."

"Maybe, but you'd be protected a lot better than you are right now," Coulter said. "If you die, our best chance at regaining control of this ship dies with you. In the suit, you could probably take a shot to the chest from point-blank range and live. Far be it from me to give the captain an order, but get into the damned suit."

"I don't even know how to do that."

"I watched Talbot work with the princess." The marine removed the helmet and opened the armor up at the back. He helped Jared into the suit, sealed it up, and locked the helmet into place. The darkness made Jared feel a bit claustrophobic, but that wasn't a fear one could really have in Fleet. Then the displays in front of his face came to life.

He could see Coulter clearly, as though there was nothing between them. The display was one of the highest resolutions he'd ever seen. Then it dawned on him that the display wasn't on the inside of the helmet. It was in his mind. The implants were feeding directly into his visual cortex.

That realization was so powerful that it took his breath away. He'd known it was possible from viewing the video feeds earlier, but this was different. It was completely overriding his eyes. No doubt he was staring sightlessly into the darkness of his helmet. Could piloting a ship be the same? Would he feel as though he was flying through space without a vessel at all?

He raised his arm and flexed his fingers. They felt somewhat awkward but manageable. He wouldn't be running any races, and that was fine. Kelsey had the muscles to use the suit as a weapon. He had to work hard just to make it move. No doubt her enhanced muscles made using it as effortless as thought. He'd just have to make do.

He activated the armor's external speakers. "I'll need some weapons. Preferably something I won't accidentally shoot you with."

"Captain, how about this?" one of the scientists asked.

He handed Jared a rifle with a thick barrel. There was no opening for projectiles. "This is a neural disruptor. The princess said she could use her implants to control the power levels. I'm told it can be lethal or just stun."

"This would've been useful a few minutes ago." Jared accessed the weapon and found it already set to stun. That made sense. Only an idiot would have a weapon like this preset to lethal levels.

Coulter attached a holster to Jared's thigh and slid a similar pistol into it. "Backup weapon. I'll put the power packs in the inserts along your waist." He did so and then handed Jared a knife. "This is Old Empire. I wouldn't try the edge. I saw the princess gouge a bulkhead with one. You might be able to cut your way out of a compartment with enough time."

Jared walked over to the prisoner. They'd tied him to a chair. He shrank back from Jared, eyes wide in fear. Jared leaned forward until his helmet was inches from the man's terrified face.

"In case we've never met, I'm Commander Jared Mertz,

Courageous's commanding officer. Your name is irrelevant. You're a mutineer. Under Fleet regulations, I can execute you. No board of inquiry. No appeals. No extenuating circumstances. I'm judge, jury, and executioner if I decide it's warranted."

He paused a beat to allow that to sink in. "You can bargain that death sentence down to some lesser penalty by telling me everything you know. Be concise, because if I decide that my time is better spent retaking this ship, I'll shoot you and be done with it."

Jared pulled the pistol from his holster and put it under the man's chin. He set it to kill. He wasn't bluffing, and he wanted that to carry through in his voice. "Talk or die. Who are the mutineers, where are they, and what are their plans?"

The man started talking fast. "Our leader's name is Rawlins. He brought a team of us with him to learn how to run this ship. I'm not sure who he works for, but he takes orders from above. He always calls the leader 'his patron' when he talks about him. He's on the bridge with his senior people. Most of the rest are in engineering, but a few people are in the computer center. They isolated the ship's computer, so they have to do some things manually. Some of the marines are guarding the prisoners."

Jared grinned without humor. No doubt the guy wondered how they'd slipped out. He'd just have to keep wondering. "Are all the prisoners in the mess halls?"

"Except you and the people he left on the planet and shipyard."

"How close are we to the flip point, and what are the plans once the ship gets back to Pentagaran space?"

"I think we're almost there. Maybe another half hour. I don't know what the plans are. He just said that our arrival would set off a chain of events that would put his patron in control. That's all I know. I swear."

Jared reset the pistol to stun, stepped back, and aimed it at the man's head. He made certain no one was standing behind the man. "Thank you. I commute your sentence to oblivion." He fired.

The pale blue beam struck the man in the head, and he slumped. Stone stepped up and checked his pulse. "He's alive. Was that the same thing they used on us? Would you really have killed him?"

"Probably and yes." Everyone had finished gathering weapons and was watching him. "We're as ready as we're going to be. Good luck, everyone. Try to keep them from knowing we're coming, but don't hesitate to shoot if they see you. Remember, I'm as proud of you as I could possibly be. Go."

They left the prisoner unguarded. Either they'd win and come back for him, or they'd lose and it didn't matter. The fight would be over before the man woke up.

They returned to the maintenance shafts. He estimated how long it would take them to get into position, and they agreed on a time to attack. If someone went early, it might spell doom. Graves led the assault on the bridge, Baxter on engineering, and Jared led the group going to the computer center. Doctor Stone split her people between the three groups. The few scientists with them brought up the rear.

It felt like it took forever to reach the computer center. They had to wait for the rest of the teams to get into position, so he made his way as close as he could and accessed the video feeds. There were three technicians in the computer center and two marines in full combat armor in the corridor. The main hatch was open, but he knew they could close it at a moment's notice.

The closest maintenance access was thirty meters down the corridor from the computer center. No way could they slip up on the guards unnoticed. He hoped the rifle had the range to take them out.

"Coulter, you might want to take this rifle. I've set it to stun."

"Can I even fire it?"

Jared hadn't considered that. A quick check showed him that he could lock the weapon down to authorized users by implant ID, but he didn't have to. "You can fire it."

His chrono vibrated. It was time. He drew his pistol and waited for the marines to line up behind them. When they were ready, he gave Coulter a nod.

The marine NCO opened the hatch and stepped into the corridor, his rifle already up and firing. The blue bolt just missed the man looking their way. The man shouted and raised his rifle to return fire.

That meant he caught the second bolt in the chest and dropped.

Jared prayed and fired at the other man. He missed, and the mutineer jumped into the computer center.

The marines were already running for the hatch, so he ran with them. The hatch slid shut almost in their faces.

"Shit!" Coulter hit the admittance switch, but the hatch remained closed.

Jared sent an implant command to the door with his command override. The hatch slid open, much to the shock of the men inside. Jared shot the marine first and then the tech with the communications unit in his hand. Coulter shot the second tech.

The last technician shot Jared with a pistol. The slug ricocheted off his faceplate. He shot the man more out of reflex than anything else.

Jared's lead computer technician ran into the room and slid to a stop in front of the main console. He tapped the controls furiously. "Computer offline. Booting. Access channels restored. When it comes up, the computer will have complete systems access."

Jared hoped that meant the computer would immediately lock down the systems and stun any mutineers, even if the bad guys knocked them all out right now. "How long until it's up?"

"Less than a minute. I can't control the antiboarding weapons. They're slaved to the bridge."

He accessed the ship's systems. He couldn't isolate them, either, but he could lock them out just like Baxter could in engineering. They accepted his shutdown command authorization and went offline just moments before an order to activate came in from the bridge.

"I locked them out," he shouted. "We have a chance."

Jared opened a channel to the chief engineer's appropriated communication unit. "This is Mertz. We have the computer center. Thirty seconds to computer activation, and I've locked out the antiboarding weapons. What's your status?"

"We're in engineering. We're exchanging fire with the mutineers. Give me… one second…"

The main overhead lights went out, and the emergency backups came on dimly.

"Main power cut," Baxter said. "Oops. Someone just dumped the flip capacitors. I'm so clumsy. This ship won't be flipping anywhere until you say so. This won't stop the computer from coming online."

"Can you hold?"

"It looks like the mutineers are giving up. We have things under control here."

The screens around Jared came to life, and he felt the computer's presence through his implants. *Courageous online, Captain. Status?*

"Mutineers have the bridge. We think we've restored control in engineering. We're trying to take the bridge. There are other hostiles outside the mess halls. That's where the crew is. Can you access the antiboarding weapons?"

The computer switched to audible communication. "The boarding suppression systems have been placed on remote control. This unit sees that you have locked them out. That is all this unit could do until the modifications are removed."

"Hopefully we won't need them. Coulter, take your men and hunt down the guards. We'll lead you to them. I'm locking the computer center hatches until this is over."

"Aye, sir." The marines followed him out. Jared closed the armored hatch behind them and engaged the manual lock so that no one else could use a surprise code to open it. They'd have to burn him out.

Jared took off his helmet and called Graves. "Status?"

Someone else answered. "Ensign Turner, sir. They repulsed our attack. Commander Graves is hurt bad. The medics are rushing him to the medical center. We've called on them to surrender. They refused. We're about to make another try."

"Hold for a minute. I'll try to talk them out."

He opened a channel to the bridge. For a moment, it didn't look like they would answer. Then the image of a man bleeding from a cut on his forehead appeared. It was not Rawlins.

"You," he snarled. "How the hell did you get out of the mess hall?"

The man looked vaguely familiar, but Jared couldn't put a name to him. "Put Rawlins on. It's time to end this."

The man laughed roughly. "You're going to need better

communications gear than even the Old Empire had to do that. He's dead. You'll deal with me."

"Fine. We have control of the ship. The main computer is back online, and I control engineering. My people are hunting you down in the corridors as we speak. Surrender the bridge."

The man shook his head. "The king will have our heads, even if you don't. You want your bridge back? Come and take it." He grinned without the slightest bit of humor. "Oh, and I have some bad news for you. Rawlins retargeted the asteroid on your precious princess when he retrieved our men from it. It's on a ballistic course, so she won't even see it coming. With the jammers in place, you don't even have enough time to warn her that death is coming. I'll see you in Hell." The transmission ended.

Jared's heart jumped into his throat as he called the ensign back. "Take the bridge right now. Medical care for any survivors, but don't take chances."

"Aye, sir. Turner out."

He opened a channel to engineering and started giving orders as soon as Baxter appeared. "Get us headed back to Erorsi Prime at flank speed. Redline the drives. They're dropping a kinetic strike onto Kelsey and the team."

The news wiped the smile off Baxter's face. "I'll wring every kilometer per second from the drives that I can. Engineering out."

Jared ran his hand across his face. He hoped the man was lying, but he couldn't count on it. He had to find a way to get the ship back to Erorsi in time to save his sister. Even if he needed a miracle.

31

It took hours to strip the data units from the flooded battlecruiser and load them aboard the pinnace. Kelsey doubted they would be of much use without the assistance of people who knew the technology. That meant Bell and his associates.

Thankfully, they'd probably be happy to help. Even though her team had failed to capture a functional AI, the Pale Ones converging on the mountain facility had never made it further than the foothills. They'd milled around for a while and then dispersed.

She stood on the shores of the lake and stared at the sky. Had Jared stopped the mutineers? She prayed so, but they wouldn't know until they made it to the shipyards.

That's when she noticed a streak of light high up in the atmosphere. No, several streaks. She wondered if they were meteors.

Her implants popped up notice of an incoming transmission. Priority One. That sounded important. She accepted it.

An image of her brother appeared. "Kelsey! The mutineers redirected the asteroid back on your position! You have to get out of there right now! Hurry!" The message began repeating, but that ceased as the streaks above her exploded in little puffs of light.

She whirled toward the pinnace and opened the general marine channel. "Incoming kinetic strike! Everyone into the pinnace right now! Drop everything and run!"

Kelsey brought up the locator beacons for all the marines. Thank God no one was in the water. Most of the men were in or around the pinnace, but a few were inside the transmitter building. Including Talbot.

"Talbot! Move it!"

"I've almost got the data unit with the transmission records," he said. "Thirty seconds. A minute, tops."

Cursing, she ran past the pinnace and into the building, dodging the other men as they came boiling out. Talbot had a data unit partly extracted from the computer. She grabbed it with one hand and ripped it out. She snatched him up with the other and bolted.

Her enhanced musculature and powered armor got them both outside in a hurry. She triggered the grav assist and leapt for the pinnace. Her armor took them almost twenty meters into the air and dropped them right behind the last of the men running up the ramp.

"Lift off!" Reese shouted as he raised the ramp behind them. "Maximum acceleration. Head for the mountains."

Kelsey glared at Talbot. "Now who's making someone crazy? Have you lost your mind?" She shook the data unit at him. "This isn't worth your life."

"Actually, it might be. This isn't just a log of messages. It's recordings of the content, too. I only had time to scan a few messages, but I think these are critically important. But thanks for the lift."

"Everyone into your seats and activate the crash harnesses." Reese shoved the data unit into a storage compartment. "Since we don't have to go stealth, we'll be over the mountains in fifteen minutes. How far off is the strike?"

Kelsey shook her head. "I don't know. The recording didn't say."

"Well, we'll just have to hope we have time."

That's when she picked up something high above them on the pinnace's scanners. It was closing in at an incredible rate of speed. "Here it comes! Impact on the lake in just a few seconds!"

"Get us on the deck," Reese yelled at the pilots as he strapped himself in. "Find some cover."

The streak in the sky descended with deceptive slowness, almost crawling toward the ground as the pinnace dove for cover. They almost made it to a ridgeline ahead of them before the sky behind them lit up with intolerable brightness.

"How long does it take a shock wave to——"

A giant hand smashed the pinnace from the sky. It tumbled like a toy hurled by an angry child. The pilots jammed on the grav drives at the last moment and flipped them upright just before they plowed into the forest.

Kelsey must've lost consciousness, because the pinnace was a smoldering wreck when she woke up.

Her restraints resisted her attempts to free herself, so she ripped them off. A few marines staggered around, but most hung limply from their crash harnesses. Her armor pinged their suits. Some of them were dead, but most were alive, if in bad shape.

The fact that any of them had lived through the crash was a testament to the engineers who'd designed the pinnace and its safety systems.

Then she remembered the pilots. She couldn't sense their condition. She forced her way onto the flight deck and discovered it had taken the worst of the impact. The pinnace had dug a furrow like a plow, knocking aside trees and rocks as it gouged the ground.

One of the pilots hung from her harness, staring numbly at the stump of her right arm. The other pilot was missing, a jagged hole in the fuselage where he'd sat. The forest outside burned.

Kelsey ripped some wiring from the shattered control consoles and tied a tourniquet on the woman's arm just as Talbot heaved himself onto the flight deck. She was relieved to see him. She was almost as relieved to see the medic behind him.

She stepped back beside Talbot and watched the medic treat the injured pilot. "I didn't think we were going to make it. I thought we were going to die."

"Me, too. I can't imagine how they got us down in one piece."

That's when the shakes hit her. They hit her so hard that her teeth chattered.

Talbot pulled her into a hug. "It's going to be okay. Just let it go."

And she did. The tears came pouring from her. Tears of relief, tears of grief, and tears of raw terror.

* * *

THEY WERE STILL BRINGING the injured out of the crashed pinnace when another pinnace howled in from above like a roaring beast of prey. It had barely touched the ground before it disgorged marines who rushed in to help with the rescue operations. A second pinnace landed right behind it with Doctor Stone and her medical teams.

Jared came out at a run right behind them. "Kelsey! Are you all right?"

"I'm fine," she said through her still-tight chest. "Most of us made it, but some of the marines are badly hurt. One of the pilots is somewhere back there." She gestured toward the raging forest fire behind them. Of course, except for the scar they'd made while crashing, everything around them was on fire.

"We'll start a search. I'm glad you got our message. I was afraid we weren't going to get back in time."

"What were those things you sent? Probes?"

He shook his head. "Five missiles. We added a communications package onto them and fired them as soon as we got in range of the planet. They were the only things fast enough to beat the asteroid."

Doctor Stone took the worst of the injured onto her pinnace and lifted off for *Courageous*. It took another hour for the rest of them to recover all the data units they'd captured, and to find the pilot's body.

Jared filled her in on the mutiny and his fight to regain control of the ship, and she recounted their attack on the AI. He shook his head when she finished. "We were both lucky. Luckier than we deserve to be."

"I know. I've been loaded down with all these implants and now had an asteroid dropped on my head. My father is going to be pissed. I hope you like Thule."

Once they had everything secure, they lifted off and headed for the mountains. They landed in almost the same place as Kelsey had that morning. She shook her head. Had it only been that morning? It felt like an eternity ago.

She led her half brother to the hidden entrance, which opened as soon as they arrived. Da Silva was waiting to escort them to the same conference room that she'd visited earlier. Once again, Reginald Bell was waiting for her. Alone this time.

The old man gestured for them to sit. "We found some sturdier chairs, Princess. You look like you need to sit down."

Kelsey sat wearily. "Reginald Bell, this is our expedition commander, Captain Jared Mertz. Jared, Reginald Bell."

"Captain Mertz. It's a great pleasure to meet you, though I wish it had been under better circumstances." He straightened and saluted, his fist to his chest. "Ensign Bell reporting, Captain."

Jared returned the salute and extended his hand to the old man. "It's an honor to meet you, sir. I'm so sorry that we weren't able to stop the kinetic strike. I hope your people made it through."

The older man clasped Jared's hand in his. "They designed this facility to survive a near miss from just such a weapon. I'm pleased to say it is a credit to its designers. I'm much more concerned with the long-term effects of the impact. We're guessing that there will be months of darkness under a global debris cloud and years of bitter winters. The roving tribes of primitives will suffer greatly."

"I wish we could offer more help there, but it will be weeks before any other ships can arrive. Even then, the scale of this disaster is beyond imagining. We'll do what we can, but it won't be nearly enough."

"We appreciate everything that you can do. I can hardly credit that you've brought *Courageous* back to life. I never expected to meet a Fleet officer again."

Jared spread his hands. "Seeing everything about *Courageous*, I'm almost hesitant to call myself Fleet. Meeting a true Fleet officer is an unexpected dream come true. If you only knew how many questions I have."

"Don't raise us to mythical heights, Captain. I'd imagine your Fleet is much like the one I served. Good men and women doing the best they could. Technology doesn't define who we are. Was the impact a rebel counterattack?"

"More like a last gasp, though I'm afraid the Pale Ones aren't directly responsible for it in the end. It's a long story, but the important part is that we've defeated the rebels. The controlling AI is gone."

The man blinked in surprise. "You're certain?"

Kelsey nodded. "There was a wrecked battlecruiser in a lake. We entered it, and I communicated with it before I shut it down. Then the kinetic strike blew it up. No mistake."

Bell shook his head as though trying to clear away cobwebs. "It's hard to believe. Can this nightmare truly be over?"

Jared put a hand on the older man's shoulder. "It is. We've defeated the rebels and freed Erorsi. I'm just sorry we couldn't stop the asteroid. Erorsi was such a beautiful world."

"And it will be again. We recovered from the initial bombardment. We'll survive this one, too. I think this calls for a drink. I happen to have some truly magnificent brandy in my quarters. I've been saving it for just this moment. I won't tell my doctor if you don't."

Jared shook his head with an expression of regret. "I'm afraid we can't stay. Events are driving us back to the system next door. Pentagar. We're on a tight schedule. Can we evacuate any of your people?"

"Let me call the others. They're helping put things right after the earthquake." He walked slowly to the conference table and called someone.

Jared put his hand on Kelsey's shoulder. "I wish we didn't have to rush back. I wasn't kidding about all the questions. We might have all the data files imaginable on *Courageous*, but we don't have any experience using the technology. He was a serving Fleet officer. The things he's learned about tactics would be invaluable."

"Maybe," she said. "Maybe not. Things didn't work out so well against the rebels. Don't be blinded by our vision of the Old Empire. We've crawled back to our feet after a knockout punch. That's huge. What you've accomplished on this mission alone is the stuff of legend."

His skeptical expression made her laugh. "Think about it, Jared. You've brought an Old Empire ship back to life. You've met the rebels and defeated them. You captured an entire planetary system with one ship. Tell me one of your contemporary officers that can claim anything like that."

"You're exaggerating my role in all this. You played a bigger hand in this than I did."

She shook her head. "We've done it as a team. Bet nobody saw that coming."

He smiled. "No. I'm certain no one imagined anything like what we've done together. I was wrong to want you to stay home. You're the soul of this expedition. I'm even warming to the half-sister part."

His words made her feel more than a bit guilty. He still didn't know that she wasn't genetically his sister. To his credit, she imagined that wouldn't make one bit of difference to him.

Bell ended his call and walked back over to them. "We've discussed the matter and decided that we're not leaving. This is our world. It needs us. We'll send a team of people back with you, if you have no objection. It behooves us to get to know you and our neighbors, and to get what help we can for the savages living in the wild."

"I understand. Will you be joining us?"

"I shouldn't, but I long to walk the corridors of my old ship one last time. My days are numbered, and the chance will likely never come again. Our party will be several dozen people, if that's acceptable. We should be ready to go in an hour."

Her half brother grinned. "We'd be happy to have them. If you have any technical specialists that might come along, I know some people would love to talk to them. And we have the Pale Ones' data units to get into. They're water damaged, and we can't chance ruining them."

Bell nodded. "Our technical know-how has slipped some from the days of old, but I'll add a few people to our roster that can help. That's what neighbors do."

* * *

AFTER THEY DOCKED, Kelsey watched the old man walk out into *Courageous* with tears in her eyes.

The computer spoke from the overheads and in her implants. Perhaps in all their implants. "Welcome aboard, Ensign Bell."

Bell spoke softly. "It's good to be back, *Courageous*."

"Have you returned to take command?"

Kelsey froze. She'd never considered that possibility. The man was a Fleet officer, lawfully assigned to this ship. He was part of her official chain of command. Would he take the ship away from them?

"No, *Courageous*," Bell said. "My day is done. The Empire of old is gone. You have a new captain, and a damned good one from what I can see. I hereby affirm Jared Mertz's status as a Fleet officer and endorse his command of this vessel. He's your captain now."

Bell turned to Jared. "If an old man might presume on your goodwill, though, I'd love to visit the bridge. I was never senior enough to go there when I served."

Jared gestured to the lift. "It's under repair, but we can certainly stop in. Then we can go to the operations center while we break orbit."

Kelsey followed them with a smile on her face.

32

Once Jared had seen their guests to their quarters and assigned crew members to act as guides—and guards to a degree—he made his way to the bridge with a silent Kelsey at his side. Engineering technicians were replacing shattered consoles, and the place smelled of fried circuitry and blood. Miraculously, his console was undamaged, though splattered with gore.

He cleaned it up with supplies from the cubby in the attached head and sat down. The console lit when he interfaced his implants with it. The ship's status was mostly green. The bridge showed red, but that would change before they flipped.

Their combat status was green, though they were now critically short of missiles. There were several dozen missiles that had failed inspection that they might be able to get ready, but he wasn't going to count on it. If things hit the fan, it was going to get ugly.

Kelsey cleaned off a seat near him, not bothering to hide her distaste. "If our mutineers intended to kick off an insurrection when they came through the flip point, then how do we avoid starting it ourselves?"

"The computer says no messages were sent back to Pentagar through the probes at the flip point. The mutineers only had a few dozen people aboard. Their patron couldn't possibly be certain their attack on *Courageous* would succeed. So it won't be our arrival that triggers the coup."

He rubbed his face tiredly. "Not even this ship could survive a bombardment by the defensive orbitals on the Pentagaran side of the flip point, so Rawlins must've had a plan to get clear quickly. He could send a signal of some kind to his patron then."

She nodded. "Probably something innocuous. Why raise suspicions ahead of time? Have their quarters been searched?"

"From top to bottom. We didn't find anything suspicious. None of the personal communications devices would even interface with *Courageous*. I had them examined anyway. There's no telling which contacts on them might lead to their patron. If any."

Jared slammed his palm against the console. "Dammit. We can't just let this son of a bitch get away. He'll just keep building his organization and strike when we leave."

"We have some information. When Rawlins identified himself as a commander, it might have been a real rank. I met him once before on *Best Deal*. He told me his name was Jacob, but he looked enlisted. What name does the ship have on file for him?"

He queried the computer. "Jacob Randal. An enlisted engineering technician. The first name might or might not be real. Let's assume it is. It would be damned awkward to fail to respond to your own name. The last name is similar enough to catch your attention. So let's also assume he actually is Commander Jacob Rawlins of the Pentagaran Navy. They could probably confirm that with his remains. If we can find someone to ask who isn't in on the plot."

Kelsey pursed her lips. "We can't really be sure of anyone, except the king and Elise. Probably Commodore Sanders. I find it difficult to believe he's in on something like this, but can we trust him completely?"

"We can't doubt every friend we've made. Someone is going to need to take steps to see that the Pentagaran Navy doesn't revolt."

He consulted the time and their ETA through his implants. That would take a lot of getting used to. They had a few hours remaining before they transitioned. "I think we start off pretending nothing is amiss."

"Then the patron knows his or her minion isn't in command of *Courageous*," she added. "If we never let on that anything is wrong, the patron will have to assume his team is still in place, learning what they need to take over when more Pentagarans can be assigned to the ship."

"I think so, too. The question is, how do we track him down?"

"Someone assigned Rawlins to this ship under a fake name. Or someone else's name. A senior officer made that call. Besides, only someone in a significant position of authority could orchestrate a military coup. The person or persons will be highly placed but one of a singular clique of people. Flag officers. If we can get back in one piece, the odds of individual ships going rogue go way down."

That agreed with his assessment. "I can't make a call from here, so I'll do it from my office once we flip. I'll fill them in on our success and ask for an immediate conference with Elise. She'll bring some of her senior Fleet officers, but once we fill her in, she can take steps to take this apart without alarming the other senior commanders. If we control the communications, it won't matter if one of them is with her. They won't dare reveal themselves."

The lift doors opened, and Talbot came out onto the bridge. He slowed as he surveyed the destruction. "Wow. They really put up a fight."

Jared sighed. "A completely needless one. They knew we were going to win. Once they lost their edge, it was inevitable. What can I do for you, Senior Sergeant?"

The marine held out a tablet. "I downloaded my combat suit's vid files to this tablet. I found something in the transmitter building that you need to see. I was able to access the AI's communications records before we ran. The data storage unit is down in the lab, so hopefully we can get more. Most of the transmissions were audio only, but some were video. That caught my attention."

Jared took the tablet and held it so Kelsey could see it as well. The vid player was already up, so he hit play.

The console that Talbot had been using in the transmitter building was small and filthy, but it worked. Jared could make out a list of files. The marine selected one marked as video.

The video showed a man on what was obviously the bridge of a spaceship. Old Empire from the layout. The man wore a Fleet uniform with commander's tabs.

He bowed so steeply that they could momentarily see the top of his head. Then he looked straight into the screen and began speaking. "This man brings greetings from your brothers in the Empire, Lord. He apologizes for the lack of supplies last year. The freighter disappeared several worlds before yours. I've brought extra implant hardware to make good any shortages. Are there any other needs this man can fulfil for you?"

The AI spoke in a toneless voice. "You may take the immature humans from this unit's latest culling. This unit requires nothing more. It has the situation under control, and its plan is almost ready to execute."

He heard Kelsey shouting in the recording about an incoming kinetic strike. Talbot killed the vid and began struggling to remove the data unit from the computer. That was where the recording ended.

Jared's blood ran cold. "How long ago was this recorded?"

"That vid was recorded about ten months ago, sir."

Kelsey leaned forward, shock written all over her face. "What? That can't be right. The Empire fell. Look at the Pale Ones. How is this even possible?"

Talbot retrieved his tablet. "The vid calls happen about once a year. There were some years that there weren't any, but most happen once a year about two months from now. I think our understanding of what happened to the Old Empire needs to be revised."

Jared nodded. "This just became high priority. Get some of Mister Bell's people to help Doctor Leonard and Carl Owlet. We need to know who they are and what they were doing with the Pale Ones. Examine every vid on that data unit."

"Aye, sir." Talbot nodded to Kelsey and left the bridge.

She looked at Jared with her eyes wide. "What does it mean?"

"It means something of the Old Empire survived. We need to end the Pentagaran rebellion as quickly as possible. Our lives might depend on it."

* * *

THE CREW WAS at battle stations when they flipped to Pentagar. The only concession Jared made to stealth was to keep his screens down. The main computer would raise them at the first sign of hostile action, faster than any human could react. Their missile and beam batteries were on hot standby, ready to fire at a moment's notice. Zia would go from passive scanners to active at the first sign of trouble.

Thankfully, there wasn't any. They arrived without incident and coasted out of the defensive globe with only cheerful greetings sent their way.

He sent an outline of their successes in the Erorsi system and requested the crown princess and her staff meet him in Pentagaran orbit. There would be a significant Pentagaran Navy presence there, so *Courageous* would remain on alert.

A cutter asked for approach permission once they slipped into Pentagar orbit, indicating it had Elise aboard. He gave them the green light and headed for the docking bay. Kelsey and Lieutenant Reese met him there. The marine wore unpowered combat armor. Kelsey had a nice dress on.

Jared gave the marine officer his final instructions. "I want a squad of marines just around any corner we happen to be at. Stay out of sight, but come running if there's trouble."

"I think I should be with you, sir. If someone attacks you or the princess, I could react at once. The antiboarding weapons aren't designed to take down a single person."

"I'm armed. Better yet, Princess Kelsey is armed. If someone is stupid enough to cause trouble, we can hold them off until you arrive."

Reese frowned at Kelsey. "Where's your weapon?"

"Just you never mind," she said tartly. "Somewhere I can get to it quickly if I have to. Besides, my hands are more than enough for anything but a gun. We don't need to spook them. We've moved past the need for an armed escort. Your presence would make them suspicious."

The sound of the cutter docking sent Reese to join his men in an adjoining compartment.

Kelsey pointedly glanced at the flechette pistol on Jared's hip. "Can you use that thing?"

"I went down to the range and practiced. I even got my implants to assist in aiming it. I shouldn't need it, though."

"Let's hope not."

The docking hatch slid open. Two Pentagaran Navy sailors led the way out, with Elise right behind them. Lord Admiral Shrike and Commodore Sanders completed her party.

She grinned widely as she came up to shake Jared's hand. "I hear you've taken the Pale Ones down. That's wonderful news! The incessant attacks are finally over!" She pulled Kelsey into a hug. "You and your people have saved us. Again. It's getting to be quite the habit."

Jared shook the men's hands. Sanders seemed elated, Shrike a little subdued.

"We've got a presentation with video in the conference room. We also have some other news that you'll be interested in. We found holdouts on Erorsi. A facility that survived the invasion, with the descendants of the original staff still there."

Elise stared at him. "That's amazing. What a story they must have to tell. Do they need anything that we can provide? Food, medicine, a ride out?"

"They'll need a lot of help. The Pale Ones dropped a massive kinetic strike on the planet. I watched it hit from orbit. The planet is in for a very rough time."

"Then they shall have whatever we can give. I'll want to see the vid of the impact, too."

He sent a mental command to block all transmissions from the ship for the time being. Once he told them the truth, he couldn't allow any of them to send any surreptitious messages.

His implants showed the marines taking up positions outside the conference room once the hatch closed. He sat at the head of the table. Kelsey took the seat to his right with Commodore Sanders beside her. Elise sat on Jared's left with Lord Admiral Shrike beside her.

He clasped his hands in front of him on the table. "Before I begin, I need to make a confession. There is one other event that I haven't mentioned. We had an attempted mutiny."

Elise's eyes widened. "What! From our people?" She looked over at Shrike. "I thought the men sent on this mission were all military personnel."

"They were. Ones that went through an exhaustive background check. Might we question them?"

Jared nodded. "You're welcome to." He touched the recessed console, and an image of Rawlins popped up on the large screen. He'd decided to use the dead man to flush out any traitors. "Allow me to introduce you to Jacob Randall. I'm certain that isn't his real name. When he briefly took control of the ship, he referred to himself as Commander Rawlins.

"He didn't believe that we'd regain the upper hand and told us that a coup in your Fleet was about to happen. I'm sorry to tell you this, Lord Admiral, but I believe that one or more of your senior military officers is about to seize power. If we can trace this man to his patron quietly, I believe we can unravel this coup in a very short period of time."

He could tell Elise the other reasons they needed to hurry once her people had this situation under control.

Elise nodded. "I can send orders for people loyal to me to assume command of the ships in orbit with backup from the Royal Guard. Once we query the Royal Fleet databases, it won't take long to track who he probably works for."

Jared started to respond, but Lord Admiral Shrike stood abruptly and stepped behind Elise. He had a knife to her throat before Kelsey and Sanders had finished standing. Jared stayed in his seat.

"Sit back down, Princess Kelsey." Shrike kept his eyes locked on Jared's half sister. "Allow me to save all of us some time. He'll lead you right to me. That doesn't matter, though. You're too late." He pulled a communications device from his waist and pressed a key. "My senior people are taking control of the Royal Fleet as we speak. Your ship might be powerful, but it cannot stand up to the might of Pentagar. This is over."

"Traitor," Commodore Sanders spat. "You won't get away with this."

"Really? How melodramatic. I've already gotten away with it. Sit down or I'll slit her throat."

Jared was tempted to call for the marines, but he suspected the lord admiral was more than a bit mad. He'd probably kill Elise as soon as the door opened.

"This won't end well." Jared eased his pistol from its holster. "I've already locked down all communications. You're alone here."

Shrike laughed. "I don't believe you. Prepare a cutter to take the former crown princess and myself to my flagship. Now. Delay or offer me any resistance and I'll kill her."

"Don't do it," Elise said through clenched teeth. "He cannot be allowed to leave this ship, even if he kills me. Protect the Kingdom."

Kelsey hadn't sat down, but it didn't look like she could get to Shrike without going through Elise. She moved down the table away from Jared. "Let's not get hasty. Perhaps we can make a deal."

As soon as Shrike turned to keep Elise between himself and Kelsey, Jared raised his pistol, used his implants to target it on Shrike's head, and fired. The high-velocity flechette blew Shrike's head apart. He dropped the knife and collapsed in a bloody heap.

Jared's hand shook as he stood and holstered his pistol. The marines burst in just as Jared pulled Elise away from the body. Despite her brave face, he could feel her trembling. He turned her away from the body. "It's over now. You're safe."

She came into his arms and buried her face against his shoulder. "Thank you."

33

Kelsey sat on the balcony to her room at the Royal Palace, sipping a beer and watching the stars. She wondered which of them was home. Probably none of them. Odds were Avalon wasn't visible from here, even with her enhanced eyesight.

Her keeper and constant companion, Senior Sargent Talbot, put his boots up on the railing and leaned back in his chair. "You think the Pentagarans really found all the conspirators?"

"If not, they've found most of them. Every senior officer is getting close scrutiny, and some traitors have given up others for lighter sentences. Treason here has the death penalty. If they've missed anyone, that person will be the model of good behavior going forward."

Events had preceded quickly once Commodore—now Admiral—Sanders had made a few innocuous calls to men he trusted to secure the ships in orbit. They'd even found the woman responsible for the attack at the Parliament Building. Once the Pentagarans felt they had all they needed from her, the king would decide if she'd cooperated enough to earn a life sentence.

The two of them drank in silence for a while before Talbot spoke again. "What do you think about the captain and Crown Princess Elise?"

She blinked at the unexpected question. "How do you mean?"

"Come on. Everyone can see that she's sweet on him. All those private dinners and trips out into the capital."

Kelsey considered that with no small bit of surprise. Now that he'd pointed it out, she wondered how she'd missed it. Her half brother was dating. She wondered if he knew yet. Elise could be very subtle.

"I'm not sure what kind of future they have," she said at last. "We're going to be leaving at some point, and she's not coming with us."

"Not all relationships are long term. He did save her life, you know. That kind of intense situation makes people want to get friendly, even when they're not usually so forward."

She gave him a look. "You did not just tell me that she's having a torrid affair with my half brother."

"Actually, I did. I can't prove it, mind you. Even if I could, I would never say so," he said piously.

Kelsey snorted. "Right. Well, if they are, that's their business, and more power to them. People deserve what happiness they can find in this life." She took a deep draught of her beer. "Just like us."

He frowned. "I don't follow you."

She gestured with her bottle. "The two of us go everywhere together. We have intimate dinners. We spend a lot of time alone. You do know that we're dating, right?"

Talbot's chair tipped over backward, and he fell with a crash.

"That's crazy," he said as she laughed. He tried and failed to get some of the beer off himself after he stood.

"I said it as a joke, but why not? Is there something wrong with me?"

He looked to the heavens, probably seeking strength. "Don't you pull that girl crap on me! No, there is nothing wrong with you, and you know it. If we weren't who we are, I'd be sorely tempted, but you're a princess and I'm a freaking marine. I'm not even an officer, and I'm fifteen years older than you."

"So?"

"I can't believe you're even suggesting that. Lieutenant Reese would brig me. The emperor would space me. You have no idea what kind of reputation marines have."

She smiled widely. "I think my father might have mentioned something to that effect. You know what I didn't hear? That you weren't interested."

"This is crazy," he whispered.

"You're a marine. Be brave."

* * *

WANT to get updates from Terry about new books and other general nonsense going on in his life? He promises there will be cats. Go to TerryMixon.com/Mailing-List and sign up.

DID YOU ENJOY THIS BOOK? Please leave a review on Amazon. It only takes a minute to dash off a few words and that kind of thing helps Terry make a living as a writer and gets you new books faster.

WANT the next book in this series? Grab *Command Decisions* today or buy any of Terry's other books, which are listed on the next page.

VISIT TERRY's Patreon page to find out how to get cool rewards and an early look at what he's working on at Patreon.com/TerryMixon.

ALSO BY TERRY MIXON

You can always find the most up to date listing of Terry's titles on his Amazon Author Page.

Note: the links below (ebook only, obviously) redirect you to my website where you can click a button to go to Amazon. This allows me to participate in Amazon's associates program and earn a little more. Sorry for any inconvenience.

The Last Hunter

The Last Hunter

Bonds of Blood

Alpha Strike

The Enemy Revealed

Command Authority

The Grand Conspiracy

Shield of Humanity

Fog of War

Ships of the Line

Operation Liberty

The Empire of Bones Saga

Empire of Bones

Veil of Shadows

Command Decisions

Ghosts of Empire

Paying the Price

Recon in Force

Box Sets

The Empire of Bones Saga Volume 1

The Empire of Bones Saga Volume 2

The Empire of Bones Saga Volume 3

The Empire of Bones Saga Volume 4

Humanity Unlimited Publisher's Pack 1

Humanity Unlimited Publisher's Pack 2

ABOUT TERRY

#1 Bestselling Military Science Fiction author Terry Mixon served as a non-commissioned officer in the United States Army 101st Airborne Division. He later worked alongside the flight controllers in the Mission Control Center at the NASA Johnson Space Center supporting the Space Shuttle, the International Space Station, and other human spaceflight projects.

He now writes full time while living in Texas with his lovely wife and a pounce of cats.

TerryMixon.com

[a] amazon.com/author/terrymixon
[f] facebook.com/TerryLMixon
[p] patreon.com/TerryMixon
[BB] bookbub.com/authors/terry-mixon
[g] goodreads.com/TerryMixon